P9-EEF-456

Palo Alto City Library

The individual borrower is responsible for all library material borrowed on his or her card.

Charges as determined by the CITY OF PALO ALTO will be assessed for each overdue item.

Damaged or non-returned property will be billed to the individual borrower by the CITY OF PALO ALTO.

P.O. Box 10250, Palo Alto, CA 94303

At Risk

At Risk

Kit Ehrman

Poisoned Pen Press

Copyright © 2002 by Kit Ehrman

First Edition 2002

10 9 8 7 6 5 4 3 2 1

Library of Congress Catalog Card Number: 2002108993

ISBN: 1-59058-036-2 Hardcover
ISBN: 1-59058-045-1 Trade Paperback

All rights reserved. No part of this publication may be reproduced,
stored in, or introduced into a retrieval system, or transmitted in any
form, or by any means (electronic, mechanical, photocopying, record-
ing, or otherwise) without the prior written permission of both the
copyright owner and the publisher of this book.

Poisoned Pen Press
6962 E. First Ave., Ste. 103
Scottsdale, AZ 85251
www.poisonedpenpress.com
info@poisonedpenpress.com

Printed in the United States of America

Acknowledgments

First off, I would like to thank Bill Tapply and Steven Havill, who helped me get it right. A special thanks goes to Susan Francoeur whose unbiased feedback gave me confidence early on. I would also like to thank Sgt. Rick McGill, (retired) of the Laurel Police Department for putting up with my numerous procedural questions. Any and all mistakes are mine. Thanks also to Donna Marsh (You were right!), Connie Kiviniemi-Baylor, Almo Smith, and Teddy Saddoris. I am especially grateful to everyone at Poisoned Pen Press, especially Barbara Peters, a.k.a. TEE [The Evil Editor], and Robert Rosenwald, without whose faith and hard work this book would never have seen the light of day.

And finally, thanks to my family and my two wonderful sons, Phil and Ray, who good-naturedly put up with the writing process.

Chapter 1

Some mornings, before darkness gives way to light and a cold wind howls across the pasture and presses against the barn like a giant hand, I wonder what in the hell I'm doing working on a horse farm.

A week earlier, the jet stream had ferried a wall of Canadian air down the eastern edge of the Allegheny Mountains, and the mercury hadn't crawled out of the single digits ever since. I yanked a second sweatshirt over my head and walked into the kitchen.

The barn's crossbeams and rafters creaked and groaned like a Spanish galleon on the open seas while familiar sounds filtered up through the floorboards. Rustling straw, the hollow thump of a hoof knocking against a wooden plank, a bucket rattling.

I opened the drawer next to the kitchen sink. Buried among a Phillips screwdriver, a past due Gas and Electric bill and a stack of old bank statements, rubber bands, paper clips, and everything else that cluttered the junk drawer, I found a dirty manila envelope with the flap crimped shut. I turned it over in my palm. My boss had printed *Stephen* in bold black letters on one side along with the horse's name and detailed instructions that I knew by heart. Inside were tubes of ophthalmic ointment that couldn't be left in a cold barn. I tucked the envelope in my pocket and shrugged into my coat.

Fronds of ice feathered across the inside of the window-panes like a crystal-growing experiment gone wrong. They might have been pretty if they didn't mean I'd be freezing my ass off in a minute or two. I scratched at the frost with my fingernails, then squinted through the glass. The thermometer read two below zero.

There were a half dozen good ways to spend my time at three o'clock in the morning, and this wasn't one of them. But corneal ulcers had to be treated aggressively, because a horse that can't see, can't jump. And at Foxdale Farm, jumping's the name of the game. Hunters, jumpers, three-day eventers. Only the dressage horses kept their feet on the ground.

Outside, I took the steps two at a time, swiped the ice scraper across the windshield, then slid behind the wheel. The vinyl creaked under my weight, and the duct tape I'd plastered over a rip in the seat shifted and stuck to the seat of my pants. I huddled over the steering wheel and cranked the engine. Listening to the starter grind, I wondered what I would have been doing if I'd stayed at college. Sleeping more than likely. Better yet, I'd probably be in Florida on spring break where the locals would be inclined to think two below zero was the name of a rock group.

When the Chevy finally coughed to life, I coaxed the truck onto the road and, ten minutes later, pulled onto Foxdale's long gravel drive. The headlights cut across the metal walls of the indoor riding arena as I swung around into my usual parking space. To the casual observer, the arena and two huge barns farther down the lane might have looked like warehouses if not for the warren's nest of paddocks radiating outward like the spokes of a wheel.

I cut the engine, and Bach's Brandenburg Concerto Number 3 in G Major died at the start of the second movement. The sudden quiet was overwhelming. So was the dark. High above me, the sodium vapor lamp was an indistinct shape against the bulk of the building. I made a mental note to have Dave replace the bulb, then I grabbed my flashlight from under the driver's seat and climbed out.

My boots scrunched on the gravel as I rounded the southwest corner of the indoor arena. When I switched on the flashlight, nothing happened. I slipped off my gloves, tightened the housing, and fiddled with the switch. Still no luck. I glanced toward the barns and froze.

A pickup and horse trailer were parked farther down the lane where they had no business being, not at three in the morning. A broad shaft of light poured from the truck's cab and reflected off the barn's metal siding, but what sent a shiver down my spine was the overall absence of light. Both sodium vapors were out.

I stood still in the cold air and shifted my weight from one foot to the other. Mrs. Hill was too efficient to have forgotten to tell me that someone was going to pick up a horse. And it was the off season. No one was showing. Certainly not in Maryland.

Besides, no one loaded horses in the dark. Not if they could help it.

There was a pay phone in the arena by the bleachers. A call to the police seemed like a good idea. Prudent anyway. I opened the door and peered inside. Couldn't see a damn thing. I stepped over the threshold and ran my hand along the wall, feeling for the phone. When my fingers touched the receiver, I heard a muffled noise behind me.

Something heavy glanced off the back of my head and crashed into my shoulder. A searing pain slammed into my brain as specks of light flashed in a dizzying arc behind my eyes. Someone grabbed my wrist and wrenched my arm behind my back. He shoved me face-first into the arena wall, into dust and dirt and cobwebs. The door slammed shut.

"Shit." I clenched my teeth.

He leaned into me and readjusted his grip. "Got that right, punk. And you just stepped in it."

"What are you gonna do?" someone behind us said. A male voice, high-pitched and tense. "You ain't gonna pop 'im, are ya?"

The guy holding me felt my muscles tense and yanked my wrist higher between my shoulder blades.

Farther back in the building, a flashlight switched on. "No. Not yet, anyway." His voice was ordinary, calm, as if he were discussing what to do with a stray piece of equipment. The beam moved down the wall and focused on our backs. "I know. Get the keys to his truck."

Iron Grip twisted my wrist and increased his leverage, then the tense guy stepped around us and clumsily searched my pockets. When he leaned forward to check my left front pocket, I got a look at him. He'd pulled his ball cap low on his forehead, but judging from what I could see of his face, I'd never seen him before.

"They ain't on him," he said.

"All right, then. Turn him around."

They yanked me off the wall. The one with the flashlight shone the beam in my eyes as he adjusted something on his face, and I realized he was wearing a ski mask. I glanced at the guy on my right. His mask's eye holes were circled in red, and the skin at the corners of his eyes crinkled as if he were smiling.

I stood there stiffly, feeling heat seep from beneath my coat collar. Except for my breathing, I could hear no sound. Not even a car on the road.

The guy with the flashlight stepped closer. "You got lousy timing, kid," he whispered. "Lousy for you, that is. For me, now, it's a whole different ball game." He paused. "I ain't got my workout today."

The guy on my right sniggered.

The blast of light shifted as he crossed over to the bleachers and balanced the flashlight on one of the planks, bathing the wall behind us in a dull wash. When he turned around, the skin on the back of my head contracted. There was nothing but malice in his eyes, his intent all too clear.

I briefly considered asking them what they wanted or telling them to let me go but knew I would get nowhere with either line. I kept my mouth shut.

He took off his gloves. As he methodically folded them and stuck them one at a time into his coat pockets, it occurred to me that he was dragging it out, trying to make me sweat. And it pissed me off. He shoved his right hand into his jeans pocket and pulled out something metallic. I couldn't tell what it was until he slid it down over his fingers and made a fist. He clenched his hand, and light glinted off the top edge of the brass knuckles.

I tried to yank my right arm free and got my wrist wrenched behind my back for my trouble. Iron Grip had a way of applying leverage that told me he knew what he was doing, that I was out of my league.

The leader stepped closer and rolled his shoulders. "You interrupted me, boy, and you're gonna pay."

I aimed a kick at his groin. It took him by surprise, and I would have done some serious damage, except the asshole on my right pulled me off target at the last second. I must have gotten the leader pretty good, though, because he groaned and doubled over as I slipped my left arm free. Before I could get away from Iron Grip, he latched onto my coat collar and flung me into the bleachers. My head hit one of the metal supports, and I slumped to the ground.

Iron Grip was on top of me almost before I'd hit the ground. He jammed his knee into my lower back and twisted my arm around. Pain stabbed through my shoulder and radiated toward my elbow. He increased the tension, and after a while, I was aware of little else. When they finally yanked me to my feet, the talkative guy wasn't talking.

Before I could react, he hit me in the stomach...hard.

He landed two more punches. I doubled over, and the only thing that kept me from falling flat on my face was the hold they had on my arms.

I gritted my teeth. "Bastard."

After what seemed like forever, I straightened up.

A mistake.

He clipped me with a backhand I didn't see coming. Before I could regain my balance, he punched me in the nose. Blood flowed down my face and dripped off my chin.

I spit a mouthful at him. "Goddamn bastard."

He nailed me with another backhand that landed above my eye. The ground tilted suddenly and slammed into my face, and I heard his voice, faint in the background.

"That'll learn ya," he said.

I was rolling downhill in a clanging metal drum, and my head was spinning. When I opened my eyes, memory returned along with a flood of pain. I was half-sitting, half-lying in a horse trailer, and I wasn't alone. Seven horses were crammed into a trailer designed for six, and I was in danger of being stepped on.

I shifted. Pain splintered through my side and snatched the breath from my lungs. Busted ribs. I'd done it before and knew the drill. I closed my eyes. I couldn't move anyway. My hands had been tied behind my back, latched together around the metal post that formed the lower portion of the stall divider.

The metal was cold. I was cold, stiff.

I pushed myself into a sitting position and rested my head against the post. The horse behind me snorted, and I realized that the big gray was Gulf Coast. One of my favorites. Lines of worry crinkled the skin above his eyes, and he was standing so close, his warm breath trickled through my hair.

"That's a good boy, Shrimpy. Everything's going to be all right," I whispered. He lowered his head in response to my voice and fluttered his nostrils. In the next stall, Steel, an open jumper, leaned against the stall partition. A good bit of white shone round his eyes—never a good sign—and his skin was stretched taut over tense muscles. His coat was patchy with sweat. Steam curled off his chest and neck and rose toward the ceiling, back-lit by the only overhead light fixture in the trailer that wasn't broken.

As I listened to the whine of tires on smooth asphalt, I realized I hurt in more places than I should have. More places than I recalled taking a hit. Then I remembered the crack about getting in a workout.

Damn him.

Why had they taken me, anyway? Why hadn't they simply left me in the arena? Something to do with my truck. Did that mean they knew me well enough to know that I drove a truck, or had they just seen me pull in off the road? I had no idea.

One thing was certain, they hadn't kidnapped me to collect a ransom. Although my father had a ton of money, few people knew I was the son of Robert J. Cline, M.D., cardiovascular surgeon extraordinaire. One of Johns Hopkins' elite super-stars. If that had been their plan, they wouldn't have bothered with the horses. And they couldn't have known I would show up at the farm in the middle of the night. But if they wanted to kill me, why not just do it while I lay helpless on the arena floor?

I decided I didn't want to hang around and find out. I yanked at whatever was binding my wrists. The horse across from me lowered his head and pawed the floor, and Steel, who was high-strung to begin with, pulled against his chains. They wouldn't hold him if he lost it, and a horse, panic-stricken and loose in the trailer, I did not need.

I reconsidered my options. What was knotted around my wrists felt like nothing more than baling twine, which I knew I could break under normal circumstances. But this was anything but normal. Between the twine and the cold, I had already lost feeling in my fingers. I jammed my fingertips into the half-inch space between the rubber matting that covered the floor and the metal post, hoping to find a way to dismantle the partition. I couldn't find a bolt to unfasten or a lever or mechanism of any sort.

I wanted out of that trailer more than I had wanted anything in my life. I drew my feet beneath me, braced my back against the post, and pushed with my legs. My side felt like it was splitting open. I clenched my teeth, gripped the post with both hands to steady myself, and made it to my feet.

I stood there shaking and sweating, swallowing against a wave of nausea. After a minute or two, I braced my legs, and when I thought I wouldn't be thrown off balance by the trailer's movement, I twisted around and examined the partition. It was made to be dismantled, but not by someone tied up in the dark with hands stiff from the cold.

The trailer lurched around a bend, and I went down on my knees. The truck slowed to a stop. I held my breath and listened. No doors opened. No one came to see if I was awake, and in a moment, the truck pulled off, swept into a wide turn, and picked up speed. I exhaled slowly as the vibrations in the floorboards increased, and the metal shell of the trailer rattled so loudly, it was hard to think. We had left the highway.

I spread my wrists and got to work on the twine.

Ten minutes into it, one of the fibers gave way and then another, so when they finally separated, I overbalanced and crashed against the horse tied in the aisle. I patted his shoulder, then ducked under his neck and squeezed around to the other side. Most older trailers have emergency exits, and this one was no exception. I gripped the lever that latched the door into place and pushed upward. It was jammed, frozen with rust and disuse. I crouched down, put all my weight behind it, and tried again.

Without warning, the lever snapped off.

I dropped it on the floor, leaned against the cold metal wall, and felt the vibrations go right through me. If I didn't get out, I was dead. I pushed myself upright and studied the door. It had been damaged in the past and no longer hung flush with the opening. Through a crack, I saw that the hinges were simply bolts slid into grooves on the trailer's frame. With a tool of some sort, I could push the bolts up and out. But what tool? I looked at the lever lying at my feet.

I wedged it into the gap and pushed upward. The bolt moved a quarter of an inch. Half an inch. I pushed harder. The lever slipped and the door slid back into its original position. I repositioned the lever and tried again with the same result. After a third unsuccessful try, I looked for another way out. All the exits were locked on the outside, and metal bars had been welded across the windows.

As I passed the side door used for loading the horses, the toe of my boot knocked against something. It rolled across the rubber mat and wedged in the angle where the wall meets the floor. I slid my fingers into the narrow groove and felt the rounded metal. Picking it up, I held it to the light and thought I had a chance after all.

The old bolt, with part of its anchoring chain still attached, had once been part of a stall partition. It was rough and discolored with rust, but it was narrow enough to do the job. I used it along with the broken lever and, after a few false starts, worked the door up and out of its hinges. Before I could get hold of it, the door swung away from the trailer.

"Oh, shit."

Even though it was still dark, if they were paying any attention at all, they would see the escape door, which now hung at an odd angle over the speeding roadway. I reached out and grabbed the lower edge, but the weight of the door caused the whole thing to break off and crash onto the road.

The driver hit the brakes. The trailer shuddered and bounced, and the horses were almost thrown off their feet with me right along with them. I grabbed the metal frame, pulled myself upright, and watched as the trailer slowed.

Before it came to a stop, I jumped out. I instinctively rolled when I hit the ground and, by some miracle, landed on my feet. Behind me, voices shouted and doors slammed. I ran past the back bumper and didn't risk a look back. Didn't dare.

A loud noise cracked through the air, and it took me half a second to realize it was a gunshot. The second bullet whined above my head. I darted to the right and stumbled across the shoulder of the road. The ground dropped off into a wide drainage ditch, and as I picked up speed, I realized too late that there wasn't any cover until I made it to the woods on the far side. I'd almost reached the bottom of the ravine, when my foot caught on something hidden in the long grass. I crashed onto my shoulder, and a layer of ice shattered like glass under my weight.

I scrambled through the water, struggled up the far bank, and lunged into the woods. Another crack. This time the bullet splintered a tree limb to my left. I stumbled uphill, crashing blindly through tree limbs and heavy undergrowth, conscious of the noise I was making and could do nothing about. I had gone about fifty yards up the steep incline, when I came to a fallen tree blocking my path. I clambered over the rough bark and dropped to the ground, then cautiously looked back toward the road.

They were closer than I'd imagined. Too close for any margin of safety. Two of them stood alongside the trailer's back fender, and as I watched, the third jumped down from the cab and ran back to meet them. When he flicked on a flashlight and pointed it toward the woods, the largest of the three snatched it out of his hand. He played the beam across the hillside, concentrating on the area to my left.

I sank farther down behind the log and tried to control my breathing. As long as I stayed still and didn't make any noise, they wouldn't find me. Just as that thought crossed my mind, the beam caught me full in the face. I stopped breathing.

The light moved off to my left, and for a moment, its afterimage was all I could see. I squeezed my eyes shut and tried to clear my sight. When I opened my eyes, the men had moved past the trailer's bumper. The glow from the taillights bathed them in red. They were no longer wearing masks. The one with the flashlight gestured aggressively, barking commands I couldn't hear. When the other two wheeled around and took off down the road, the skin on the back of my neck tingled. Though I doubted they knew where I was, the image of them sneaking up behind me was overpowering.

I scrunched deeper into the leaves, pressed my shoulder against the log, and waited. When I next heard voices, I lifted my head and squinted toward the road. The two men had returned with the escape door and were loading it through the opening.

Light flashed in the woods to my left.

He was part way up the hill with his damn flashlight, shining the beam across the wooded slope behind me and to my left. If he moved much farther uphill and swung the light to his left, he'd see me. I watched as he ducked under a tangle of tree limbs and came closer. Another thirty feet, and he'd be level with my hiding place. He moved off to the right, toward a downed tree. As he crept around the base of the stump, light glinted off his gun.

If I ran, he'd see me, and he was too close to miss. But if he checked behind my log, I was as good as dead.

The cone of light cut across the ground just beyond my head. I waited for it to refocus on me. Waited for the shouts. When neither happened, I cautiously lifted my head. The flashlight was out, and as I listened, I realized why. A car was approaching. The engine's whine dropped a notch or two as it slowed to pass the trailer. After the car moved off, he switched on the flashlight, studied the hillside above my head, then turned and started back down the slope.

I kept my head down until I heard noises by the trailer. The one with the flashlight swept the beam in broad tracts across the asphalt, and I wondered what he was up to. Twice, he reached down and picked something up.

"Son of a bitch," I whispered.

Evidence. He was making sure they didn't leave anything behind. He found the third shell casing along the shoulder of the road. A pickup sped past as they climbed into the cab. Doors slammed, the truck dropped into gear, and they drove off. They probably figured they didn't have much to worry about, and they were right. I couldn't identify them. Even without the masks, it had been too dark.

As I watched the taillights fade into the distance, the thought of what I had narrowly escaped made my stomach do a quick one-eighty. I began to shake and not just from the cold. I stared at the vacant road, and pain I hadn't noticed since I was free of the trailer reawakened with a vengeance. Ribs, face, head.

I pushed off the log and stood up. My jeans were stiff and unyielding. They had begun to freeze. I'd be next if I didn't hurry. I turned my coat collar up with fingers that felt as if they belonged to someone else and stumbled down the slope. The drainage ditch was too wide to jump, so I waded through the icy water and climbed the embankment. I started walking.

A vehicle rounded the bend in the road ahead and accelerated toward me. I stood, frozen in the bright headlights. I hadn't noticed whether it was a car or a pickup or a dualie pulling a horse trailer. I staggered into the woods and dropped to the ground.

It whizzed by. A car...only a car.

I hung my head and listened to my pulse pound in my ears. After a minute or two, I stepped onto the pavement and tucked my hands under my armpits. My fingers felt like blocks of ice, and my teeth were chattering so hard, my jaw hurt. The idea of curling up in the leaves and going to sleep seemed attractive, and the fact that I was even considering it scared me. I had to get somewhere warm, and fast. Given the right circumstances, cold could kill as effectively as bullets.

I kept walking.

By the time I reached safety, in the form of an all-night convenience store, the sky had lightened into a dull gray.

The police arrived, as they typically do, followed by the medics and later, at the hospital, a detective—all of them asking questions, most of which I couldn't remember afterward. At first, like the convenience store clerk, the cops thought I was drunk and had upended my car in a ditch somewhere. But the ER doctor told them that hypothermia did that. That they shouldn't be surprised that my speech was slurred, reactions nonexistent, memory faulty.

Chapter 2

Sunday afternoon, my doctor signed my release papers.

"You're not allergic to any medications, right?"

"Far as I know."

"You're employed?" I nodded, and he said, "Take off for a day or two, and when you go back, take it easy for a couple weeks." He pulled a prescription pad from a pocket in his lab coat and began to scribble. "Occupation?"

"Barn manager...at a horse farm."

He looked up, his pen hovering over his paperwork. "Better take off a full week, then start back slow. Give the ribs a chance to heal."

I didn't tell him I couldn't afford to, that there was just too much to be done, not to mention the fact that I needed every penny I earned.

He saw what I was thinking, tore up the prescription, and wrote a new one. "This will give you more relief. If you have any questions or problems, get in touch with your family physician." He tried to suppress a yawn as he initialed the chart. "You *do* have a family doctor?"

"Err, no, actually."

He shook his head. "Well, find one, will you?" He straightened and tucked the pen back into his breast pocket. "Have the police finished with their interviews?"

"Last night."

"Thought so. You weren't very coherent when they brought you in."

The entire police thing had been more tedious and involved than I ever would have imagined and something I would just as soon forget. Besides requiring a more detailed statement, they had taken my fingerprints—for elimination purposes, they'd said. And they had photographed my injuries. Need to have proof an assault happened, you know? The only thing they still needed, and were unlikely to get, were suspects.

He dropped the prescription on the bedside table. "Good luck." He grinned. "And stay out of trouble."

I watched him stroll out the door, then I called the farm and arranged for a ride home.

For the next two hours, I stared out the window at a dreary expanse of black rooftop, thinking unproductive thoughts while the relay switch in the heating unit clicked wildly. At a quarter to five, Marty slouched into the room, and it was only from long acquaintance that I noticed the brief hesitation in his face as he took in the bruising and the gown and the bandages around my wrists.

He called over his shoulder. "He's in here."

Dave, Foxdale's handyman, appeared in the doorway as Marty hitched a hip on the footboard.

"Tell all," Marty said.

Since I'd started at Foxdale, Marty and I had become best friends. An unlikely union as we were more opposite than alike. He was easygoing and coarse, vulgar at times, and seemingly without ambition. "You first," I said. "What's happening at Foxdale?"

Marty shrugged. "What you'd expect. Phone ringing off the hook. Outrage, paranoia, tears." He grinned. "On the boarders' part, that is. 'Cause the guys are thrilled to death having seven less stalls to muck out."

"That won't last."

"Suppose not. But some folks'll be afraid to trust their horses to us now that somebody's taken off with a trailer full. So give with the details. Whatju run into?"

I sighed. It was going to be a long week.

He waved his hand. "Come on, man. The cops were crawling all over the place yesterday. You'd of thought you were dead," he glanced around the room, "or dying."

"It's true," Dave muttered but kept his gaze on the floor. He'd been checking out the pattern in the tiles ever since he'd walked into the room.

"Anyway," Marty said, "the boys in blue had Mrs. Hill holed up in her office for about an hour, and when they finally hightailed it out of there, she was madder'n hell. But, Mrs. Hill being Mrs. Hill, she wouldn't tell us a goddamn thing. And, get this. A fucking reporter showed up this morning. Mrs. Hill sent him packing, though," Marty added, and it was clear the thought amused him.

I just stared.

"So, what happened? Rumor has it, the shits who took the horses took you, too."

"That's right."

"Fuck, man. How'd you get away?"

"I just did. So, why'd Mrs. Hill send both of you?"

Marty stood and stretched. "She thought you might be wantin' your truck, so we dropped it off at your place when we got the clothes you asked for."

"Oh," I mumbled.

"What were you—"

"Marty, shut up," Dave said. "Let Steve get dressed so we can get outta here." He handed me the paper bag he'd been holding which I saw contained a fresh change of clothes.

"I knew you were weird," Marty said. "But goin' to the barn naked?"

I grinned. "My clothes got soaked. The medics cut them off."

"How'd they get—" Marty said as Dave pushed him out of the room, "wet?" he finished as the door swung shut.

It was after six and dark by the time Marty swung his old Firebird round the parking lot behind the loft and jerked to a halt at the base of the steps. He looked over at my Chevy parked under the dusk-to-dawn light. "We couldn't find your keys. Hope you got a spare. And you'd better check your battery 'cause it was dead. You left the door open, and the dome light was on."

But I had closed it. I distinctly remembered how loud it had sounded. "Then how'd you get it over here?" I said.

"Jumped it."

"But—"

"He hot-wired it," Dave said from the back seat, and I thought I heard a hint of disapproval in his voice.

Marty turned in his seat and grinned at me.

"Well, who'd of thought." I levered myself out of his low-slung car, then watched Dave struggle out of the back seat and plop thankfully into my spot.

Marty ducked down so he could see me through the passenger window. "Need help with anything?"

I told him I'd be fine and waved him off, but by the time I made it to the landing, I was doubtful. By the time I reached the deck and walked into the kitchen, I knew I had lied. I was exhausted and hungry, but too tired to bother with it. I swallowed some pain pills, turned off the lights, and crawled into bed.

I was running down a long dark tunnel. Running as fast as I could and getting nowhere. There were no footsteps. No sound.

I came to a door. Didn't open it. Didn't want to.

Just the same, I ended up inside a room. A room without walls.

The ground felt solid but somehow wasn't. With dread, I looked at my feet. The floor was liquid. It didn't make sense. I looked closer. Not water. No, it wasn't water.

It was blood.

Ripples lapped against my boots as something moved on the edge of my field of vision. I tried to turn my head to see what it was but couldn't.

Couldn't move. Couldn't breathe.

I forced myself to look. It was a head. A horse's head. Others floated past in the current, rising to the surface like huge, hideous bubbles. One drifted past my feet. I could see the dull, lifeless eye staring up at me.

Tight bands constricted around my chest, and my heart was pounding so hard, I was afraid it would explode.

Someone cried out.

The sound woke me. Even though the air was chilly, I lay trembling between sheets soaked with sweat. The pain medication had worn off.

I sat up, braced my hands on the edge of the bed, and worked to slow my breathing. One of the cats leapt onto the bed and leaned against my arm. Her purring sounded loud in the quiet dark. Ignoring her play for attention, I nudged her off the bed and stood up.

I walked stiffly into the kitchen, washed down a pill, and set the glass on the counter. It had snowed, and I could see quite easily into the night. Dark shapes were scattered on the hill above the lake. I picked up the binoculars and adjusted the focus. Deer, six of them. In the muted light, the fencing rose and fell like a roller coaster, enclosing pastures that were otherwise empty, their inhabitants snug in the barn below. On the frozen lake in the south field, the snow was even and stark.

I glanced at the clock on the stove. Three-ten. I had slept for a long time. I walked into the bathroom and switched on the lights. The plush expanse of teal and navy wallpaper and matching carpet seemed foreign after the cold sterility of the hospital. The loft seemed different somehow. Nothing tangible, but a change nonetheless. Or maybe it wasn't the loft that was different but my perspective of it.

I turned on the shower and looked in the mirror. Despite the fact that I had two impressive shiners and my cheek was mottled with purple, black, and yellow, the swelling around my eye had improved considerably in the last twenty-four hours.

When I took off my clothes, the view there wasn't much better. Under the bandages, worse still. Deep red grooves dug into my wrists. In places the skin was raw and oozing.

Bastards.

I stood under the spray of hot water, and as the tension in my muscles drained away, I thought about the horses. They had been chosen for one characteristic and one characteristic only. Size. The larger and heavier, the more money they would command at slaughter. I thought about Shrimpy with his huge, intelligent eyes. I had watched him in a jumper class once, when he had slipped going round a turn. He'd regained his balance, zeroed in on the next fence, and jumped it without a rub. His rider, all the while, had been grossly out of position, simply struggling to stay on. The horse had a heart of gold, and now he was heading down a frightening path to annihilation.

I braced my hands against the wall and watched the water swirl down the drain, thinking I could have met the same fate.

I stayed in the shower until the hot water ran cold.

I spent most of the day in bed, listening to music and trying not to think. Not about the horses, or the men, or what they had done. Around four in the afternoon, I got the coffee machine going, made some toast, and sat on one of the barstools. I slid a magazine across the counter and leafed through the pages until I came to an article on pastern lameness.

Behind me, someone banged on the kitchen door. My hand flinched, and coffee sloshed over my fingers and spread across the page.

"Damn."

I wiped my hand on my sweats and walked across the cold white tiles. My landlord was standing on the doormat, blowing on his hands and shifting his weight from one foot to the other.

He looked up when the door creaked open. "Oh, man."

"Hi, Greg."

He closed his mouth with a snap. "Marty said you'd tangled with them, but I didn't think…"

Cold air and a couple of snowflakes eddied in through the open door. I backed up. "Come in."

He stepped into the kitchen and stood just inside the door while the snow on his boots melted and formed an irregular brown puddle on the tile.

"Susan knew something was up," he said. "She saw someone drop off your truck Sunday afternoon and thought that was kind of weird, especially when we didn't see any lights on last night. You know how she is, the motherly, over-protective type."

Motherly would not have been my first choice when describing his wife. Beautiful, yes. And sexy. Motherly? No way.

"Then Foxdale's my first stop this morning, and I hear about the horses." He ran his fingers through his light brown hair. "What happened?"

As I told him, I thought that I should have handled the situation differently. Should have gone back to the truck and driven somewhere else to call the police. Put up a better fight. Hell, I didn't put up any fight.

Greg rubbed the back of his neck. "Jesus. Are you all right?"

"Yeah, I'm okay." I gestured to the coffee pot. "Want some?"

He glanced at his watch. For answer, he opened the cabinet door closest to the phone.

"Next one over," I said.

Greg let the door thump closed and opened the one beside it. He took down a mug and filled it, then sat on one of the stools and rested his elbows on the counter. He had the loose-limbed build of a basketball player, and at six-foot-three, he had a good three inches on me. He kept his hair layered and long in the back, and he had what many considered Hollywood good looks. But being a horse vet was about as far from glamour as it got. He'd once told me he might have reconsidered his career choice if he'd realized it meant spending half the day with his arm buried to the shoulder in a horse's rectum.

"What they did," Greg said. "I've been thinking about it all day."

"How's Sprite's eye?"

Greg raised his eyebrows. "You sure like to change the subject, don't you?"

I smiled.

"The cornea's healed," he said. "No thanks to your crew. No one's bothered to medicate it. You must've treated it aggressively in the beginning, like I told you."

"Yeah, I did."

He unbuttoned his coat and cupped his fingers around the mug. "Doesn't anyone over there do medications besides you?"

"No."

"Two hundred horses, and no one else does medications?" Greg shook his head. "What are they going to do when you go on vacation?"

"You assume a great deal."

He shot me an amused glance, then took a tentative sip of his coffee.

I sighed. "Nobody else takes the initiative, and management cuts corners wherever they can, whenever they can. As long as the boarders won't notice." I dropped two more slices into the toaster. "How often do horses get stolen around here, anyway?"

"I'd bet it's more prevalent than any of us realize. They don't always make the papers, but I hear about them on my rounds sometimes. Foxdale's more vulnerable than most operations because no one lives on the premises." He smoothed his fingers through his hair. "Someone out there doesn't mind taking risks for what I would have thought was a small profit."

"Maybe they like the risk more than the profit," I said.

His gaze sharpened on my face. "What makes you say that?"

I shrugged. "Firsthand knowledge."

Greg shook his head. "Jesus."

I pulled the slices out of the toaster and dropped them on my plate. "So, what kind of profit are we talking about?"

"Well, let's say the bottom'd dropped out of the meat market, and all they were getting was fifty cents to the pound. For a thirteen-hundred pound horse, that would be about six hundred and fifty bucks. Round up seven good-sized horses, and they'd end up with about forty-five hundred. That's not bad for something that didn't belong to them in the first place. As the price gets closer to a dollar a pound, it just plain gets more tempting."

"What's the price right now?"

Greg shrugged. "Haven't heard."

"How hard would they be to sell? They're some nice-looking horses. Wouldn't they stick out?"

"Put 'em in a crowded lot for a week or two, and they'd look like nags by the time they turned up on the auction block or, more likely, at a packing plant."

I spread some margarine across the toast. "Then they get slaughtered?"

"Yeah, but probably not in the states. Most of them are hauled to Canada first. Then the carcasses are shipped to Europe."

"Why there?"

"Because horse meat is a common…Well, people eat it."

I made a face. The idea seemed alien, like eating the family dog. "What about proof of ownership? Wouldn't they need that?"

"Some outfits aren't very careful with the paperwork end of it. And if the thieves have a connection somewhere, it would be easy."

I slid the plate down the counter and perched on the edge of a stool, hoping I didn't look as stiff as I felt.

Greg eyed me across the rim of his mug. "What goes wrong with people that they'd do something like that?" he said, and I knew he was no longer referring to the horses.

"Things don't go wrong, people do. It was their choice," I said and was surprised by the anger in my voice. "Nobody forced them."

Greg looked at me with an expression I couldn't read. Guess he hadn't expected Philosophy 101. Not from me anyway. He sighed. "I suppose you're right."

He glanced at his watch, then fished his wallet out of a pocket. "Here's my card. Pager number's on the bottom. If you need anything, let me know. The clinic's closed today, so we should be eating around seven. Why don't you come over? Susan would love to have you."

I almost smiled at his choice of words and tried to suppress my runaway imagination by blocking her out of my mind as best I could.

"Come on, Steve." He glanced around the loft—an actual hay loft that he'd converted into a spacious apartment for his teen-aged daughter before she'd decided at the last minute to attend college out of state. I'd considered myself lucky when Greg had offered to rent it to me. "It'll do you good to get out of here, have a home-cooked meal for a change."

"Some other time, thanks."

He downed the rest of his coffee and stood up. "You sure?"

I nodded, and Greg reached over and placed his hand on my shoulder. His palm pressed down on an area of bruising that was still tender. I flinched, and he dropped his hand to his side and stared at me.

"Nothing a Percodan won't fix," I said.

He shook his head and ambled over to the door. "That's strong stuff. Make sure you follow the directions."

"Yes, Mom."

He grinned as he pulled the door shut.

The sky had cleared, and the brood mares, heavy with foal, were grazing in the field where the deer had been. I walked back to the counter and fingered the toast. It was cold, and the margarine had congealed into an unappealing film. I decided I wasn't hungry after all.

◇◇◇

Five days after the horse theft, I went back to work.

I nosed the pickup down the long gravel lane, swung the truck around into my spot, and switched off the engine. It was a quarter of seven, and as usual, I was the first one there. Except for a row of trailers parked along the fence bordering the southwest field, the lot was deserted. I listened to the pings and clicks as the engine cooled and tried to ignore the tension that had crept into my shoulders and settled at the base of my skull.

I climbed out of the truck and slammed the door. As I walked down the lane past the entry door by the pay phone, for a brief second, it was the middle of the night, and I was back inside and scared half to death. Scared half to death and hurting. Hell, I was hurting.

I shook my head and tried to lose the sensation as I unlocked the office door with the new set of keys Dave had dropped off at the loft the day before. I scooped up the scraps of paper in my bin and flipped through them—a list of horses to be medicated, a reminder to leave Mary Anne's gelding in so he'd be ready for an early morning lesson, a note from Mrs. Hill that Lori's mare had thrown her bar shoe again. She'd scrawled that one in red ink and had underlined "again" three times. I added the mare's name to Nick's list, jammed the slips of paper into my coat pocket, and walked down to barn B.

Overnight, it had warmed up to a balmy thirty degrees, and the barn was fragrant with the long familiar smells of horse, hay, and sawdust. Listening to the usual chorus of nickers and whinnies, I loaded medications and supplements into the feed cart and was halfway down the aisle, when I felt as if someone had kicked me in the gut. Fourth down the med list was a name I wouldn't need to worry about.

"Gold Coast—vit. supp.," it read. Poor Shrimpy. He wasn't going to need a vitamin supplement anymore. Neither were six other horses.

I rubbed my face. I hadn't thought it would affect me like this. Hadn't prepared myself for any of it. I glanced at my watch when I heard a thump in the barn aisle across the way.

"Yo, Steve. That you?" Marty's voice.

"Yeah."

He cut through the small arena and strolled down the aisle toward me. "There's the man hisself. Our hero. Defender of horses everywhere."

"Give me a break."

He came closer and inspected my face. "Pretty."

I ignored him.

"You got a nice rainbow going—black, purple, green, yellow—kinda clashes with your blond hair, though."

I shoved the scoop into the grain, then emptied some of the pellets back into the cart until I could see the three-quart line. "How'd it go while I was out?"

"The usual circus. You shoulda been here Monday. Mrs. Gardner came back from some cruise Sunday night and found out about her horse secondhand," Marty said through a yawn. "She had a fit, and Sanders made a scene, like he actually gives a shit about his horse."

"We know better, don't we?" I said. "He doesn't get a horse, and fast, he won't be able to show off for his girlfriends."

"Man, oh man." Marty slapped his thigh. "That's right. You missed it. The Monday you were off, before the horses got pinched, Sanders brought this blonde to the barn. I swear, the girl had secretary printed on her forehead."

"Administrative assistant."

"What?"

"Never mind."

"She was really hot, man. If her skirt'd been any shorter, I'd've been checkin' out her underwear, assumin' she was wearing any."

I snorted. "What in the hell do they see in him?"

"His money, what else? The guy's got no redeeming qualities. Anyway, I happened to be hayin' down at the far end of the aisle when she—"

"Happened to be? Yeah, right. You were scopin' her out, man."

"Hey. I had to hay down there eventually, didn't I? Anyway, they're lookin' in at that stud of Whitey's, and he's hangin' like he always does. Well, she just about pees her pants when she sees how big his dick is."

I chuckled.

"And get this," Marty said. "Sanders has the nerve to compare hisself. Like he's even close."

"What an asshole." I scooped out an ounce of biotin and dumped it on top of a helping of grain. "How'd the crew do for you?"

"Brian let things slide a bit, and I caught him smoking."

"Damn." I rolled my shoulders. "Where?"

"Out behind barn A. Thought he was on vacation, you not being here and all."

"Yeah? Well, he'll earn himself a permanent vacation if I catch him at it."

Marty chuckled.

I dumped the grain through the opening in a stall front. The pellets slid down the bay's nose and clattered into the feed tub. "What's that sign about, at the corner of Rocky Ford and Stonebridge?"

"Farm got sold." Marty pushed the feed cart farther down the aisle. "Some big-time developer's gonna build a bunch of fucking mansions on puny two-acre lots."

"Oh, no," I said, but it wasn't a surprise. Everywhere you looked, what had once been prime farmland was now a housing development or shopping center or office complex.

It also wasn't a surprise, because the brothers who owned the farm were getting up there in age, and their kids wanted nothing to do with farming. Although I had been drawn into lengthy conversations with them on more occasions than I cared to remember, the old guys were good neighbors. They were as generous lending their equipment as they were dispensing free advice. And most astonishing of all, they had ignored the present-day free-for-all when it came to litigation and had given Foxdale's boarders permission to ride on their property.

"Well," I said, "at least we still have the park land."

"Yeah. In a couple years, it's gonna be the only place where there won't be houses standing eyeball to eyeball." Marty stretched and yanked off his hat. His black hair stood up from his scalp, full of static electricity. He smoothed it down with his palms. "Want me to finish graining, Steve?"

"No. This is easier than haying. I'll leave that to you guys this morning."

Marty grunted. "Why'd you come back so soon? Mrs. Hill would've let you take more time."

"If I'd stayed in the loft another day, they'd be hauling me out of there in a straightjacket."

Marty rolled his eyes and headed for the door, muttering under his breath. Though he kicked butt when he was at work, he would have taken full advantage of a shot at some time off, most of which he would have willingly spent in the sack. And he wouldn't have been lonely, of that I had no doubt. Marty had inherited his father's height and his mother's Latin American looks, and this time of year, he made the rest of us look anemic.

At twenty-two, he was a year older than me, and he made me feel old.

Chapter 3

By nine o'clock, I'd had my fill of similar comments from both crew and boarders alike. I went outside and stood in the alleyway between the barns. All morning long, geese had been flying so low that the beating of their wings was clearly audible, their distinct voices urgent. I walked up to the office, put my hand on the doorknob, and paused. Sanders was standing in front of Mrs. Hill's desk with his back to the door. His posture was rigid with tension as he stabbed a finger in the air, and I could hear him easily through the glass. I stepped inside and clicked the door shut.

"I can't believe you let this happen," he was saying. "You're all incompetent. Why didn't—" Sanders must have sensed someone behind him, because he whirled around. When he saw me, he clamped his mouth shut.

Although he was in his late forties, his skin was unnaturally smooth and moist-looking, like he'd just splashed after-shave lotion on his face. With what I hoped was an impassive expression, I watched a muscle in his jaw twitch as the silence in the room lengthened.

Mrs. Hill cleared her throat. "As I was saying, Stephen tried to stop the thieves but couldn't. He wound up in the hospital for his troubles. He's lucky to be alive."

She was pushing it a bit, but it seemed that my timing and appearance couldn't have been better. Mr. Sanders, Steel's owner, or should I say ex-owner, snatched a paper off Mrs. Hill's desk and almost bumped into me when I didn't move fast enough. He slammed the door on his way out.

What an arrogant s.o.b. I wouldn't miss him if he didn't replace his horse, but I could sympathize with him. I was sad and angry, too, every time I thought about the horses.

"Stephen, my poor boy." Mrs. Hill clambered to her feet. "You look absolutely horrid. How do you feel, dear? You should have stayed home longer."

I turned toward her as she hurried around the corner of her desk. "I'm fine, Mrs. Hill."

"Good, dear." She patted my arm.

The level of her distress took me by surprise, and that, in and of itself, was a sad commentary on my life. I tried to keep from fidgeting under her gaze.

Mrs. Hill patted my arm one last time and returned to her desk. She straightened the hem of her blouse before she lowered herself into the chair—a kind of symbolic redefining of boundaries. She would have been thrilled if I'd been more willing to accept her as a motherly substitute. God surely intended her to be one, unlike my own mother who was more adept at managing fund-raisers and organizing charities for strangers than caring for her family.

"What did Mr. Sanders want?" I said.

"Oh." She flapped her hand. "He needed insurance papers signed."

We discussed the daily operations of the farm, and when she finished bringing me up to speed, I said, "Any word on the horses?"

"No. We've sent their descriptions to all the rendering plants and auction houses we could think of, but we haven't heard anything."

"How are the owners holding up?"

"As well as expected, I suppose. Jill Gardner's taking it especially hard." Mrs. Hill stretched across her desk and plunged her thick fingers into a Foxdale mug filled with candy. "She was in here yesterday, saying she'd never buy another horse. You know how some people are when they lose a favorite pet and think they'll never get a replacement. Well, I told her she would eventually, and she thought I was saying that just so I could talk her into bringing it here when she did. Anyway, she started screeching like she does when she's upset."

Mrs. Gardner I wouldn't miss, either.

As barn manager, I'd been on the receiving end of her screeching more times than I cared to remember, but Muffy was a nice old mare. Never gave us a bit of trouble, even when she'd developed a rare blood infection and had needed antibiotic injections twice a day for a month.

Mrs. Hill absentmindedly unwrapped the plastic from a butterscotch candy and popped it into her mouth. "She said we'd never see her business again and that she was going to sue us for not keeping her precious Muffy safe." She held up the mug. "Want some?"

Trying to keep a straight face at her rendition of the story, I mumbled "No, thanks" and said, "Do you think she has a case?"

She rolled the candy from one side of her mouth to the other and frowned. "Don't know. It's not my concern. Not unless I get dragged into some silly court proceeding."

Mrs. Hill might have been the farm's manager, but she didn't have final say when it came to finances. The purse strings were controlled by the farm's owner—a Baltimore-based millionaire who, as far as I knew, had never set foot on the place. And that was half the problem. Foxdale had been on a downhill slide ever since the last nail had been driven home. Only in the past year had things turned around.

"Is there anything else?" I said.

"No, dear, carry on." She slid a stack of mail across her coffee-stained blotter and flicked on the computer.

When I found the crew, they'd already begun mucking out barn A. Cliff was perched on the John Deere 960, twisted around in the seat as he inched the tractor down the aisle. A skinny sixteen-year-old, Cliff was hopelessly undereducated, hardworking, and so enthusiastic I sometimes wondered if he was on something. He wore his blond hair spiked—effortlessly achieving the just-stuck-my-finger-in-an-outlet-look—and he liked his jeans baggy. I figured it was only a matter of time before one of us found him hanging from the tractor with his pant leg snagged on the gear shift, not to mention the fact that the color and style of his underwear had become a running joke with the crew. Checking had become reflexive. Today's choice: purple jockeys with a black waistband.

He'd just about gotten the manure wagon lined up with the next group of stalls when he caught sight of me. "Hiya, Steve."

"Where's Brian?" I said.

"Takin' a leak."

I nodded and turned, ready to retrace my steps back toward the lounge, when Cliff said, "Wrong way. He's out back."

I clamped down on my response and started around the tractor when Cliff looked beyond me and did a double take. I turned to see what he was looking at. Not what, but whom. Mrs. Elsa Timbrook had cut through the wash rack, which was surprising, considering the elegant knee-high suede boots and fur jacket she was wearing.

She walked up to me and stood so close, I figured she'd never heard about personal space. The musky scent of her perfume overpowered the pervading odors of diesel fumes, sawdust, and horse.

"Steve, I need Lite brought in for a training session with Anne."

"Yes, ma'am," I said. "Cliff, go get him for Mrs. Timbrook."

Cliff's grin widened. "Sure thing." He switched off the engine, swung his leg over the steering wheel, and jumped to the ground with a degree of agility I wouldn't have thought possible with those jeans.

Mrs. Timbrook frowned as Cliff skirted past us.

"Excuse me," I said. I squeezed between the wagon and a jumble of pitch forks and rakes that leaned against a stall front. As I approached the doorway, Brian sauntered into the aisle. He stopped abruptly when he saw me.

"Go back outside," I said. I pulled the doors closed and turned to face him. "What do you think you're doing?"

"Takin' a piss, man. Whataya think?"

"What I think is that we have restroom facilities for a reason. One of the boarders walks out here and sees you, I don't think she'd be too impressed with Foxdale's professionalism."

"Depends on which one," he said with a smirk that pissed me off.

"And another thing—"

"Oh, let me guess," Brian said. "Marty ratted me out."

"You get caught smoking on the premises again, and that's it. You can find a job somewhere else."

"Is that all?" His voice was sullen.

"Yeah."

I put my hands in my pockets and waited for him to head back, and in a moment, he did.

◇◇◇

By Friday afternoon, a week after the theft, three boarders had taken their horses somewhere safer. We were down ten horses, but I wasn't concerned. Owners who kept their horses at pasture for the winter would be looking for a facility like Foxdale as the show season drew nearer.

I walked into the implement building and yanked my keys out of my pocket. Dave, who had been hunched forward over his workbench, rhythmically rubbing a sheet of sandpaper along the length of a two-by-four, looked up when he heard me.

"How's it going?" I said.

"I'm 'bout finished with the fan jump combination. Doin' the standards right now. Wanna see?"

"Sure." I squeezed between the bush hog and an old manure spreader we no longer used and stood beside him. "They look great. I see you've finished the Liverpool."

He nodded.

I gestured to the piece of wood he was working on. "Why don't you use the sander for that?"

"Already did. I like to finish up by hand."

I ran my fingertips along the smooth wood. The show jumps he created were as much works of art as they were obstacles for the horses to negotiate. I was, as usual, impressed.

"Supplies'll be arriving next week for that cross-country jump you want built in the southeast field," Dave said. "When you want to work on that?"

"Maybe in a couple weeks." I walked over to the tractor, thinking I could do without that chore just then. "If the ground isn't frozen."

When he saw me struggling to hook up the drag, he stepped in front of me, snapped on the lynchpins, and adjusted the hitch. The man did everything with precision, without fuss, and I would miss him when he decided to retire for real.

I looked over my shoulder as I steered the tractor out of the building. Dave stood motionless, his face blank as he watched me drive off. Wisps of his thin white hair stuck out from beneath his Orioles cap, and he was sucking on his lower lip, giving an impression of the ordinary, but there was nothing common about Dave.

I got to work on the largest outdoor arena and soon found that what I had hoped would be an easy job was more difficult than I'd anticipated. The big old John Deere was difficult steering through the heavy sand at the best of times, and it didn't take long before my ribs began to ache. I swung the tractor around to the north. A cold wind stung my face, and diesel fumes, caught in a down draft, wrapped around the back of my throat.

I maneuvered the tractor through the one-stride in-and-out and made another sweep around the diagonal line of fences. As I pulled out of the turn, I almost ran into my favorite jump. I gritted my teeth and hauled on the steering wheel. The weights in front came within an inch of crashing into the rust-brown jump standard with a fox's head carved out of the middle. Mrs. Hill's sister had painted an impressive hunt scene on the wide middle panel of the jump, and my boss would have been majorly pissed if I'd creamed it.

Someone yelled, and I looked over my shoulder. A bunch of kids were running toward the barn, just goofing around. But it was not they who held my interest.

A car braked to a stop alongside the office door, ignoring an official-looking sign at the mouth of the lane that prohibited vehicular traffic of any kind. The driver climbed from behind the wheel and scanned the grounds before he walked into the office where I was certain Mrs. Hill would lay into him. I swung the tractor into another turn and made one last sweep down the outside line, then drove around to the far side of the judge's stand.

A half-hour later, I pulled out of a tight corner and glanced toward the buildings. Mrs. Hill was standing outside the office door with her arms wrapped around her chest. When she saw me look over, she signaled that she wanted to see me. Wondering what was up, I drove across the arena, parked next to the gate, and climbed stiffly to the ground. I'd had enough. Dave could finish in the morning.

I cut across the lane, head bowed, hands in my pockets, shoulders hunched against the cold, and wished I were going home instead. The driver watched my approach, and I had the distinct impression he was waiting for me. He stepped aside as I walked into the office. I glanced from him to the door between the office and lounge and frowned. It was closed, and what was more, it was locked. Mrs. Hill always left it open.

She was standing behind her desk, her face tinged with color from the brief moment she had stood in the wind. Through the side window that looked into the arena, I saw that Karen's three o'clock was in full swing, the horses cantering by in a quiet, orderly line. Voices filtered in from the lounge, which was packed that time of day with students and boarders.

"Stephen, this is—"

Someone knocked on the lounge door.

"Wait a minute," Mrs. Hill yelled. She frowned at her visitor. "Could you take this somewhere else? I need my office back."

Take what, I wondered? I looked at him with growing curiosity. Tall and broad-shouldered, he had sandy brown hair like my own and pale hazel eyes. I glanced around the room and couldn't figure why she wanted us out.

"My car will do," he said, his gaze on me, and there was a light in his eyes that spoke of nothing if not intelligence, and interest. Interest in human nature.

Outside, a strong breeze cut across the open pasture and funneled between the buildings. Like so many winter days, when the sun begins its descent, so does the temperature. I looked more closely at his car, a dark green Crown Victoria with three whip antennas sticking out of the trunk. The guy was a cop. No wonder Mrs. Hill had wanted us out. Frequent visits by the police were definitely not on her list of boarder confidence builders.

"I'm Detective James Ralston with the Maryland State Police." He pulled his identification from an inner pocket and flipped it open and shut too fast for me to read.

I wondered if he'd done it on purpose. Like a police or psychological tactic of some kind. Or a test. He'd be able to draw a different set of conclusions based on whether or not his subject asked to see it more closely. I decided I wasn't going to play.

He gestured to his car, and I climbed in, happy to get out of the wind.

Detective Ralston lifted a pair of aviator glasses off the dash, put them on, and thumbed to a blank page in a worn notebook. "I have some questions regarding the horse theft and your assault and abduction which occurred Saturday morning, February the 24th."

Ralston covered all the questions the detective in the hospital had asked, then added a few of his own. He made sporadic notes with a chewed on pencil, and I didn't think I had told him anything he didn't already know. He popped the latch on a briefcase that was wedged between the seat and a bank of controls that straddled the transmission hump, then pulled several tightly folded sheets of paper from a compartment built into the lid. He smoothed them out on his thigh. I watched him flip through the pages until he found what he wanted.

"This is a printout from the MVA." He handed me the top page. "I had them compile a list of people who own white or off-white dual-wheel pickups and a separate listing for six-horse gooseneck trailers. The one you're looking at consolidates both. As you see, there aren't many matches. Do you recognize any of the names?"

I studied the list, then shook my head.

"All right. Take a look at the list of truck owners."

He handed over a more substantial printout. The tractor-fed pages were still linked together. I took my time over the list, and before long, Ralston switched on the engine and cranked up the heat.

Many of the registered owners weren't individuals, but companies. Rose Acre Farms, Smith Landscaping, T&T Industries, Murray Construction. "I had no idea there were so many white dualies on the road," I said.

"And that's just from the surrounding counties. Howard, Montgomery, Carroll, Baltimore, Anne Arundel...Thought I'd start locally and expand the search if need be."

"Well, I think you struck out." I handed him both lists, which he laid face down in the briefcase. "I don't know any of them," I said. "How come you think I'd recognize them, anyway?"

Ralston ignored my question and handed me a smaller list. "These are the trailer owners. The list isn't broken down as well as I would have liked. Some of these trailers are probably smaller than what they used."

I studied the list and shook my head. "Sorry."

He shrugged. "It was a long shot. How about this list?" He handed me another printout. This one, however, was not from the MVA.

I scanned the sheet and told him the names I was familiar with—one farrier, two grain outfits, a fence company, and Greg, Foxdale's vet. As I read through to the end, I became conscious of the fact that he'd been watching me.

"Does Raymond Crump work for Foxdale?" Ralston said, referring to the farrier whose name I had recognized.

I shook my head. "No."

"In the past?"

"Not that I know of."

"How do you know him, then?"

"I don't. Just heard of him." I shrugged. "He doesn't hotshoe, so we don't use him."

He glanced at his notes. "What about the two feed suppliers?"

"I've heard of them, but we haven't used either company, not since I've worked here."

"How long's that been?"

"Two years in June."

"And the fence company?"

"We buy supplies from them." I shifted in my seat and leaned my back against the door.

"Do they deliver the supplies?"

"Yes."

"When were they here last?"

I thought back to our last project. "In October."

"Where do they unload? Would they know the farm's layout?"

"Yeah, probably. We have them unload different places, depending on what we're working on."

"And Gregory Davis?"

"He's Foxdale's vet." I handed Detective Ralston the sheet. "And my landlord."

He tossed the printout into his briefcase and scribbled something in his notebook. "He'd know Foxdale's routine, then?"

"I guess so. He has a whole slew of clients, so I wouldn't say he's an expert on what goes on here." I gestured to his briefcase. "You don't think they have anything to do with what happened, do you?"

He glanced at me over the rims of his glasses. "I'm checking everyone."

Ralston shifted in his seat and looked toward the barns, and I couldn't begin to guess what he was thinking. When he said nothing further, I leaned my head against the vinyl headrest and stared unseeingly at the sun visor. After several minutes, I looked over at him. He was jotting down notes in a neat, controlled script. His fingernails were clean and well manicured, his hair cut military short. Everything about the man was neat and tidy, right down to his expertly polished shoes.

I looked at my hands. Dirt was permanently ingrained in skin that was mostly chapped, and my fingernails weren't too clean, either. Come to think of it, my clothes were filthy, and I was certain I smelled like a horse, or worse.

I cleared my throat. "Why has the case been referred to you? I thought someone else was handling it?"

He shifted in his seat so that he was facing me, rested his arm on the backrest, and absentmindedly turned the pencil over in his fingers. With effort, I kept still under his gaze.

Finally, he said, "The detective who interviewed you in the hospital, Gary Linquist, he responded to a teletype I'd sent out to surrounding counties in the hope of connecting with anyone who's investigating a case similar to one I'm working."

"What kind of case?" I asked.

He gestured to the indoor. "Is that where the assault took place?"

I glanced at the huge building. "Yes."

"I need to look at the scene." He stopped fiddling with the pencil. "And I need you to walk me through what happened that night."

I looked out the windshield.

"I also want to see each stall a horse was taken out of and the location of the fuse box."

"Fuse box?"

"They didn't break the security lights," Ralston said. "Shooting them out would have made too much noise. Turning all of them off would have attracted attention. Based on Howard County's report, it looks like they just flipped the circuit breakers for half the security lights and nothing else."

I nodded. The light behind barn A and the one down the side lane to the implement building had been on. I remembered seeing them from the road.

I showed him each stall and, for the first time, realized that all of the stolen horses had been housed in barn A. Next, we went into the utility room. The fuse boxes were covered with a layer of black dust and smudges that I assumed were the result of fingerprinting.

He examined both boxes, then stooped down and angled the beam of his flashlight across the floor, even going as far as peering behind the water heaters and heating unit. "Was this room locked?"

"I don't know. It should have been." I looked at the floor. From one end of the room to the other, hoses snaked across the cement. We had stepped over them when we'd first walked into the room. "I guess the door could have been left unlocked. The crew's always coming in here to get the hoses since we can't keep them in the barns this time of year without them freezing."

"Do you remember locking it that night?"

"No."

He straightened and glanced at me but said nothing. After he examined the entire floor of the small room, I showed him where the truck and trailer had been parked between the barns, then we walked toward the parking lot.

As we neared the southwest corner of the indoor, I turned around and looked down the lane. "I was about here when I saw the rig."

"How much time passed from the time you pulled off the road until you first saw the truck and trailer?"

I glanced toward the road and shrugged. "I wasn't in a hurry. Five minutes. Probably not that long."

Ralston jerked his head toward the indoor. "You went in there to use the phone?"

"Yeah."

"Through there?" He pointed to the entry door by the bleachers.

"Yes."

"They moved fast." He crossed his arms over his chest and rubbed his chin. "Probably had a lookout posted. When he saw you turn off the road, he signaled the others, and they moved into position behind you. Except you walked into the building and surprised them. It still worked, but their strategy was risky. There's no other entrance to the farm?"

"No."

"Okay, show me what you did after you saw the truck and trailer."

I looked across the grass to the door. "Lessons are going on right now," I said. "We'll be disturbing them."

He looked me in the eye. "We won't actually be standing where the horses are working, will we?"

I shook my head.

"Well, come on then. Let's go."

I wiped my face with the sleeve of my coat, then strode across the grass. When he followed me into the arena, I said, "I left the door open, but I'd better shut it so we won't distract the horses."

"All right."

Across the arena, the school horses were lined up, waiting their turn while a cute bay pony with a naturally well-balanced stride negotiated the course of fences with ease. I pulled the door inward until the latch clicked.

"I was standing here." When I pointed at the pay phone, I was dismayed to see that my finger was trembling. I jerked my arm down to my side and stuffed my hands in my pockets, hoping he hadn't noticed. I cleared my throat. "Anyway, before I could pick up the phone, someone hit me over the head."

"Do you know what they used?"

"No…except it was hard."

Ralston's head shot up at the tone of my voice, and the corners of his mouth twitched. "Did it feel like wood, metal?"

"Oh. Wood."

"Then you fell?"

He had his flashlight out again, and if he could make anything of the jumble of footprints in the dirt, he was Sherlock Holmes incarnate.

"No. I lost my balance, but one of them shoved me against the wall there." I made a conscious effort at keeping my hand steady and pointed to the space between the door and pay phone.

Ralston stepped closer and angled the beam across the siding. Even though we kept the arena floor watered down, the horses kicked up a lot of dust. Except for a few smudge marks at shoulder height, it looked like ten years' worth of dust and dirt coated the walls, and the spiders had been busy, too. I backed out of his way and pulled my coat collar up around my neck.

After a moment, he straightened and pocketed the flashlight, then walked behind the bleachers and paused alongside the large sliding door the students used to bring their horses into the arena. Because of the cold, it was open only a foot or two, just enough for a person to squeeze through.

He looked around. "Notice anything missing? Out of place?"

I scanned the area. Except for the bleachers and two fifty-five gallon drums we used for trash, the spectator space was empty. "No. Everything looks the way it always does."

Ralston peered into one of the drums. "When were these cans emptied last?"

"I don't know. Dave empties them when they get full enough to bother with."

"Dave Wade?" Ralston said, and I saw he'd done his home-work.

"Yeah."

"Into the Dumpster out front?"

"Yes." I looked at the accumulation of empty soda cans, paper cups, and candy wrappers. Someone had even tossed a frayed crop into the trash. "The truck comes every Friday."

"It's been here already?" Ralston said.

"Uh-huh. Around one o'clock."

"Could you get Mr. Wade over here?"

"He's already gone home."

Detective Ralston compressed his lips in annoyance. When he couldn't get Dave on his cell phone, he pulled on plastic gloves and carefully emptied both drums into a large plastic bag that he'd dug out of the trunk of his car. Dressed in a suit and tie, he looked as incongruous rooting around in the trash as he had earlier walking through the barn.

He taped the mouth of the bag shut, scribbled on a label, and chucked it into the trunk. When he noticed my expression, he said, "If Mr. Wade hasn't emptied them since the theft, it's worth a closer look."

I nodded and tried to smother a grin as I followed Ralston back into the indoor. When he asked to see where I'd collapsed, I pointed out the spot alongside the bleachers.

Ralston unhooked his flashlight and flicked it on. He scanned the ground and angled the beam under the bleachers near the metal uprights. I pulled my cap off and yanked my coat open. At the sound of the snaps popping apart in quick succession, Ralston glanced up from where he was crouched. I crossed my arms on one of the planks at shoulder level, rested my head on my arms, and wondered what was taking him so long. My skin felt clammy, though the air temperature was close to freezing.

"What happened next, Steve?"

I squinted at him, then reluctantly lifted my head and told him the rest.

Ralston folded his arms across his chest. "And you don't—"

A sharp crack split the air and echoed off the metal walls. I jumped as if I'd been shocked with a cattle prod. It was just one of the horses rapping the top rail of a jump.

Just one of the horses.

I rubbed my forehead.

"Okay," Ralston said. "I think we're done in here. Let's finish up in the car."

"Finish up?" I mumbled.

"Yes. I have a few more things to go over."

Back outside, the white metal siding glowed pink as the sun neared the horizon. It wouldn't be long before it disappeared behind the tree line, and as so often happens, the wind had died down with the sun's descent. I climbed back into Ralston's car and wondered when I'd be getting back to work.

He slammed his door and flipped through the ever present notebook. "I have a list of the owners of the stolen horses. I want you to tell me what you know about each one, okay?"

I nodded, and he started checking off names. I hesitated when he got to Sanders.

He looked over at me, his pencil poised, waiting. "What's the deal with him?"

I shrugged. "Nothing. I just don't like him much."

"Why?"

"No particular reason. It's more a personality conflict than anything." I sighed. "I don't really know why I don't like him....He's not a good horseman."

"What do you mean?"

"Oh, stuff like not cooling out his horse after he's worked him, being too aggressive when he rides. Things like that. It's more like he uses his horse, treats him like an object instead of a living, breathing animal."

Frowning at my explanation, Ralston switched on the engine and slid the control levers into position for maximum heat output. I listened to the purr of the engine and thought about how Sanders used his horse as a bizarre sort of aphrodisiac.

Ralston must have seen something in my expression because he said, "What are you thinking?"

"Nothing....Nothing to do with this."

"Tell me anyway."

He'd said it like I didn't have a choice. Like I wouldn't be getting out of his car if I didn't tell him what he wanted to know, which kind of pissed me off. But it wasn't any big deal, so I told him.

When he checked off the last name, he said, "The evidence clearly shows they were familiar with the farm's layout and routine."

"Um."

"Tell me about the employees. Anyone have a gripe with management?"

I thought about Brian and decided that his grumpy attitude didn't make him a suspect. "No. They're a pretty good group."

He shifted in his seat and leaned against the door. "And you didn't recognize their voices?"

I shook my head. "The guy with the ball cap," and a whine in his voice, I thought but kept to myself, "I've never seen him before. I'm sure of that. As for the other two, far as I remember, they always spoke in a whisper. I don't know whether I could have recognized them under those circumstances."

"Maybe you do know them, and they were trying to disguise their voices."

I didn't like that thought one little bit. That someone I knew could be so callous. Could hate me so much. Someone I knew, maybe even liked and trusted. I didn't believe it. I turned in my seat to face him and said, "So. What similarities?"

"What?"

"You said there are similarities between the case you're working on and this one."

He looked at me with an expression that would have served him well in a high-stakes poker game. When he spoke, his voice was flat. "Six months ago, seven horses were stolen from a farm in Carroll County. Not far from here, actually. The owner was murdered."

Chapter 4

I couldn't breathe. Couldn't speak.

He, however, continued. "A white or off-white pickup, pulling a dark-colored horse trailer, was seen in the vicinity around the time we estimate the owner was abducted. A month later, two boys were hiking a trail that parallels the western bank of the Patuxent when they discovered the partially-buried body of a white male. He was later identified as the farm's owner. Before he died, he had been beaten and," he paused, still watching me, "his wrists had been bound with baling twine. It was still on what was left of the body."

I leaned my head against the side window and closed my eyes. A humming noise filled my ears, and I felt as if I were sinking, the blackness behind my eyelids spiraling out of control.

"Mr. Cline...you okay?"

I swallowed. My throat was dry. My tongue felt like it was stuck to the roof of my mouth. I opened my eyes. "Yeah, sure," I mumbled. "How the hell do you think I am?" I couldn't keep the anger out of my voice. Or was it fear?

He didn't say anything, just looked at me with that damn uninformative expression of his, and I wondered if anything rattled him.

I shifted in my seat and stared out the window. A dozen riders were circling their horses, waiting to go inside for their lesson. Behind us, the sun cast long shadows down the lane. The light had an orangish late-afternoon quality to it. Voices drifted on the cold air while some of the horses, impatient to be going, blew down their noses and pawed the ground. Farther down the lane, the barns looked warm and inviting… and safe.

He cleared his throat. "So, now you see why it's important that you carefully think through everything that happened, every detail."

"I already have." I rubbed my face. "I didn't see enough or hear enough to be a threat to them. They took me anyway, and I learned more because of it." Though what good it would do, I couldn't imagine. "Once I was out of the trailer, I could see them better. The leader had light brown hair, maybe blond." I licked my lips and turned to face him. "So, if they wanted to kill me," I paused and hoped he couldn't hear the tremor in my voice, "why didn't they just do it here, on the farm? When I was out?"

He closed his notebook and slid the pencil through the channel formed by the spiraled metal wire. "These guys are smart. In the first place, their timing would have been perfect if you hadn't interrupted them. Under normal circumstances, they wouldn't have been disturbed. In the first incident, in Carroll County, it was just pure luck that we got a description of the truck and trailer, as vague as it is. Howard got zilch when they canvassed this neighborhood. Montgomery County didn't do any better at the location where you escaped. Whatever they used to hit you with, they took with them. They didn't leave fingerprints. The ground was too frozen for tire tracks. You saw how careful they were after you got away from them. That's rare. I'm surprised they didn't double back after they lost you in the woods."

I groaned.

Ralston compressed his lips and studied me with an otherwise dispassionate expression. "And what do you think would have happened Saturday morning, when the rest of the employees arrived to find seven horses missing and you nowhere to be found?"

I looked at him and didn't think I liked the implication.

"Your boss and fellow employees might have been certain you had nothing to do with it," he said. "But sure as I'm sitting here, the police would've been looking for a suspect, not a body. If these guys were really smart, they would have gotten rid of your truck. Then you would have been on top of our list, without question. Not until the connection was made between the two cases would we seriously have considered that you'd been abducted, and by that time, we would've been lucky to find your body. In the other case, we never found the murder scene. We were damn lucky to find the body, and after a month's exposure in the heat and humidity we had last summer, much of the forensic evidence had been destroyed."

I shifted in my seat. Such a casual discussion of inhumanity was more than a little unsettling.

Ralston reached inside his jacket. "Here's my card. Call me if you think of anything else, no matter how insignificant."

He dropped the gear into reverse, and as I put my hand on the door latch, it occurred to me that they had tried to move my truck. I told him how Marty had found it. That they must have been unsuccessful because the starter was acting up. That I was certain I hadn't left the door open, which had drained the battery. I refrained from telling him about Marty's hot-wiring capabilities.

He tossed his notebook into the briefcase and lowered the lid but left it unlatched. "You need to be careful when you come here outside normal business hours."

"Why?" It came out high-pitched. I cleared my throat. "Why would they come back?"

"I doubt they will. As long as they stay smart they won't, but..."

"But what?"

He shrugged. "Just a thought."

"Oh, great." I shoved his card into my jeans pocket. "Who was the man who was, eh...killed?"

"James Peters. Ever heard of him?"

I shook my head.

"He and his wife owned and operated a horse farm. Hunter's Ridge. He went out to check on a sick horse and never came back."

I climbed out of the car and watched Ralston drive off. With him went any confidence I'd been able to scrape together in the past week.

The lane was deserted now. All the horses had gone inside for their lesson, out of the wind, out of the cold. The glare from the sodium vapors was taking over in the fading daylight, and after the warmth of the car, the air felt bitterly cold. I pulled my collar up around my neck, got back on the tractor, and drove to the implement building on auto pilot.

I parked next to the manure spreader and didn't bother unhitching the drag. Someone else could do it in the morning. I stopped alongside Dave's workbench and smoothed my fingers across the expertly sanded wood. The sweet aroma of freshly cut lumber still hung in the air.

He never came back.

My legs buckled, and I collapsed onto Dave's chair. I wrapped my arms around my waist and hunched forward to keep from shaking. I felt like I had when I was a kid. Felt as helpless and as scared and alone as I had the day my old man dropped me off at a dude ranch in West Virginia a week after my eleventh birthday. I'd stayed the entire summer. Learned more about horses than I'd thought possible, and that seemed to piss off my father even more. The following year, I'd gone off to soccer camp, then lacrosse. Being on my own like that, I'd learned how to take care of myself. By the time I was thirteen, I had grown used to the routine. Actually looked forward to it. Hell, it was better than staying at home with him, with them, where I wasn't wanted, both of them too caught up in their own lives to parent.

I'd thought I could handle anything. Until now.

After a while, I squinted at my watch and waited for the numbers to come into focus. I was late for evening feeding. I wiped my face, blew my nose, and hoped no one had missed me. As I hurried down the rutted lane, I saw that the horses had already been brought in for the night. The winter day had come to an end.

Marty was standing in the middle of the feed room, staring at the cart. He turned with a start when I walked through the doorway. "Where the hell've you been? I was ready to grain the horses myself."

"I'll do it."

"Good. I don't know how you stand it. All those damn supplements." He squinted at me. "Hey, you don't look so good, Steve. You comin' down with somethin'?"

"No, I'm fine." I rubbed my face. "Any problems this afternoon?"

"Nope. Everything's done. Was that a cop you were talking to?"

"Uh-huh."

"What'd he want?"

I glanced at Marty then looked down at the feed cart. "Nothing much."

When I said nothing further, Marty said, "Well, seein' as you're gonna do the feeding, can I leave now?"

"Sure...have a good night."

"I always do. Jessica's off," he added with a grin that could only be described as wicked.

I chuckled. Marty had the pursuit of happiness down to an art form. The pursuit of sex, more like.

"You sure you're all right, Steve?"

I told him to get the hell out before his girlfriend found a replacement and watched as he strolled out of the feed room, whistling under his breath.

◇◇◇

Saturday afternoon, when the last batch of private turnouts were in their paddocks, I went into the feed room and lifted my clipboard off the shelf above the workbench. I leafed through the pages until I came to the medications list. There were no wounds to clean, medicate, and bandage, no eyes to apply ointment to, no injections to give. I was caught up until it was time to grain. I replaced the clipboard and walked up to the office.

The last lessons of the day were winding up, but the farm was busy as usual. I grabbed a magic marker off Mrs. Hill's desk, pulled some paper out of the printer, and printed in bold black letters:

> NOTICE. A white or light-colored dualie and an older dark-colored, six-horse gooseneck were used in the horse theft at Foxdale Farm on February 24th. If you have any information regarding the identity of the rig's owner, or know anything about the theft, contact Steve Cline.

I added Foxdale's phone number and my home number in the lower right-hand corner and made a couple of copies. I thumbtacked a sheet to the bulletin board in the office and walked into the lounge.

I tacked a copy squarely in the center of the cork board by the soda machine. Across the room, Maryanne, Sheila, and Mrs. Curry had pigeonholed Mrs. Hill by the coffee machine. Because of the horse theft, they were planning another boarder meeting. I left before they drew me into what I knew from experience would be a long conversation and headed back to barn A. I stopped at the cork board in the aisle near the wash rack, rearranged some advertisements, and pulled off several outdated announcements. I pinned up my notice.

"Cline, tack up Bethany for me."

I turned around as Whitcombe, one of Foxdale's trainers, looked over my shoulder. As his gaze flicked over the wording, I noticed a momentary tightening around his eyes. His thick, curly red hair, which he had the good sense to keep cut short, was damp with sweat from his last ride, and his freckled, weather-wrinkled skin reminded me of a prune.

"Fall off a horse?" he said, referring to the faded bruising under my right eye.

"No." I edged past him and started down the aisle toward the tack room.

"I'll be in the lounge," he called after me. "And, Cline?"

I stopped and pivoted around. "Sir?"

"I want a dropped nose band and a Dr. Bristol bit, and this time get it right."

Get it right? Who was he kidding? I turned away from him and wondered when he'd grow tired of his stupid little control game and give it up, always asking for one thing, then telling me I'd gotten it wrong when I hadn't. Trying to make me look stupid. Maybe he wouldn't stop until I reacted. Got myself in trouble.

"Cline?"

I slid my hands into my pockets and turned around. Movement behind him caught my eye. Marty. Marty bouncing into the aisle, swinging a lead rope in his hand.

"I didn't hear you," Whitcombe said.

I refocused my gaze on Whitcombe's ugly face. "Yes...sir."

He smiled as he spun around and headed for the exit. Marty suddenly became interested in the floor. As soon as Whitcombe passed him, Marty looked up at me and grinned, and I could have killed him. He caught up with me, glanced over his shoulder, and whispered, "The asshole likes to ride more than horses, don't he?"

"Marty, don't." I cradled my arm along my ribs and tried not to laugh. "It hurts too much."

"Awh, Stevie, don't cry."

"Damn it, Marty, stop." I walked into the tack room and heard his footsteps behind me. "Don't you have something to do?" I said over my shoulder.

"No."

I spun the combination on the supply locker.

"I can see it now," Marty said. "One day you're gonna let 'im have it and get your ass fired."

"Won't happen. He's not worth it." I creaked the door open and stared at the pile of brushes, curry combs, rub rags, and cans of hoof oil. "Help me out, Marty. Grooming's a pain right now."

"Sure."

"Hope Bethany's not too dirty."

"She's turned out."

"Oh, shit. I forgot."

"I'll go get her," Marty said.

"Thanks. Bet that's why he wanted to ride her in the first place, 'cause he knew getting her ready would be more work."

"The guy's a genuine, fu—" Marty glanced at me and shut his mouth. "Be back in a sec."

He ended up doing most of the grooming and all the tacking up. When he was finished, I led Bethany into the indoor and waited for Whitcombe. I could see him in the office, talking to Mrs. Hill and one of the boarders. He saw me but pretended he hadn't—typical Whitcombe. I was ready to walk over and tap on the glass, when he pushed out of his chair and walked around to meet us.

He carried a crop in his right hand and absentmindedly slapped it against his boot. Bethany moved away at his approach, subliminally voicing her opinion of who was preparing to climb on her back. I steadied the mare while he checked the girth and stirrups, gathered up the reins, and stood next to the horse with his knee bent, waiting for a leg-up.

Damn. The guy weighed a good one-eighty, and—

"Give me a leg-up, Cline."

"I can't...sir."

"What do you mean, you can't?"

"I, eh…hurt my ribs," I said, trying to keep the distaste I felt for him from showing and conscious I wasn't succeeding.

"You're stinking useless. Here." He jerked on the mare's mouth. "Hold her by the bleachers."

Whitcombe stepped onto the plank. I held Bethany in position, put pressure on the stirrup so the saddle wouldn't slip, and wished he'd get on with it. The ribs were hurting more than I cared to admit. Whitcombe grunted as he hauled himself into the saddle. He swung his leg over the mare's back and almost kicked me in the face.

I glared at him as I stepped back. He wisely didn't look at me, but busied himself with getting organized. He'd done it on purpose; although, to anyone watching, it would have looked like a careless accident.

I left before I said or did something I'd regret.

I went home early, and around eight o'clock, Marty showed up unannounced at my door with a cardboard box loaded down with an assortment of booze.

I fingered a cheap bottle of Gordon's vodka and whistled. "What's all this?"

"Ale for what ails ya."

He thunked the box down on the counter by the sink, and I shook my head.

"Contrary to what those boys in white think, the medicinal qualities of alcohol are highly underrated. This'll have you straightened out in no time."

"Let me guess. Jessica's at work."

"You fuckin' slay me." He hefted two twelve-packs out of the box.

"Christ," I said. "You intending to break the world record for alcohol consumption, or what?"

"Hey, I knew you wouldn't have shit in this joint."

"Just some wine."

Marty rolled his eyes as he popped the top of what I determined was his second Budweiser. An empty lay in the bottom of the box. He'd gotten a head start on the drive over. I watched as he rooted through the refrigerator and cabinets, found what he wanted, then grabbed a spoon out of the drawer by the stove. He dumped a quart of Land O' Lakes sour cream into a bowl, followed by two packets of dip mix.

"Hungry, are we?" I said.

Marty lifted a bag of UTZ potato chips out of the box, looked at me, and grinned. "Not for long."

I sloshed some vodka into a tall glass and topped it off with some orange juice.

"You always put your mail in the trash?" Marty had dropped the empty sour cream container into the can and was holding a letter from my father between his fingers. "You forgot to open it."

"I didn't forget."

He looked up from the envelope. "Damn, Steve. Don't you wanna know what it says?"

"I know what it says. 'Come back home and go to this college and major in that subject, and I'll get you in at Johns Hopkins or Yale or wherever, and you can have whatever you want as long as it suits me.'" I sat cross-legged on the floor.

"Ain't nothin' wrong with a little bribery, as long as you get what you want in the end. So what if he wants you to follow in his snotty, condescending, ivy-leagued, scalpel-wielding footsteps."

I thought I was going to choke. "How'd you like somebody telling you how and where and when to take a piss?"

Marty shrugged. "Depends what I get in return, I suppose."

I picked up the remote and turned on the CD player.

"Why didn't you finish school, anyway?" Marty said. "With your smarts, not to mention your old man's connections, you could've gone anywhere, done anything, even if you did have to kiss his ass from time to time."

"That's exactly why I didn't." Not to mention the fact that I had felt rudderless, without purpose, and most devastating to me…without passion. Then there was that sour taste I knew I'd have in my mouth if I let him run my life. I swallowed some orange juice, set the glass on the floor, and closed my eyes. I didn't know what I wanted to do with my life, just knew I didn't want to live his.

Marty dragged a kitchen stool around onto the carpet, then perched on it with his heels hooked on the lower rung. "Plus, you'd still have that sweet, motherfuckin' ride of yours. Hell, I would of stayed just for that."

I stared at him and wondered where all this shit was coming from.

"I can't believe he kicked you out just 'cause you quit school."

"He liked control, Marty. Quitting college was only half of it. What really pissed him off was that I went to work on a horse farm. It didn't go with his image, having one of his sons slinging shit for a living. What would his colleagues think? Guess he figured if he kicked me out, I wouldn't make it on my own, and before long, I'd be back home, following his marching orders like a good little boy."

"I don't know," Marty said. "It just don't figure. You'd've thought you'd whacked somebody, the way he treats you. Here you get the shit beat out of you, and you can't even talk to him, can't even go to your own parents for help or—"

"Marty…"

"—support. He's an asshole. He should be proud of you instead of—"

"Marty, quit."

"You're even defending him, for Christ's sake. And all because you made the wrong fucking career choice."

"I'm not—"

"He pisses me off. Doesn't he care?"

I was on my feet, and I think that only then did Marty realize what he was doing. "No." I glared at him. "He doesn't care." I walked over to the audio system, cranked up the volume to some rock 'n roll, and said under my breath, "He only cares about himself."

Marty was behind me then, and I hadn't heard him. He put his hand on my shoulder, wanting me to turn around. "Steve?"

I shrugged him off. I felt like hitting him, but it wasn't Marty I wanted to hit. I stood there and stared at the throbbing green and red lights arcing across the panel in sync with the music. If I stared at them long enough, they blurred together, everything else in the room dissolving into non-existence.

"They killed him, Marty." I said softly.

"What?"

"They went to steal some horses, and they killed him."

I told him about James Peters and watched the animation die out of his face.

At some point, I must have drifted off, because I woke on the floor, in the dark, with a stiff neck. I moved to check my watch and realized Marty had dropped a blanket on top of me. Two o'clock. I staggered to my feet and saw him lying on my bed, on my pillow, under my blankets.

"Fuck."

Well, at least he'd had the sense not to drive home. I took some pain pills, which I probably shouldn't have, pulled out my sleeping bag, and went back to sleep.

◇◇◇

It took all of Sunday to recover from that stunt, but by the time Tuesday morning rolled around, I was halfway to normal. Even the rib pain had settled into a dull ache, noticeable, but no longer annoying.

Like clockwork, Foxdale's farrier bumped his pickup down the lane at precisely seven-fifty-nine on the first Tuesday in March. He swung the truck around, backed up to the barn door, and braked to a halt.

"What've you got for me today, Steve?" Nick asked as he lowered the tailgate.

"Thirteen. You've done them before." I pulled a crumpled sheet of paper out of my back pocket and handed it to him.

He skimmed the list, grunting at a name or two, then tossed it back at me. I leaned against the barn door and watched him rummage through an assortment of shoes, pads, and nails. Anything an equine athlete might require to produce a winning performance.

Nick was a short, compact man with wiry black hair and a heavily muscled back from years spent doubled up under the bellies of countless horses. I'd never seen him without a twisted bandanna tied around his head, even in winter, and his thick neck always looked sunburned. Unlike Foxdale's last farrier, Nick always had what we needed in stock, even for the most complicated job. But what I appreciated most was the fact that he actually liked horses. I'd known more than one farrier who behaved as if they didn't like horses at all.

Nick hopped off the tailgate, reached back into the bed, and dragged the anvil toward him. The resultant screech of metal against metal caused me to grit my teeth. When he switched on the forge, I brought out the first horse, a bright chestnut gelding with exceptionally thin soles. He had been one of the most difficult horses I'd ever held for Nick.

"Well, this ol' boy's finally come round," Nick said, reading my thoughts.

"Thanks to you," I said.

"No...I think it was your singin' that did it," he said straight-faced.

I groaned. "Don't remind me."

"Well, come on now," Nick drawled in a hillbilly twang that I had long since concluded was mostly act. "It was torture all right, but it calmed 'im down. Must have a twisted sense of music." He ran his hand down the gelding's neck. "He's finally recovered his trust. Who did 'im before me?"

"Barren."

"Well then, that explains it. He's screwed up more of 'em than a hooker on a Saturday night."

I snorted.

We were on the second horse of the day when I heard the hay truck pull down the lane. Since Nick was working at the forge, I cross-tied the mare and told him I'd be back in a minute. I ran outside and caught up with Marty before he got to the truck.

"Marty, wait."

"What's up?"

"I want you to supervise the unloading. Get some of the guys to help you. Count every bale they throw off that truck. And," I paused and caught my breath, "I left a scale in the implement building. It's hung up and ready to go. I want you to weigh bales, say, at twenty-bale intervals. Let me have the figures as soon as you're done."

"What, they're ripping us off?"

"I think so."

"Stupid bastards," Marty said through a yawn. "How come it don't surprise me?"

"Thanks…oh, and did Brian come in yet?"

"Nope. Called in sick."

"All right. And let me know what the tonnage on Harrison's paperwork is, too."

"Sure thing, boss." I watched him head for the truck, knowing full well Marty couldn't care less about little scams like that. I wondered why I did.

Forty-five minutes later, we were almost finished with horse number three, and Marty still hadn't come back.

"Nick," I said. "Do you know anyone who owns a white dualie and an old, dark-colored, six-horse? A gooseneck."

He straightened and stretched the kinks out of his back. "Not offhand. Why?"

"Here you go, boss," Marty said in my ear. He handed me a slip of paper. "Anything else?"

I shook my head, and Marty spun around and headed back to barn B.

I worked out the sums. The tonnage was off. Somehow, Harrison was altering the figures from the weigh station. In the past, all I'd had were suspicions. Now I had proof. Unfortunately, bringing this to Harrison's attention would not be pleasant. He was irritated with me anyway, because I didn't hesitate to return moldy or poor-quality hay and demand credit—services he touted, but when it came to the actual case in point, he did grudgingly.

"What about that trailer, Steve?" Nick said as he clinched a nail flush against the hoof wall.

"Oh. A rig like that was used by whoever stole the horses."

"From Foxdale?" he said.

"Yep."

"I didn't think the police had any leads."

"They don't. Not if they can't figure out who owns the trailer." I watched Boris, Foxdale's lone barn cat, make his way down the aisle. When he saw me, he trotted over and leaned against my leg. I pushed him away with my foot, but he came right back, not getting the hint. "Damn it."

Nick paused with the rasp in his hand. "What's that?"

"Oh, nothing," I said. "Just that this stupid cat won't leave me alone. Have you heard of any other horse thefts or—" I glanced over my shoulder.

Mr. Harrison had squeezed between Nick's truck and the barn door and was walking down the aisle toward us. A tall, plain-faced man, he kept his thinning blond hair combed across his scalp in a misplaced effort to hide the fact that he was balding prematurely.

He nodded to Nick, then handed me his clipboard. "Any return bales?"

"No." I hesitated. "There's a problem, though."

"What?"

I looked from the paperwork to his face. He had narrowed his eyes, and I had a sudden impression that the muscles in his face had settled into an arrangement they were accustomed to. Deep wrinkles creased his forehead, and his eyebrows had bunched together into a straight line that shadowed his gray eyes.

I cleared my throat. "There's a discrepancy between the tonnage stated on the invoice and what we actually received."

"What are you talking about?" His face was turning red, and he'd clenched his hands.

"By my calculations, we're about twelve hundred pounds short, give or take a bale or two. And that's just this one delivery," I said and saw he knew exactly what I meant.

He looked so angry, I thought he might hit me. Instead, he grabbed the clipboard, scratched out his figure, wrote in a new one, and shoved it back into my hand.

I looked at the invoice. He'd pressed so hard, the pen's tip had ripped through the top sheet. I checked it, signed it, gave it back to him.

He stood there for a couple of seconds, staring at me with eyes that had become oddly vacant. The muscles along his jaw were bunched with tension, and I still thought he might slug me.

He turned abruptly and headed down the aisle. His shoulders were hunched forward under his stained coveralls as he walked out of the barn and into the flood of sunlight.

Behind me, Nick chuckled. "You sure know how to make friends."

"I wouldn't want him for a friend," I said quietly.

"No. He's a creepy bastard. Mean too, what with that incident a while back."

"What incident?"

"You didn't hear about that?"

I shook my head.

He slid the hoof knife into its slot on his leather apron and picked up a rasp. "Well, about a year ago, there was a stink about him beating a horse—"

"He has horses?"

"Yep. Owns a farm west of here. Can't remember the name right now. Anyway, some horse did somethin' that pissed 'im off, so he tied it to a post and beat it with a whip. Cut the animal up good, so they say. Blood everywhere. Somebody reported him to the Humane Society. Course, by the time they showed, the horse was nowhere to be found." He spit a glob of chewing tobacco into an open stall. "Nothin' ever came of it."

"What kind of farm's he run?"

"Hunter/jumpers, lessons, sales, anything, I imagine…. Got his hand in everything. Makes 'im feel important."

"You shoe for him?" I said and wondered whether Harrison would have the nerve to continue supplying us.

"Yep. For 'bout a year now. But I'm thinkin' of droppin' him."

"Why's that?"

"Guy's got a major cash flow problem." Nick flipped the rasp over in his hand. "Ol' Steel use to board at his farm."

"You mean Mr. Sanders' horse?"

"Yep."

"He's one of the horses that was stolen," I said.

"I know. Sanders had him insured for twenty grand while he was at Harrison's."

"You're kidding?"

"Nope. My sister works for the insurance company that issued the claim. Agent who sold 'im the policy had a couple of tense minutes over it, 'cause in retrospect, it appears the horse ain't worth as much as all that."

"I wouldn't have thought so."

By the time Nick's truck disappeared down the road, my side was throbbing, and I was beat. Thinking about Mr. Sanders' little insurance policy, I left a message for Detective Ralston and headed home. As I climbed the steps to the loft, a trace of light lingered in the west, conclusive evidence that the days were getting longer.

I closed the kitchen door behind me and dropped my mail on the counter. The loft was oppressively quiet, the air stale.

I dumped everything I'd been wearing onto the floor in the closet. Nothing smelled worse than burnt horse hoof. Even I couldn't stand myself. I took a long, hot shower, then sloshed some Jack Daniels' over ice and downed a Percodan. Between the two of them, the rib pain didn't stand a chance.

Chapter 5

Wednesday morning, I could have done without. The combination of whiskey and pain medication that had successfully obliterated feeling of any sort the night before had mutated into a sledgehammer of a headache between my temples. And it didn't help that the first person I ran into was Brian.

"What'n the hell'd you tell that cop?" he asked before I'd even unlocked the feed room door.

"What cop?"

"That cop that was here, Ran…"

"Ralston?"

"Yeah, him."

"What about it?" I said. "He's investigating the horse theft."

"I know that," he snapped. "He was here again Monday, day you was off. Questions he was asking, you'd of thought I was guilty or somethin'."

I shook my head. "Brian, I didn't say anything about you."

"You must of said something."

"No," I said and knew I was wasting my breath. "I didn't."

Brian sulked off, and I wondered if he'd ever see that he created his own reality. And I was impressed with Ralston. He'd pegged Brian pretty quick, and I wondered how he had classified me.

The morning dragged on. Boarders came and went. Horses were shifted from stall to paddock or paddock to stall. A third of the stalls had been mucked out by lunch time, and the headache had disappeared without my being aware of it. I walked into the lounge, got my lunch out of the fridge, and checked the office. Mrs. Hill had gone home to eat, and everyone else had gone out. For something to do, I switched on the TV, sank into the sofa cushions, and flipped through the channels. The news was a repeat of the day before; only the names had changed. The soaps were a farce. The talk shows worse. I hit the play button. Someone had left an instructional video in the machine, and though it didn't much interest me, it was better than nothing.

I had almost finished my lunch when the door to the lounge opened. I looked over my shoulder.

Mrs. Elsa Timbrook walked into the room. Well, she hadn't walked, not really. I doubted she walked anywhere. More accurately, she strode with long lithe legs, like a cat. Or a tigress. She stood just inside the doorway and surveyed the room as the door swung shut behind her. Satisfied that we were alone, she looked at me and smiled, and I felt my pulse pick up.

She had long blond hair that tended to frizz when it rained, stunning green eyes, and a body so sensual in design and proportion, she ought to be illegal. I looked back at the television and tried to ignore her. She crossed the room and sat next to me. I glanced at her and managed a weak smile, then looked at the apple in my hand and couldn't imagine finishing my lunch.

She wriggled around on the sofa and slid her leg onto the cushion, like she was going to sit Indian-style, but she left the other leg where it was so that her knees were spread apart. She made sure her shin was pressing into my leg. My gaze drifted downward. Her skin-tight breeches left little to the imagination, and I felt frozen, sitting there like some damn idiot, completely under her control.

"Hi, Steve," she said in that husky voice of hers that always got me wondering what she sounded like when she wasn't putting on an act. Or maybe she'd played it for so long, the act was the only thing that was real.

"Hello, Mrs. Timbrook."

"Elsa."

I cleared my throat. "Elsa."

"Oooh, you've hurt your face." She leaned forward and brushed my cheek with her fingertips. "What happened?"

I was surprised she hadn't heard, but the rest of the boarders, the majority being female, left her strictly alone. "I, uh…got hurt."

She leaned closer, and the scent of her perfume filled my nostrils. "Poor honey."

Elsa put her hand on my knee, and it was then that I noticed her ring. I'd often wondered what her husband was like, though she probably never did it with him—the thrill for her was the chase. The more you resisted, the more determined she became. The woman liked control as long as she was the one who had it, and I almost felt sorry for him.

She looked at the TV. "What are you watching?"

"'Rider Position and Technique,'" I mumbled.

"You don't need to watch that." She slid her hand farther up my leg. "I can teach you everything you need to know about position and technique."

Christ. I bet she could. I felt my face flush, and it was getting damn uncomfortable sitting there like that. I needed to adjust myself in the worst sort of way. Maybe she'd do it for me, and imagining that made it worse.

I shifted on the cushion just as she slid her hand off my leg in a slow upward movement. Her fingers brushed across my crotch. I exhaled sharply.

Elsa's eyes were strangely unfocused under heavy lids, and she was breathing through her mouth. She straightened and unzipped her coat, then reached up with both hands and shifted it off her shoulders. It tumbled onto the cushion behind her and slid to the floor in slow motion. Her sweater was softly luminescent under the fluorescent lights, the swell of her breasts pressing against the fabric.

She reached over and stroked her fingers across the top of my hand. Her touch sent a jolt through my body, like electricity was coursing through my veins instead of blood.

Elsa moved her hand beneath mine and took hold of the apple I had forgotten was there. My grip was so tight, I had to force my fingers to relax as she pried it from my grasp. As she turned it in her hands, I noticed that her nail polish was the same deep red. She had great hands. Long slender fingers, long nails, a light touch. I bet she was good with her hands. Practiced anyway.

When she had the apple just so, she gazed into my eyes, slid her tongue across the skin, and took a bite where I'd last taken one. I imagined our saliva mixing together, and one thought led to another.

I grabbed her wrist. She started, then I watched transfixed as the expression in her eyes and on her face shifted from surprise to daring. She parted her lips, and her warm breath brushed my cheek.

I laced my fingers in her hair and kissed her roughly on the mouth. She pushed her tongue between my teeth, and I was vaguely aware of the taste of apple. When I moved my hand over her breast, she sighed. A quiet sound, barely audible. Beneath the gauze-like fabric, her nipple hardened under my palm. I smoothed my hand over her flat stomach and curled my fingers under her sweater.

She clamped down on my wrist and pushed my hand away. "Well. It's about time you came around, Stevie. But not here, silly. Your Mrs. Hill might—"

The door opened.

I jerked upright. Marty came in along with a blast of cold air. Elsa didn't bother to check, and I couldn't believe her composure. Practice probably had a lot to do with it.

She licked her lips. "See what I mean."

Marty was stomping his boots on the mat when he looked up and saw the expression on my face. He paused in mid-stomp and stared with his mouth open. I looked away from him, and he burst out laughing.

"Steve…a horse in barn B," he choked on the words, "…is colicky."

I jumped to my feet. Elsa stood more slowly, behaving as if Marty wasn't even there. He had been a previous conquest, easy by anyone's standards. Elsa lowered her gaze to my crotch and smiled. When I yanked my jacket off the back of the sofa and held it at waist height, I thought Marty was going to have a seizure, he was laughing so hard. And he was making a damn ass of himself. I glared at him as Elsa reached over and took my hand in hers. She placed the apple in my palm and closed my fingers around it. She didn't let go, at least not right away.

I had a sudden vision of Eve in the garden of Eden. Poor Adam. He hadn't stood a chance.

I cleared my throat. "I'll be right there," I said to Marty and was relieved when he spun around and went back outside.

As I leaned forward and picked Elsa's coat off the floor, I became intensely aware of her body's proximity to mine. My hair brushed against her thigh when I straightened, and I was afforded a slow-motion, close-up tour of her body—legs, crotch (couldn't help but pause there), waist, breasts (another pause), lips, eyes.

I held out her coat.

She squeezed my hand as she took the coat. "Later, Stevie."

I shrugged. Couldn't think of anything intelligent to say, and with a conscious effort, I walked slowly to the door.

Outside, Marty was waiting for me, and he was still laughing. "Fucking shit. Another couple minutes, and you'd of done it."

"Marty…be quiet."

"Why don't you put your coat on, Steve?"

"Shut up," I said. And amazingly, he did.

We walked past the restrooms, and I dropped the apple into a trash can. I was no longer hungry, not for food anyway, and the hunger I felt, I could do nothing about.

Too bad I hadn't brought a banana for dessert. Now, that would have been…interesting. I gritted my teeth. "Which horse?" I said.

"Horse?"

I looked at him. He was grinning wildly, his imagination running away with him, too. "Yeah, Marty, you know the one. Four legs, mane, tail, whinnies. Which horse is colicky?"

"Oh, Sandstone." He walked into the barn ahead of me. "She'll get you yet. Why you just don't give in and get it over with, I'll never know."

"She's not my type."

He whirled around. "Looked like she was 'your type' just a second ago." When I didn't say anything, he said, "Loosen up, for Christ's sake. Have some fun."

"Marty."

His eyebrows rose. "Yes-s-s?"

"When a boarder's around and there's a problem, wait until we're out of hearing range before you tell me what's wrong."

"What're you talkin' about? She don't care 'bout no horses. She only cares about fuckin' your ass. Only reason she's got a horse in the first place is so she can expand her territory. Though when I think about it, it was a bad move on her part, 'cause mostly it's girls 'round here, and the guys, well, some of 'em are more than a little questionable, if you know what I mean. My cousin works at that new health club by Wilde Lake, and he knows Elsa. She's a member, and he told me—"

"Marty. I don't want to hear about it." I sighed. "It's general operating procedure I'm talking about. And you need to watch your mouth."

"Yes, sir." He rolled his eyes and pulled the stall door open with exaggerated subservience.

I stepped into the gelding's stall. "Your mom never use soap in your mouth, or what?"

"My momma dishes out slop at a truck stop sixty hours a week. Compared to her," he grinned, "I'm a fucking angel."

"Then heaven help us."

Sandstone, a washy palomino, stood at the back of the stall with his head lowered. His eyes were a dead giveaway. He was so preoccupied with his pain, he hadn't even bothered to look at us when we entered his stall.

I checked his vitals. Capillary refill time was normal. Pulse and respiration right on the mark. His gut sounds were slightly louder on the left. I pinched the skin on his neck, and it snapped back fast enough. He wasn't dehydrated.

"Who noticed he wasn't feeling well?"

"I did," Marty said.

"Good work. I'm impressed. You were on top of it to have noticed that anything was wrong at all."

"Yeah." He grinned wickedly. "You oughta get on top of it."

"Damn. I stepped right into that, didn't I?" I turned away from him to keep from cracking up. "I'll give him some Banamine and monitor his vitals. Do me a favor and check on him whenever you're over here, and let me know if he gets worse?"

"Sure. You need help with the shot?"

I shook my head.

"I'm gonna go switch the horses, then."

I got what I needed from the feed room, prepared the syringe, and injected the gelding in the neck. He began eating his hay almost immediately. I looked at the syringe and rolled it between my fingertips. He couldn't have felt better that fast, not from the drug, anyway. Given intramuscularly, it takes twenty minutes before it kicks in. He knew what the injection was about. He felt better in his mind, if not his body.

"You junkie, you," I said, softly.

He stopped in mid-chew, with wisps of hay sticking out the side of his mouth, and looked at me with inquisitive brown eyes. When I said nothing further, he lost interest and turned his attention back to lunch.

Satisfied that he was okay for the time being, I spent the rest of the afternoon dragging and hosing down the indoor arenas. In truth, what I really wanted to do was take a nap, but with Mrs. Timbrook on the premises, who knew what would happen if she found me in a prone position? I smiled to myself and spent some minutes thinking about that. It did nothing to satisfy but helped pass the time.

Thursday morning, I woke around four and couldn't go back to sleep. Hanging around the loft didn't appeal to me, and lying awake in bed was worse still. For the past two years, it had been my routine to go in early and ride one of the school horses, and it would have been nice to think the only reason I hadn't done so in the last twelve days was because I was too sore. I got dressed and headed to Foxdale.

It was pitch black when I turned the corner and eased the pickup down the lane toward the indoor. I backed into a spot under one of the security lights, turned off the engine, and cracked open the window. I sat there unmoving and tried to ignore the tension in my shoulders. After several minutes, I got out and shut the door.

The mournful hoot of an owl carried clearly in the still air. After a moment, the call was returned by its mate, or an enemy. I didn't know which. I walked down to the barns.

No trailer was parked where it shouldn't have been. No one was lurking in the dark with a mask over his face. I was being childish. It wouldn't happen again. They wouldn't be back.

I slipped through the space between the partially opened barn doors and turned on the lights. Some of the horses were lying down. Others were standing, dozing. They all squinted at the light. I strolled down the aisles. Soon the barns would be noisy with the activity that went along with caring for two-hundred-plus horses—raised voices, the bass throb of a radio, the clatter of horseshoes on asphalt. But for now, the barns were quiet, the air filled with pungent odors of sawdust, hay, and horse. My favorite time of day.

I stopped in front of stall 36. An elegant gray mare pricked her ears and watched me with wide-spaced, blue-brown eyes. She was a replacement for one of the stolen horses, and she'd settled quickly into the farm's routine. I cut through the wash rack, headed back to the lounge, and got the coffee machine going.

By mid-morning, after the horses had been grained and hayed and the first batch was unenthusiastically plodding across pastures thick with frost, I took the rest of the day off. Mrs. Hill didn't question it, and I didn't offer an explanation. But the previous evening, with Mr. Sanders' insurance windfall in mind, I'd given Nick a call. He'd conferred with his sister, and thanks in part to Nick's guarantee that I could be trusted to keep what I learned to myself, she'd agreed to meet with me.

Traffic was light on I-95, and I made it downtown with an hour to spare. I drove past Camden Yards, where I'd watched my share of Orioles games, and found a parking space a block from the Inner Harbor. I strolled down the wide cobblestone steps to the water's edge. Exhaust fumes mingled with an underlying odor of stagnant water, while above my head, seagulls swooped and cried, ever watchful for a handout. I squinted at a distant sailboat as it skimmed silently over water that sparkled under the winter sun and thought how appearances could be deceiving. Up close, where the waves lapped against the bulkhead, the greasy white body of a fish floated between rotting pieces of lumber and the plastic rings from a six-pack. The water was coated with an oily film, and I wondered how anything could live down there.

I walked past one of the pavilions that had been boarded up for the season. Tacked alongside the entrance, its faded corners curling back onto itself, was a poster announcing a performance by the Baltimore Symphony Orchestra. The event itself had long since come and gone, and if my sister hadn't up and moved to California, her attendance would have been a sure bet. I had spent countless hours listening to her music filter through the bedroom wall as she worked her way through a piece, her brow furrowed with concentration, the smooth wood of the violin tucked under her chin.

I sat on a park bench facing the water and stretched my legs. A man and little boy were at the far end of one of the piers. The kid squatted on his haunches and inspected something at his feet.

Sherri and I had been close, growing up in a family that discouraged closeness. Mother and Father had provided nannies, expensive toys, and precious little personal attention. I'd often wondered why they'd bothered having children at all, unless it made them look good.

The little boy stood and stepped closer to the edge, so he could look into the murky water. His father grabbed his hand, and the kid squealed as he leaned out across the water, windmilling his free arm as if he were falling.

Unlike Sherri, Bobby, my older brother by eight years, had thought of me as a nuisance. He had repeatedly referred to me as an accident, and I couldn't now remember how old I'd been when I figured out what he meant. But I would never forget the hurt. Bobby was a carbon copy of the old man in looks and aspirations. The last I'd heard, he was a financial adviser for some blue-chip company. He'd divorced his first wife, a smart move by all accounts, considering she was higher up the soci-eco food chain and possessed the arrogance that went with it. Together they'd produced two snot-nosed little brats who I imagined would grow up to be just like him.

I hadn't seen Sherri since the wedding, and I wondered when I ever would. I closed my eyes and felt the chill in the air and the warmth of the sun on my skin. Behind me, a bus accelerated through the intersection, and a grate rattled under the heavy wheels of a truck. As far as I was concerned, the harbor and Foxdale could have been on different planets.

The man and boy headed toward Rash Field, and after a while, it was time for me to go. I left the harbor behind and headed north on Calvert Street.

Five blocks later, I stopped in front of the wide plate-glass windows of a jeweler's store and glanced at the sign above the door. Geoff and Teal Jewelers. Behind me, a horn blared, followed by the high-pitched squeal of poorly adjusted brakes. The sound bounced and ricocheted off high walls of concrete and glass. I looked at my watch and saw I was ten minutes early.

"Steve?"

I turned around.

She held out her hand. "Marilyn," she said. "Nick's sister." She kept her blond hair short, and a pair of large wire-rimmed glasses couldn't hide a dusting of freckles scattered across the bridge of her nose. Based on Nick's comments, I assumed she was in her early forties, but the animation in her eyes made her appear younger.

"Thanks for taking the time to meet me," I said.

"No problem. Let's go inside." Marilyn turned without waiting for a response and strode briskly down the sidewalk.

She was wearing a navy blazer with gold piping and a skirt that reached her knees. The cut looked expensive, but the length accentuated her thinness. She looked prim and professional, the opposite of Nick in every respect. And she was my height. Taller than her brother.

At the corner, she pulled open the door to a dingy-looking cafe and chose a table at the far end of the room. Only then did the logistics of our meeting become clear. I sat across from her, realizing she was taking a chance talking to me and didn't want anyone to overhear our conversation. If she was nervous, though, she didn't show it.

She shifted in her seat, crossed her legs, and opened her menu. "How do you like working on a horse farm?"

"I like it." I thought about how frustrated I would have been if I'd gone through two or even six more years of college only to find that I hated the actual job. "It suits me."

She nodded. "Nicky, too. Now, me." She crinkled her nose. "By the time I was eighteen, I'd trudged through enough mud and muck to last me a lifetime." She saw the blank look on my face and said, "Dad used to train timber horses and steeplechasers. He even trained a Maryland Hunt Cup winner."

"I didn't realize."

"Nicky loved it, of course. Anyway," she said, "what do you want to know about insurance fraud?"

"Well, uh, for a start, how would Mr. Sanders profit—"

She raised her hand. "Hold on a sec. It would be unethical for me to talk specifically about one of our clients, but there's nothing wrong with discussing insurance in general, is there?"

I grinned. "I suppose not."

A waitress came over and took our drink order—iced tea for Marilyn and a Coke for me—and before she could leave, Marilyn ordered a chicken salad sandwich on wheat. I asked if they could do a BLT. They could. She scribbled down our order, then tucked her pencil behind her ear and the pad under the ties of her apron.

"Okay," I said when our waitress was out of hearing range. "If I had a horse I wanted to…"

"Defraud an insurance company with?".

"You said it."

She grinned. "Of course, like everything else, there's more than one way to skin a cat, or should I say, lead a horse to water?"

"Ugh."

The wrinkles that radiated from the corners of her eyes when she smiled disappeared as her gaze swept the room. Except for an elderly man in a booth by the front window, we were alone.

"One of the most common frauds in equine mortality insurance starts out innocently enough," she said. "You buy a horse with no thought of defrauding anyone, then the horse's performance, for whatever reason, starts to slide. The horse suffers an injury of some sort, or develops a subtle lameness, or some condition becomes evident that you know won't respond to treatment. The horse is no longer doing his job, and you know you'll never sell him for what you dished out. Instead of taking it in the teeth, you eliminate him before the problem becomes too obvious and collect on the insurance. As far as everyone's concerned, you're just another poor slob with bad luck. A victim."

"And if the original owner knowingly passed on a horse with a problem," I said, "that's exactly what I would have been...in the beginning, anyway."

"Yep. So you have the horse killed or, more likely, kill it yourself. Pretending it was stolen involves more risk."

I frowned "Why?"

"The police aren't going to do anything about a dead horse, unless it's obviously the result of a malicious act. And with horses, the two most common methods, electrocution and suffocation, aren't that easy to spot. But with theft, you're likely to become a suspect."

"Yeah, but if I board my horse in a public stable and take a bunch of other horses with it—"

"You'd be less of a suspect," she agreed. "Any reason you think a certain someone's guilty of anything underhanded, I'd like to hear about it."

I shook my head. "No reason. I'm just fishing."

Marilyn relaxed into her chair. "Though it doesn't happen as often, thank God, some people purchase a horse with the deliberate intention of defrauding an insurance company. If you're cautious and not too greedy, you buy an inexpensive horse and inflate the purchase price on the bill of sale. Not much, but enough to make it worth your while. If the horse is doing okay at the shows, his inflated price won't be questioned. Putting a value on an animal is fairly subjective at the best of times, and you've got your fake bill of sale to back you up. So when you dispose of the animal, you collect on the policy, less any deductible. It's a nice little fraud that's hard to prove unless you've made some glaring mistakes. Clear?"

"As glass."

Marilyn rolled her eyes.

"But it doesn't seem like you'd make all that much," I said. "Not when you consider the actual purchase price, the insurance premium, plus the usual board and upkeep of the horse."

"And don't forget the vet exam the policy requires," she said.

"So, where's the profit?"

"There's not much. But if you insure your horse with more than one company…"

"Oh, wow."

"There's more risk, but the profit's considerably higher." Marilyn shook her head as if she couldn't believe she was telling me this. "Let's say you and a couple of your buddies have this horse that can do the jumper circuit. He's nothing great, but he makes do. You take turns 'buying' him, insuring him, then stealing him. Between each 'theft,' you take him home for a while, then send him to another stable where he does a little showing to substantiate that he is in fact a jumper. Then he gets stolen again. Each time, the owner's name is different, the stable where he's boarded is different, and of course, he gets a new name at each barn."

"But doesn't the insurance company review the horse's show record when they determine its value?" I said. "And what about the registration papers?"

"Sure. You send the company paperwork on someone else's horse that's doing well in competition."

"But—"

She raised her hand. "Let's say you have a chestnut Hanoverian gelding that you're competing in open jumper classes—there are hundreds of them on the show circuit. He's doing okay, enough to play the part, but in the grand scheme of things, he's a pretty mediocre animal. But you know of a more successful Hanoverian the same sex and color, similar markings, and chances are, he's not insured with the company you're dealing with. So when you apply for insurance for your horse, you write away for the show record—"

The waitress plunked down our drinks and sandwiches and laid the check face down on the checkered tablecloth. "Anything else?" she asked as if she didn't expect to be bothered.

Marilyn shook her head, and the waitress returned to the kitchen's swinging doors, where she'd been chatting with someone just out of our line of sight. Marilyn leaned forward and said, "Where was I?"

"You write away for the show record..."

"Oh, yeah." She bit into her sandwich. "You get the show record of a successful Hanoverian, put his name on all your paperwork, do a little creative forgery on a copy of your horse's registration papers, and viola, you now have one expensive animal, at least on paper. But not so expensive that he's going to raise a flag. When you get rid of him, no one's the wiser."

"But wouldn't someone figure it out?"

"It's a riskier fraud, I'll admit, but if it's uncovered, it more than likely won't be the insurance company that catches on." She sipped her iced tea. "Most agents wouldn't know a Hanoverian from a Clydesdale. Consider the thousands of horses competing today, and the hundreds of insurance companies that provide equine mortality insurance, and it's pretty easy to see you'd go unnoticed, unless you did something stupid, like pretend you owned a world-class horse like Charisma. The real threat comes from someone on the show circuit noticing that the horse you're masquerading as Rocket isn't Rocket at all, because Rocket's down at ol' Charlie's place in South Carolina right about now."

"So you've got to be careful where you place your horse," I said.

Marilyn nodded. "That's right, and you don't keep him there long, and though you'll probably have to give the barn owner his fake show name, you make sure everyone else around the barn knows him as plain ol' Jake."

I swallowed some Coke. "Why's he have to be the same color?"

"For the vet exam."

"But if one of your buddies is a vet, then it wouldn't matter what the horse looked like. You wouldn't even need a horse, would you?"

"Your buddy the vet could fill out a fake report, sure. But when it came time to 'steal' the horse, you'd need a police report, and for that, you've gotta have a stable owner that can witness the fact that there actually was a horse. Too many thefts from one farm won't be noticed by different insurance companies, but the cops would eventually catch on."

I grinned. "Guess it would be too farfetched to think you'd have a crooked vet, cop, and stable owner as friends, wouldn't it?"

She looked at the ceiling. "Let's hope so. Course, I imagine if you were smart enough and had the connections, the entire scam could be done on paper without there ever being an actual horse."

We ate in silence. Despite the dreary decor and poor service, the food was surprisingly good. Eventually, I said, "It's a pretty unscrupulous industry, isn't it?"

Marilyn shrugged. "It's everywhere. Kinda makes you wonder about human nature, doesn't it?"

"Yeah. So, is Sanders' policy being questioned?" I asked, not sure that she would tell me.

She glanced around the room. "No. He'd signed up three months before the theft. That might've caught someone's attention, but it happens. In this case, what really got the ball rolling was pure and simple fate. Nicky happened to be shoeing at the barn the day the horse was vetted for the policy, and he overheard the figure, which he thought excessive. He mentioned it to me when he heard the horse was stolen, and," she caught her breath, "since I just so happen to work for the insurance company in question, the underwriter had a tense moment or two because the policy did appear to be on the high side. But after an investigation, he was cleared." Marilyn leaned back in her chair and eyed me speculatively. "And you have no suspicions?"

"No. I'm just trying to figure out who'd gain by taking the horses."

"Besides the thieves, you mean?"

"Yeah." I thought about James Peters and figured she was right. It was just too farfetched to think that Sanders had anything to do with what had happened at Hunter's Ridge. "So he's going to get a check?"

"Sure. No reason why he won't. Thirty days after the date of the theft, we'll cut his check."

"Why thirty days?"

"SOP."

"What?"

"Standard operating procedure."

"What if the horse shows up after he collects?"

"Then the company has the right to take title and possession of the animal." She glanced at her watch. "Anything else?"

"I don't think so."

"If I hear you're going around collecting on insurance claims," she said with a grin, "I'll wring your neck."

I chuckled. "Yes, ma'am."

"Don't 'ma'am' me, boy. Makes a girl feel old." She wiped her mouth with a napkin, tossed it on the table, and stood up. "I'm late. Thanks for lunch."

I stood also and thought that I'd gotten the prim part wrong. "Thanks for the education." I hesitated. "Any chance I could get a look at my friend's paperwork?"

She tilted her head. "I'll think about it."

We shook hands, and I watched her walk out of the cafe.

Chapter 6

Five-thirty Saturday morning, and already bands of color had spread across the eastern horizon. The horses watched as I walked down the barn aisle, flipping through my farm keys, looking for the right one. I had too many damn keys. Even with color-coded tape, I was still sorting through them when I stopped outside the tack room door.

Sensing something wrong, out of place, I looked up. I wouldn't be needing my keys. Not that morning, anyway.

The door was half open, and the jamb was cracked and splintered and dented with pry marks.

With nerves on high alert, I pushed the door inward with the toe of my boot and flipped the light switch with my key.

Locker doors hung askew or lay on the floor. Most of the saddles were gone. I walked into the center of the room and surveyed the damage. Some of the more expensive bridles were missing, too. I checked the other boarders' tack room. Everything of value that could easily be sold was gone. On my way out, I stopped outside the school horses' tack room. It was still locked. I frowned at the undisturbed door and considered the implications.

I walked over to barn A, knowing I'd find the same thing.

I pushed the door in with my boot, hit the light switch, and froze. A thin trail of blood snaked across the floor and disappeared around the corner of the central island of lockers.

I looked at my hand. Blood darkened my fingertips. The light switch had been smeared with blood, and it was still tacky.

The lockers were eight feet tall. I couldn't see around them. I inched toward the first row of lockers.

Before I made it around the corner, a hollow thump resounded in the barn. The muscles in my gut tightened. I looked back at the doorway. No one was there. The sound had come from one of the stalls. It was simply one of the horses across the aisle, knocking a hoof against the wall.

I looked down at the floor, realized I was holding my breath, forced myself to breathe. I stepped around the corner and followed the trail with a gaze so intent, I could see nothing else.

Something touched my hair.

I jumped back. The heel of my boot caught on the edge of a broken locker door, and I crashed backward into the row of lockers. Hanging from the rafters, and now gently swaying, was Boris the barn cat. Baling twine was tied around the tip of his tail, and his throat had been cut. His head dangled from a thin ribbon of flesh and matted fur. My stomach lurched, and saliva flooded my mouth. I swallowed and stumbled out of the room.

My muscles felt rubbery from the flood of adrenaline. I rubbed my face, then remembered the blood on my fingers. I wiped my hand on my jeans and looked up and down the aisle. Everything looked peaceful. Normal. The horses were watching, wondering what I was up to.

"Just having heart failure, guys," I said and didn't recognize my own voice.

After a minute or two, I went back in. Most of the saddles in that barn were ridiculously expensive. They were all gone. I crossed the room and examined the door that opened into aisle two. It was still locked. Blood had been smeared on that light switch, too. Whichever door I chose, I would have put my hand on a bloody light switch.

I walked back into the center of the room. The flies hadn't taken long to find the cat. They buzzed and flitted around the gaping wound in his neck and crawled over the matted fur. He'd been the only cat on the farm—a mascot of sorts—and wasn't aloof like most of them. Many of the boarders brought him treats. I doubt he'd ever caught a mouse. He wasn't going to now.

I thought about the room's layout and how his body had been strategically placed for maximum effect. I hadn't seen him until I was right on top of him. Someone had a very sick, twisted mind. Tack theft was all too prevalent, but this was cruel, wicked. Designed to terrify. Judging by my physical state, it had been, on the whole, entirely successful.

I headed for the office. The buildings were bathed in an early-morning wash of gray, and a ground-hugging mist had settled in the swales that cut through the pastures. The farm looked like a latent photograph come to life. As I walked down the sidewalk, it occurred to me that the office and lounge weren't immune to vandalism, either. I quickened my pace.

I peered through the glass as I unlocked the office door and saw that everything was secure. In the quiet room, my footsteps echoed hollowly on the cheap linoleum. I snatched up the phone and punched in the familiar number.

Mrs. Hill answered in three rings, fast for her. I glanced at the clock. Five-forty-three.

"Yes?" An element of dread in her voice.

"Mrs. Hill, this is Steve...." When she didn't respond, I said, "There's been more trouble at the farm—"

"Oh, no."

I told her about the saddles and Boris and the blood. She didn't say anything...not a word.

"Mrs. Hill?"

"I can't believe this. Are you okay?"

"Yes, ma'am."

"Are any of the horses missing?" Her voice was tight.

"No, ma'am."

"Well, there's that at least. I'll be in as soon as I can. It'll be a while, though. I have to wait until the bus comes for the kids."

She told me to notify the police, and I could hear her yelling to her husband as she hung up the phone. I slumped into her chair and rubbed my face. It was too much. Too damned much. I sat up, tapped my fingers on the blotter, and looked at the phone. Made another call.

The voice at the other end said, "C.I.U., Ralston."

"This is Stephen Cline from Foxdale Farm. You interviewed me last week, about—"

"What's up?"

"Last night, someone broke into the tack rooms on the farm. Most of the saddles are gone, and I think it might be the same people who took the horses."

He cleared his throat. "What makes you think that?"

"Well, whoever was here last night couldn't keep it simple. They killed a barn cat and smeared its blood around. Then they hung the body from the rafters." Christ, I had walked into the damn thing.

"How?"

"How what?"

"How was the cat killed?"

"Oh. They slit its throat."

After a pause, he said, "Did you see anyone when you arrived?"

"No, sir."

"You're sure no one's there now that shouldn't be?"

I glanced reflexively at the door. "Yes."

"Okay. I'll give Howard County a call." He paused, and I could hear papers rustle in the background. "And I think I'll drive over there myself. Do me a favor, Steve. Keep everyone clear of the barns. Don't let anyone drive all the way down there, okay?"

"Sure."

He disconnected, and I thought about the exhaustion I'd heard in his voice and didn't envy him his job.

I grained the horses early—they didn't object—then lugged hay bales out of the storage area at the end of the barn and spaced them down the center of the aisle. I slid my hand into my pocket and wrapped my fingers around the knife that was successfully wearing a hole through my jeans. The smooth plastic sheath was warm from my own body heat. It wasn't until I pulled the blade out that I thought how someone, just hours before, had used a knife to slit the cat's throat.

◇◇◇

Shortly before seven, a police car pulled down the lane and jerked to a halt between the barns. As the officer climbed out and grabbed a clipboard off the dash, a dirt-streaked white Taurus parked alongside the grain bin. I answered questions that had become increasingly familiar in the past two weeks, while the driver of the Taurus popped the trunk and levered himself out of his car. He wasn't in uniform, and judging by the equipment he'd hefted onto the asphalt, I guessed he was a technician of some sort. When he joined us, carrying a black duffel bag with HCPD stenciled on the side in one hand and a heavy-looking aluminum case in the other, we walked into the barn.

I glanced over my shoulder when one of them whistled.

The uniformed cop adjusted his mirrored sunglasses. "How many horses you got in this place?"

"In both barns, one hundred and ninety three."

He whistled again, then grinned at his partner. "Look like they're in jail, don't they?"

The plainclothes cop didn't respond, and I wondered what was eating him. We stopped at the tack room door.

"They broke in here," I said. "But we can get in through the undamaged door in the other aisle. I nailed this one shut, because I didn't want the employees or boarders to see what's inside."

"And what's that?" the uniformed cop said.

I glanced at my reflection in his glasses and realized how disconnected I felt because I couldn't see his eyes. I told him about Boris. "I was hoping to keep it quiet. Some of the boarders loved that cat."

"Did you touch anything?"

"No. Oh, yeah. The light switch."

"Humph. We'll start processing the scene, but I can't guarantee we'll be done in time for what you want."

I skirted a puddle in the wash rack and ducked under the divider that allowed two horses to be bathed at once. "We can cut through here," I said over my shoulder, "to get to the other aisle." I turned in time to see them hesitate. The grumpy guy crinkled his nose and proceeded as if he were in alien territory. Smiling to myself, I took the opportunity to rinse my hands under the spigot. A minty scent, left over from liniments and leg braces, clung to the walls.

The uniformed cop stood beside me as I unlocked the door. "You'll need to make a preliminary list of the items that were stolen and their estimated value."

"It'll be a rough estimate," I said. "Very rough, like not even in the ballpark kind of rough."

He grinned. "That'll do for now. You can submit a more accurate inventory later."

As I opened the door and stepped back, a dark green Crown Victoria pulled alongside the patrol car. Detective Ralston climbed out and clicked the door shut. His wrinkled suit hung loosely off his shoulders. He looked as if he hadn't made it to bed the night before, or if he had, he'd slept in his clothes.

He introduced himself to his Howard County counterparts, mentioned Detective Linquist, then looked at me. "What've we got, Steve?"

For an answer, I pushed the door open with my boot. Detective Ralston walked inside, looked around, and came back out.

He yawned. "Did you touch anything?"

I rubbed my thumb across my fingertips. "The light switch." I pointed across the room. "Over there." He looked at me as if I should have known better. "I didn't in the other tack rooms, though," I said and thought I saw a glimmer of amusement in his eyes.

"How many people have access to this room?"

"Fifty-plus."

Ralston grunted, and the plainclothes cop, who was standing behind him, scowled. His expression said loud and clear that he thought he was wasting his time.

"If the burglars had any sense," Ralston continued, "they wore gloves."

"Even if they didn't," the plainclothes cop said, "with all that traffic, it won't matter."

Ralston looked at the man, and a muscle twitched in his jaw. "When's Gary gonna show?" he said.

The cop shrugged.

After the Howard County team stepped into the tack room and dumped their equipment on the floor, Ralston went back to his car. I separated out four flakes of hay, fed the last two horses at the far end of the aisle, and squinted at Ralston's car. He was on the phone, and I would have bet half my paycheck that he was bending Detective Sgt. Gary Linquist's ear.

Five minutes later, Ralston strolled back into the barn and stood looking into the tack room. He folded his arms across his chest and watched the uniformed officer take pictures. The glare of the flash bounced off the walls and the ceiling... and Boris. I checked my watch. Seven-ten. It would be a miracle if the crew didn't end up standing around with their mouths open, gawking at the cat, then telling everyone they could think of about it, and the story would become unnecessarily sensationalized and blown out of proportion.

I stuck my head in the doorway. "Would you let me know when you're done in there? I want to clean up as soon as possible."

The uniformed cop looked up and nodded. "No problem."

Ralston started in on the questions. I hadn't seen anyone. The sodium vapors were still on. The place had been dead. He rubbed his face. "You're the first person here every morning?"

"Usually."

"How common's that knowledge?"

"I have no idea."

"What did you think when you saw the blood?"

"That there was a person around the corner." I looked him in the eye. "A dead person."

He grunted. "What did you think when you saw the cat?"

I blinked. "Think?"

He waited.

"That someone was playing a game," I said and felt that Ralston could read my every thought. Was sure he could imagine every damn feeling I'd had the pleasure of exploring earlier that morning. "A mind game."

"You think it was directed at you personally?"

I shrugged.

"If it's the same crew, they probably had you in mind." When I didn't respond, he said, "When, exactly, did you discover the burglary?"

"Around five-thirty."

He frowned. "Was the blood dry?"

"It was damp. Kind of tacky."

"They hadn't been gone long."

I looked at the floor and kicked at a few wisps of hay with the toe of my boot. Someone hadn't done a very good job sweeping up the night before.

"You might want to change your routine."

Change my routine. Easy for him to say.

"So," Ralston said. "You think the events are related because of the excessive brutality."

I nodded. "They didn't need to do that."

Ralston shifted his weight and leaned on the doorjamb. "Burglars normally don't waste time leaving such an elaborate message, not unless there's a reason for it. Especially since they must have known they were running out of time." Ralston poked his head into the tack room. "Did Gary tell you this case might be related to an open homicide?"

The uniformed cop looked up from where he'd been trying to enhance a print, a small brush poised in his hand. "Yes, sir. He did."

"Also," I said to Ralston. "It looks like they knew the layout of the farm. They didn't touch the school horses' tack room. The saddles in there are cheap."

I glanced over Ralston's shoulder. Marty was strolling into the barn, a questioning look on his face. I hurried to cut him off.

"Steve, what the fuck's goin' on?"

"Someone made off with a truck load of saddles and—"

"No shit."

"No shit. The police are collecting evidence now, so please stay away from all three tack rooms. If you see the guys before I do, let them know. Oh, and the school horses' tack room wasn't touched, so you can do whatever you have to in there."

"Wow. I don't believe it. First the horses, now this." He calmly looked at my face. "Someone doesn't like us very much, do they?"

"Apparently not. By the way, has this happened before? A tack theft I mean?"

"Not that I know of. Not since I've been here."

I sighed. The morning seemed to be going on forever. "Let's get to work. Most of the haying's done over here. Go help out in barn B, then we'll start turnouts."

"Okay, boss."

I watched him saunter off without a care in the world, and I envied him.

A half hour later, the uniformed cop told me they were finished in the tack room.

"How'd it go?" I asked.

"Everywhere they would've touched, we got nothin' but smudges."

"They were wearing gloves," I said.

"Looks that way. We do have some good tool marks to work with, which reminds me. I need your signature." He handed me the clipboard and showed me where to sign.

"What good are tool marks?"

"Aren't good for nothin', not until Detective Ralston figures out who did it. Then we can compare their tools with the impressions."

"Oh," I said, and he could probably see I wasn't impressed.

I watched him head to the other barn. Out in the lane, Ralston and Detective Linquist were talking to Brian, and I wondered when I'd hear about that.

I was leaning against a locker, working halfheartedly on the inventory, when Mrs. Hill marched into the room. I pushed myself off the locker and straightened my spine. She circled the room with her hands on her hips.

I closed one locker, squatted down, and was checking the locker on the bottom row when I became aware of a stillness in the room. I looked over my shoulder. Mrs. Hill was standing in the middle of the room with her hands in her pockets and her head bowed. I stopped what I was doing and stood up.

"Oh, Stephen," she said. "What a mess. I hate to think what Mr. Ambrose is going to say when he hears about this. He's going to have a fit."

I doubted Mr. Ambrose would care one little bit. Although he was Foxdale's owner, his wife had been behind Foxdale's inception. A talented rider who had represented the United States in numerous Olympic and World Cup competitions, she had died of cancer a month after the ribbon-cutting ceremony.

"He doesn't care about the place," I said.

"Oh, that's not true, dear. He likes anything that makes a profit, which we do. And I must say, you've helped tremendously in that department. I tell him all the time what innovations and improvements you've come up with. He's quite pleased." She frowned. "He won't be now."

"No." I slid my pencil under the clasp on the clipboard and thought about money and insurance...and tax write-offs. Contrary to what he tells her, what if Ambrose wanted Foxdale to lose money? Even if he was rolling in the stuff, I found his avoidance of the place a little strange. "Who do you send the payroll information to?" I said.

She frowned. "Farpoint Industries in Baltimore. Why?"

"Just curious."

"What are you doing?"

"Working on a list for the police." I looked at my scribbled notes. "But without the boarders' help, it won't be complete. I don't know the saddles' values. All I can do is write down the names of everyone who's had a saddle stolen. And if by chance they've taken them home to clean, I've got that wrong, too."

"You're right. I'll start making calls. We'll need an accurate itemization from each boarder."

I looked at her face and saw by her expression that she'd already shifted into high gear. Making plans, working out procedures, focusing on the days ahead. She turned and left with a characteristic "Carry on, dear," floating over her shoulder.

I carried on but with little enthusiasm.

The resultant uproar was predictable and worsened by the fact that Foxdale was holding a schooling show the following morning. Two boarders gave notice that they were taking their horses and belongings elsewhere. I overheard more than one boarder asking Mrs. Hill about a night watchman and privately wondered how she would fare with the frugal Mr. Ambrose.

Three boarders asked if I knew where Boris was. I didn't. No one seemed to notice that he had disappeared along with the saddles. Dave spent all of the afternoon and most of the evening restoring the tack rooms to their former perfection, and life went on except, of course, for Boris.

◇◇◇

Sunday afternoon, "the schooling show that wasn't" was thankfully half over. Some of the boarders had borrowed saddles, but most had stayed home. Sitting around, watching competitors from other farms win all the ribbons, was no one's idea of fun. I walked into the southwest field that served as a parking area during show days and scanned the rows of trailers.

Checking had become a habit. Checking locks, checking horses. Checking trailers, looking for the elusive dualie and old trailer, my personal introduction to hell.

There were far too many trucks and trailers in the pasture to check them from a distance, so I walked up and down the rows. Quite a few saddles had been left sitting on their stands. On the off chance I might recognize one of the more distinctive saddles that had been stolen from the tack room, I took note of them, too. More checking.

There were few people in the parking area—most had gone to lunch—so I was surprised to hear heavy, quick footsteps behind me. Before I could react, someone grabbed my shoulder and spun me around.

He tightened his grip on my jacket. "What in the hell do you think you're doing, snooping 'round out here?"

I looked up at him. Had to. He had a good four inches on me. Maybe thirty-five, and overweight, I had never seen him before. He didn't look like a rider or a trainer.

"You looking to steal somebody's stuff?" He shook my shoulder with each inflection of his voice. "Is that it? What're you doing? Speak up."

He hadn't given me a chance. I resisted an urge to kick him in the shins and said with irritation, spitting my words out slowly, "Actually, I was looking for stolen tack…not trying to steal any." I exhaled and made an effort to relax. "I'm Foxdale's barn manager. Somebody cleaned out our tack rooms Friday morning, and I was hoping to find a lead of some kind."

"Oh." He let go. "Sorry, then. I heard about that."

I smoothed out my shirt. "Have you had any tack stolen?"

"Yeah, as a matter of fact, I have. I run a show barn in Pennsylvania, and right before Christmas, our tack room was broken into." He ran a hand through his hair and stared off into the middle distance as if reliving the event. "We couldn't believe it 'cause our house sits across the road from the barn, and somebody had the nerve to go in there with a truck and empty the place out. We never thought it would happen to us."

"No," I sighed. "Have you had any horses stolen?"

"Hell, no."

"Do you know anyone who has?"

"Yeah. Come to think of it, I do. A buddy of mine had four of his horses stolen right from under his nose."

"When?"

"Two years ago. Maybe longer. Don't rightly recall."

"Where does he live?" I asked without much hope.

"He runs a dressage barn in northern Carroll County, just south of the Maryland-PA line. Four of his best horses, gone without a trace, and he didn't have any damn insurance on them, either."

Carroll County. James Peters had lived in Carroll County. We weren't far from Carroll County. The world wasn't that small a place.

"What's your friend's name?"

"George Irons. Why?"

"I'd like to talk to him. Do you know anyone who owns a white dualie and an old, dark-colored six-horse?"

"No."

He'd answered quickly, without thinking. "Are you sure?" I said. "It's important."

He smoothed a hand over his hair and down the back of his neck. "No, can't think of anyone. Why?"

"In February, someone stole seven horses from Foxdale with a rig like that. And last June, seven horses were stolen from James Peters' farm in Carroll County. Ever heard of him?"

"No."

"Apparently the same truck and trailer were used. If you see a rig like that, could you let me know? Just call Foxdale. Ask for Steve."

"Sure, but you aren't ever gonna get your horses back."

"I know. But whoever did it, whoever stole the horses... murdered James Peters."

His mouth fell open, and he gaped at me like a fool.

I knew intimately how he felt.

He gave me an idea, though. A risky idea, nonetheless. From that day on, I would tell everyone I met the same thing. Many of the exhibitors traveled a circuit. Who's to say the thief slash murderer wasn't doing the same thing elsewhere? With luck, I might learn something useful. Consequently, I spent the rest of the day, not watching the show, not working, but talking. By the end of the day, there wasn't a soul on the grounds who hadn't heard of James Peters, the stolen horses, and the white dualie and old six-horse.

Chapter 7

Late Monday afternoon, I pointed the truck northward and soon found myself negotiating a narrow, winding road in northern Carroll County. I slowed to a crawl when I saw a three-story brick home set close to the road. One hundred feet beyond, I braked to a halt next to the wide doors of a bank barn. I got out and stretched, then lifted my notebook off the dash and looked around. The pasture's tidy four-board fence dipped and rose with the hilly terrain, and the trees that were clumped on hillsides too steep to be mown were in full bud, their colors an echo of autumn.

I heard a scuffing noise behind me and turned to see a tall, broad-shouldered man, going fat round the middle, walking toward me down the steep, gravel drive across the road. The driveway led to a red pole-building that served as an indoor riding arena. A girl on a heavily muscled gray with a naturally high head carriage trotted past the open doorway.

He held out his hand. "George Irons. You're Foxdale's manager?" His eyebrows rose, and I saw in his brown eyes a rapid assessment of my age and a hint of surprise.

I shook his hand. "Barn manager, yes."

Although it had been warm enough at Foxdale, it was chilly here, where the steep wooded hills channeled cooler air along the valley floor. My T-shirt felt inadequate, and I noticed wryly that my host wore a long-sleeved, flannel shirt.

"Lemme show you the layout." He continued past me, down the sloped lane alongside the barn, and entered the lower level. "They just led the horses out of these stalls, pretty as you please. Took 'em on up the path we come down on and loaded the lot into a trailer. Right across the road from the house like that, took some balls, I'll tell you. The wife and I slept right through it. Didn't know the horses were gone 'til I came out in the morning to feed."

"What time was that?"

"Five-thirty."

"Do you always come out that early?"

He nodded. "Yeah. I work off the farm. First shift. Always feed 'em before I leave, then all Nancy's gotta do is turn 'em out when she gets up."

The lower level of the barn was three-sided, open to the wind on the south, and decidedly dank. Deeper within the bowels of the old barn, ten stalls surrounded a common area. With its low ceiling, the barn was more suited for cows than horses.

"Had a full barn one second," Irons said, "then I'm down five horses the next."

"I thought they took four," I said.

"Four were mine. The biggest ones which, as it turned out, happened to be the best." His voice was bitter with the memory. He ran his fingers through his thick, windblown hair and sighed. "Other one was a boarder's. The thieves must of tried for seven, though."

"Why?"

"When I came out that morning, I found two of 'em on the lawn behind the house, and they had their halters on."

"They don't normally?"

He shook his head. "Those two are the devil to load, so I'm not surprised they gave up on 'em and just let 'em go. They ran back into the barn and got into the bags of grain I keep on the pallet over there," he gestured to a far corner, "before they tore up the garden and went strollin' round the back yard. I was damn lucky they didn't colic."

"When did you last check on them?"

"I come out before I go to bed. Make sure everybody's okay. Must of been around ten 'cause I had to work the next day."

"Six and a half hours," I mumbled. "Which night? Do you remember?"

"Lemme think." He tugged upward on his jeans. It didn't do him any good, because his belly was in the way. "Oh, yeah. It was a Sunday. I lost a bunch of overtime 'cause I didn't go in that morning like I'd planned."

The weekend. Why wasn't I surprised?

He slid two fingers into the breast pocket of his shirt, pulled out a sheet of loose-leaf, and unfolded it. "Here's the information you said you wanted. Grain supplier, vet, farrier. Anybody I could think of who comes here regular and would know what's what." He handed me the list.

I scanned the page, recognized several names, questioned a few. Nothing jumped out as significant. With growing disappointment, I said, "How long ago was this?"

"Be two years in June, and I'm still not full up. People get scared when somethin' like that happens. Word gets around, and before you know it, your customers are lookin' for some-place safer to keep their horses."

He didn't know anyone who owned a white dualie and dark-colored six-horse. Didn't have a clue who was behind the theft. I thanked him for his time. As I drove home, I thought about his parting comment and the frustration I'd heard in his voice. "With the barn so close to the house, Nancy and I always thought we'd be safe from this sort of thing."

Everyone thinks they're immune. Until it's too late.

By the time I pulled into my parking space behind the foaling barn and climbed the steps to the loft, I'd decided that there was one other question I should have asked Mr. Irons. I fished the sheet of loose-leaf out of my back pocket and punched in his number.

His wife picked up. I explained who I was and waited nearly five minutes before he came on the line, out of breath, his voice husky.

I twisted the phone cord round my fingers and hoped he had never heard of my landlord. "I forgot to ask. Have you ever used Gregory Davis as your vet?"

"No."

I let out a breath.

"Only 'cause he lives so damned far away. I keep tellin' him we need a good vet up here, but he don't wanna move away from his rich clients."

I rubbed my forehead. "How do you know him then, if he's not your vet?"

"We're neighbors."

"Huh?"

He chuckled. "That's right. Our cabins butt right up against one another on the banks of the St. Martin. We go motorin' up and down the Isle of Wight Bay, slip on over to the Ol' Woman's Ass when we're wantin' to get in some crabbin'—"

"Woman's…ass?"

He chuckled again. "Assawoman Bay. Indian name. Good crabbin'. Fair fishin' if you don't mind the sunnies."

"If you say so." I learned more than I cared to about the teeming waterways and ecosystems of the Eastern Shore, and by the time I hung up, I had decided that his knowing Greg was simply a coincidence.

I called Detective Ralston, gave him the name of the guy I'd run into at the show who'd had tack stolen from his barn, then I told him how someone had stolen five horses from George Irons' farm in Pennsylvania and that they'd tried for seven.

He questioned me closely, and when he disconnected, I wondered why I hadn't told him about Greg.

◇◇◇

The next morning, two of the guys called in sick. Since Marty was in the other barn tacking up a horse for Anne, Foxdale's other trainer besides Whitcombe, the barn was unnaturally quiet. No rock 'n roll blaring from a cheap boom box, or worse—country. No arguing over who was going to do what. Only the muted rustling of a horse moving in his stall. A bucket being nudged. A soft exhalation like a sigh. I flung a load of manure into the wagon, and it hit the bare wooden floor with a dull thud. Despite the soreness in my ribs, I was already halfway down the aisle.

Unlike most of the crew, I didn't mind mucking out. The job took little concentration, so there was plenty of time to think. I raked the wet sawdust into a pile, forked it into the wagon, and wondered who had it in for Foxdale and what, if any, connection existed between Foxdale and James Peters. If the horse and tack theft at Foxdale were committed by the same people, then all three events could be linked. But the police had no conclusive evidence, and without it, the connection was pure speculation.

I smoothed out the sawdust with my rake, moved on to the next stall, and thought about motive. If it wasn't greed, then what was it? Maybe someone had a grudge against Foxdale. An ex-employee, perhaps. In the past two years, I had fired four employees. I'd also been responsible for Foxdale's discontinuing the services of two farriers, one vet, and several suppliers. But it was absurd to think they had anything to do with what was going on. Anyway, what did they have against James Peters?

Foxdale and Hunter's Ridge could have been the targets of random theft and nothing more. I leaned the rake against the wall, pulled a tattered notebook and chopped-off pencil out of my back pocket, and made a list. I didn't have enough information. I didn't know enough about Hunter's Ridge or James Peters. But ignorance could be deadly.

I ripped the page from my notebook, crumpled it into a ball, and flicked it into the wagon. Hopefully, it would be

smooth sailing from now on. No horses going to slaughter…
no cats hanging from the rafters with their throats slit…no
bodies in shallow graves.

"Hey? Whatju doin'?"

I jumped.

Marty was watching me through the stall's grillwork. "You
look like you've seen a ghost."

I swallowed. "Just thinking."

The mischievous grin faded from his face. "Uh-huh." He
propped his shoulder against the doorjamb and crossed his
arms. "You want me to muck out or do the school horses?"

I checked my watch. "Damn, we're running behind."

Marty looked down the aisle.

"Brush off the school horses first," I said. "Then—"

Marty's easygoing features had dissolved into a look of
pure dislike as thoroughly as if someone had reached up and
wiped the expression off his face. I poked my head into the
aisle and saw the reason for the transformation.

Whitcombe stopped alongside the wagon. Marty pushed
himself upright and took a step backward.

"Cline, I want…What's so funny?"

I cleared my throat. "Nothing, sir."

"I want to ride Fleet." He glanced uncertainly at Marty,
then looked back at me. "Get him ready."

"Yes, sir."

I stepped out of the stall. Whitcombe was standing in the
narrow space between the wagon and stall front, twirling a
riding crop between his fingers. I walked the long way around.
"Marty, could you—"

"Now, Cline."

"Yes…sir." I gritted my teeth and gestured for Marty to
follow.

"So," Whitcombe said. "It takes two of you to tack up a
horse, does it?"

I paused and looked him straight in the eye. "No, sir. I
was giving Marty instructions." Before you interrupted me,

you shithead, I wanted to say, and for a brief second, I was sure he could read my thoughts. I started down the aisle.

"Oh, and Cline?"

Keeping my face neutral, I turned around.

"I want a segunda bit on him today."

"Yes, sir."

"Hurry it up. And Cline..."

"Sir?"

"I'll be in the lounge." He turned and strolled down the aisle.

I watched the departing view of his back and wholeheartedly wished I could fire his ass. Disgusted, I walked into the tack room and spun the dial on Whitcombe's locker.

Even though Whitcombe was long gone, Marty stood next to me and whispered, "What a fucking asshole. You better do what he says though, Stevie," he said with an exaggerated lisp, "or he might have to spank you with that crop of his."

I went right past the last number on the combination. "Christ, Marty. Quit before we both get in trouble." I leaned my forehead on the locker and concentrated on the dial. "The way you backed away from him, I thought I was gonna lose it. You wouldn't be homophobic, now, would you?"

"Me?" Marty said. "Well, correct me if I'm wrong, but more than once, I've seen you change course when you were headin' to the men's room and saw Whitcombe go in first."

I grinned. "This may be true."

"He sure likes to keep on going and going, don't he? Likes to jerk you around, see if he can piss you off."

"Yeah," I said. "Like the Energizer Bunny. He keeps going and going and—"

Marty snorted.

"—going. He sure likes his little games." I rummaged through Whitcombe's locker. "You know, he threatened to get me fired last week."

"What the fuck for?"

"For nothing." I sorted through the crate until I found the segunda. "Guess he didn't like the way I said 'sir.'"

"Bet Mrs. Hill'd pick you over him if it came down to it." Marty said. "Who cares about his reputation? He's nothin' special."

I shrugged. "He thinks he is. My only hope's that he'll get a job offer somewhere else, and seeing that trainers usually don't stay in one place for long, especially trainers who aren't as good as they think they are, I might luck out."

"I heard him chewing you out the other day for the way you tacked up Nightshade."

I grunted. "Ever notice how he makes sure he has an audience? I wouldn't be surprised if half the people around here think I'm an idiot."

"Nah," Marty said. "It's pretty obvious who the idiot is."

I selected one of Whitcombe's bridles and switched the bits. "I'll bet you a thousand to one, when I take Fleet down there, he'll find something to complain about."

"Why don't you say somethin' to Mrs. Hill?"

"She doesn't need that. Anyway, I have a game plan of my own when it comes to dealing with our Mr. Pretentious Whitcombe."

Marty's eyebrows rose. "And what might that be?"

"The more I keep my cool and don't respond to his digs, the more pissed he gets. It's almost comical."

"Jesus. Remind me not to get on your bad side."

I pulled Whitcombe's saddle off the rack and ran my fingers across the smooth, supple leather. The rich, earthy new-leather smell filled my head. "Damn, money must not be a problem for him. He's already replaced his old saddle, and this one's expensive big time."

"Maybe he wiped out the tack rooms and used the money to buy hisself a new load of shit."

I spun around. "Why do you think that?"

He grinned. "No reason. Just that he's jerk enough for it. Why don't you mention it to the police?"

"Yeah, right. I can see it now. Officer, I think he did it. And why do you think that, Mr. Cline? Oh, nothing substantial, sir. It's just that I can't stand the guy."

Marty arched his eyebrows. "Guy?"

I chuckled. But Whitcombe did have opportunity and knowledge and connections, not to mention the fact that he was a jerk. I draped the bridle and girth across the saddle and lugged the armload of tack into the aisle.

Marty cut in front of me and plopped the tote of grooming supplies on the floor outside Fleet's stall. "I still don't see how you put up with him," he said.

"I'm not going to let him ruin this job for me, though most days I'd like to ram a pitchfork up his ass."

"Awh, man. Don't do that. He might like it."

"Christ, Marty, you're sick." And I almost didn't get Whitcombe's saddle onto the rack before I dropped it on the floor, I was laughing so hard.

I handed Fleet over to Whitcombe—amazingly he kept his mouth shut—and went into the lounge to get a cup of coffee. Voices floated in from the office, and I walked over and leaned against the doorjamb. A scrawny-looking guy, dressed in a suit, tie, and wrinkled overcoat, had his hands pressed down on Mrs. Hill's desk, his fingers splayed on the blotter. His mousy brown hair was windblown, and his face was pinched with displeasure.

"You'll have to talk to Mr. Ambrose about that," Mrs. Hill said.

"But I can't get past his assistant."

Mrs. Hill shrugged. "Well, I'm sorry. I can't help you."

He snatched his card off her blotter, glanced at me, and stalked out the door.

"What was that about?" I asked.

"Real estate agent. Vultures. That's what I call 'em. That one's been here before. Now that they're building next door, I imagine they'll be crawling out of the woodwork."

The brothers' farm was now dotted with survey flags, and I imagined it wouldn't be long before the heavy earth-moving equipment rolled over the fallow fields.

"Thank God for the park," I said.

◇◇◇

Early the next morning, the wheels of Greg's truck hadn't slowed to a stop, and already some of the horses were uptight. I rolled a utility cart out of the feed room and parked it alongside the tailgate.

Greg popped open a side compartment on his red vet-mobile. "Well, Steve. You up to this?"

"More or less." I leaned against the back fender.

"What's it been," he said, "three weeks since you got pummeled?"

"There about." I watched him sort through a bin and wondered if I was up to the day ahead. "Want me to do anything?"

"Not yet. Just give me a minute to get organized."

"Hey," a voice said in my ear.

I looked over my shoulder.

Marty was standing behind me, grinning. "Boy, I hate this shit. Nothing like restraining a hundred one-thousand-pound, pea-brained animals to liven up your day."

"Oh, come on, Marty," I said. "They aren't that bad."

"Wasn't it you that got knocked down last time?"

"No. Cliff." I pulled a crumpled sheet of paper out of my pocket and handed it to Marty. "What do you think of the people on this list?"

He squinted at my printing and ran his fingers through his black hair. "Well, for one thing, they're the wrong sex."

I rolled my eyes. "I mean, do you think any of them could be behind what's going on around here?" I waved my hand. "The horse theft and all."

He frowned. "I don't know, Steve. I'd put my money on Sanders or Whitcombe. Well, maybe not Whitcombe. Not personally, anyway. He doesn't have the balls for it."

I snorted.

"And don't forget Tony and Mark," he said. "They both swore they'd get even after you fired them."

"That was almost two years ago."

Marty looked at me and shrugged.

"And they aren't organized enough for it," I added.

"All right, gentlemen."

I turned around.

Greg had the cart loaded down with enough paste wormers and vaccinations to do half the farm, and he was watching us with a devilish grin on his face. "Ready?"

Marty and I groaned in unison.

While the rest of the crew mucked out the other barn, the three of us worked our way down one side of the aisle and up the other. Greg dropped an empty paste wormer and two used syringes in the trash bag hanging off the cart and went into the next stall, where Marty was already restraining a bay mare. I walked past them and realized I'd come up with the short end of the stick. The next horse in line was Chase. Most of them offered little resistance, but that particular gelding was difficult about everything. I got the chain on his halter without too much trouble and clamped the twitch on his nose before he realized what I was up to.

When Greg slid the door open, the gelding ran backward, bumped into the corner of his stall, then reared. He lifted me off my feet. He was still balanced on his hind legs, when he pivoted and crashed against the wall. My back smacked into a support post. The sharp edge slammed into my back right between my shoulder blades. I held on, knowing instinctively that it was safer to go with him than end up on the floor under his feet. When he came back down, he lunged forward, and I ran with him. Marty and Greg were in the stall then. Greg cursed as he jabbed the gelding with a needle.

"Let go of the shank and get out," Greg yelled.

The three of us jumped out of the stall, and the horse spun around as Marty rammed the door home.

"You all right?" Greg asked.

I nodded and tried to catch my breath. "What about the other shots and the wormer?"

"That wasn't a vaccination. I gave him a tranquilizer. We'll come back in a little while and finish the job." He peered at me. "You sure you're okay?"

"Yeah." I rolled my shoulders. "Next time, bring a tranquilizer gun."

"How about a real gun?" Marty said, and I didn't think he was joking.

Twenty minutes later, we went back and looked in at Greg's patient. The gelding seemed unaware of our presence. His legs were splayed, head lowered, nose close to the sawdust.

"Greg," I said. "Did you know James Peters?"

"Who?" He was watching the horse, lost in thought.

"James Peters. Owned Hunter's Ridge Farm."

"Oh…yeah. I used to work for him, but it's been ten years or better. He'd call me out to check on the status of one of his mares or to check for uterine infections, that sort of thing."

A breeding operation hadn't been what I'd expected. "I thought he boarded show horses."

"Used to. About twenty years ago." Greg rubbed the back of his neck. "They switched to breeding. It was easier on them as they got older. No boarders to keep happy. Just their own stock to take care of."

"How were they making out?"

"Good. As I recall, they were getting ready to add on to their barn when he was killed."

"You didn't work for him…near the end?"

"No. You know, it's one thing to die, we all face that, but to be murdered." Greg shook his head. "You never think you'll know someone who's been murdered. What an awful fate, and for what? He was a nice man. Never hurt anyone in his life."

"Is his family still running the place?"

"No. I don't think they had any children, and his wife had a nervous breakdown after what happened. She's in a nursing home, I think. They weren't young. Both of them had to have been in their sixties when it happened."

"Do you recall who their barn manager was?"

"They didn't have one. The place wasn't all that big. They hired school kids to muck out. Far as I know, Peters did everything else."

"Did they have any tack stolen before the horse theft?"

"Not that I heard." Greg was no longer idly watching the gelding but had turned around and was studying me with his piercing blue eyes. "What's this about, Steve?"

"Do you know anybody who worked for him just before he died, anybody I could arrange to talk with?"

"Not offhand." He glanced at the gelding. "You're thinking the people who stole his horses were behind what happened at Foxdale, aren't you?"

"The police consider it a possibility."

"Shit."

I dreamt I was lying in the woods.

The earth was hard and damp and cold, the world thickly black. I tried to touch my face, to see if my eyes were open, but my arms were stuck to my sides. I couldn't move. Couldn't move because I was buried. Buried alive.

I bolted upright. Above me, the familiar knotty-pine ceiling rose toward the ridge beam. Vast empty space. I was safe in my own bed, not suffocating in a shallow grave. I breathed in a great lungful of air and felt my heart pounding against my ribs. The dream had been too real.

After a minute or two, I got up and walked over to the kitchen sink. I turned on the tap, let the water run until it was icy cold, then took a swallow and felt the chill settle in my chest. I picked up the copy of Sanders' insurance papers off the counter. I had been surprised when they'd arrived in the mail and disappointed when I'd leafed through them. They looked unremarkable, and I could see why the claim hadn't been contested. The only thing that had caught my attention was Greg's signature on the vet exam.

I set the glass on the counter and walked around the loft. I paused at the north windows. The world was quiet and still, everything peaceful and safe. So, why didn't I feel safe? I got back in bed and thought about James Peters. Thought about the awful terror he must have felt before he died. Like Greg had said, no one deserved that.

Chapter 8

After the schooling show, when I had checked the competitors' trailers and had almost gotten my teeth rearranged for it, I had called Detective Ralston and told him what I had in mind. We had agreed that preparations would take at least a week and a half. So it wasn't until a windy afternoon toward the end of March that I headed north to Westminster.

I pushed through the double glass doors of Maryland State Police Barracks "G" and signed in at the desk. The corporal handed me a pass that I pinned to my jacket, then I rode the elevator to the second floor. Each door down the brightly lit hallway had an identifying sign protruding from the transom that reminded me of a miniature street sign. Interview One, Two, and Three, Storage, Records, Properties, Holding One and Two, and directly across the hall, C.I.U. From the spacing of the doorways, it looked like the Criminal Investigations Unit had been allotted a generous slice of floor space.

C.I.U. was stenciled across the pebbled glass in black rimmed with gold. I opened the door and stepped inside. Two rows of pale blue partitions formed a wide central aisle that stretched to the back wall. The room was freshly painted in a creamy yellow, and the slate gray wall-to-wall was new. A strong odor of new carpet still hung in the air.

A heavyset black man with a pair of bifocals perched low on his nose glanced up when he heard the door swing shut behind me. He was leaning back in his chair with his ankles crossed on the edge of his desk, a handgun magazine propped on his belly. A glossy advertisement for a Sig Sauer P239 covered the back page. I told him who I was looking for, and he directed me to Ralston's cubicle.

Two other detectives were at their desks midway down the room, one on the phone, the other writing on a legal pad. Neither looked up as I walked past. Ralston's cubicle was the last one on the left, and he was on the phone. He motioned for me to join him. I sat in the chair alongside his desk and half listened to his end of the conversation.

"No. There's no way we won't get an indictment....Tuesday at the latest."

Ralston's desk looked spare and neat. He'd covered his blotter with Plexiglass, which he used to anchor lists of information, and he'd angled his computer monitor so that whoever sat in his visitor's chair couldn't see the screen. Above his desk, a calendar featured a glossy photo of a dirt bike jockey catching air as he flew over the edge of an embankment. The rider, dressed in neon yellow and lime green, stood out against a cloudless blue sky.

"Guerra won't play ball, but—" Ralston frowned and shook his head impatiently. "No. He can dick around all he wants, but we're running with it. We've got Menza locked in good and tight."

A collection of pens and pencils filled a navy blue mug with "The Man" printed in gold. The man himself looked professional in a crisp white shirt and paisley tie. The only thing that distinguished him from the rest of the business world was the gun strapped into a shoulder harness.

Except for the mug, and maybe the wall calendar, there was nothing of a personal nature in evidence. No family photographs, no trinkets, and I wondered if the separation of job and personal life extended to his home and thought it probably did.

"He doesn't have to like it, and there's no disputing the—Relax, Martin. You'll see….Not this time."

Directly across from where I sat, a bank of windows stretched across the back wall. I glanced at my watch. Although it was only five-thirty, the glass behind the vertical blinds was dark. Heavy black clouds hung low in the sky, and gusts of wind whipped the top branches of a nearby tree. As I watched, the first drops of rain splattered across the glass.

Below the windows, conference tables had been shoved against the back wall and were loaded down with computer monitors, a printer, and stacks of binders and reference books. Cardboard boxes were jammed under the tables, and a collection of wall maps, white boards, and rolled up posters leaned against the wall in the corner.

"Yeah, Monday." Ralston hung up and filed the sheet of paper he'd been taking notes on into an open binder. "Thanks for coming in, Steve."

"No problem."

He wedged the binder in among the others that lined the right side of his desk. Each one had a card slipped into a slot on the spine with a name and date typed in bold black letters. Peters, James S. was third from the left. The binder he'd been working on had McCafferty, Margaret A. hand-printed in blue ink. The date was a week old.

Ralston stood and stretched. "Want some pizza? This is going to take a while."

"Sure."

He put in a call to the local pizzeria, then hefted a cardboard box off the floor. I followed him into interview room number two. Crumbs were scattered across the metal table. The room smelled like fried onions and pastrami.

"I haven't received a response from everyone, yet," Ralston said. "But we have more than enough to get started." He lifted a bulky manila envelope out of the box. "Start with this one while I get the MVA lists."

Ralston went back to his office as I emptied the contents of the first packet onto the table. Even though I hadn't recognized the make and model of the trailer used in the theft, I'd been able to eliminate some trailers at the schooling show. With a little effort and attention to detail, I figured I could narrow down the field, even if I had to do it on paper. When I'd suggested this to Ralston, he had enthusiastically sent requests to every trailer manufacturer in the country.

I scanned the pamphlets sent in by Equifleet Manufacturer and saw they'd been more than happy to comply. Equifleet produced top-of-the-line horse trailers in fourteen different models, both bumper-pull and gooseneck, depending on trailer size and customer preference. Their best-selling model was a simple two-horse bumper-pull with a tapered tack room in the front. All of their trailers featured optional living quarters for the competitor who preferred to sleep on the show grounds. Currently, the largest trailer they manufactured was a popular four-horse slant load with an expanded camper section. No six-horse.

I flipped through their brochures and saw that they had switched to an aluminum shell a decade earlier. I hadn't thought about it at the time, but the trailer I had been imprisoned in had definitely had a steel shell. That, in and of itself, wasn't significant. In the past, all but a few elite brands had used steel.

It wasn't until I opened an older Equifleet pamphlet that I spotted a trailer that was a possibility. As I studied the trailer's floor plan, memories of that night unexpectedly crowded my mind, and the walls in the small, windowless room seemed to close down on me. For the first time, I thought about James Peters being in there, too. In the dark, alone. Tied to one of the metal partitions. And I wondered what it had been like for him. Maybe he hadn't been able to untie his hands, or maybe he had been unconscious. Or it simply could have been that I was the lucky one. The one who had found the old bolt.

The hum of the ventilation system seemed to grow louder, but the room felt airless.

Ralston opened the door, dropped the MVA list and a notepad on the table, and paused before handing me a Coke. "What's up?"

I shook my head and looked back down at the brochure. "Nothing."

Ralston hitched his chair up to the table and grabbed another envelope out of the box. After a few seconds, I sensed that his attention was on me and not the packet in his hands. I looked up and saw that he was watching me, a slight frown on his face. When I leaned back in my chair and popped the tab on my Coke, Ralston opened his envelope and dumped the contents on the table.

"What are we looking for?" he said. "I don't know the first thing about trailers, or horses for that matter."

I rubbed my forehead and sat up straighter. "First of all, the trailer has to have a steel shell. Most if not all of the companies are using aluminum nowadays, but their older models, like the trailer I was in, were steel. It's gotta be a gooseneck, too, with a loading door and ramp on the right side—"

"Right side? You mean the same side as a car's passenger door?"

"Yeah. The escape door's across from that and a little toward the front, on the driver's side. And see this?" I swiveled the Equifleet pamphlet around and pointed at the diagram I'd been studying. "The layout's very much like this one. It's called a six-horse head to head. The loading door accesses a wide central aisle, and the horses are brought up the ramp and are either backed into one of the three stalls in the front of the trailer or into one of the three in the back. The horses face each other as they travel, and it's easy to unload them. You just lead them out of their stalls and down the ramp."

"Okay. Could that be the one?"

"I don't think so. It's fancier than the trailer I was in, and it has a rear tack room. I'm pretty sure the one I was in didn't."

I looked up from the diagram. "But I'm not one hundred percent certain."

Ralston drew two lines down the top sheet of his notepad and labeled the resultant columns "unlikely," "possible," and "positive."

I opened the last pamphlet Equifleet had sent and scanned the diagrams. "This is the same layout. The same floor plan, anyway."

Ralston stepped around the table and looked down at the diagram.

"But the windows are in the wrong place," I said.

"What about the escape door? Is it the same kind?"

I studied the photograph of their oldest six-horse. "I can't tell."

"Wouldn't details like the style of the escape door and window location be optional?"

"I suppose so," I said.

"And they might make minor changes to the design without going to the expense of printing a whole new batch of pamphlets. I'll list them as a positive for now."

"Sounds good to me."

I was on my third packet from a company named Kennsington, when the door opened.

"Delivery." The detective who'd directed me to Ralston's desk laid a pizza box on the table and began to back through the doorway. There was a look of amusement in his eyes that Ralston picked up on immediately.

Ralston yanked up on the lid. Several slices of pizza were missing. "Schnauz, what's this?"

The detective grinned and began to pull the door closed. "Delivery perks."

"You're a shyster, you know that?" Ralston yelled as the door clicked shut.

We worked steadily for the next two hours. By the time we'd finished, the packets from the trailer manufacturers were separated into three piles that matched the columns on

Ralston's list. Thirteen names on the MVA list were now highlighted in yellow. The only positives. I commented on the low number.

"It only takes one," Ralston said. "And don't forget, I haven't heard back from all the companies yet. He lowered the "unlikely" pile into the box.

Phase one completed, now we actually had to look at the trailers in person, and I had the impression Ralston would have been happier if he could have proceeded without a "civilian" in tow. But it couldn't be helped.

"I hope the companies sent us all their old pamphlets," I said. "Otherwise, we could have missed it."

"We'll start with the positives and work our way down the list. If we don't get a hit, I'll contact the companies again." Ralston rubbed the back of his neck. "Or, if it comes to it, we could resort to checking all the names on the list in person and hope we don't have to widen the search to the counties I haven't run off."

I groaned. "It's going to take forever."

Ralston grunted. "Contrary to the public's perception, detective work's ninety-nine-point-nine percent tedium. Speaking of which, when can you start?"

I thought about the next two days. Besides the usual workload, Foxdale was hosting a party Saturday to kick off the show season. I told him the earliest would be Sunday morning, late, and we agreed to meet at the farm.

Lunch time Friday, I spent at a nursery, watching the bumper of my pickup sag closer to the ground as an assortment of shrubs and flowering plants were loaded into the bed.

On the trip back to Foxdale, I braked as I approached the sharp curve on Rocky Ford. A pickup was half in the road. I slowed even more and saw why the driver had parked where he had. Three men were unloading a fancy wooden sign for what would soon be the new housing development. A flatbed with a hoist had delivered a load of bricks the week before, and decorative columns already flanked the entrance.

As I pulled into Foxdale, I saw that a crew from the local rental company had erected a huge yellow and white striped canopy between the indoor and barn A. I bumped the pickup across the grass, toward the rows of banquet tables and folding chairs that had already been set up.

Marty and I unloaded my truck. Afterward, I gestured toward the potted plants that we'd positioned to keep the guests from walking into the guy wires. "We'll use them around the jumps next weekend if it's not too cold."

"Don't tell me. The first A-rated show of the season."

"That it is."

Marty hung his head. "Man. The winter break was too damn short."

I wiped the sleeve of my shirt across my forehead. "Awh, come on, Marty. Think of all the overtime."

"What overtime?"

"Oh, yeah." I grinned. "Being salaried's the pits, isn't it?"

"Got that right."

We both turned around when a heavy vehicle rumbled down the lane.

"Damn it." I stood and peeled my shirt off the back of my neck. In the last two weeks, the weather had gone from winter to spring. "I forgot about the hay delivery."

Marty lifted the Chevy's tailgate and slammed it home. "Want me to count and weigh the bales?"

"I don't know." I sighed. "Let's take a look at the load and paperwork, then decide."

"Why don't you find another supplier?" Marty said.

"Harrison might not be the most honest guy around, but he's got the best quality hay in the area, and he was only shorting us thirty-five bales or so. I'm hoping random checks will be enough to keep him honest." I sighed. "I don't know. If he tries it again, I'll dump him."

"I have no doubt."

The driver jumped down from the cab and scanned the party preparations with apparent irritation. "Alfalfa-timothy mix like you wanted," he said.

"Good," I said. "Could you drive on over to the implement building? Someone will be down to help unload in a minute."

He stared at me for a second, then wordlessly climbed into the cab.

"Unfriendly sonofabitch," Marty said as the truck lumbered out of sight behind barn B. "I think his face would crack if he smiled."

Marty, I thought, was diametrically opposite. I looked at my watch and frowned. It was later than I'd thought. "Marty, I'll get Cliff and Billy to help me stack the hay. Round up the rest of the guys to do turnouts, okay?"

"So, you're going to check?"

"Might as well."

"You never give up, do you?"

"Go on, Marty."

"Yes, sir...boss." He grinned, and I wondered if he found it odd calling someone younger than he "boss." I knew I was caught off guard whenever he said it.

The driver threw the bales off the flatbed, and I tossed them up a level where Cliff and Billy were stacking them in the mow. The quality was good throughout. Even though it was last year's hay, the aroma was sweet. I started to throw a heavy one up to Cliff, when my glove got stuck under the baling twine and almost came off. I set the bale down, straightened the glove, and bent over to grab the twine. The next bale slammed into my back and almost knocked me off my feet.

I spun around and glared at the driver. Before I could say anything, he said he was sorry, but he wasn't. He was pissed. Except for the last time, we'd never checked his shipments, and my counting the bales was shoving it in his face. I resisted the urge to rub my back, threw the bale to Cliff, and left the one that had tumbled to the ground where it was.

After we stacked the last bale in the mow, I sat down on a row of hay and did some quick calculations while the driver dragged heavy chains across the flatbed and dumped them into piles just behind the cab. I glanced up in time to catch his stare. He had been staring at me the entire time, or so it seemed. I stood and stretched, trying to get the kinks out of my neck, and decided I was getting paranoid. I signed his paperwork without comment, then watched him drive past the muck pile. He ground the heavy truck's gears as he pulled onto the side road on his way back to the office.

◇◇◇

Saturday morning dawned warm, and by late afternoon it was downright hot. I took off the flannel shirt I'd been wearing over my T-shirt and ran it across my face and down the back of my neck, then tossed it through the Chevy's open window. I leaned against the back fender and watched Marty unload the last case of soda into one of the plastic tubs under the canopy. That done, he walked past me, reached across the tailgate, and picked up a bag of ice.

"Here. This'll cool you off." He tossed the bag at me.

I caught it, just.

"Oooh, good reflexes." He grinned, then hoisted another bag out of the bed.

We made a race out of filling the tubs, and by the time I'd dumped my last bag of ice on top of cans of Coke and 7-Up and root beer, my arms were frozen.

Marty ripped open his last bag and dumped the ice into the nearest tub. "You know," he said, "warm as it is, this won't be enough."

"I know. Terry and Cliff are going to haul in some just before the party."

I went into the lounge and bought a soda. When I walked back outside, Marty had already helped himself to a 7-Up.

"Isn't that warm?"

"A little."

I made a face, parked my soda on one of the picnic tables, and sat down. The clip-clop of horseshoes echoed off the barn siding, and a mild breeze rustled the canvas above our heads. I took a swig of Coke and rested my elbows on the table. The day had been a long one, just a taste of what lay ahead with the show season right around the corner.

I looked up in time to see one of the new boarders walk past on her way to the barn. Her name was Rachel, and she'd hauled her horse in two weeks earlier. Since she rode in the evenings, I'd been staying at work later and later with each passing day. She looked in our direction and waved. I waved back. Marty, ever observant, took it in.

After she walked out of sight beyond the corner of the barn, he said, "Holy shit. You're alive after all."

"What are you talking about?"

"I was beginning to worry about you Steve, ol' buddy, ol' pal. Is that the new boarder?"

"Yeah."

"How come I haven't seen her 'til now?"

"She comes in after you leave." I grinned. "She must of heard about you."

He chuckled and, as if proving my point, said, "Man, oh, man. That's the best part of this job. More girls here than flies on shit. Girls and their horses. And the way they move their hips when they're riding, wearin' those tight britches like they do. Man, it's enough to make a guy crazy. What's her name?"

"Rachel."

"She's got a great ass. Must have somethin' to do with all that ridin'. Bet she's good in—" Marty looked at my face, correctly read my expression, and rephrased his statement, "eh...a lot of fun. Fun to be with, I mean." He sat on the edge of the table. "I was wondering when you were gonna wake up. You gonna ask her out? After that girl of yours, what's her name...Melanie..."

"Melissa."

"You haven't gone out since she dumped you, have you? I get dumped all the time. Matter of fact, Jessica dumped my ass the other night. But I don't let it stop me. There's always a honey out there somewhere. You shouldn't let it get to you. I don't."

I fingered my Coke can. "Sorry about Jessica."

Marty shrugged it off.

"And you're wrong," I said. "I didn't let it get to—"

"Yeah, Steve. Right. Anything you say. But I know you."

I picked up my Coke and smeared the ring of wetness across the varnished wood. As much as I hated to admit it, Marty was right. I'd been devastated, though I'd pretended otherwise. Almost believed it. But what really bothered me was that I'd gotten it so wrong. I wasn't going to let that happen again, and yet, here I was, crashing headlong into those old, overwhelming feelings. At least Rachel wasn't attracted to me because she thought I was loaded, like Melissa had been. Being poor had its advantages.

"So. You gonna ask her out, 'cause if you aren't—"

"We already have."

"Have what?"

"Gone out. Three times, in fact." I grinned at him.

"You're shittin' me?"

I shook my head.

"Well, fuck me." He jumped off the table, extended his arms toward me, and wiggled his fingers. "He no longer slumbers," he said with what he hoped was a spooky-scary voice. "He's—"

I threw my empty Coke can at him.

With the party clearly on everyone's mind, the crew wrapped up the day's work in record time. I drove home, shaved and showered, brushed my teeth, then struggled over what to wear. I decided on a striped Oxford that I'd always liked, pulled on a reasonably new pair of jeans, and found a pair of clean socks that actually matched. The nights were still chilly, so I topped everything off with my old leather jacket.

I went back into the bathroom and looked in the mirror. My hair was too long. The warmer the weather, the shorter I kept it, and it wasn't behaving. I combed it again, without effect, then leaned over the sink and squinted at the scars on my face. Even though they'd faded since my stay in the hospital, they were still depressingly noticeable.

I thought about Rachel, combed my hair one last time, and grinned at my reflection.

Damn, you're a fool to be liking her so much so soon.

At Foxdale, cars and pickups and even a motorcycle or two were jammed into every conceivable space. I parked on the grass shoulder close to the road and, with an almost forgotten feeling of lightheartedness, walked down the lane and joined the party. The last trace of daylight had seeped from the sky, and the Christmas lights Mrs. Hill had strung in the dogwood saplings beyond the indoor twinkled in the gentle breeze. The sound system was impressive, and the food smelled great. I looked for Rachel. When I couldn't find her, I loaded a plate down with barbecued chicken and steamed shrimp, grabbed an ice-cold Coke, and sat on the grass.

I was thinking about seconds when the crowd shifted. Mrs. Hill was standing under the canopy, talking to a distinguished-looking man with gray hair and a salt-and-pepper mustache. He was wearing an expertly cut three-piece suit that went a long way toward disguising his bulging middle-aged gut. He bent forward, cupped his hands around the end of his cigar, and struggled to keep his lighter from going out in the breeze. I watched his cheeks work as he puffed on the stogie and idly thought that he shouldn't be smoking so close to the barn. Someone stepped in front of me, blocking my line of sight.

"Hello there." Rachel crossed her arms and grinned down at me. "I was wondering if you were going to show."

I stood up. "Wouldn't have missed it." I ran my fingertips along the corners of my mouth and hoped I didn't have any barbecue sauce on my face.

When she looked over her shoulder and checked out the crowd, I put the opportunity to good use. She'd ridden earlier, so I was surprised to see that she'd changed her clothes. She was wearing a soft-looking sweater and a pair of jeans that were snug enough to get my pulse racing. Her hair was no longer confined in a ponytail and hung well past her shoulders. I wouldn't have minded running my fingers through it. Wouldn't have minded kissing her, either.

She tilted her head back and gazed at the night sky. The line of her neck was immediately stimulating. Long, taut lines. Creamy smooth skin. Form and function blended in such a way that could only be viewed as sexual by an adult male.

"It's turned out to be a nice evening, hasn't it?" she said.

I imagined what it would be like to slide my hand into that sweater of hers. "Um-hum."

"I can't believe how many stars you can see out here. It's beautiful." When I didn't respond, she turned to look at me, and I thought it was a damn good thing she couldn't read my mind.

"Um-hum, beautiful," I mumbled.

She looked at me strangely, and I figured she wouldn't need to be a mind-reader if I kept acting like an idiot.

I cleared my throat. "Have you eaten?"

She nodded. "The food's delicious. How often does Foxdale have these parties?"

"Several times a year. The next one'll be in June, at the start of the four-day A-rated show. Then there's a Halloween party for boarders and students. That one's a blast. It's held in conjunction with a fun-day horse show for the kids. They wear costumes and compete in silly games. Then there's the Christmas party. The boarders' committee plans and organizes that one."

"Very impressive. It must be a lot of work for you."

"Yeah, but it's fun." I ran my fingers through my hair.

We were standing close, the goings-on around us oblivious, at least, to me. Mrs. Hill chose that moment to walk over and say hello. I didn't hear her at first.

"...Stephen?"

I turned around. "Mrs. Hill?"

"Stephen...this is Mr. Ambrose. Mr. Ambrose," she said with a look of amusement in her eyes that I think only I noticed, "Stephen Cline."

Wow. The man himself, and after all this time.

"Hello, Stephen." Ambrose held out his hand, and I shook it. "I've heard a great deal about you from Mrs. Hill. According to her, you're the driving force behind Foxdale's recent success. Well done, young man."

"Eh...thank you, sir."

He took a puff from his cigar and uninhibitedly looked me up and down. "How old are you?"

"Twenty-one, sir."

He grunted. "I don't mind telling you I'm pleased with how the farm is prospering just now. When my wife decided to have it built, I thought it a foolish idea. I continued to think so for a long time, but when she passed away, I held onto it in honor of her memory. Now, it is no longer a burden but an enterprise I don't mind having my name connected with."

I glanced at Mrs. Hill and wished I hadn't. She was grinning at me with what I could only read as motherly pride.

"Well done, young man." Ambrose clapped me on the shoulder.

"Thank you, sir."

He gave me a curt nod, glanced at Rachel, then put his hand on Mrs. Hill's shoulder and steered her toward the parking lot. I heard his voice clearly over the crowd. "Imagine, losing a tax write-off because of a twenty-one-year-old kid."

Chapter 9

When I looked back at Rachel, I realized I'd forgotten to introduce her. I apologized.

"That's all right." Her eyes twinkled with humor. "You were too busy being run over."

I snagged one of the servers, got a beer for myself and wine for Rachel—served in a plastic cup, nonetheless—and said, hoping it didn't sound idiotic, "To the future."

"To the future." She hesitated before taking a sip. The Christmas lights reflected in her dark eyes, and I thought that maybe, just maybe, the future would be an improvement over the past.

We carried our drinks into the barn and checked out the inhabitants. I stopped at the second stall on the right. "This is Jake, one of my favorites."

Rachel grasped one of the bars on the stall door, and the gelding tentatively stretched his neck and nuzzled her fingers with his velvety black nose.

"Yep," I said. "He's as sweet and as docile as a lamb, but boy, can he jump. Jumps like a jackrabbit."

We drifted down one side of the aisle and up the other. Kids were running and squealing in the aisle across the way, turning the barn into a playground. Most of the horses were eating their hay, some were dozing, none seemed disturbed by the activity. When I was satisfied that they were fine with all the commotion, we crossed over to barn B and eventually stopped at her horse's stall. The gelding tilted his head to the side, the way they do when they think they're going to be fed, and tried his damnedest to look cute.

"You're embarrassing. You know that?" Rachel stretched her fingers between the bars and rubbed his nose. He pulled back in annoyance.

Just then, Marty, obviously a shade drunk, strolled into the barn with his arm slung around the shoulders of a tall blonde and a beer dangling from his hand. I had never seen her before, but I wasn't surprised. With Marty's dark good looks and outgoing personality, he was never alone for long. They came to an abrupt halt in front of us. The blonde swayed from the unexpected maneuver. I glanced at my drink and wondered if I'd be driving them home.

"So-o-o, there you are," Marty slurred. "Was wonderin' where you'd got to. Steve, this is Angie." He paused, and I noticed a mischievous glint in his eyes as he added, "Jessica's sister." He gestured with his hand and beer sloshed down his fingers. "Angie, Steve."

So Marty's new honey was his ex's sister. Damn, he didn't worry about anything. I tried to keep a straight face. "Nice to meet you."

Angie pushed a handful of bleached-blond hair out of her eyes and mumbled something indistinct. She was heavy into jewelry and makeup—unappealing to my eyes—but Marty never sweated the details. His only concern, as he frequently lectured me, was the main course. And actually, the main course looked pretty good. She was built a lot like her sister.

Marty gulped some beer, then licked his lips. "Yep, ol' Steve here's the main man. Our hero. Defender of horses everywhere. Yep. Got the crap—"

"Marty!" I cut him off. "Marty, this is Rachel...Rachel, Marty. He works here, too."

Marty looked her up and down with evident approval and swayed when he leaned forward to shake her hand. "Nice to meet you." He looked past her and winked at me.

I sighed inwardly. Marty, sober, was not the epitome of tact. Plastered, he was much worse. Pulling his girl along with him, he stepped over to me and hooked his free arm across my shoulders.

"Rachel," he said, "take good care of this guy. I'm happy to see there's life in him after all." He squeezed my shoulder, then let his arm drop to his side. "Come on, Ange." He guided her toward the exit. "See ya later," he yelled over his shoulder.

I leaned back against the stall door, thinking that Marty could be so embarrassing, when Rachel said, "What was he going to say when you interrupted him?"

The overhead lights shone like silver in her dark hair. "What?"

"What did he mean by 'defender of horses'?"

Damn Marty and his big mouth. "Nothing," I mumbled. "It's just something silly he likes to say."

She frowned.

Rachel, I saw, was not a girl to put up with evasion. I wondered what I should tell her. If I should tell her.

I sighed. "In February...some guys stole seven horses from the farm. I ran into them. That's what he was talking about." And damn him.

"Is that what happened to your face?" she said.

"Yes." It came out a whisper.

"It must have been horrible."

"It's history. No big deal." My voice sounded convincing enough, and it was over and done with, but not in the middle of the night. Not in my dreams. Annoyingly, I still dreamt about it. Dreamt about him. And in those dreams he was disturbingly real.

"You're strong," she said softly.

I snorted. If she only knew. There was compassion in her eyes, I thought, and understanding. We were standing close. I wrapped my arms around her and pulled her against me.

As I'd been ignoring Foxdale's policy of non-fraternization with the boarders, a policy no one paid attention to anyway,

I said, "I know you get up early, but would you like to go to dinner and the movies"…and bed…"Thursday evening?"

She looked at my face, her dark eyes serious. "Sure."

I kissed her on the lips and thought the evening couldn't get any better.

We walked back outside to the party, or what was left of it. The caterer's wagon had been locked up tight, and many of the guests had gone home. As we crossed the grass, I heard someone shouting above the music. His back was toward us, his muscles rigid with tension, and he was flailing his arms. I groaned when I saw his target.

Of all people, he had to be arguing with Mr. Sanders, who was so anxious to get away from the guy, he was practically squirming. His face was red from embarrassment or anger. I couldn't tell which. It hadn't taken him long to replace Steel, though I imagined the twenty-thousand-dollar insurance claim had helped considerably. A week after the theft, he'd purchased a large blood-bay hunter with an ugly head and surly disposition. The new horse didn't take well to mistakes or roughness from his rider and was teaching Sanders a thing or two about finesse and tact, having bucked him off whenever Sanders' aids weren't precise.

I asked Rachel to stay where she was, then walked down the alleyway between the barn and canopy. The troublemaker was waving a beer bottle in the air and shouting increasingly vulgar obscenities. Sanders backed up, reminding me of a horse ready to bolt.

I stepped closer. "Excuse me."

The troublemaker wheeled around and lurched sideways. "What the fuck do you want?"

I was surprised because I knew him. He drove Harrison's hay truck more often than not, and he hadn't been invited to the party. I thought about the bale he'd slammed into my back and wondered what his problem was.

"You'll have to leave," I said.

In a low, menacing voice, he said, "Make me, you little boot-licking, cock-sucking, creepy bastard."

Conscious of the attention we were attracting, I stood very still, knowing full well that my lack of reaction was pissing him off.

I should have seen it coming...stupid, really, that I didn't. I had started to turn, to make sure Rachel hadn't followed, when he punched me in the face. I crashed backward against the barn siding. I was still scrambling to get my footing when he swung the beer bottle at my head.

I ducked it...just. The bottle exploded against the ridged metal siding, inches above my head.

He now held in his hand a jagged, lethal-looking piece of glass which he held close to my face.

I didn't move...didn't dare.

He couldn't be stupid enough to use it in front of all these people, could he? But he was drunk. "Drunk and disorderly" came to mind as I looked in his eyes. Nothing reassuring there. Nothing at all.

I couldn't think of a way out. I was afraid to move. Was sure he'd use it if I did.

"Hey!" a loud voice boomed. Marty.

The driver looked at Marty. I didn't. When his gaze was off me, I hit his arm hard. The glass flew out of his hand and bounced across the grass.

He spun back around. His eyes had the glazed-over look of the truly inebriated and were wild with hate. An ugly vein that ran across his temple had become distended and throbbed visibly. I rammed my fist into his ear with a fierceness that surprised me. He yelped and cupped his hand over his ear.

I tackled him, and we crashed into a picnic table. He hit the wooden edge hard. The momentum carried us across the top, scattering paper plates and half-filled cups.

When we landed on the grass, I got to my knees fast and rolled him onto his back. I straddled him and slammed my fist into his face. My knuckles connected solidly with his nose, and I felt the cartilage give. I got in two more swings before he got his arms up and covered his face. I punched him in the solar plexus, then swung my arm back for another go.

Someone grabbed my wrist and hauled me to my feet. I whirled around.

"Jesus Christ," Marty yelled. "What's the matter with you?" He glanced down at the driver, who was rolling over onto his hands and knees, and pulled me across the grass. "What'n the hell do you think you're doin'?"

"Get off me." I yanked my arm free and spun around. The driver was staggering between a table and a half-empty tub of soda on his way to the parking lot. I started after him.

Marty latched onto my arm. "Give it a rest for crying out loud."

"Let go!" I pulled against him, but his grip was like steel. "Let go of me, Marty."

"Forget him."

"Fuck you." I slammed my hands into Marty's chest and pushed him backward, but he held on like a leech. I looked after the driver and saw that he'd already disappeared around the corner of the indoor.

Marty moved around in front of me and blocked my view. "Steve, you're making a mistake."

"No, Marty." I glared at him and said through clenched teeth, "You're making a mistake if you don't fucking turn me loose."

I looked down at his fingers wrapped around my arm, at my hands clenched into fists, at the blood smeared across my jacket.

"Okay, Steve." He released my arm. "It's your call." His voice was so calm, it took me by surprise. "Just don't be stupid."

I glanced around. The remaining guests were clustered in little groups, whispering to each other with sidelong glances, trying not to be too obvious. I sat down at a nearby picnic table, braced my hands on my knees, and watched blood drip from my nose and splatter onto the grass between my feet. I closed my eyes and felt dizzy.

"Come on, Steve." Marty slipped his hand under my arm. "Let's go into the lounge. Okay, buddy?"

I yanked my arm free. "I can stand up, dammit."

It wasn't until I was on my feet that I noticed Rachel. She was hovering behind Marty with her arms wrapped around herself, looking like she didn't know what to do.

She walked over to me. "Are you all right?"

I nodded.

◇◇◇

It took forever for my nose to stop bleeding. We had gone into the lounge, which thankfully was deserted. Once I'd successfully squelched the flow, I tossed the wad of paper towels in the trash and took off my jacket. Shards of brown glass cascaded to the ground.

Marty reached down and picked up a fragment. "What the hell?"

"It's from the beer bottle." I ran my fingers through my hair and rubbed the back of my neck. "My hair's wet, too."

"What beer bottle?"

I grabbed hold of my shirt collar and peeled the wet fabric off my back. I smelled like a brewery, but at least the glass hadn't worked its way into my shirt. "The bottle Harrison's driver had."

"What are you talking about?"

"That's what he had in his hand when you yelled at him."

"It didn't look like a beer bottle."

"Guess not. Not after he'd tried to smash my head in with it, it didn't. He missed and broke it on the side of the barn. Then, I suppose he figured he might as well redecorate my face while he was at it."

"Son of a bitch. If I'd known, I'd've laid into him, too." Marty walked across the room and dropped the piece of glass into the trash. He opened the freezer door. "Son of a bitch," he said again, more to himself than anyone else.

I sat down and wondered how many other people had only seen the tail end of the fight and thought I had gone stark-raving mad. Marty returned and unceremoniously plopped some ice, wrapped in a towel, on my face.

"Thanks." I held the bundle on the bridge of my nose and tilted my head so I could look at him. "And, Marty...I owe you an apology."

"Damn right you do," he said. "Pull that shit again, and I'll...I'll have your job."

I grinned at him. "I thought you didn't want my job?"

"Oh, yeah. I forgot." He crossed his arms over his chest. "So, what started the whole fucking thing?" When I finished telling him, he chuckled. "Shit, Steve, you should of given him a medal for bothering Mr. Hotshot Sanders. That asshole sure could use some puttin' in his place."

I glanced at Rachel.

Marty continued. "Come to think of it, I saw them talkin' earlier, thicker 'n flies on shit, and Sanders didn't look too happy then, either."

"Well, it makes sense they'd know each other. Sanders used to board at Harrison's farm." I readjusted the ice. "Wonder what's up."

"Who the hell cares?"

I scrunched down into the cushions and concentrated on balancing the ice while keeping the pressure as light as possible. Several minutes later, Marty was still pacing around the room. Angie was sprawled on the adjacent sofa and looked bored, and Rachel was watching me with a worried expression on her pretty face.

I tried a smile. "Well," I said, "so much for an uneventful party."

Rachel shifted on the cushions. "I thought he was going to kill you."

"No. He wasn't that stupid," I said, convincing myself as much as her. "Anyway...everything worked out okay."

She frowned. "Your perception of okay's kind of skewed."

"Yeah." Marty plopped down next to Angie. "Just wait 'til Monday morning."

"Monday morning?" Rachel looked from Marty to me.

"Yeah," Marty said. "When Mrs. Hill finds out about our wild man here."

I listened to the grin in his voice. "What was I supposed to do?" I said. "Just stand there and let him cut me?"

"No, Steve. But you didn't have to pound him into the ground, either. Not that I blame you. Hell, I might of killed the bastard."

I slid my spine deeper into the sofa and rested my head on the cushions.

Marty said, "Is the ice making any difference?"

"Yeah. Now, not only does my nose hurt, it's cold."

He snorted.

After a minute or two, I shifted the ice pack. Marty had his arm draped across Angie's shoulders. Their heads were turned toward each other, their voices indistinct murmurs. Rachel's arms were stiff at her sides, and her shoulders looked tense. I took the ice off my face, sat up straighter, and put my hand on hers.

"I'm sorry," I said.

"For what?"

"Sorry that this whole stupid thing happened." I squeezed her hand.

"Well, we're outta here." Marty levered himself off the sofa. "You gonna be all right, Steve?"

"Yep."

"Good. See you Monday, if you still got a job."

I groaned. "And, Marty…thanks."

He slid his arm around Angie's waist and grinned wickedly. "We'll discuss my fee later."

I watched them head toward the door and decided he looked fit enough to drive. The evening's events had no doubt gone a long way toward sobering him up. "Hey…drive carefully," I yelled over my shoulder.

"Yes, Mom," he said with mock disgust.

After the door had swung shut, I thanked Rachel.

"For what?"

I shrugged. "For being here."

"You're welcome. It's been...different."

She was sitting close. The place was deserted, and given any other circumstance, it would have been perfect.

"Are you really going to get in trouble?"

"I hope not."

"Can I get you something?" She rose to her feet and scanned the lounge. "Don't they have a first aid kit around here? Some aspirin would help."

I started to get up.

Rachel put her hands on my shoulders. "Stay put. I'll get it."

She looked so serious, it was all I could do not to grab hold of her and pull her into my lap. I smiled at her instead and sank back into the cushions. "In the office. On the table along the back wall."

While she went on her search, I closed my eyes and tried to ignore the throbbing in my head. Listening to her rummage around in the office, I thought about the following morning, when I was expected to come in early and clean up after the party. I didn't feel like it, and I doubted six hours were going to change my outlook any. I checked my watch. Eleven-forty-five. Make that five hours. When I opened my eyes, Rachel was standing in front of me with three Tylenol caplets in one hand, a Coke in the other, and a worried expression on her pretty face. A grin from me was met with a frown, and I found I was liking her more and more.

"Three?" I said.

"It won't hurt, and you look like you could use it." She watched me swallow the pills, then sat down beside me. "Do you think your nose is broken?"

"Probably not, but if it is, there's nothing much to be done about it. The last time I...eh." Damn, why'd I have to bring that up? I sure as hell didn't want to talk about that. "It probably isn't."

"Um." Rachel swiveled around to face me, much as Elsa had done, minus the sexual come-on. She reached over and lifted the ice pack off the armrest. "Here, you should keep this on your nose. Somehow, I figure when you get home you won't bother."

Rachel scooted around so that she was on her knees beside me on the sofa. She braced her left hand on the backrest next to my shoulder and held the ice on my nose. Any closer and she'd be in my lap. I wanted to take the damn ice off my face and wrap my arms around her, but my stomach had other plans. My gut was churning like a cement mixer, and I thought I'd probably swallowed more blood than I'd realized.

"Rachel." I reached up and took the ice pack out of her hand. "Thanks for all your help. I think—"

"You're welcome."

"It's the last thing I want, but I really need to head home."

"It's getting late, isn't it?" She lifted her hand off the back of the sofa to check the time and lost her balance. I caught her as she toppled forward. We stared at each other, our faces almost touching. Her eyes were wide with surprise, and I couldn't help but grin at her. I slid my hands around her waist and helped her get vertical, though horizontal would have been a hell of a lot more fun.

I let her go, and she stood up. "I'll walk you to your car, if you like," I said.

"I like." She ran her fingers through her hair, and if I wasn't mistaken, her face was flushed.

If she was embarrassed, she had no reason to be. Not with me. I struggled to my feet but got to the door before she did. When I held it open for her, she brushed past me and smiled as if at some private joke, or so it seemed.

Rachel slid behind the wheel of her Toyota Camry and wound down the window. Except for her vehicle and mine, now looking ridiculous parked by the road, the place was deserted. She looked at me looking at my truck and grinned. "Would you like a ride to your truck?"

"No thanks. I need to go back and check the barns before I leave." I stepped back as she started the engine and slipped it into gear. "Have a safe drive home," I said.

"You, too."

I watched her drive off, checked the barns, then broke every speed limit home, all the while wishing that Mrs. Hill wouldn't find out about the fight but knowing she'd hear about it one way or the other.

◇◇◇

The clock radio clicked on, and I groped for the off button. When I didn't find it right away, I yanked the cord out of the wall. Monday morning, and rain was hammering the tin roof above my head and slashing against the windows as gusts of wind battered the barn. But what did I expect? It was, after all, April first.

On the drive to Foxdale, the dreary, rhythmic scrape of wipers across windshield grated on my nerves. I turned on the radio—loud—and mulled over yesterday afternoon's unsuccessful trailer search with Detective Ralston.

Based on Ralston's premise that "the obvious is oftentimes the most likely" and assuming that the horse thieves had been taking me to territory they were familiar with, we had worked in concentric circles that radiated outward from where I'd escaped the trailer. Almost half of the trailer owners weren't home. Most who were kept their trailers on the farms where they boarded their horses, necessitating yet another trip on our part. All reacted with genuine surprise at a police detective's appearance on their doorstep.

On the positive side, working down the list produced the expected domino effect we'd hoped for. Knocking off just one trailer's make and model immediately eliminated several names on the list. We worked through all of Montgomery County and part of Howard before calling it a day. Even still, the results were disappointing.

When Ralston had asked when I could take off for another attempt, I selfishly avoided sacrificing any part of my next scheduled day off. Rachel and I had a date planned, and I'd justified my decision with the knowledge that I had some sleuthing of my own in mind.

Rain moved in sheets across the pavement. I squinted through the spray of water droplets and felt the beginnings of a headache. As I pulled off Rocky Ford and headed down the lane toward the parking lot, something in the large outdoor arena caught my eye. One of the jumps looked different, but I couldn't make out why from so far away. I backed into my usual space and pulled on a rain poncho. Cold rain stung like needles on my face as I trudged across the lane. I unlatched the gate and walked into the arena. The going was deeper, but as usual, the drainage system was doing its job. Even in a downpour, the footing was good for the horses.

I stopped at the base of the jump, or what was left of it. The message was bone-chillingly clear. The Foxdale jump, the one that most represented Foxdale, had been burned to the ground, the intricately carved fox heads and hunt scene reduced to a pile of charred rubble and ash. Standing there as the rain splattered loudly on the plastic of my poncho and pounded in a deafening roar on the arena's metal roof, I'd had enough. I would have to find them, stop them. They wanted to play with fire, I'd make sure they got burnt.

I looked for additional damage and found none, but the message was poignant all the same. I grained the horses and started haying. When the crew straggled in around seven, I left them to finish up and went into the office. I pulled a worn card out of my back pocket and dialed Detective Ralston's number. After six rings, I was thinking about hanging up when he picked up.

"This is Steve Cline, at Foxdale."

"What's up?" He sounded wide awake and enthusiastic if not downright cheerful.

"Someone torched one of the jumps in the outdoor arena last night. I didn't know if you'd want me to call you or not, but the jump they chose was one with Foxdale's logo on it. I took that to be a message of sorts." When he didn't respond, I said, "Assuming it's the same crew, it seems there's been a shift in their focus."

"What do you mean?"

"Profit." I rubbed my forehead. "There wasn't any profit in what they did last night. Only malice."

"There was malice with the cat," Ralston said. He was right, of course. "Is it raining there?"

"Coming down in buckets."

"I'll call Linquist and let him know. The rain's probably destroyed any evidence, but it'll be good to get the incident on record."

"All right."

"Any other damage?"

"No. Nothing else has been touched."

"Good. Someone will be out."

When Ralston disconnected, I stared at his card lying on the blotter. What was I going to find next? What if they decided that torching a jump wasn't enough?

Chapter 10

I left a note for Mrs. Hill, emptied out my bin, and walked back to the barn.

Later that morning, after the crew had turned out the first batch of horses and we'd started in on the stalls, I grabbed a push broom from the storage area at the end of the aisle. When I turned around, I almost bumped into Dave.

He opened his mouth to say something, then hesitated. He hadn't gone to the party. Hadn't heard about the fight. Hadn't seen my face.

I looked more closely and saw he was angry, and I didn't think it had anything to do with me. "What's wrong?" I said.

"What happened to the Foxdale jump?"

I crossed my arms and leaned on the broom. Not one of the crew had noticed except him. "Someone was up to no good last night."

Dave looked affronted. Probably couldn't believe that someone had dared touch his artistic handiwork. He glared at me. "You seem to be takin' it lightly."

"Err…" I straightened. "Sorry. It was a magnificent piece of work, but at least it wasn't the barn they burned down."

"Well, shoot. Hadn't thought about that." He rubbed his hands down the front of his grubby overalls and strode out of the barn. Five minutes later he was back, and if anything, he was more agitated.

"What's wrong, now?"

"Somebody's been messin' about in my workshop," Dave said.

"What?"

"My tools are all right." He kept them locked up tighter than Fort Knox. "But paint's been spilled all over the place and somebody's painted obscenities on the walls."

"Damn it." I hadn't thought to check there. "Let's go see."

I hopped into Dave's rusted-out Ford, and he wrenched on the steering wheel and bounced the pickup into the side lane that led to the implement building. He had the wipers on high, even though the downpour had slackened to a drizzle, and there must not have been a shock absorber on the damn thing. I braced my hand on the dash and was still in danger of being bounced off the seat.

"Messing about" was an understatement. Every surface in the workshop was covered with paint, including both tractors. And what was printed on the walls was unbelievable. Filled with rage. Whoever had done it must be literally sick with hate. Dave leaned over to pick up an empty paint can.

"Don't touch that," I said.

He straightened and looked at me, his face blank.

"Don't touch anything, at least not yet."

"What about cleanin' up? The paint's still damp," Dave said. "It'll be easier to get off."

"The police are coming out because of the jump. They'll want to look at this, too." I looked at the walls. "Maybe take pictures. What were you going to work on, anyway?"

"I was gonna work in here 'cause of the rain." He looked out at the gray sky and, after a moment, said he might as well go back home.

"Dave, hold up. Could you buy some supplies, instead?"

He squinted at me and pursed his lips. "What kind of supplies?"

"Anything you need to make the place more secure, go out and buy it. Like better locks for all the tack rooms and the feed room. Maybe you should reinforce the locks on the lounge and office doors, too." I started for his truck. "And is there some type of lock we can put on the feed bin, the big one outside?"

Dave caught up with me by the front bumper. "Don't know."

"Well, if you can't rig something up, call the manufacturer. See if they have any suggestions." I walked around to the passenger's side and opened the door. "Get more fire extinguishers for all the buildings, too. And I think we'll install a gate across the lane to the road. What do you think...two 12-foot gates latched in the middle?"

"That'll work." Dave frowned. "What about where the side lane empties into that old road down by the manure pile?"

"There, too."

"Then we'll need to put up a line of fence."

"Oh, yeah. You're right. Let's just get the other things done first. We'll do that later, when we have time." I slid onto the seat and waited for him to climb behind the wheel. "If you think of anything else we can do to improve security, do it."

He simply nodded, and I wondered how much effort he would put into improving security against an unseen enemy.

"Oh," I said. "And get whatever you need to clean up that mess. When you come in tomorrow, find me. You can show me what to do, and I'll clean up while you install the locks, okay?"

Dave stared at me as if he couldn't quite remember who I was. "Sure," he mumbled before dropping the truck into reverse. He backed down the rutted lane without bothering to look over his shoulder. When he jounced the truck onto the asphalt lane between the barns and pointed the nose toward the road, I wished I'd walked.

"Shit, Dave. You can't drive like that around here."

He grunted and drove off at a more sedate pace but put his foot heavily on the brake pedal when we pulled up alongside the office door. The Ford jerked to a stop, and I just about slid off the smooth vinyl seat. I jumped out and slammed the door, thankful to be on firm, unmoving ground.

Dave sped off as abruptly as he'd stopped. The truck's bald tires sluiced through a large puddle, and I wondered how he'd lived to be so old.

After I called Ralston and was told he was out, I dialed Mrs. Hill's number with dread. Her answering machine picked up. I left a message and, for good measure, dropped another note on her desk.

◇◇◇

Notwithstanding the rain pounding on the metal roof above our heads, we easily heard Mrs. Hill's voice crackle over the PA system. She did not sound happy.

Her message for me to report to the office ASAP elicited a variety of remarks from the crew, mostly obscene and, as far as I was concerned, said with far too much pleasure. All morning long, they'd been debating whether or not Mrs. Hill would have heard about the fight and had been taking bets on her reaction. Ignoring them, I propped my pitchfork and rake in the corner of the stall I'd been mucking out and headed for the office.

By the time I got to the office door, I was sopping wet, which, when I thought about it, was kind of appropriate for the upcoming discussion. As I put my hand on the rain-splattered doorknob, I had a knot in my stomach reminiscent of visits to the principal's office. When I stepped inside, Mrs. Hill looked up from her paperwork and compressed her lips.

I took off my hat. Rainwater dripped off the ends of my hair and slid down the back of my neck. "Mrs. Hill?"

"Stephen..." She tapped a finger on my notes. "What's all this about?"

I looked out the door. It was raining so hard, I couldn't distinguish the pile of rubble from the line of the arena fence. "Last night, someone torched the Foxdale jump. They stacked it into a heap and set it on fire. There's nothing left but charred wood."

"But why?"

I slowly turned to face her. "I don't know."

I told her about the vandalism, and her face grew stiff with disbelief. She stared at me and absentmindedly clicked the top of her ballpoint pen against the desk blotter. The sound acted as a metronome, measuring each passing second, intruding on the lengthening silence, and I found standing still under her gaze difficult.

"You called the police?"

I nodded.

"Another thing…" She did not look pleased. No pleasure anywhere. I shifted my weight from one foot to the other. "Mr. Sanders told me that you got into a fight with someone at the party." Her face was flushed with anger.

Damn Sanders. He hadn't walked away like I'd thought but had hung around to watch. And when I'd had that damned piece of glass shoved up my nose, he hadn't done a thing to help. But he had the balls to imply that I'd started the whole thing. I hoped his horse would dump him on his ass. Into a puddle would be even better.

"Well?" she said.

"I don't know what he told you," I tried to keep my voice even, "but the guy I fought with hit me first. He was bothering Mr. Sanders, and I walked over to see if I could do anything to help. The guy was yelling obscenities, so I asked him to leave, and that's when he hit me. So I…defended myself."

She picked up a piece of hard candy and fingered the wrapper. "Who was this person?"

"He delivers hay for Mr. Harrison."

"What?"

"He drives the hay truck for Mr. Harrison sometimes," I said.

She swiveled around in her chair, pressed a couple of keys on her computer keyboard, and scrolled down the screen. When she found what she wanted, she snatched up the phone, punched in a number—Mr. Harrison's, I presumed—and unleashed some of her anger in his direction. More than likely, the poor guy didn't have the foggiest idea what she was talking about.

Mrs. Hill seldom got angry, but I saw that when she did, she didn't hold back. Personally, I was happy to be removed from target status. She demanded he dismiss his driver. He must have disagreed, because she said she "could be responsible"—her exact words—"for getting a different supplier." Here we go, I thought. Mrs. Hill listened without speaking, then disconnected.

She looked up at me. Her face flushed as patchy red blotches spread up her throat. "I'm sorry, Stephen. Mr. Sanders gave me the wrong idea. I should have known you wouldn't start anything."

"That's all right."

"No it isn't." She rubbed her forehead. "Mr. Harrison's going to dismiss his driver. He had the nerve to say he wasn't responsible for what his driver did when he was off. I tell you." She slapped her palm on the desk blotter. "He can be responsible for the type of person he employs, can't he?"

I struggled to keep a straight face. "Yes, ma'am."

She waved me off. I cut through the lounge, wondering what Harrison's driver and Sanders had been arguing about and, more to the point, whether he had purposefully been trying to get me in trouble. And if so, why?

The crew had moved on to barn B, and they almost seemed disappointed that I hadn't gotten my butt in trouble. Marty's opinion of Mr. Sanders was, as expected, unrepeatable. I didn't spend much time thinking about it, or the torched jump, but chose to think about Rachel instead.

I checked my watch. Lunch time was half over, which explained the lack of activity on the farm. I went into the lounge, grabbed my sandwich out of the fridge, and switched on the television. I was still channel surfing when I heard a vehicle pull up to the office door. The engine cut off and doors slammed. When someone opened the door and stepped into the office, I pushed myself off the sofa and strolled over to see who it was.

A uniformed cop and another man dressed in ratty jeans and an Orioles warm-up jacket stood on the square of carpet in front of Mrs. Hill's desk. They turned toward the door at my approach.

The uniformed cop glanced at the pocket-sized notebook he held in his palm. He was a lanky black man, a good four inches taller than me, with close-cropped hair and a narrow mustache. "You Stephen Cline?" he said.

"Yep." I explained about the burnt jump and briefly described the events of the past five weeks.

He gestured to my face. "Who you tangled with got anything to do with why we're here?"

"Nope. Someone was drunk at a party."

"Uh-huh. But not you?"

There was a look of amusement in his eyes which negated any irritation I might have otherwise felt. I glanced at his name tag. DORSETT was printed in all caps. "Nope. Not me."

"Let's take a look, then."

I dropped my orange into my jacket pocket, picked up my half-eaten sandwich, and switched off the TV. Outside, the air smelled of rain and moist earth. The cloud base was low and black, heavy with the threat of more rain. In the east, wispy tendrils of cloud broke free and scuttled across the sky in a wedge of fast-moving air.

We stood in a semicircle around the jump. I lowered the brim of my cap and huddled inside my jacket while Dorsett's partner crouched down and peered at the pile of charred, soggy wood.

I said to Dorsett, "Did Detective Ralston send you?"

"Indirectly, through Linquist."

"When I talked to him on the phone this morning, I thought this was the only damage on the property, but afterward, we found more vandalism in one of the other buildings."

"You finished here?" Dorsett asked his partner.

He nodded.

"Show us the way then, Cline."

"It's that building." I pointed. "Down there."

"We'll take the car."

I climbed in the back and found it a bit like sitting in a cage. A metal screen separated the back seat from the front.

Officer Dorsett glanced in the rear view mirror and laughed. "A bit unnerving back there, ain't it?" He slowed to make the turn onto the side lane that led to the implement building. "Every kid should take a ride in the back seat. See what it's like."

Kid?

He parked nose to nose with the John Deere 960. They got out. I couldn't. The doors in back wouldn't open from the inside. Dorsett and his partner stood by the car, and the black cop was grinning.

I tried to keep a straight face. "Funny, real funny," I said through the glass.

He unlocked the door, and we stood just inside the building's entrance.

Dorsett whistled. "Could be worse. They could've smashed up everything." He slid a flashlight from a loop on his belt.

"We had to pull the muck wagon and one of the tractors out of here this morning," I said, "so we could get some work done. Hope that was okay."

He had angled the cone of light along the walls and was reading the graffiti. "Do you have any enemies, someone who hates you personally?"

"No....Not really. Not like this."

"Pretty disturbing stuff," he said. "And the guy ain't no genius either."

"You mean the 'y-o-u-r dead' bit?"

Dorsett glanced over his shoulder and grinned. "Right-o. Can't spell, but he's sure into anatomy and bodily functions, ain't he."

"Yeah. But most of it's physically impossible." I watched Dorsett's partner walk back to the cruiser and pop the trunk. "You gotta hand it to him though," I said. "He did get a 12-letter word right."

"Probably had lots of practice. You sure this ain't directed at you?" Dorsett had turned to face me. "It sounds personal."

"Shit, I hope not."

He stepped closer to the wall and played the light across the dusty ground. "We might have some footprints here, Mark."

I edged along the 960 and stopped beside him. Sure enough, a row of prints was distinct in the soft dirt, and what caught my attention most was the fact that they pointed toward the wall—consistent with someone having stood there, painting their sick little message.

Dorsett squatted down. "Steve, these look familiar?"

"No. They're sneakers. Everybody around here wears boots. Especially when it's wet." I looked closer. "There were two of them. See over there?" I pointed to a different pattern tracked through the dirt near Dave's storage room.

"Okay," Dorsett said. "We'll take photos and make casts of both sets."

I leaned against Dave's workbench. "Now you just need the owners."

"Yeah, but we find 'em, we'll make the case." He pointed to a particularly clear print of a left shoe. "See the wear pattern in the tread on that one? There's a notch out of the edge on the inside heel, see?"

"Uh-huh."

"We get the guy, and he's still got the shoes, we got 'im nailed."

I sat on a row of hay and, with increasing fascination, watched them make casts, take photographs, and dust for prints. Maybe we were getting somewhere after all. I finished my lunch and glanced at my watch. I was way behind schedule, and they looked like they were going to be awhile.

I told them where they could find me and hopped off the hay bale. "After you're done today, can we clean up?"

"Don't see why not." He straightened up from where he'd been working on one of the footprints, a packet of plaster of Paris in one hand and a wooden stick in the other. "Just to be on the safe side, though, I'll talk to Linquist and get back to you."

I got a cup of coffee from the lounge and wondered if a drunk gate-crasher counted as an enemy. Maybe since I'd started checking hay shipments, he was an enemy, but he wasn't *the* enemy. The horse theft had happened before I'd confronted Harrison, and the burnt jump felt like the same old campaign against Foxdale.

I cupped my fingers around the Styrofoam and realized that the headache I'd been nursing for the last couple of days had disappeared. Only later did I realize how easy it was to take things for granted.

◇◇◇

Toward the end of the day, I set my grooming tote on the ground outside Chase's stall. As soon as the realization that I was going to do something with him seeped into his tiny brain, he pinned his ears flat against his head. I unlatched his door, and he swung sideways so he could shift his hindquarters toward me. I grabbed the noseband on his halter and stopped him before he had the chance. He curled his neck around and tried to sink his teeth into my arm.

"You stupid son of a bitch," I muttered. His ear flicked at the sound of my voice.

I threaded the chain shank through his halter and cross-tied him in the center of his stall. I hadn't groomed him for three days, but damned if his coat didn't shine like copper. He was one beautiful horse. Too bad his mind was screwed. He bobbed his head as I worked the curry comb in small circles down his neck.

"Who's this?"

I turned around. Rachel was grinning at me through the grillwork. "Cut to the Chase," I said. "He's an open jumper."

"Kind of nasty, isn't he?"

"Yeah. But with his talent, nobody cares."

"Humph, poor thing. He seems so unhappy."

I snorted.

"What do you think his problem is?"

"Life."

"Steve…"

I paused and considered him. Wrinkles creased the skin around his worried eyes, and his jaw was tight with tension. Hell. His entire body was tense.

"Damned if I know," I said. "He's hell on the ground, totally unpredictable, but point him at a jump, and he's one happy puppy. It's like he was born to it." I ran my hand down his neck, and he ground his teeth. "He lives for it."

"Hum. Looks like he lives for getting a piece of your hide between those molars of his."

"Yeah, but he can't help himself. If I discipline him, he gets worse, he's so strung up." I sighed. "He'll kick you as soon as look at you."

She groaned. "And you're the lucky one who gets to do him."

"I'm the *only* one who gets to do him. He's gotten used to me a little. I really think he hates men."

"So, why not have a girl groom him?"

"Right now, we don't have any girls on the weekday crew. Only the weekend."

"I pity whoever rides him," Rachel said.

"Oh, he's not so bad then, 'cause he knows he'll be jumping."

"So, did you have a nice day slopping around in the rain and mud?" She wrapped her fingers around the metal bars and grinned at me. She had a great smile. Straight, white teeth, gorgeous lips, a dimple in her left cheek.

"Cute, Rachel."

"No matter how awful the weather is," she said, "I love getting away from the office. Where I work, we don't have any windows. None you can see out of, anyway. That's one reason why I like riding so much, being outside and doing something physical. Maybe that's his problem."

Maybe that was *my* problem. I sure wouldn't have minded doing something physical with her.

"...And an indoor arena makes it even better." She reached up and worked her hair into a ponytail. "Where I boarded last, the footing was lousy most of the year. The ground was either frozen, sloppy with mud, or dry and hard as rock. I couldn't work on anything consistently."

I knocked the curry against the wall and dislodged a build-up of dirt. "Do you show?"

"Only at local shows. And when I can bum a ride off someone. Well, I'd better get going. I left Koby tacked up in his stall." She adjusted a pair of headphones over her ears. "Music helps me concentrate," she said when she noticed me watching her.

From what I'd seen, she didn't need help in that department. She tuned out everything when she rode. I, on the other hand, was thoroughly distracted by her and found concentrating on anything else difficult when she was around.

After I transferred Chase into Anne's capable hands, I grained the horses, then went in search of Rachel. She had finished cooling out her horse and was in the tack room. I leaned against the locker next to hers and watched her stow her gear. Her face was damp with sweat, and loose wisps of hair clung to the back of her neck. She bent over and rifled through the clutter in the back of her locker. Her britches clung tightly to the full curves and narrow crease of her backside, and there was a nice gap between her thighs. I wanted to take her in my arms and kiss her. Wanted to feel her body against mine. She squatted back on her haunches and looked up at me. A quizzical expression crossed her face, and I supposed I must have appeared odd just standing there.

I rubbed my face and relaxed the muscles in my jaw. "Is Thursday still good for you?"

"Yes." She stood up. "I think so. Where were you just now?"

"Wanting to kiss you," I said.

"Oh." She turned her back to me and slid the lock through the clasp on her locker, then pushed the shaft down into the housing and spun the dial. Strange, even ordinary, everyday things could be exceedingly sexual.

She turned back around. We were standing close. I could smell her scent, imagined that I could feel her breath on my skin. The air around us felt curiously charged, enveloping us in a private world without sound. Her gaze rose slowly to my face. I brushed her bangs from her eyes and felt the dampness of her skin beneath my fingertips. I rested my hands on her shoulders and kissed her lightly on the lips. When I straightened and dropped my arms to my sides, I was no longer breathing normally. She smiled briefly, then lifted her jacket off the bench that separated the rows of lockers.

I cleared my throat. "Tomorrow. Is four-thirty too early?"

"No, that'll work." We made plans to meet at the farm, then she rooted around in her jacket pocket and pulled out her car keys. "I'd better go," she said, and there was a shyness to her smile that I found captivating.

I watched her walk toward the parking lot. The place felt empty without her.

◇◇◇

After the day's work was done, and with security high on my list of pressing concerns, I methodically walked around the farm, looking for weaknesses in our defenses. First stop, the implement building. I crossed over to the wall that enclosed the small storage room and flicked on the lights. Because the fixtures were widely spaced and partially blocked by the hay mow, the work area was poorly lit with heavy, deep shadows under the equipment.

I squeezed behind the row of tractors, ducked under the hay elevator, and looked up at the massive wall of hay. Large quantities of it. All highly combustible. For that reason, even though it was a pain in the ass to haul, we only stored a day's worth in the barns. I would get Dave to hang more fire extinguishers near the entrance, but what good it would do, I couldn't imagine. If they decided to burn down the building, it would be at night when no one was around. If they decided to burn down a barn.…Well, I couldn't even think about that.

The smeared, sick graffiti seemed even more threatening at night. I backtracked, switched off the lights, and wondered if they'd been bold enough to turn them on while they spray-painted their little message. For the umpteenth time, I wondered who they were and why were they messing with Foxdale. And would they be back?

I followed the lane past the implement building and looked toward the old paved road. It dead-ended to my left, at a barricaded fire road that marked the western boundary of a wide swath of state park land. All of those unspoiled acres and the river that wound through them attracted boarders as much as anything else. Only Foxdale's employees and an occasional truck from the mushroom farm frequented this part of the farm. It wouldn't take much fencing and a couple of gates to prevent anyone getting onto the farm from the road, but if someone really wanted to hurt Foxdale, chains and locks and gates across the driveway wouldn't make any difference.

As I turned to go back, something moved in the pine grove that screened the muck pile.

I started, then saw it was just a fox. I exhaled slowly through my mouth and listened to the wind whistling through the boughs. Above my head, stars shone through breaks in the clouds, and in the west, the moon was a chalky smudge behind a thin veil of fast-moving cloud. Away from the farm's lights, the sky seemed vividly alive and close. Close enough to touch.

I slipped my hands into my pockets and headed back. A horse was being led into barn A, his figure back-lit by the soft light that poured through the open doors. Even at that distance, I could clearly hear his shoes scraping the asphalt.

I checked barn B. Beyond installing better locks and adding more fire extinguishers, I couldn't think of anything else we could do to improve security. Outside, I looked at the grain bin that towered high above my head and thought about poison. If someone wanted to contaminate the grain, they would have to climb up a narrow ladder to reach the valve at the top. Thirty feet up. Thirty feet of flimsy metal ladder in the dark.

There were easier ways to ruin Foxdale. With a match, for one.

I walked into barn A and cut through the wash rack. Footsteps echoed behind me, and I spun around.

"Jumpy, aren't we?"

"Hello, Mrs. Timbrook," I said.

Elsa had come out of Satellite's stall, and she'd stopped so close, I thought she might bump into me. I resisted the urge to back up. Her eyes were a deep green, and I wondered if she was wearing colored lenses. She moved closer. Her musky perfume filled my head, and her closeness was overwhelming. I stepped back, forgetting myself, and her smile broadened.

"Stephen, there's a nail sticking out of a board in Lite's stall. I'm afraid he'll cut his smooth, beautiful skin."

Christ. "I'll get a hammer." I took a step backward to avoid bumping into her as I turned and went over to the other barn.

I unlocked the feed room door. "I'm afraid he'll cut his smooth...beautiful...skin," I mouthed. Give me a break. I scanned the pegboard—screwdrivers, pliers, wrenches, all neat and organized thanks to Dave—and spotted the Craftsman hammer with the leather grip. As I lifted it off its bracket, I sensed subtle movement behind me. A slight shifting of air current. I spun around.

Elsa had followed me into the room.

Chapter 11

She closed the door and smiled. She had every right to. She'd set her trap, and I'd unwittingly walked right into it. Stupid. Decision making time. I'd been half playing around with it for long enough. I hadn't totally pushed her away. Hadn't actually made up my mind one way or the other. Elsa took off her jacket and let it drop to the floor. It seemed to float in slow motion before landing in a disorganized heap on the dusty cement. I couldn't take my eyes off it. Didn't feel as if I were breathing properly, either. My legs felt wooden, my feet stuck to the floor.

I dragged my gaze upward, looked at her face, and figured I was about to make up my mind. Her eyes were dreamy-looking, compelling, holding me in a trance. She parted her lips with a hint of a smile. Nothing to do with friendship, however.

She reached up and unbuttoned her blouse, slowly, deliberately, one button at a time. Dragging it out, making me wait.

She wasn't wearing anything underneath, and she made sure I knew. Made sure I saw. I inhaled sharply. She walked over to where I stood, pressed her body against mine, and laced her fingers behind my neck. She stood on tip-toe and kissed me on the mouth. Her lips tasted of peppermint, and when I opened my mouth to tell her we shouldn't be doing this, she flicked her tongue between my teeth.

Well, to hell with it. I stepped backward, pulling her with me, until I bumped into the workbench. I reached around, dropped the hammer onto the plywood, and moved my hands over her breasts. It was cold in the room, and her nipples were hard.

She let go of my neck, slipped her blouse off her shoulders, and let it drop to the floor. I explored her breasts with my hands and eyes and thought for about the millionth time that women's bodies were just so damn fascinating.

Elsa moved her hands between us, and for a second I thought she was going to stop me, but I'd misjudged her. She undid my belt buckle and unzipped my jeans, and somewhere in the back of my mind, it registered that she'd done it with practiced ease. She smoothed her hand down my belly, eased her fingertips beneath the elastic, and slipped her hand into my shorts. When she wrapped her fingers around me, a shudder coursed through my body.

I grabbed her breast hard and moved my mouth over her throat. Her skin was soft and smooth and tasted slightly of salt.

She moaned.

The sound was a physical jolt to my senses, and I was afraid I would come then and there if I didn't do something. I pulled her hand away.

She rubbed against me. "What's the matter, Stevie-boy?" she whispered. "You too quick on the draw?"

"Shut up."

She giggled. "Or am I just too hot for you?"

I'd show her what hot was, damn her. With trembling fingers, I fumbled with the snap on her pants.

"Here, let me do that." She pushed my hands away. "It's been a long time, hasn't it, Stevie?"

"Don't call me that."

I watched her strip. She wriggled out of her tight britches faster than I thought possible. Nothing underneath them, either.

"Cute guy like you should be gettin' it all the time. You shy, Stevie-boy? Is that it?"

"Damn you." I grabbed her wrist, pulled her down on the floor, and straddled her, my hands on either side of her shoulders, her legs between my knees. She lay naked beneath me with a smirk on her face and a glint of challenge in her eyes, and for an instant I felt more like hitting her than fucking her.

"Come on, Steve, I was just playing around." She slid one leg out from between my legs, then the other, planted her feet alongside my knees, then reached down and touched herself. She moved her hips rhythmically and whispered, "Come on, Steve. You know you want it."

Damn right I did. I pushed myself upright, yanked off my jacket, and shoved my jeans down to my knees. I lowered myself and thrust into her, feeling the mind-blowing sensation as if for the first time. She moved with me aggressively, and I realized I needed to concentrate on something, anything, to make it last. I studied her face.

She had closed her eyes. Her lips were parted, her breath coming faster. I watched as she arched her back and turned her head to the side, the movement causing light from an overhead fixture to flash across a horseshoe-shaped gold earring. I admired the line of her neck, the way it blended into the v-shaped depression at the base of her throat, the way her breasts looked, round and firm above a faint line of ribs, the nipples hard and pointy.

When I slid my tongue along her throat and bit her just below the ear, Elsa grabbed my butt. She wrapped her legs around me and tilted her pelvis upward, pulling me in deeper. I bit down harder. She laced her fingers in my hair and redirected my mouth to hers. I pushed my tongue into her mouth while our bodies moved in urgent, frantic rhythm.

The release was incredible, intense, explosive. I collapsed on top of her and tried to catch my breath. After a minute or two, she put her hands on my chest and rolled me off.

"Oh, my. You're still hard. Even after all that."

She slid on top of me and rubbed her crotch against me in a slow, rhythmic grind. I lay there and enjoyed watching her, and by the time she came, I wanted to start all over.

When she moved to get up, I grabbed her arm. "Ride me."

She looked from my face to my fingers holding her tight. "I only do it once, honey."

I didn't let go. "Before, you said you were just playing, not trying to jerk me around....Prove it."

She didn't say anything. I let go of her wrist, and she stood up.

"Guess you're too tired," I said, and she turned to look at me. "Can't last more than one time."

For a minute she stood there motionless, staring at me, her eyes in shadow. Then she squatted over me, reached down, and grabbed my cock. My breath caught in my throat, and I tensed, wondering what in the hell she was going to do next.

"By the time I'm done with you, you won't be able to get off the damn floor." She began to stroke me, slowly at first, with an expert touch. Then she guided me into her.

Damn, the woman could ride more than horses. When she finished, I felt like I had been worked over. Felt like I couldn't lift my head off the floor.

She crouched next to me and touched the bridge of my nose. "How'd you get this bruise?"

"A fight at the party," I mumbled and didn't bother opening my eyes.

"Who with?"

"One of the guys from the hay delivery service we use. His driver....He was drunk."

"Oh." She leaned over and kissed me on the lips. Her silky hair fell across my face. "Don't fall asleep on the floor."

I almost smiled. Opened my eyes instead. She stood and dressed, all the while looking down at me without expression. She had won, or maybe it was a tie. I couldn't tell.

Wordlessly, she walked over to the door and put her hand on the knob. She stood there for a second, then slowly turned to face me. "Stay away from him, Stevie. He's a dangerous man." I propped myself up on my elbows. "What do you mean?" "Honey, I know lots of things about lots of people, especially men. Just stay away from him." She turned and left, closing the door firmly behind her.

I stood and clumsily pulled up my jeans, tucked in my shirt, and looked around the room. I had been completely oblivious to my surroundings. Now, as I stood in the middle of the room, I could still smell her, smell myself. The musky odor of sex mixing with the sweet smell of molasses and grain additives. I could hear the horse moving around in the stall next door and, in the distance, a car engine turning over. I looked down and saw where our bodies had smudged the dusty floor. My clothes were covered with dirt.

I brushed off my jeans, switched off the light, and closed the door behind me. I flipped through my keys until I found the right one—a new key with bright yellow fluorescent tape. Dave's doing, no doubt. I slid the key into the lock and the tumbler snicked smoothly into the jamb.

Someone walked into the barn.

I looked over my shoulder. It was only Karen. I glanced at my watch. Almost ten o'clock. Lessons were over, the barns were closing down for the night, and I hadn't had a clue it was so late.

She looked at me as if she'd never seen me before, and I wondered if I'd forgotten to pull up my zipper or something. I glanced down. Nope. I hoped I didn't look as if I'd just been rolling around on the floor and suddenly felt transparent.

"What are you still doing here?" Karen asked. "I thought you'd left a long time ago."

"No, eh…just doing a few things."

She crossed her hands over her chest, and her eyebrows bunched together the way they do when she's pissed off about something, which just about all the time. I felt my face getting hot.

"Would you check everything then…since you're still here?"

"Sure." It came out a whisper.

She gave me a sideways glance, then departed.

By late afternoon Wednesday, Dave had put his wizardry into effect. A formidable gate stretched across the lane to the main road, and I had spent the better part of two days in the implement building, cleaning paint off every conceivable surface (no one's idea of fun) while my thoughts swayed between Elsa and Rachel, between ecstasy and guilt. As Marty liked to put it, I'd given control to someone else and gone along for the ride. I didn't particularly like it, but hell, I hadn't minded the ride, had I? No. I'd jumped right on.

Earlier that afternoon, I had avoided Rachel by graining the horses when she was riding, because I had this uncomfortable feeling that she would know what I had done just by looking at me. Now, I was finally finished with the cleanup. I gathered together the filthy rags, brushes, and cans and tossed everything into the trash. Dave wouldn't approve, but I couldn't care less. I gave the work area one last cursory glance and walked outside into sunlight and air not laden with fumes. I headed to the men's room, bent over the sink, and turned on the tap.

I was waiting for the water to get hot when someone opened the door.

"Finished with the paint removal yet?"

I glanced over my shoulder as Marty strolled into the room. "Yeah," I said. "Finally."

"What did the inspector say?"

"That horse barns were almost always a total loss if a fire breaks out." I soaped my hands and looked at Marty's reflection in the mirror. "Shit. There's so many horses in one barn, just the thought of it makes me sick."

"Jesus." Marty leaned against the wall and crossed his arms over his chest. "Did he have any suggestions?"

"Not really. We've done everything we can short of installing an overhead sprinkler system, and—"

"That'll be the day."

"Got that right. No way in hell will Ambrose shell out that kind of money. He said no to hiring a night watchman, too."

"I heard."

"Mrs. Hill did talk the local cops into driving by after-hours to give the farm a once over. Who knows how long that'll last."

"Or how open their eyes'll be."

I rinsed my hands and splashed water on my face. "Well, I'm finally caught up." I yanked some paper towels out of the dispenser and started to dry my face.

"Er…maybe not."

I paused. "What do you mean, maybe not?"

"Whitcombe's added two more horses to your list."

"Shit."

"And he's in a foul mood. Motherfucker needs to get laid."

I wadded the towels into a ball and hooked them into the trash bin that stood in the corner of the room. "Damn. Would you do one for me?"

"Sure."

"Thanks."

"Speakin' of needin' a good lay," Marty said. "You've been awfully tense lately."

I made a noncommittal noise in my throat and turned for the door, not trusting my expression. "See ya," I said over my shoulder.

I was heading for the lounge to get a Coke when Whitcombe called after me. He had already jumped off the horse he'd been riding and was leading it across the ring. I glanced at my watch. He'd quit early.

I wound my way through a bunch of kids who were waiting for the three-thirty lesson to begin and stood by the arena gate. The horse's sides were heaving, and despite the chilly air, he was damp with sweat.

"Got lead up your ass, Cline?" Whitcombe said. "I don't have all day."

I glanced over my shoulder. Everyone was watching and no wonder. The man was hard to ignore. But, it was his grave he was digging if Mrs. Hill caught him talking like that. I reached out to take the horse's reins. Whitcombe didn't let them go, so I dropped my hand to my side.

"You don't know jack shit about horses do you?" he said. "I asked for a figure-eight noseband, and I get a flash attachment."

"Your figure-eight was—"

"And I wanted a Dr. Bristol, and you can't figure that out, either."

I clenched my fists. I hadn't messed up, and he knew it.

"You ought to be ashamed of yourself, Cline. You have no business working here. You're an incompetent, ignorant, lazy"—and then he lowered his voice so only I could hear—"son of a bitch who wouldn't be able to find your own fucking asshole without a map." He continued again with increasing decibels. "That you're barn manager blows me away. You're too damn stupid."

What a goddamned jerk.

He was down to a whisper again. "What'd you have to do, screw Mrs. Hill to get the job?"

I felt my face getting hot. I snatched the reins out of his hands. "What's wrong, Lawrence?" I whispered. "Can't find any boys to fuck?"

He narrowed his eyes and clamped his mouth shut. A film of sweat glistened on his skin, and he glared at me with such hatred, I felt as if a cold ball of ice had settled in my gut.

I turned away from him and led the horse back to the barn.

Damn it. I'd crossed that line, and worse, I had let him push me over it. I should have known better. Should have kept my damn mouth shut.

After Razz had cooled down, I tied him in his stall and began the tedious job of brushing the sweat out of his coat. I was working on the matted hair along his stifle when I heard someone stop in the aisle outside Razz's stall. I looked over the horse's rump.

Marty took note of my expression and grinned. "Expecting somebody, Steve?"

"You could say that."

He came into the stall. "I hear Whitcombe's at it again."

"Got that right. And shit, Marty. I let the asshole get to me."

"Damn…you're human after all. What'd you do?"

"It's not what I did, it's what I said."

"Well?"

"I called him a fag, more or less."

Marty snorted. "When you lose it, you do it with style. Anyway, thought I'd better warn ya. He's in the office, whinin' to Mrs. Hill."

I swiped the brush down the horse's rump. "He's prob—"

Mrs. Hill's voice came over the PA system loud and clear, calling me to the office. Marty chuckled.

"Here, Marty." I tossed the brush at him. "You think it's so funny, you finish Razz."

"Give 'em hell, Steve."

"Damn it, Marty. Don't look so happy."

"I'm not. It's just that you're so damned serious."

I walked into the office. Mrs. Hill was sitting behind her desk, and what surprised me was that she didn't look angry. I glanced at the door to the lounge. It was locked.

Whitcombe had claimed the one and only comfortable chair in the room. He crossed his legs and brushed the horsehair off his britches. His own hair was freshly combed, and I could have sworn he'd changed his shirt.

I crossed the room and stood facing him with my back to a row of filing cabinets. Leaning against the cool metal, I hooked my thumbs in my pockets and crossed my ankles.

"Stephen," Mrs. Hill said. "I want you to apologize to Larry for what you said."

I looked at her and tried to keep anything from showing in my face. She was watching me with calm eyes, certain that I would do as she asked.

I turned back to Whitcombe. His blue eyes glimmered, and the corners of his mouth twitched. He was enjoying himself. Gloating. I felt like wringing his scrawny neck. But if and when I left the job, I wouldn't let Whitcombe have the satisfaction of thinking he'd had a hand it in.

I unclenched my jaw and took a deep breath. "I'm sorry I lost my temper," I mumbled. It wasn't exactly what Mrs. Hill had in mind, but it was all she was going to get.

A small smile crept across his fat-lipped mouth. "That's more like it, Cline. Remember who's—"

"And, Larry," Mrs. Hill interrupted. "I want you to apologize to Stephen for the way you've been treating him."

"But—"

"In the past month, more than one person's complained to me about your actions. Stephen's the best barn manager we've ever had, and you don't give him the respect he deserves."

Whitcombe's, or should I say "Larry's," face deflated like a punctured balloon. His smug, self-satisfied smile dissolved, and his eyes widened with astonishment. His mouth hung open, and when I realized I was mirroring him, I snapped my mouth shut.

Whitcombe jumped to his feet. "Mrs. Hill, I beg to differ. I owe Cline nothing. He's insubordinate and insolent and disrespectful, and I will do nothing of the sort."

He started for the door, spun back around, and whisked his coat off the back of the chair. He raised a finger and pointed in my direction. "They make fun of me."

His eyes were moist, and I wondered if he was going to cry. He turned around abruptly and slammed the door on his way out.

I stared after him. As much as I disliked the guy, I'd never intended for him to overhear the things Marty and I said.

"Stephen," Mrs. Hill said.

I pulled my gaze away from the empty doorway.

"In the future, please keep your opinions of Larry to yourself."

"Yes, ma'am."

"You may go."

"Thank you." I walked outside, half expecting to find Whitcombe waiting for me. But he was nowhere in sight.

I didn't see Whitcombe for the rest of the day, and when I opened the door to the loft, the phone was ringing. I dumped my notebook and mail on the counter and snatched up the receiver.

"Aren't you ever home?" Kenneth Newlin said before I'd gotten two words out.

He'd gone by Kenneth ever since I'd known him. No one in his right mind would have called him Kenny. Kenneth was, pure and simple, a geek. Until we'd met during fifth period Physics class in tenth grade, I'd never thought anyone actually wore a pocket protector. The only thing he lacked was tape on his glasses, and for all I knew, he could have lowered himself to that by now.

"No," I said. "Not much."

Kenneth grunted. "Well, you were right about the tax write-off. Farpoint Industries has been listing Foxdale as a liability ever since they broke ground on the place, but they won't be able to this year. Foxdale's now in the black by a narrow margin. But I don't see how losing the write-off's gonna make any difference whatsoever in FI's end-of-year balance sheet."

"Why's that."

"The company's making money hand over foot. Losing the write-off's penny-ante stuff to them."

"What about money laundering?" I said.

"Well, I'm no accountant, but based on the files I accessed, I didn't see any indication of that."

"How'd you get into them?"

"The files?" Kenneth said.

"Yeah."

"You don't want to know. Oh, and even though they've lost the write-off, FI's still getting a hefty tax break because of the Green Space Act."

"The what?"

"Some bleeding heart liberals in the Senate and EPA are promoting it. In certain parts of the country—and your Foxdale just so happens to be smack in the middle of one of their grids—the government's granting landowners a hefty tax break for every acre they leave undeveloped in a futile effort to slow urban sprawl. At five hundred and seven acres, FI's doing itself some good just by owning the land."

"So you don't see any way Ambrose would benefit from Foxdale losing money?"

"Nope. If someone wants the place to go belly up, it's not him."

"Okay. Thanks, Kenneth."

"No sweat."

"What're you up to these days?" I asked.

"I'm starting at NASA in May."

"Don't you have two more years before you graduate?"

"Nah. I crammed the four into two. Hell, I could have taught the classes I've been taking in my sleep, they're so basic."

I chuckled.

Kenneth told me about the artificial intelligence project he'd soon be cutting his teeth on, and by the time we said goodbye, the dull ache behind my eyes that I'd been nursing all evening had turned into a full-blown headache.

I knocked the cap off a bottle of beer and swallowed some ibuprofen. After I'd opened a box of Cheez-Its, I flipped through the pages in my notebook until I came to the scribbled notes I'd made at the library, where I'd stayed until closing time. I was fast becoming a pro at scanning micro-fiche, but I'd come away empty-handed as far as news coverage on horse and tack theft went. More depressing, however, was the lack of details on James Peters' death.

I unfolded the photocopies, smoothed them out on the counter, and read the blurred print for the third time.

STABLE OWNER MISSING
ALONG WITH SEVEN HORSES

Berrett: Police were called to Hunter's Ridge Farm on Martz Road shortly after seven a.m. Saturday morning, when Gwendolyn Peters discovered that seven of the farm's horses were missing from their stalls and presumed stolen. Police could not locate her husband, James S. Peters, though it is unclear at this time whether the events are related.

BODY FOUND IN PATUXENT
RIVER STATE PARK

Damascus: The partially decomposed body of an unidentified adult male was found in the Patuxent River State Park just south of Long Corner Road early Friday morning. Two fourteen-year-old boys from Dorsett, Maryland discovered the body while hiking along a trail west of the Patuxent River. Police determined that the body had been buried, but recent heavy rains had washed away the loose soil. The cause of death was not immediately known.

BODY IDENTIFIED

Damascus: A body found in the Patuxent River State Park early Friday morning has been identified as that of James S. Peters of Berrett, Maryland. Peters, 64, who owned and operated a horse facility near Piney Run Park, disappeared

August 4th, the same day seven horses were stolen from the farm.

Detective James Ralston, who is heading the investigation, said preliminary findings indicate that Peters interrupted the intruders and was murdered. Ralston refused to comment on other details of the investigation except to say that cause of death was determined to be blunt force trauma to the head. Peters is survived by his wife.

Those three clippings, combined with a brief write-up in the obituary column, were, as far as I could determine, the total coverage devoted to the life and death of James S. Peters. I downed the last of the beer and threw the empty into the trash.

Chapter 12

Thursday morning, I visited Gwendolyn Peters.

The only other living relative mentioned in Peters' obituary had been a nephew, and after a bit of detective work with the phone book the night before, I'd tracked him down. He knew little about the events surrounding August fourth and next to nothing about Hunter's Ridge. He did, however, point me in the right direction as far as his aunt was concerned. Shortly after her husband's death, Mrs. Peters had suffered a nervous breakdown and seemed destined to live out the remainder of her days in a nursing home.

"What about the farm?" I'd said. "Do you think anyone still works or boards there who knew your uncle?"

"You're outta luck there, pal. Place got sold and is being bulldozed as we speak."

"Bulldozed into what?"

"A housing development, what else? Nice, too. The land backs right up to Piney Run."

Shortly after eight, I pointed the Chevy's nose northward. After a few wrong turns, I found the town of Wards Chapel and, on Eighth Street, Shady Grove Nursing Home.

They must have recently polished the floor, because my shoes squeaked with each step I took down the long, depressing corridor. I had always hated hospitals, and nursing homes were close enough to elicit the same adversionary response. I turned a corner and nearly walked into an elderly man with disheveled yellow-gray hair. His back was so stooped, he reminded me of a tree limb, ready to snap. Even his skin looked like bark. I continued on.

Most of the doors were open, but I did not look in any of them. I paused just before I got to room 309 and wished I was anywhere else. The air stank of strong disinfectant that couldn't mask the stench of urine and was nauseating. I wiped my hands on my jeans and stood in the doorway.

Mrs. Peters sat unmoving in a chair that had been placed so she could look out the window. Early morning sunlight shifted and winked in the branches of a nearby mimosa and angled through the glass like a moving kaleidoscope. The view was pleasant enough—manicured lawn, a hedge of forsythia bushes that had probably been spectacular a week earlier, a patch of blue sky. A breakfast tray sat on the bedside table, and by the looks of it, Mrs. Peters ate very little. The room was cheerless and drab with institutional furniture and empty walls, except for a still-life print that hung above the bed. The only personal possession in evidence was a photograph on the night stand.

I cleared my throat. "Mrs. Peters?"

She didn't respond.

I walked around the bed and stood by the window where she could see me. "Mrs. Peters?"

She turned her head slowly and looked at me with pale, watery eyes, her expression blank. Her skin was deeply wrinkled and hung slackly from her bones. She no longer looked like a woman in her sixties as her nephew had said she was.

I introduced myself and asked if she would mind answering some questions about Hunter's Ridge.

"Hunter's Ridge?" Her eyes widened, and her hands clutched at the knitted afghan draped across her lap. "You know Hunter's Ridge?"

"Yes, ma'am."

"Is it a job you want?"

I blinked. "Uh…"

"Because you'll have to ask Jimmy. He's the one does the hirin'."

I didn't say anything. Couldn't.

"Have you seen him?"

I shook my head and swallowed. "I wasn't looking for a job. I wanted to know who worked for, uh…is working for him."

"Oh, well, Maryanne and Crystal come in the afternoons and on weekends, and Vicky gives lessons."

According to Greg, it had been years since they'd switched from boarding to breeding, and I wondered what time frame Mrs. Peters' mind was stuck in. "What are their last names?"

"Oh, heavens, I don't have the vaguest. Jimmy would know. He keeps the records. You just go on over and ask him. He'll know."

"What about boarders?"

"Oh, well there's Jenny and Sue Ellen, Linda and—"

"Their last names?"

"Oh, my. I don't rightly recall. They come and go, you know? You'll have to ask Jimmy."

I asked her who shod their horses, delivered their grain and hay, and anything else I could think of, and I learned that Mr. Peters had done with as little help as humanly possible. She mentioned a Buddy Harrison who may or may not have been related to John Harrison; otherwise, none of the names were familiar. If she was talking about twenty years ago, then I supposed it made sense.

"And your vet?" I said.

"Greg Davis." She nodded to me. "So young and handsome, like yourself. At first, I told Jimmy I thought Greg was too inexperienced, but Jimmy had great faith in him. Said he knows how to time a breeding better than Morgan ever did. Course, Morgan was always half in the bottle. Couldn't tell a one from a three if his life depended on it.

And if you don't read the follicles right, you end up breeding too early or too late and have to wait another whole month."

"Morgan?"

"Doctor Morgan. Passed away, God rest his soul."

I glanced behind her, at the photograph on the night stand, and she followed the direction of my gaze and twisted around in her chair. She picked up the gold-framed photograph, then settled back against the cushions and balanced the frame on the folds of her afghan. It vibrated in her trembling hands. A network of blue veins and tightly strung tendons threaded their way under skin that looked transparent, and her knuckles were swollen, fingers misshapen with arthritis. A gold wedding band hung loosely around a bone-thin finger. I stepped to her side with sick fascination.

Peters had been a tall, gangly man with a broad forehead and easy smile. His arm was casually draped around his wife's shoulders as they stood in front of a split rail fence. A group of yearlings had gathered on the far side with their ears pricked curiously toward the couple. Mrs. Peters was leaning against her husband with her arms around his waist, her head tilted back as she gazed into his face. She looked young and carefree and exceedingly happy.

She touched the glass with her fingertips, as if she could bring back the moment. "Have you seen Jimmy?" she said without looking up.

I swallowed. "No, ma'am."

"I told him he shouldn't have reported it." Her voice caught in her throat. "But he always does what's right."

"Report what?"

She didn't answer.

"Mrs. Peters, who did he report?"

"Do you know when he'll be back?" Her voice was high-pitched with strain. "Dinner's almost ready."

"Mrs. Peters. It's important that you tell me. What did he report?"

She covered her mouth with a trembling hand.

"Who, Mrs. Peters? Who did he report?"

Tears spilled down her cheeks. "No, no, no-o-o." Her voice rose in a wail that filled the tiny room.

I put my hand on her bony shoulder. "I'm sorry, Mrs. Peters."

A nurse bustled into the room. "You. What are you doing?"

I straightened.

"You'll have to leave." She stood aside so I could move around her. "Now."

I walked out into the sunlight and tried to imagine all the possible things Mr. Peters might have reported that had anything to do with horses. As I drove back to Foxdale, I couldn't stop thinking about the fragility of the human mind. Under normal circumstances, I imagined, Gwendolyn Peters could have been reduced to such a state by senility or Alzheimer's or whatever, but I had an overwhelming feeling that she had been pushed. Pushed by the horror of her husband's sudden, violent death.

The man who was behind this, whoever he was, had destroyed more than one life on that hot summer night.

Rachel beat me to Foxdale by half a minute. She stretched back into her car as I idled my pickup down the row of parked cars and came to a stop behind her back bumper. She straightened and turned quickly, and I was rewarded with a welcoming smile. I hopped out and opened the door for her as she slipped on a sweater.

She reached up and flipped her hair out from under the collar. "Sneaking up on me?"

I grinned. "Me? Never."

"Uh-huh."

I checked out the rest of her outfit with growing appreciation. A short, brown skirt, secured around her waist with a wide, yellow belt, revealed a lot of good-looking leg. The only surprise…she was wearing tennis shoes.

Rachel smiled. "I like to be comfortable."

"So, you're a mind-reader."

"It's a girl thing. Or, I suppose you could say it's a guy thing. 'Cause you guys are easy to read."

"Oh, come on. Okay." I crossed my arms over my chest. "Where would I like to be right now?"

"Somewhere horizontal and...private."

"Damn. You are a mind reader."

She grinned, then climbed into the truck. The skirt rode up on her thighs. I reluctantly shut the door and walked around to the driver's side.

We headed south and, as it happened, the route I'd chosen took us past Greg's farm. I pointed it out.

"You live in that house?"

I shook my head. "No, I live in the barn."

"The barn?"

I glanced sideways at her. "Yes. Where the hay loft used to be. It was remodeled into an apartment. Very nice, too."

"Can we stop?"

I briefly wondered if she was initiating the horizontal and private thing but dispelled the idea as wishful thinking on my part. I pictured how I'd left the place and decided it would be acceptable. I'd picked the clothes off the floor a couple of days earlier, and I'd even thrown the bedspread back across the mattress.

She must have sensed my hesitation, because she said, "Oh...I shouldn't have asked."

"No," I said. "I'd like to show you."

I turned around, and we headed back. As I pulled onto Greg's farm, it struck me how elegant the place looked. Pin oaks lined the drive on both sides along with an immaculate four-board fence. The three-story brick house looked as stately as ever, and the barns were constructed of rich wood siding instead of the usual steel, which I found cold and dreary.

I pulled into the parking area behind the foaling barn, and we climbed the steps to the loft.

A dead mouse lay on the doormat.

"You have cats, I see." Rachel said.

"No. Well…yes. Actually, they're not mine. They sort of came with the place. They're barn cats, really. I probably shouldn't have let them in at all, but they're insistent."

She grinned at me, and I wondered why I couldn't shut the hell up. When I opened the door for her, she said, "You don't lock your door?"

"Nah. On a farm like this, there's always someone around. I don't worry about it."

Rachel walked inside and stood in the middle of the kitchen. "Wow. This is nice."

She turned slowly, taking it in, her brown skirt and the sweater's warm shades of tan, orange, and yellow a vibrant splash of color, intense and alive.

She spun around and walked onto the carpet. "What a great place. It's so cool and big and on a horse farm with such great views. I envy you. I live close to the Baltimore City line. Not even in a neighborhood."

Rachel paused at my stereo system. It was stacked on an old, wooden crate and had cost me a fortune. She picked up a stack of CDs and shuffled through them like they were a deck of cards. "Kenny Wayne Shepherd, Vivaldi, Kid Rock, Mellencamp, Bach, Matchbox Twenty." She looked up at me and raised her eyebrows. "You've got quite an eclectic collection here, don't you?"

I shrugged and told her about my sister. "With her room next to mine, it was either get used to it and like it, or live day after day in misery."

She smiled, then walked to the end of the loft and looked out the north windows at the tree-lined drive. When she turned around, it seemed to me that she had noticed my bed for the first time. She glanced from it to me and walked purposefully back into the kitchen. The long-haired cat squeezed out from under my bed and trotted over to her.

"Oh, what a beautiful cat." Rachel crouched down, and the cat rubbed against her legs.

I didn't look at the cat, however, having a definitely more interesting view elsewhere. Rachel's skirt was very short.

I cleared my throat. "You've made a life-long friend."

"I've never seen a cat that's so friendly." Rachel laughed when the cat flipped onto its back. "What a wiggle worm. What's her name?"

"Far as I know, she doesn't have one."

Rachel was on her hands and knees, and her hair had fallen forward over her shoulders. "How could you have a cat and not name it?"

"But it's not *my* cat."

Rachel shook her head and rose to her feet. She put her hands on her hips. "Don't you ever pet her?"

"Of course I do. That cat has an insatiable desire for affection." Not unlike my own, I thought.

We spent the afternoon paddling around Lake Kittamaqundi. We checked out every cove, risked getting stuck in the shallows, and went to dinner when the sun dipped below the horizon.

The food was delicious, but I couldn't, for the life of me, remember eating it. Rachel had candlelight in her eyes, and her hair glowed with a warmth and vibrancy of its own. We talked about everything and nothing while light seeped from the sky, the glass turning black with the night.

When the crowd thinned, and one of the waiters started pushing a sweeper across the carpet in the next room, I said, "Are you ready to go?"

She nodded.

Outside, it was chillier than expected, and neither one of us had dressed for it. Ignoring the cold, we followed the path as it hugged the shoreline. Where the woods thinned, we paused and looked across the lake. A half moon hung low in the east and reflected off the water's surface. A sure, straight path, cutting across the lake.

"How beautiful," Rachel murmured.

I took her in my arms and kissed her, not a drop-down-and-do-it kiss, but a gentle one that she returned in kind. When I felt her shiver, I wrapped my jacket around her, and she rested her head on my chest and slid her arms around my waist.

Above our heads, a gentle breeze moved through the trees. It would have been peaceful except for the primitive feelings brought to life by her body's closeness to mine. I felt the quiet rhythm of her breathing against me; yet, I was having a hard time controlling mine. I smoothed my fingers through her silky hair and breathed deeply. Her scent was barely perceptible on the shifting air currents. She looked up, and I kissed her again.

After a while, we headed back to Foxdale. Ignoring the fact that the roads weren't all that great, I put my arm around her shoulders, which I probably shouldn't have done. All I could think about was sliding my hand into her blouse. After maneuvering the truck out of a particularly sharp curve, I decided I'd better keep my eyes on the road and my hands on the steering wheel.

I clamped both hands on the wheel and glanced down. Shouldn't have done that, either. If I lowered my hand just a few inches, I would be touching her legs. And with that short skirt, one thought led to another, and I was right back where I'd started.

I was almost relieved when I turned into the lane at Foxdale.

I clenched my teeth. "Damn it."

Rachel shifted in her seat. "What's wrong?"

"The gates aren't locked." I glanced at my watch. It was almost eleven.

"Is that a problem?"

"I hope not. I forgot to ask Karen to lock up, but she should have thought about it. Everything else better be locked up, or—"

"Maybe she didn't know what to do because my car was still in the lot."

I glanced at her. Pale light from the dash shone on her face. "Yeah," I said softly. "You're probably right."

I pulled in alongside the Camry and scanned the grounds before I got out. Rachel swiveled around on the seat to face me. When she slid down to the ground, quite a distance for her, the skirt hung up on the vinyl bench for a brief second. Damn, she looked good. I pulled her to me and gave her an open-mouthed kiss. She felt perfect in my arms, and I thought I had better send her on her way before I wasn't as controlled.

Rachel unlocked her car. As she slid behind the wheel, I checked the back seat. We said goodbye, then I watched her drive away until her taillights disappeared around the bend.

I walked through every building, checked every corner, every horse, jiggled every doorknob, and felt bone tired by the time I climbed into the Chevy. As I slotted the key in the ignition, light flashed across the windshield. I swiveled around as a car headed down the lane.

A cop car. The cruiser angled across the parking lot and pulled in behind my truck. The driver lit up the interior of my truck with a spotlight and approached the truck with an interesting blend of confidence and caution. I kept my hands on the steering wheel.

He shone his flashlight in my face, then lowered the beam. "What are you doing here this late?"

I recognized him from Monday. Officer Dorsett, tall, lean, black, with a thin mustache and a gold hoop in his left ear that didn't quite go with the otherwise military turnout. "I was on a date," I said. "We met here. I dropped her off a little while ago, then checked the barns."

His radio crackled. "One-twenty-three, status?"

Dorsett keyed his mike. "One-twenty-three. Ten-six. No need to check further."

"Clear."

Dorsett switched off his flashlight. "You leaving?"

"Yep."

He followed me off the parking lot, waited for me to lock the gate, then followed me part of the way home. I stayed within the speed limit.

◇◇◇

By late Friday afternoon, new locks had been installed wherever possible. I flipped through a ridiculously large bunch of keys, thanks to Dave's brilliant idea that multiple keys would confuse the enemy, and tried to remember which color tape went with the new feed room lock. Pink? No, yellow. I unlocked the door and pulled the feed cart away from the wall. I had organized the supplements and medications and was turning the cart around when I heard Marty yell my name.

I ran outside and found him standing between the barns, his back toward me. "Marty. What's wrong?"

He spun around. "I'm surprised you didn't hear."

"Hear what?"

"Whitcombe was riding that gelding of his. The plain bay…"

"Rennie's Luck?"

"Yeah, that's the one. Well, Lucky wasn't so lucky."

"What do you mean?"

"You know how he's been stoppin' at the jumps lately?"

I waited for him to get on with it.

"Well, Whitcombe took a whip to him and cut 'im up pretty—"

"Where is he?"

"Whitcombe?"

"No," I said. "The horse."

"In his stall."

I turned and started toward Lucky's stall.

"You'll be needin' to medicate him," Marty said. "And guess what?"

"What?"

He jogged up alongside me. "Mrs. Hill fired him."

I paused. "She fired Whitcombe?"

"Who else?"

"Fucking shit."

"Wait a minute." He cupped his hands behind his ears. "Did I hear you right, or was I just imaginin' things?" He crossed his arms over his chest. "You know, you really should watch your mouth, young man. Foxdale—"

"Geez." I turned and left him there.

"—has an image to uphold," he yelled at my back.

We stood outside Lucky's stall. The gelding was standing near the back wall, his eyes wide, muscles tensed.

"Goddamn it."

"You should of seen him, Steve. Whitcombe had ol' Lucky here so worked up, gallopin' full out, I thought he was gonna wipe out in the turn...or crash through a fence."

I slid the door back and walked into the stall. Lucky was drenched with sweat, and the muscles along his flank trembled in spasms. I examined the cuts and was relieved to find they weren't as bad as I'd first thought—more gore than actual damage. I collected the supplies I would need, then we cross-tied him in the wash-rack.

"Damn Whitcombe," I muttered.

I stepped toward Lucky's shoulder, and he bobbed his head. The chains rattled hollowly against the wall.

"Marty, hold his head for me." I patted the gelding's neck and kept my hand on his body as I moved toward his flank.

"His ears are pinned, Steve."

"I'll be right back."

I grabbed a bag of carrots out of the feed room and fed him a couple.

"Poor guy." I broke another carrot in two. "Marty, what happened exactly?"

"Well, when Lucky here refused the Liverpool for the third time, Whitcombe just laid into him. I can't believe the shit was stupid enough to do it in front of everybody."

"What a fool."

"One of the boarders ran into the office and told Mrs. Hill what was goin' on. She saw the end of his little temper tantrum and fired his ass."

I grinned. "Good for her. It couldn't have happened to a better person." I glanced down the aisle. "Eh, where is Mr. Whitcombe, anyway?"

"He had a few words with Mrs. Hill, then drove off." Marty grinned. "Oh, and the little shit's got a new ride."

"What?"

"A fucking new Mustang convertible."

"Wonder where he got the money for that? He sure didn't earn it here."

Marty shrugged.

"Too bad I missed it. I would've liked to have said goodbye."

"I bet you would of."

"There's justice after all. Whitcombe loses his job, maybe now he won't be able to make his car payments." I ran my hand down Lucky's face and cupped my hand around his muzzle. His old, soft lips searched my palm for another piece of carrot. "Except ol' Lucky here'll be going with him."

I was leaving for the day when Mrs. Hill stopped me on the sidewalk just outside her office door.

"I have a favor to ask," she said. "After you've had your supper, would you come back and stay here until Mr. Whitcombe picks up his horses and tack?" She looked at my face and could see I was less than thrilled. "Please, Stephen… here's some pizza money—"

"No, thank you. You don't need to do that."

"Take it, dear." She shoved the folded bills into my palm. "I know I'm asking a huge favor, but he said he'd be back later tonight, and to be honest, dear, as angry as he was when he left, I don't trust him." She peered into my face. "I know everything will be all right if you're here."

I exhaled. "I'll be back in a little while, then."

"Oh, thank you, dear. Thank you so much. I'll stay until you get back. I told him you'd be here to lock up when he was finished, so he knows he won't be able to get away with anything."

I shoved Mrs. Hill's pizza money into my pocket and headed for the parking lot. It wasn't until I'd climbed into my truck that I realized I'd lost my appetite.

Chapter 13

More than one of the crew had overheard Whitcombe blaming me for what happened, so as soon as I was certain I'd catch Marty at home, I closed the door between the lounge and office and used the phone.

"Shit, Steve. I have a date."

"Come on, Marty." I swiveled around in the chair until my back was to the door and rested my chin on my hand. "Bring her along. You can hang out in the lounge."

"Not for what I got planned. Not unless you wanna watch."

I groaned.

"Man, I can't stand it when you whine....Oh, all right, but I won't be over until ten, maybe eleven."

I didn't say anything.

He sighed. "Okay. Ten o'clock and not a minute before, and you owe me."

"Thanks."

"Sissy," he said, and I could hear a smile in his voice.

"Got that right. Whitcombe's PO'ed, and I'm not on his top ten list."

"Depends what list you're talkin' about."

◇◇◇

Ten o'clock came and went, and no Marty. Karen and Judy left for the evening, and all the boarders packed up and drifted home. The place was deserted, yet the newly installed gates by the road stood wide open so Whitcombe could drive down to the barn, and Marty.

Where the hell was he? I could imagine where he was, damn him.

At eleven-thirty, I picked up the phone. No answer.

I had never thought much about the presence or absence of courage. Apparently I was lacking in that department, and I didn't like it. Not one little bit. I was tempted to call Mrs. Hill, or just go home; instead, I sat on the sofa and switched the channel to a late night talk show that was only marginally entertaining.

◇◇◇

Someone gripped my shoulder and shook me.

I scrambled off the sofa and just about fell on my butt. "Damn, Marty. You almost gave me a heart attack, sneaking up on me like that."

He laughed. "'Sneakin', my ass. You were sound asleep."

"God." I shook myself. Every muscle in my body was strung tight, and my heart was pounding so hard it hurt. Waking up like that couldn't be healthy.

"Nervous, Steve?"

"A little.…So where the hell've you been?" I looked at my watch. "It's one-fifteen."

"Sorry. Fell asleep."

"In whose bed?"

Marty grinned. "Wouldn't you like to know." He yawned and rubbed his face. "I take it Whitcombe hasn't showed?"

"No. Even if he got past me while I was asleep, he still needs to come in here and pick up his paperwork before he can get his deposit refunded."

"Think he's gonna show?"

"Who knows," I said. "This is the last thing I feel like doing right now." I looked at Marty. "Or you, either. Thanks for coming in."

"Well, I would of felt like shit if Whitcombe planned some pay-back and you were here all by your lonesome."

"Didn't know you cared."

"I don't." Marty dropped down onto the sofa. "I just don't like guilt."

"Now, that sounds like the Marty I know—"

"And love?"

"Not on your life," I said. "Not in this life. Not in any life." Marty was still chuckling when I walked over to the soda machine and slotted some coins into the machine. "I think you're confusing me with Whitcombe. Want a Coke?"

"No, I'd be awake half the night. Speakin' of sex—"

"I thought we were speakin' of love," I said. "Or sleep."

"Whatever. Anyhow, that Rachel's sure cute." He leaned back against the sagging, worn cushions and hooked his leg over the armrest. "Maybe she'll wake you up."

I grinned.

Marty lifted his head off the cushions. "Well, hallelujah. I was afraid you were gonna turn into a monk or somethin' and be celibate for the rest of your godforsaken life."

I swallowed some Coke, and we both looked up when a horse van rumbled down the lane past the lounge door.

I lowered the can from my lips. "Party time." I grabbed the paperwork off Mrs. Hill's desk.

The van had parked in the pool of light between the barns. As Marty and I approached, Whitcombe hopped down from the cab and turned toward me with a smirk on his face that disappeared when he saw Marty.

Marty worked out every day. Excluding the opposite sex, it was his passion, and I'd often thought that I wouldn't want to find myself on the wrong side of his anger.

The passenger's door opened. Someone got out and walked around the front bumper. He stopped behind Whitcombe, and I thanked my lucky stars I'd had the sense to get reinforcements. He looked like a goon—all muscle, no brain—and he didn't look like a horseman. Light glinted off his bald head, and despite the chilly night air, he was wearing a muscle shirt that showed off his tattooed biceps to best advantage.

"Get the horses for me, Cline," Whitcombe said.

"Get them yourself."

Marty snorted, prompting a scowl from Whitcombe and a grin from me. Whitcombe turned and strode into the barn, followed obediently by his friend. I took a swig of Coke. When they finished loading the horses, I handed Whitcombe the forms.

He creased them in half and wedged them into his jacket pocket. "Unlock the tack room, Cline. I need to get my gear."

I walked down the barn aisle, sorting one-handed through the keys, and thought how nice it was not having to say "sir" to that creep anymore. When I paused to unlock the door, I glanced at Marty. My own personal bodyguard, I saw with amusement, was checking out Whitcombe's friend. Marty winked at me when he saw me looking.

I suppressed a grin and flicked on the lights. Whitcombe and his friend followed me into the room. Before I realized what was happening, his friend closed and locked the door.

Damn.

My bodyguard was on the wrong side of the door, and I doubted he had his key.

Marty yelled and banged on the door.

Whitcombe and friend closed ranks. I backed up until my back was pressed against a row of lockers. They stopped short of bumping into me, and I felt like a damned idiot, standing there with a soda in one hand, keys in the other, and without a useful thought in my head.

Whitcombe leaned in closer. His hot breath stank of beer. "You caused me to lose a damn good job, you little shit, and I'll get even."

"You didn't need my help, losing your job," I said. "You did it all by yourself."

His eyes narrowed to slits, and his lower lip looked fatter than ever. "When you first started here, I thought you were different. But you're just like all the rest. Afraid of anybody who's different than you."

"No, I'm not."

"Don't kid yourself. You make me sick."

He signaled to his friend, and I tensed. Instead of laying into me, he walked across the room and unlocked the door. Marty stood glaring at them with hunched shoulders and clenched fists.

Whitcombe walked over to his locker as if nothing had happened and hauled his stuff out to the van. Marty and I watched in silence until they'd finished loading Whitcombe's tack and had driven away.

"What happened?" Marty said.

"Nothing."

He frowned at me. "He say where he's going?"

"Nope," I said and couldn't help but wonder if he'd be back.

Seven-thirty Sunday morning, and the first A-rated show of the season was half over. Cliff started up the John Deere 960, shifted into gear, and hauled the overflowing manure wagon out of the barn. I walked outside and looked down the lane toward the arenas.

Exhibitors were already warming up their horses, lunging them in the pasture alongside the road and hacking them in the ring. In the chilly air, the horses' breath formed misty plumes that shimmered with gold in the early morning light. The entries were double what they had been the year before. Figures for the day would be comfortably in the black.

Soon, the quiet, surrealistic moment would be replaced by the hustle and bustle of dozens of people competing against each other, a civilized modern-day imitation of mounted warfare. Risk was noticeably absent.

When the tractor pulled into the lane between the barns, I headed back. After we mucked out the next group of stalls,

Cliff pulled the wagon farther down the aisle, adding diesel fumes to the dusty haze kicked up from cleaning stalls. I picked up the push broom and began sweeping the aisle where we had just finished working. Marty was in rare form, singing a country song rather badly. Some song about somebody losing somebody.

I looked up when I heard someone walking toward me. Elsa. My muscles tensed. It was the first time I'd seen her since the feed room. I bent over and jabbed the broom toward a tangle of hay and sawdust.

As she walked past, I glanced sideways at her. Without breaking stride, she slapped my butt—a blatantly clear message to anyone who was watching.

Marty was watching. He stepped into the aisle and stared at me with his mouth open.

"I can't believe it," he said. "You fucked her, didn't you?"

I unclenched my teeth. "Shut up."

"After all this time—"

"Shut up, damn it."

I leaned the broom against the stall front and turned toward the door. One of the boarders had walked into the barn, and she had undoubtedly heard at least part of the conversation.

I went outside, sat at one of the picnic tables, and rested my forehead on my knuckles. What a mess. I should have known better. Should have left Elsa alone.

"Sorry." Marty's voice.

I looked up. There was no humor in his face. No laugh lines crinkled the skin around his eyes. "Never mind," I said.

He sat across from me. "You're only human, Steve....I know what she's like. The woman's relentless. 'Course all she had to do was look my way."

"Man." I rubbed my face. "I really screwed up. Rachel will dump me if she finds out, and the thing is, I had no intention, none at all of...Oh, damn it."

He shook his head. "You worry too much. Rachel's a smart girl. Anybody with half a brain can see what kind of woman Elsa is. I mean, it's kind of understandable what happened. And the two of you haven't been going out all that long, right? It's not like you've agreed that you wouldn't date other people, right?"

"I know."

"Well, see. She probably won't find out, anyway. Elsa ain't the kiss and tell type. I'll bet—"

"Could of fooled me."

Marty grinned. "I think the only reason she made an example of you was because you were a challenge."

"Ha. Hardly."

My timing had been awful. A month earlier, and it wouldn't have made any damn difference.

Monday morning, I fixed a bowl of corn flakes, and while I ate, I made a list of people who might, for whatever reason, be waging a hate campaign against Foxdale. Or maybe the evil-mindedness was directed at me, though I couldn't guess why.

I started with the people I had fired. Mark, Tony, Bobby, and most recently, Alan. I wrote out a second heading.

Discontinued Services:
Dr. Weston—vet
Rick Parker—farrier
Luke Barren—farrier
East Pence—grain dealer
Schultz—hay dealer

I added Harrison's name. Even though he still supplied us, he was pissed at me, and so was his driver.

The list looked ridiculous. I couldn't imagine any of them having a grudge strong enough, and where was the connection to James Peters? I doodled in the margins and thought about motive. I wrote that down, too.

Greed, jealousy, hate. I thought about Boris the cat and added psychosis.

What was their motivation, if not simple, straightforward malice? Maybe Foxdale's success was hurting someone, possibly another horse farm with the same hunter/jumper focus. Maybe they were losing clients while we were flourishing. They would be jealous, envious, hateful. Maybe they were losing clients to *us*.

Maybe, maybe, maybe.

I ran my fingers through my hair and stared at the lists until the words blurred. So far, Foxdale had prospered despite the campaign. It wouldn't last forever. There was only so much the boarders would overlook.

I yanked the calendar off the wall and tossed it on the counter. It hit the surface with a resounding smack. The loft was too quiet, and it was getting on my nerves. I switched on the audio system, turned up the volume, and tried to work the kinks out of my neck

As best as I could remember, I listed all the events I'd learned about in the past six weeks.

George Irons, horses stolen	two summers ago
James Peters, murdered	Saturday, August 4th (last year)
tack theft, S. Miller, PA	Saturday, December 21st
At Foxdale:	
horse theft	Saturday, February 24th
tack theft/Boris	Saturday, March 9th
burnt jump, graffiti	Monday, April 1st

Assuming the events were related, our man liked to work on the weekend.

In the past week, I'd scanned old headlines until my eyes glazed over, yet I had only uncovered two other horse thefts. I'd discounted both out of hand. A boarder had stolen his own mares and skipped town without paying his board, and in the other case, only one horse had been taken.

As of yet, I hadn't discovered a connection between Foxdale and Hunter's Ridge. The rig was the only lead, and that was looking more and more like a dead end.

At ten o'clock, I walked into the office and stood in front of Mrs. Hill's desk. I pulled the lists out of my back pocket, unfolded them, and handed her the wrinkled sheets.

She glanced at them. "What's this?"

I wiped my hands on my jeans. "Foxdale really needs to hire a night watchman. I'd say it's become a necessity."

She started with the list of chronological events. "What's this? James Peters, murdered?"

"Did you know him?"

She shook her head. "No. But his name's familiar." She tapped her fingers on the desk blotter and stared at the office door as if she'd find the answer there. "Oh, yes. That detective asked about him, but I can't now remember...."

"He owned and operated a horse farm in Carroll County." I paused. What happened to him was hard to think about, much less talk about, especially with someone who knew what had happened to me.

"Stephen?"

I cleared my throat. "Someone stole seven horses from his farm, and when they did...they murdered him."

"Oh, no. But—"

"The police believe his murder, the horse theft here, and possibly the tack theft, were committed by the same people."

"But that...that means that you—"

"Then there are those other incidents on the list, which may or may not be related."

She stood and walked around the desk. "You could have been murdered," she gestured to my lists with a flap of her hand, "just like this man."

A slight tremor worked at the corner of her mouth, and she wasn't telling me anything new. That depressing fact had been hovering in my subconscious for the past month and a half. I looked down at my feet, at the square of blue carpet in front of her desk. It needed to be hosed off. Too many muddy feet trudging in from the barns.

She sighed. "I'll ask Mr. Ambrose about a night watchman again." She paused, then picked up my list of names. "I can't believe any of these people would do such a thing, Stephen. It's absurd."

"I know, but I can't think of anyone else."

"Leave it to the police. They'll find out who's behind it." She held my lists out to me and, mistaking my silence for agreement, switched to discussing preparations for the dressage clinic Foxdale was hosting over the weekend.

I studied the wall alongside Mrs. Hill's desk, which was, in effect, one gigantic calendar. She had covered it with white board, and every weekend for the next three months had some event or other scheduled. I felt tired just looking at it.

"Stephen, are you listening?"

"Yes, ma'am."

"And you'll have to move all the school horses…"

Last night, I had spent more time than I'd care to admit lying awake, unable to sleep, which was ironic, considering how physically tired I'd been. Telling everyone about James Peters and the rig used in the horse theft was fine as far as it went, but inefficient. I could do better.

"Stephen?"

"Yes, ma'am. I'll make sure it gets done. Tonight, can I use the computer and printer?"

"Of course, dear."

"With your permission, I'd like to send a letter to everyone in the address files—boarders, suppliers, contractors, everyone on the show mailing list—all the individuals and organizations we deal with."

"Whatever for? There are hundreds of them."

I told her.

"But that could be dangerous."

"I'll use an anonymous post office box, then. Not Foxdale's, and I won't sign it."

She shook her head but gave me permission in the end. She didn't seem concerned about what my letter might do to Foxdale's reputation. Maybe she saw, as I did, that if the attacks didn't stop, there might not be anything left worth saving.

Eleven o'clock Monday night, and I was still peeling labels and stuffing envelopes with what I hoped would be an effective attempt at finding James Peters' murderer. Mrs. Hill had been wrong. There were more than a thousand names once I'd opened all the files. But like Ralston had pointed out, it only took one.

Someone out there knew who owned a white dualie and dark-colored six-horse. But that wasn't all I was after. I was looking for information from anyone who had been the victim of horse or tack theft or unusual vandalism in the last five years. Maybe a pattern would emerge. I set aside a stack of letters to give to Greg and Nick.

As I switched off the computer, light flashed across the office door. I crossed the room and peered through the glass. It was only a police car. Officer Dorsett climbed from behind the wheel as I unlocked the door.

He stepped inside and looked me up and down. "I'd've thought you spent all your time in the barns."

I glanced down at my jeans. They were filthy, and when I did get around to doing the laundry, I used the machines on the farm, which were used for washing the horses' leg wraps, saddle pads, and blankets, so whether I realized it or not, I probably smelled like a horse.

"Yeah," I said. "I generally steer clear of the office if at all humanly possible." I walked behind the desk and noticed him eyeing the cup of coffee I'd just made. I pointed toward the lounge door. "Want some, help yourself."

He returned moments later with a Styrofoam cup in his hand. Steam rose from the cup's rim and curled toward the ceiling in lazy spirals. "What're you working on?" he said. "The place is usually dead this time of night."

"Just some paperwork."

He strolled around the office, his gaze drifting over the clutter that blanketed every flat surface.

I stuffed the last stack of envelopes into a cardboard box and set it on the floor by the door. Dorsett's patrol car was parked under the glare of the sodium vapors. A nice touch as far as security went. Maybe I'd get Dave to make some official-looking signs about guards or attack dogs.

Officer Dorsett said, "Doing a little sleuthing?"

I turned around and saw he'd been reading the stack of fliers. "Nosy, aren't you?"

"Comes with the job."

I picked up the fliers and wedged them in alongside the envelopes.

"I'm serious," he said. "Have you told Detective Ralston you're doing this?"

I straightened. "Why should I?"

"He's talked to everyone who has Foxdale on their post," Dorsett said. "Apparently he's frustrated with the case he's working, and frankly, I think he's worried about you and—"

"What do you mean, he's worried about me?"

"Come on, be your age. Whoever's been doing this," he gestured to my letter, "is probably going to keep on doing it until they're caught."

"Shit."

"Damn straight. You should tell Ralston about it." He glanced at his watch. "How much longer you going to be here?"

"I'm done." I pulled on my denim jacket. "I just have to check the barns."

"I'll go with you."

I lugged the box of letters outside, dumped it on the sidewalk, and locked the doors.

When we walked into barn B, Dorsett said, "Damn, I've never seen so many horses before. And they're not your ordinary plow horse, either."

I chuckled, "No, they most certainly are not."

"How much are they worth?"

"It all depends." I jiggled the tack room lock. "Anywhere from a thousand to forty thousand. Often more."

"Shit."

"Damn straight."

His eyebrows rose. "You don't miss much do you?"

"Yeah, right."

After checking both barns, we walked down to the implement building. I flicked on the lights and rattled the doorknob to Dave's storage room, then I walked around to the back of the building. We still hadn't gotten around to fencing in the lane. It was wide open to anyone who might drive in off the back road. Officer Dorsett unhooked his flashlight and switched it on. There was nothing to see.

He followed me out like the last time and waited while I closed and locked the gates, except this time he didn't follow me halfway home.

Chapter 14

Despite Officer Dorsett's warning, I mailed the fliers Tuesday afternoon and didn't give them another thought. At quitting time, I poured myself a cup of coffee and went into the office. I fished a couple of aspirins out of the first aid kit and swallowed them. Through the Plexiglas, I watched the six o'clock warming up. Vicki Lewis was riding Jet, Foxdale's most recent addition to its string of school horses, and the mare was giving her a fit, shying in the corners and breaking into a canter at the slightest provocation. Mrs. Hill was huddled in her coat, talking to Karen. I blew across the coffee cup and wondered what I was going to eat for dinner.

Corey Claremont, one of Foxdale's boarders, walked into the office, said hello, then dropped an envelope on Mrs. Hill's desk. She turned to leave and paused. "Oh, Steve. You made me think of something. You know that notice you put up on the bulletin board? The one about the trailer."

I nodded.

"Well, there's a trailer like that off one of the trails." She told me how to find it. "Unless you know it's there, you can hardly see it, but I hacked out that way a lot this winter, so I know the area pretty good. Thought you might want to know."

I thanked her, and after she left, I dug Mrs. Hill's county map out of the supply cabinet and sat down at her desk.

Corey was an experienced eventer, and when she went on a trail ride, she covered a lot of territory.

Even though her directions were a bit complicated, after a few false starts, I pinpointed the section of park land she'd indicated. Two roads were close to the location, but without seeing it for myself, I wouldn't know which was the right one. I leaned back in the chair. Detective Ralston and I had covered that part of the county already, so why hadn't the trailer been on the MVA list?

I called Ralston's number and was told he was unavailable until Thursday. I went home and emptied a can of Campbell's Hearty Beef Stew into a pot. After it had heated through, I took it and a bag of pretzels out on the deck. I sat with my back to the wood siding and watched the colors fade from the day. Above my head, a full moon shone in a cloudless sky.

I'd never been much good at waiting. I dumped the dishes in the sink, slipped a flashlight into my jacket pocket, and headed back to Foxdale.

I caught Karen between lessons and told her I was taking Jet on a trail ride.

"She's never gone on the trail alone," Karen said, "and you're taking her out at night?"

"It's light enough with the moon."

"She doesn't even know the trails."

"She'll be fine," I said. "Besides, she needs the work."

"Only because half the students can't handle her," Karen snapped. She lowered the jump cup on the standard and repositioned the rail. "Which trail are you taking?"

"The one to the north."

"North?"

"To the left, Karen."

She put her hands on her hips.

"I'll follow the river for a while, then bring her back."

"You get her hurt, it's on your head." She looked across the arena when one of the ponies faked a shy in the corner and yelled, "Don't pull back on the reins! Inside leg! Use your inside leg and push him forward."

I left Karen to her class, tacked up Jet, and swung into the saddle. We headed down the corridor that runs between the rows of paddocks. When we reached the woods, I reined her to the left, and after a moment's hesitation, she followed the trail as it zig-zagged downhill toward the river. She strode out well, eager yet relaxed, and it was obvious she was enjoying herself.

Moonlight filtered through the woods, and after a while, my eyes adjusted to the light. Tall, thick-trunked oaks towered above us, their dark tangle of branches dramatic against the moon-washed sky. Where the trail dropped into a deep ravine, I leaned back in the saddle and let her choose where to put her feet. The cool air was curiously still in the shelter of the woods, her footfalls silent, the creaking leather and our breathing the only sounds.

When we came to the first stream crossing, I slipped the reins through my fingers. Jet half-slid, half-jumped down the slope, then scrambled up the opposite bank. She lowered her head and cantered down the trail with exuberance, all the while subtly trying to bounce me out of the saddle. Grinning at her enthusiasm, I brought her back to a walk.

The mare was still keyed up when we reached the place where the trail empties into a wide meadow down by the river. Jet wheeled around, and I almost came off. She bolted into the woods, and by the time I managed to get myself vertical and her stopped, she was standing in a grove of pine trees. Her body was rigid with tension. I could feel her heart pounding in her chest, and my own was doing a fair job at imitation.

A heavy pine branch arched across her neck, inches above her mane. If she took a step or two forward, I would be knocked off. There was no way around it, and I knew she wouldn't back up in that mess. I gathered the reins in my left hand, slipped my stirrups, and slid to the ground.

Even with the care I'd taken, she threw her head up. When she felt the branch brush against her mane, she ran backward. I ran along with her. Just as I reached the conclusion that I would have to drop the reins or be dragged across the ground, she came to her senses and stopped.

It took ten minutes to calm her, five more to pick our way through the woods, and one second to swing up onto her back. I had used the time in the woods to check for cuts or scrapes, and amazingly, she had none. I pointed her in the direction of the meadow and nearly laughed when I spotted the cause for her concern.

Deer were browsing among the thick grass and scattered saplings that grew by the river's edge. They noticed us immediately but seemed undisturbed by our presence. I stroked Jet's neck and made her stand until I felt her muscles relax and saw the lines of tension around her eyes soften. When she was thoroughly bored, I reined her to the north, away from the deer.

Wooded hills sloped upward on both sides of the river, and except for a faint gurgling, where fast-moving water tumbled over a natural dam, the meadow was quiet. I might have found it peaceful except for the night's objective. I looked at my watch. Seven-fifty-five. I had two hours before the last lesson was over, before Karen would check to see if we'd made it back.

When we came to a stretch of meadow where the footing was safe, I bridged the reins together over the crest of her neck—to act as a brace in case she stumbled—then crouched low over the saddle. She automatically lengthened into a ground-covering canter, the instinct for speed there for the asking. Her body rocked beneath me, her muscles straining, footfalls muffled, breath coming faster, louder, filling my ears. I pressed my knuckles into her mane and relaxed into her stride. The brisk air stung my face and pulled tears from the corners of my eyes. The ground beneath us was a blur, the speed intoxicating for both of us.

Where the meadow narrowed into a track not much wider than one of the old logging roads, with trees thick on both sides, I brought her back to a walk. Jet swiveled her ears and tossed her head in irritation.

"Sorry, girl. Can't run here." I patted her neck. Steam eddied through her coat, curling upward in tendrils, and I could smell her sweat, stirringly primitive. A link to the past. The result of countless years of man and horse working together.

It took me half an hour to find the trail, but when I did, I had no doubt I'd found the right one. Corey's directions had been dead on. "Right at a wide fork, go two hundred yards to another fork, make a left. The trail rises sharply, then follows the crest of a narrow ridge that runs north to south with a fence line just visible on the western slope." We followed the trail for several miles, and it was there, where the trees thinned, that I saw the trailer.

I reined Jet to a stop. Fifty feet down slope, the woods gave way to pasture land that backed up to an old, white farm house and dilapidated bank barn. A trailer that looked remarkably like the one I'd had my ride in was parked behind the barn in a rickety-looking corral out of sight from the road. I studied the house. Lights were on downstairs, casting yellow squares across the grass, but the back porch light was dark.

I spent all of five minutes making up my mind.

I slid off the mare, tied her to a tree, and squeezed between strands of rusty barbed wire. It was only six hundred feet to the trailer. Six hundred feet of open ground under a full moon. But if no one was looking, it wouldn't matter.

I took off at a dead run. Midway between the woods and corral, a drainage ditch I hadn't noticed stretched blackly through the tangled grass.

I vaulted over it, landed on my knees and scrambled up the other side, wondering what else I might have missed.

By the time I got to the old split-rail fence, my lungs were burning. I reached out to grab the top rail and brushed my hand against an electric wire. Inhaling sharply, I jerked my hand back, then wasted precious seconds looking for a place where I could squeeze between the rails. I slipped through where one of the rails had sagged and crossed the rough ground to the trailer.

Standing with my back against the trailer, I tried to catch my breath and listened for distant voices, barking dogs, anything that would indicate I'd been seen. All I could hear was my own breathing. The escape door was on the side closest to the barn. I pushed myself off the cool metal, moved to the front of the trailer, and peered around the corner. The barn was dark and silent and blocked my view of the house. I crouched down and crossed under the nose of the trailer, between the trailer's body and hitch. As I inched my way down to the escape door, I curled my fingers around the flashlight.

I flicked on the light. The sheet metal was smooth and straight, not misshapen and dented. The workmanlike hinges were free of rust. The escape door, on the whole, was in much better repair than the rest of the trailer. I ducked down and peered at the lower edge of the door. The thin strip of metal, hidden from casual view, was blue not green.

A tingle went up my spine.

The door had been painted.

But I wouldn't know for sure unless I looked inside. I flicked off my light and edged around to the side door used for loading the horses. Thinking that I didn't want my fingerprints plastered all over the trailer, I slipped my hand under my T-shirt and unlatched the heavy ramp. I lowered it toward the ground, letting the springs do most of the work. They twanged and hummed under the stress, and the rusty hinges screeched until the lower lip of the ramp settled into the grass.

I nearly lost my nerve then, but the barn would muffle most of the sound, and the house was a good fifty yards beyond. I swallowed.

Heavy plywood partitions lay folded across the ramp. Normally, they would be raised on either side of the ramp, then slotted and bolted into place to form sidewalls for guiding the horses, but I didn't bother with the ramp. I stepped around the ramp, grabbed the edge of the door frame, and scrambled into the darkened trailer.

The air was chillier inside than out and smelled strongly of cows. I switched on the flashlight. Someone had removed the stall dividers and stacked them against the back wall. I looked at the window placement, at the shape and size of the storage space over the gooseneck, at the design and positioning of the overhead lights, and was certain I was standing in *the* trailer. Details I hadn't remembered came flooding back— the missing bar in the left-hand window, the six-inch crack in the yellowed light fixture over the back stalls, the tufts of torn baling twine that stuck out like a bad hairdo from the tie ring in the central aisle, the way the rubber matting under the escape door curled at the edge.

I examined the interior surface of the escape door. It, too, had received a paint job, but not as thorough. The original color was evident in the crease along the hinges and in the lower right-hand corner. I thought about how I'd escaped from the trailer and searched the floor. The old bolt was lying in a crevice where the fibers in the rubber matting had separated. Three links of chain still hung from one end. I bent down to pick it up, then hesitated.

I left it where it was, scrambled out of the trailer, and raised the ramp. I slid the latch home, spun around, and walked straight into the business end of a double-barreled shotgun.

The barrel jerked upward, and I felt my scalp contract.

"What'n the hell are you doin'?" He held the gun at the ready, pointing straight at my chest. "Well?"

I tried to work some saliva into my mouth, but all I could do was stare at the gun, at his hand steadying the barrel, at his finger fidgeting over the trigger guard.

As he stepped back, I heard a deep, guttural sound that rose into a menacing growl. I glanced down. A huge, broad-shouldered Rottweiler crouched in the grass next to the man's legs. His lips were pulled back from razor white teeth, his hot gaze locked on mine. The fur from the nape of his neck to the base of his tail stood on end, and I was sure, given half the chance, he would tear me to shreds.

"Well, boy, speak up. What're ya doin' lookin' in there?"

"I...I was looking for my dog, and I thought I heard something down here, and—"

"What?"

"I was following his tracks on the trails back there behind the pasture, when they broke off and headed down here toward your barn."

"Tracking a dog?" His eyes narrowed. "The hell you were. You were running across the field like the devil was fixin' to light up your ass."

"It's true, sir. I was looking for my dog."

"Put your goddamn hands up."

I looked at his dog and slowly raised my hands. The Rottweiler stepped sideways, and his growl, if anything, grew louder.

"We're gonna go talk to the police." He motioned to me with the shotgun. "Go on back round the trailer. Don't do anything stupid, now. Ain't nothin' gonna stop me from shootin' your ass. Understand?"

I nodded.

"Go on."

I stepped backward and tripped over something hidden in the tall grass. I landed flat on my back. The dog lunged forward, and I was sure I was dead. He bounced to a stop and lowered his head. A growl rumbled deep within his chest, and I watched, transfixed, as drool slid off the tip of a fang. It seemed to fall in slow motion before it landed on my face. The warm saliva trickled down my cheek into my hair.

"Get up."

I couldn't move. Every muscle in my body had seized, and I wasn't sure I was breathing.

"Get up, damn it," he yelled, and I wondered which would hurt more, being ripped apart or shot to death.

Finally, he must have realized I wasn't going anywhere with his dog breathing down my throat. He called to it and damn if the thing didn't listen. It trotted off, circled around behind its master, and stopped beside his leg. I slowly got to my feet and stood there feeling lightheaded.

"Get your damn hands up." I put them up. "Go that way." He jerked his head. "Walk through that gate there, the one over by the barn, and head on up to the house."

I turned and stepped through overgrown grass, praying that he wouldn't trip and end up shooting me in the back.

"Keep moving," he said.

When I got to the house, I stumbled up the back steps and stood where he told me, facing the wall. Out of the corner of my eye, I saw that he was careful to keep the shotgun leveled my way as he pulled open the screen door. He fumbled with the doorknob, then pushed the storm door open and told me to go inside. I turned to face him. He was standing awkwardly, his leg braced against the screen door that was hanging out of plumb with the frame. I hesitated and wondered if I'd be walking out under my own power.

"Go on in, damn it. I don't got all night."

I took two steps. He pointed the gun to the side to give me room to walk through the doorway, and I thought it might be my only chance. I could jump him. Then I looked at his dog. I wouldn't get two inches.

I walked into the kitchen.

He slammed the door so hard, the window panes rattled behind their thin, ratty curtains. The farmer kept his gaze on me as he strode across the room, dragged a chair away from the kitchen table, and told me to sit. I sat. The dog must have felt I was a welcomed guest then, because he nonchalantly walked into a half-collapsed cardboard box,

circled twice, then lay down on a dirty, rumpled quilt. He
lowered his head onto his front paws and sighed.

The farmer snatched the phone off the wall. "Keep your
hands where I can see 'em," he said as he punched in a
number. A long one. He hadn't dialed 911.

He leaned his butt against the kitchen counter and tucked
the shotgun under his arm. His grip looked relaxed. The
muzzle was pointed toward the floor, but there was no way I
could cross the space between us before he brought the gun
to bear.

"Wes? This is Randy." His gaze was steady on my face,
listening, impatient.

The muscles in my belly constricted, and a rising wave of
panic flooded my veins. I had made a big mistake. He wasn't
calling the cops. I should have made a break for it when I
was outside. Shouldn't have walked into this house.

"All right, fine. Listen, I caught this kid here, trespassin'.
Snoopin' round the trailer out back....He's sittin' right here,
at the kitchen table....I don't know. Could be. Can't tell for
sure....All right, and come to the back door." He hung up
the phone and raised the shotgun in one fluid movement,
then he stepped past the sink and flicked on the porch light.

I swallowed. "I thought you said you were calling the police."

"I did. So...you wanna tell me what you were doin'?"

When I didn't answer, he shrugged, pulled off his cap,
and tossed it on the counter. His red hair was full of static.
As he flattened his hair with the palm of his hand, I felt like
I'd been kicked in the gut. In the glow from the pickup's tail
lights that night, I easily could have mistaken red hair for
blond. He was the right build, too.

And that barn. It would be perfect for keeping horses out
of sight until they were ready to be shipped to Canada. If he
and his buddy on the phone were the horse thieves, I
wondered what they were going to do with me and thought
I already knew.

A clammy wave of nausea swept over me. It was hot in the kitchen, and I was sweating under my jacket. I rubbed a hand across my forehead, and that simple movement got the dog's attention. His head popped up, and he eyed me suspiciously.

Swallowing, I looked at the door. Light from the porch filtered through old towels that were tacked to the wood frame. I wouldn't be able to see who was at the door until he actually walked into the room, and by then it would be too late.

I cautiously turned my head to the right. There were two doorways. One opened into a dining room, dark and lifeless, giving an impression of disuse. From the other, a narrow hallway led toward the front of the house where a faint light shone. With each passing minute, the silence in the old house deepened—no television, no radio, no voices, not even a ticking clock.

The farmer—what was his name? Randy?—seemed content with guard duty. He had shed his jacket and was leaning against the counter, the shotgun wedged in the crook of his elbow. I looked at the dog. His head once again rested on his paws, eyes closed, but I doubted he was sleeping.

Someone rapped on the kitchen door, and all three of us jumped. The dog hit the linoleum at a dead run. His paws slid out from beneath him as he scrambled toward the door. Randy yelled, "Come in," and every muscle in my body tensed. I could hear my pulse pounding in my ears, even above the dog's frantic barking, and I decided to try and get away. Run through the house, out the front door, and away...if I could.

The door was creaking in on its hinges when I jumped to my feet. By the time the chair I'd been sitting in clattered to the floor, I was around the table.

"Hey," Randy yelled, but I was halfway down the hall, praying he wouldn't let loose with his gun inside the house.

Behind me, another voice yelled, "Stop," but I kept running. Where the hallway emptied into the living room, I almost ran into the back of a sofa. I vaulted it and landed on a coffee table. Piles of magazines and a coffee mug scattered across the polished wood, and the whole thing tipped over. Somehow, I landed on my feet. I sprinted for the front door.

Without warning, something jerked my leg backward, and I crashed face first onto the floor. The impact knocked the breath out of my lungs. I gasped, trying to inhale and feeling like I couldn't, when a knee jammed into the small of my back. A strong hand gripped my neck and pressed my face into the carpet. He was yelling at me, screaming, but I barely heard him. Grunting with exertion, he tried to get hold of my right arm with his free hand.

I reached behind my neck, grabbed his wrist, and yanked as hard as I could. It broke his grip, and he overbalanced. He toppled forward. I twisted and jammed my elbow into him and tried to roll him off. He was too quick. He pinned my shoulders to the floor, and the farmer walked over and ground his boot into the back of my neck like he was squashing a bug. I lay there for a second, panting, unable to move, and realized that something was wrong with my leg.

The dog. It was the damn dog.

The guy on top of me shifted his weight and latched his fingers around my wrist. He yanked on my arm and tried to get my hand behind my back, but he was going to have to work for it.

"Come on, kid," he grunted. "Give it up." He pulled harder, but it didn't do him any good. "Randy, put your weight into it."

"I am." Randy increased the pressure on my neck.

"Relax, kid," the guy on my back panted. "You're just making it harder on yourself." He changed his grip, jackknifed my arm around, and pinned my wrist between my shoulder blades.

He shifted, and I realized he was groping for something. A gun, a knife?

Fueled with desperation, I wrenched my arm free, grabbed Randy's ankle, and twisted at the same time. It threw him off balance. His boot scraped across my neck, and he landed heavily on the carpet. I rolled and twisted, trying to get to my feet, when I caught sight of the guy behind me and froze. He was squatting, bringing his arm down in a wide arc, and in his hand, he held a shiny black stick. It cracked into my arm, just below the shoulder. The blow shuddered through my body, and my arm went numb.

He pushed me back onto my stomach and clamped something on my wrist. The ratchetting sound was unmistakable, and I had probably just gotten myself into a whole lot of trouble. He pulled my left arm into position, slapped on the other cuff, and pushed to his feet. I twisted around.

They stared down at me, both of them out of breath, and sure enough, the glimpse I'd caught of a uniform hadn't been a mistake. He was a cop. A sheriff's deputy, at least from the waist up. From the looks of it, he had thrown on his jacket and gun belt in a hurry. Otherwise, he was wearing jeans and sneakers. I closed my eyes and groaned.

"Randy, call off your dog."

Randy motioned to his dog, and I looked toward my feet. The dog had his huge jaws clamped around my right ankle. His legs were braced, and he was pulling against me, his nails digging into the carpet. He turned his head to the side, struggled to open his mouth wider, and let go of my leg. He shook his head as if disgusted, then walked behind Randy and sat dutifully beside his master. I flexed my ankle. It burned, but I was pretty sure I had escaped any damage. His teeth had sunk into my boot, not my skin.

I moved to get up, and the cop put his foot between my shoulder blades and pushed me back down. "Don't move." He was still panting. "You're already in enough trouble." After a minute or two, he squatted beside me and checked my jacket pockets.

"What's your name?"

"Stephen Cline."

"Why'd you run, Steve?"

"I didn't think you were a cop."

He rolled me onto my side and began to empty my jeans pockets. "Who'd you think I was? Santa Claus?"

"Funny."

"You know you could of got yourself shot?" He checked my waistline, then felt between my legs.

I tensed.

"What? You never been frisked before?"

"No." I unclenched my teeth. "What in the hell are you checking for."

"Guns, knives, hand grenades...suspicious bulges." He chuckled at his stupid joke and rolled me back onto my stomach. "Ever been arrested?"

"No."

When he finished his search, he grunted to his feet, then snatched his hat off the carpet. He stood in a wide-legged stance, his gut protruding over his belt. It had been a long time since his police academy days. A long time since he'd done anything more vigorous than drive around in his cruiser. He brushed off the hat's brim and adjusted it on his balding head. That done, he hooked his hand under my arm and pulled me to my feet.

"Settle down, Steve. Gettin' angry ain't gonna help you any." He tugged on his belt. "Now, what were you doing on Mr. Drake's property?"

I told him. I told him about the horse theft and about being beaten up and abducted and about Detectives Linquist and Ralston. I told him about James Peters and everything else I could think of because I had to. By the time I ran out of things to say, Randy no longer looked pissed off, and Deputy Thompson had been on the phone several times, running a check on me and verifying my story.

Randy chuckled. "No wonder you looked so scared." He was leaning against the kitchen counter, chewing on a toothpick, and I was back in the chair I'd started out in.

Thompson shook his head as he fitted his key into one cuff, then the other. "You could of got yourself killed. What if you'd stumbled into the murderer. Next time, leave it to the professionals." He jerked his head at the farmer, and they walked over to the hallway. The deputy crossed his arms over his broad stomach and talked quietly to Randy, all the while keeping his gaze on me.

I rubbed my wrists and listened to their low, indistinct voices. The dog was back in his box, asleep this time. I glanced at my watch. Ten after ten.

Damn. Karen would be wondering where I was, and I hoped to God Jet was all right. I looked up as Thompson strode across the worn floor and stopped in front of me.

"Mr. Drake isn't gonna press charges for trespassing, son. You'd better go on home."

Press charges? I wondered what charges I could get Mr. Drake in trouble with. "Mind if I look at the trailer on my way out?"

Thompson's eyebrows rose. "Don't see why not." He turned to Randy. "Got any objections?"

Randy shook his head. I made a quick call to Foxdale and told Karen to go home, then the three of us trudged outside.

At the corral gate, I paused and looked Randy in the eye. "You had no right to hold me at gunpoint."

His back tensed under his jacket. "I got signs posted up and down my fence line, and you kids just keep doing what you please."

"I've never been here before," I said, and even I could hear the anger in my voice.

"Now, son. It's over." Thompson stepped closer. "Go on home. Mr. Drake was just protecting his property."

Wordlessly, I turned away from them and walked around to the trailer's back bumper. I pushed a clump of tall weeds out of the way. The license plate had been issued in Pennsylvania, which explained why Drake hadn't been on Ralston's list. As I straightened, I noticed my cap lying in the grass. I picked it up and dusted off the brim.

Deputy Thompson stood with his arms crossed over his broad belly and his chin tucked against his neck, waiting for me to leave, while Randy dug around his teeth with his toothpick. By all accounts, he looked bored. And I didn't understand it. If I wasn't mistaken, I had just found the trailer; yet the owner was clueless.

"You have any repairs made to your trailer in the past two months?" I said.

Randy shook his head. "I hardly ever use it."

I jerked my head toward his house. "I got turned around in the woods. What road do you live on?"

"Mink Hollow."

I told him I was sorry I'd bothered him, then crossed the corral and vaulted the fence.

I found Jet where I'd left her and turned her for home. She didn't need any encouragement. It wasn't until I pulled her up between the barns that I realized what I felt was no longer anger, but confusion and an overwhelming feeling of futility.

After I untacked Jet and brushed her off, I checked the barns. I was on my way out when I paused at the bulletin board outside barn A's tack room. I tore down the class schedule from the past weekend and crumpled it into a ball. Underneath was a crinkled copy of the announcement I'd tacked up weeks before, the one that described the rig used in the horse theft.

The paper was discolored from being in the barn so long, and someone had scribbled across the lower right-hand corner in red ink. As the words registered, I felt as if I'd been drenched with ice water.

"A cat has nine lives. You don't" was scrawled across my name.

An image of Boris swinging from the rafters with his throat cut crowded my mind.

No one knew about him except the cops.

And the killer.

Chapter 15

"Brian, jiggle the chain to distract him," I said over my shoulder and hoped he'd understood what I meant. Whether he would oblige was anyone's guess.

I had the end flap of a roll of Vetrap between my teeth, a wad of sterile gauze coated with Betadine in my right hand, and the gelding's hind leg wedged between my forearm and thigh. The bandage I'd wrapped around his hoof yesterday lay on the ground beneath his tail.

Monday afternoon, he'd clipped the bulb of his heel, and he hadn't cared for my ministrations ever since. I hiked his leg higher up my thigh and placed the gauze over the gash. I felt the horse's head come up and realized that someone must have walked into the aisle and spooked him.

I anchored the end of the Vetrap in place with my thumb and got in four good wraps before the gelding tried to snatch his hoof out of my hands.

"Whoa," I said to the horse and, with irritation, to Brian, "Don't let him move forward." Like you did yesterday, I wanted to add but knew better.

I unwound the last of the Vetrap, then clamped my hands over the sole of his hoof to mold the bandage to itself. When I let go of his leg, he kicked out before placing his hoof on the ground where it belonged.

I straightened. Detective Ralston was standing just inside the doorway, and he was watching Brian.

"Couple more minutes," I said, "and I'll be done."

I had waited to hear from Ralston all day yesterday, but he hadn't returned my call until ten, when he'd arranged to meet me at the farm in the morning. I had slept poorly and had come in early to get a head start on the day's work.

I reinforced the Vetrap with duct tape and snipped through the top margin of the bandage to alleviate pressure over the coronary band. The horse didn't like that, either.

"Okay, Brian. Put him back in his stall." I slapped the gelding on his rump as he moved off, and he flattened his ears.

After I'd washed up in the men's room, I found Ralston standing on the grassy strip that borders the outdoor arena. Beyond the fence, a handful of riders were working their horses. As I joined Ralston, Anne pointed Chase down the outside line. The gelding flew the jumps, covering the six-stride line in a ground-eating five, clearing the fan jump with a foot and a half to spare.

I whistled under my breath.

Halfway through their approach to the next line, Anne pulled the gelding off line. They galloped past so close, I felt the vibrations from his hoof beats through the soles of my boots. Ralston stepped backward. I pretended not to notice.

Anne turned the gelding toward the center of the ring. His hooves sluiced through the footing and spattered the fence boards with sand. The instant Chase realized they were heading for the diagonal line, he pricked his ears and sailed effortlessly down the line, a streak of liquid gold.

Ralston turned and looked at me over the rims of his sunglasses.

"Can we talk in your car?" I said. "The office is crowded."

"Sure."

"First, there's something I want to show you." I led him back into barn A and stopped at the bulletin board. "I found this the other night."

Ralston read the scrawled words and looked at me. "How long's this been up?"

"The beginning of March. I tacked it up as soon as I started back to work."

"When do you think they left the message?"

I shrugged. "I don't know. Marty stapled last weekend's show schedule over the top of it Friday afternoon, and he didn't notice it, but that doesn't mean it wasn't there."

"What about the boarder who told you about the trailer? She notice anything?" Ralston said.

"No, she'd read the copy I'd posted in the lounge, not this one. I've asked around, but no one noticed the writing."

Ralston went back to his car and came back with an evidence bag and a pair of gloves. He dropped the wrinkled sheet into the bag, and I followed him back outside. He'd parked his car next to the office door. I guessed when you were a cop, you got into the habit of parking wherever you damn well liked.

Ralston turned the key in the ignition and powered down the windows. "Okay. Tell me about it."

I told him how I'd learned about the trailer and how I'd been caught trespassing.

He listened without interrupting, his expression unchanged, but I sensed his irritation from the stiffness in his shoulders and his overall stillness.

I told him about the Pennsylvania tags and why I thought it was the right trailer. "But the thing is, Drake didn't act like he was guilty. Either he's an extraordinary actor, or he's not involved, which doesn't make sense."

Ralston stared straight ahead, his gaze fixed on some point beyond the windshield. "Your impulsiveness negates your intelligence. If it *is* the trailer, besides the immediate danger you put yourself in, they've more than likely moved it by now."

I looked out the passenger window. "I didn't think anyone would see me."

"And you went inside?"

I nodded.

Ralston turned in his seat. "Do you realize what you've done?"

I didn't answer.

"You've contaminated any evidence we might have retrieved." His voice was as near to yelling as I'd ever heard it.

"How do you mean?" I said. "I didn't touch anything."

"Trace evidence. Proving that you were in that trailer on February 24th was of primary importance. Now the defense will say anything we find was left behind Tuesday, not two months ago. Without that link, we don't have a case."

"Oh."

After a minute or two, he sighed. "I do appreciate what you're trying to do. But if you hear something, fine, phone it in. When it comes to chasing down leads, leave it to us, all right?"

I nodded.

"How'd Drake act when you asked him about the repairs?"

"It was weird," I said. "He didn't react at all."

"Maybe it's not the trailer."

"It is." I rubbed my forehead. "What are you going to do?"

"Get a warrant. Check it out."

Ralston popped open his briefcase and handed me a form. Under his direction, I wrote out a statement, stating that, to the best of my knowledge, the Wellington trailer parked on Mr. Drake's property, 10471 Mink Hollow Road, was the trailer used in the February twenty-fourth theft of seven horses from Foxdale Farm. In addition, I had been held in the trailer against my will. Ralston had me list the trailer's characteristics that enabled me to make a positive ID. Then I signed and dated it.

Afterward, Ralston headed north to fill out the necessary paperwork to obtain a search warrant for the property and belongings of Randor L. Drake.

◇◇◇

I spent Thursday night sitting on a hay bale in a school pony's stall. The brown mare had colicked late in the afternoon, and when a dose of Banamine hadn't set her right, I'd called Greg.

He had gone over her vitals, pumped mineral oil into her stomach, and instructed me to watch her overnight in case she got worse.

So far, she hadn't, and by two in the morning, she was dozing in her stall with her head lowered, eyes half-closed, ears at half-mast. I stretched, then leaned against the stall's rough wooden planks and closed my eyes. The crickets and tree frogs had quit their singing sometime earlier, and the barn was deeply quiet.

As dawn approached, I watched the sky lighten. By the time the rafters glowed red, touched by the nearly horizontal sunlight cutting through the windows, the mare was nosing around her stall, searching out stray wisps of hay. I got to work, and Ralston caught me in the middle of morning turn-outs. Mrs. Hill hadn't come in yet, so we went into the office.

"Did you arrest him?" I said.

Ralston smiled, I assumed, at my naiveté and shook his head. He closed the door and crossed his arms over his chest. "He's on a fishing trip in West Virginia."

"What?"

"Relax. It was prearranged. I don't think he's running yet. I talked to his neighbor. The guy feeds Drake's cattle when he's away, which according to him is most weekends of the year. Drake's got a girlfriend in West Virginia, and when he isn't there, he's training."

"Training?"

"Yeah. He's with the Guard."

"When's he due back?"

"Monday. I'm on my way to see his C.O. now. What were you wearing when they put you in the trailer?"

I thought back. "Jeans, T-shirt, a flannel shirt, boots—"

Ralston held out his hand. "I mean, do you remember specifically which flannel shirt? And can I have it?"

"Well, no. I was hypothermic, and my clothes were wet. The medics cut them off, and when I got them back, I threw them away."

"Damn."

"You found something?" I said.

Ralston shook his head. "It'll be weeks before results come back from the lab, but I needed your clothing so they can try to match it with any fibers they do find." He rubbed his face. "What about a coat?"

I nodded. "I still have that."

Ralston lowered his hand and looked at me with interest.

"And it's got a fleece collar."

"Perfect," he said. "When can I have it?"

"Now. I'll go get it."

"I'll drive," he said.

Ralston pulled out onto Rocky Ford. "I've been thinking about what I said yesterday, about your contaminating the scene. I think we still have a chance, even though we messed up."

I noticed his use of "we" but didn't comment on it. "How?"

"Let's say the techs find a couple of strands of hair they can prove came from you. The defense will say their presence has nothing to do with any alleged abduction back in February. Well, there's this forensics guy in Anchorage who performed an experiment that demonstrates the gradual deterioration of hair left in the environment. In that case, it was the opposite scenario he had to prove, but that doesn't matter."

"How do you mean?"

Ralston slowed the Ford as he approached the sharp curve at the entrance to the future housing development. "In that case, the defendant was accused of murdering his ex-girlfriend in her apartment. Forensics found hair and other fibers that linked him to the scene on the bed where the woman was strangled, in the bathroom, in the living room carpet. He used to live there, so the defense simply claimed that any of his hair found in the apartment was old."

"Makes sense."

"Yeah," Ralston said. "He swore up and down that he hadn't been there for at least three months, but ultimately, that claim was his downfall because, while they were waiting to go to trial, this forensics guy vacuumed his house every day with one of the special vacuums they use at crime scenes—"

"The murder scene?"

"No. His house."

"I bet his wife loved that," I said.

"Yeah, I imagine so." Ralston yawned. "Anyway, he demonstrated how hair deteriorates over time but is still identifiable. So, from any given sample, he could show which hairs had been in the environment for an extended period of time and which hairs had been newly shed. He proved that some of the defendant's hairs found at the crime scene were fresh."

Ralston took off his sunglasses and pinched the bridge of his nose. "Look at it the other way around. We can prove that any older hairs of yours have been in the trailer long enough to substantiate the claim that you were in that trailer two months ago as well as the other day."

"And if they find fibers from my coat, which I obviously didn't wear Tuesday, that'll help."

Ralston nodded.

I thought about the condition of the trailer and the fact that it had been forked out at least once since the theft. "What are the chances of forensics finding anything?"

"Not as bad as you might think. The overall lack of cleanliness might actually work in our favor. It's when the bad guys get out a hose and vacuum that it gets tough."

"What about James Peters?"

"I'm hoping we'll get something there, too. It's a crap shoot. You just hope you get something good." Ralston looked at me a little longer than was prudent for the narrow back road we were traveling. "Kind of an unusual job for someone with your background, isn't it?" he said.

I shrugged.

"I'd've figured you for Notre Dame or Harvard or Yale." He paused for emphasis. "Or even Johns Hopkins."

I shifted in my seat. "Done your homework, I see." When he didn't respond, I said, "I took a break from school and got a job here because I thought the idea of working with horses would be fun."

What I hadn't counted on was the old man kicking me out. Out of his house and out of his life, each of us waiting for the other to change his mind.

I sighed. "For a while, anyway."

Ralston accelerated into a curve. "But you stayed."

I adjusted the sun visor. "I kind of got caught up in it. I don't know. I like it a hell of a lot more than sitting in some lecture hall." I rubbed my eyes and said, "Do you think whoever stole the horses has someone inside Foxdale?"

"Hard to tell. Why?"

"Just wondered. One of our trainers got fired Friday. Whitcombe. The one I told you about before, who showed up with an expensive saddle right after the tack theft. He has a brand new Mustang convertible, too." And a baldheaded friend who resembled a eunuch, but I didn't tell him that.

"He inherited a chunk of change a while back, from an aunt," Ralston said, "but some family members contested the will. The ruling went in his favor. He received a check sometime in February. More than enough to cover that new saddle and a Mustang."

"Well then, that explains that. And maybe it explains his mood, too. He's always been…difficult, but in the last three or four months, he's been downright obnoxious."

"Money or love. Does it every time," Ralston said. "Know anything about his love life?"

"No," I said, "I do not."

The detective grinned, and I realized he must have known about, or at least suspected, Whitcombe's sexual preference.

"One of the other employees," I said, "Brian Denning. There's something up with him, isn't there?"

"He's in the system."

"What for?"

"Residential burglary, theft from a motor vehicle, DUI. He's on probation for another eight months."

"What's that entail?"

"Besides keeping his nose clean, staying off the booze, *and* holding a job, he's gotta attend A.A. and submit to drug testing. And he can't miss a meeting with his PO."

I pointed to a mailbox up ahead. "Turn in there."

I retrieved my coat, and Ralston lowered it into a plastic trash bag and sealed it shut with tape. He then rested a pad on the hood of his car and filled out a label which he pressed down across the bag's seam like a seal. "What about a hat? Gloves?"

I shook my head. I hadn't seen them since that night. Ralston handed me a receipt for the coat and dropped me off at Foxdale. I watched him back down the lane and hoped that something good would come from my screw-up.

After lunch, I fell asleep on the sofa in the lounge. When I next became aware of noises, someone was working at the computer keyboard in the office.

I hadn't slept for thirty hours, and lying down, even for a moment, had been a mistake. My legs and arms felt heavy, as if they were weighted down.

The lounge door opened.

My entire body felt as if it were sunk into the cushions.

Whoever had opened the door, hadn't walked on through to the office.

I opened my eyes.

Mr. Harrison was standing alongside the sofa with a clipboard in his hand. His face was stiff, and I had the distinct impression he was clenching his teeth.

I checked my watch. Lunch time had ended without my knowledge. The crew was back at work, and no one had bothered to wake me.

When I pulled myself into a sitting position, Harrison handed me the paperwork. I glanced at his figures and saw that Marty had already initialed the invoice. I scrawled my name across the bottom of the sheet just the same and held out the clipboard. Harrison stared at me for a second, his eyes flat and expressionless, then he snatched it out of my hand and walked into the office.

Nick had described him as creepy. He wasn't far off.

Harrison could have left by the office door, but he chose to cut through the lounge on his way out. I was still sitting on the sofa when he stepped outside. He turned back around as the door swung shut and stared at me through the glass with that tight, expressionless face of his before he headed for his truck.

What a jerk. He was the one who had tried his stinking little scam. It was his damn luck he'd gotten caught.

I opened the lounge door as the flatbed lumbered down the lane. Harrison sat motionless in the passenger's seat. I glanced at the driver and realized I didn't know him and wondered if Harrison had fired the other guy. Harrison had seen me check. He scowled at me through the glass as the truck jostled past.

I rubbed my forehead and felt an overwhelming tiredness deep within my bones. And to top it off, it was going to be a late night. After the last lesson, the school horses had to be turned out and their stalls cleaned because we would be leasing the space to the clinic participants. If Rachel wanted to hang around, she'd have to watch me muck stalls.

There had to be a better way to impress your girlfriend.

I took the rest of the afternoon off, went home, and took a nap. Just before four o'clock, someone knocked on the kitchen door. I squinted through the glass.

Rachel was standing on the other side of my door.

Chapter 16

I swung my legs over the edge of the bed and stood up. My jeans were on the floor halfway across the room, and the gray cat had curled into a ball on top of them. When I grabbed a pant leg, the cat dug her claws into the denim. I dragged her across the carpet until she gave it up and abandoned ship. When I straightened, I saw that Rachel was laughing.

"Ha, ha," I mouthed.

I zipped up my jeans, didn't bother with the snap, and opened the door.

Rachel was wearing a form-fitting T-shirt along with skin-tight riding breeches and boots. Very sexy. She'd pulled her silky dark hair into a loose pony tail. Wisps of hair had worked free and hung along the side of her face and down the back of her neck. She stepped inside, and I reached behind her and clicked the door shut.

A thin breeze drifted through the open window and stirred the dust that hung in the air. Her perfume smelled faintly of vanilla.

Rachel reached out and touched my skin. I looked down at her hand. Her fingertips brushed across my waist, close to the snap on my jeans.

"Marty told me you'd pulled an all-nighter." Her gaze rose slowly to my face. She was concerned…and something else.

I nodded.

She stood very still, and she was breathing through her mouth.

I took her hand in mine and embraced her, then leaned into the counter and pulled her against me. Rachel wrapped her arms around my waist, and the feel of her hands on my bare skin was electrifying. I traced my fingertips along her jaw and kissed her mouth. Her lips were cool and tasted of cinnamon. I smoothed my hand down the front of her shirt and tugged it out of her pants. When I ran my hand across the small of her back, she twisted her fingers in my hair and kissed me hard on the mouth.

The loft seemed unnaturally quiet and still, the air around us charged.

I turned her around until her buttocks were pressed against my thighs. Flattening my hands on her belly, I slid my fingers under her shirt, lifted it out of the way, and cupped my hands over her breasts. She arched her back, and every time she shifted, her ass brushed against my crotch.

Rachel turned her head toward me, and her hot breath fanned across my cheek. Her breasts rose with each inhalation, her nipples erect under the thin fabric of her bra. I rubbed against her, and after a moment, I slipped my fingers under the elastic.

She gripped my hand, then stepped away from me. She flicked down her shirt and turned to face me.

"I can't." She crossed her arms over her chest. "I'm sorry, Steve. I'm not ready."

"You don't have to be." My voice sounded hoarse. "I'll get dressed."

I walked into the bathroom, braced my hands on the sink, and hung my head. She'd been sending out subtle messages all along that she needed to go slow, and I'd blown it. I sucked in a lungful of air. After a minute or two, I splashed cold water on my face—it didn't help—finished dressing, and brushed my teeth.

When I went back into the kitchen, Rachel had made herself at home on one of the barstools. She looked composed and relaxed, and she'd tucked in her shirt.

I kissed her on the cheek and rested my hands on her knees. "I need to go back to Foxdale, I'm afraid."

"To feed the horses?"

I nodded.

"Marty's taking care of it."

"Wow," I mumbled.

"He couldn't get you on the phone—"

"It's off the hook."

"So I see." She brushed her bangs off her forehead. "Anyway, he wanted to tell you to stay home. They're going to do whatever they can tonight to get ready for the clinic and finish up in the morning. So I offered to drive over to tell you, but I see Marty was wrong." She glanced at my crotch and seemed surprised that her eyes had betrayed her. "You're not at all impaired from lack of sleep, are you?"

"Wide awake now that you're here."

She giggled. "So you don't mind my dropping in unannounced?"

I grinned. "Come anytime."

Rachel rolled her eyes. "Are you sure this wasn't an elaborate plot between the two of you to get me over here," she glanced around the loft, "in your apartment?"

I grinned. "No, we're not that clever."

Her eyes were so dark, they were almost black.

"Would you like something to eat?" I said.

She hesitated. "Dinner only."

"I promise."

"Who colicked?"

I told her about the pony while we ate grilled cheese sandwiches—the only thing I had left suitable for human consumption—and some stale pretzels. I didn't spend all that much time in the loft and rarely had company. The place would feel empty when she was gone, and I hoped her presence would become routine. But it wouldn't happen if I kept behaving like a sex-crazed lunatic.

I turned sideways on my stool and watched her. She took a bite of her sandwich and looked up at me. A smile shone in her eyes, and I couldn't help but wonder what her past experiences had been like. I swallowed some Coke and realized that I really didn't know all that much about her.

Despite what Marty had said, we decided to go back to the barn at ten-thirty. As I followed Rachel's Camry down Foxdale's lane, barn A's lights flicked out. Barn B was already dark. I pulled into a parking space as three of the four vehicles still in the lot started up and headed toward the exit. Only Karen's car was left. As Rachel and I walked around the corner of the indoor, Karen was locking the office door.

"Getting everybody out of here's a pain in the ass," Karen said when we met on the sidewalk. "Especially on weekends. They wanna hang out and socialize, they oughta go somewhere else to do it." Karen's gaze flicked over us, and she took in the fact that we were holding hands. "I have a life, too, but they never think of that."

"You gonna catch any of the clinic?" I said.

"You kidding? I have a weekend off, the last place I wanna be's here."

"Well, good night," I said.

"Oh, I almost forgot," Karen said. "Marty got all the stalls done except the eight that were in the last lesson, so you lucked out."

"Great."

With my blessing, Rachel bent Foxdale's rules (Karen would've had a fit) and worked her horse in barn B's arena while I started on the stalls. I was mucking out the second to last stall when she joined me.

"How much longer will you be?" Rachel said.

"At the pace I'm going, another twenty minutes."

"I'll keep you company."

"You don't have to do that."

"I know." She leaned against the doorjamb. "But I want to. Anyway, I don't have anything better to do."

"I might be longer. You're distracting me."

"Oh...I'll leave then." She backed into the aisle.

I hopped out of the stall, took her in my arms, and kissed her. There was passion on her part, I was happy to see, and less poised control.

In actuality, it took me half an hour to finish up. Afterward, we walked out to the parking lot. As we stood by her car, a police cruiser out on the road slowed and turned into the lane. The tires crunched across the gravel, sounding loud in the quiet darkness. He pulled alongside Rachel's car and left the engine running.

Officer Dorsett climbed out of his cruiser. "Jesus. You live here?"

"Just about." I made introductions.

Dorsett flicked his gaze over Rachel, pausing, I noticed, at the more compelling parts of her anatomy. Even with a jacket to ward off the chill, she couldn't disguise her figure. I wondered if she'd noticed, but if she had, nothing showed in her face.

"Were you leaving?" he asked us.

"Yes."

He looked directly at me and said, "Have you walked around yet?"

"No."

"I'll go with you. Nothing much going on right now."

Rachel and I said good night. Not the good night I'd envisioned, however, thanks to Officer Dorsett watching our every move. After she'd driven away, I started toward the barns. I'd taken several steps before I realized Dorsett hadn't moved.

I turned around and looked at his face. "What's wrong?"

"I've heard something that might be connected with your case."

A muscle twinged in my gut.

"Last weekend, just off Route 30 across the Maryland-PA line, some horses were stolen from a hunter barn. The woman who owns the place heard something and went outside to investigate. No one's seen her since."

I groaned. "Did anyone see the rig?"

Dorsett shook his head. "So far there aren't any leads, and her live-in boyfriend didn't hear a damn thing."

I swallowed.

"The farm's secluded. You can't see it from the road, and the barn's not close to the house." His portable radio clattered. Dorsett listened, then dismissed a broadcast that was mostly unintelligible to my ears. "They probably thought they wouldn't be interrupted."

"What about the boyfriend?"

"He remembers that she went out. After that, nothing. They'd been drinking, and he was pretty much wasted."

"What's Ralston think?"

Dorsett shrugged. "He's up there now."

We checked the farm, but afterward, I couldn't remember one damn thing I'd seen or done.

I lay awake for hours. When the clock radio switched on at four o'clock Saturday morning, my skull felt as if it had been squeezed in a vise. I walked over to the window and rubbed my eyes. Light had already begun to seep into the eastern horizon.

Despite a lack of enthusiasm on my part, the clinic started without a hitch, and by lunch time, both barns had been mucked out. I walked behind barn B and stood by the pasture gate. The school horses were exiled to the field for the duration of the clinic, and any change that interfered with a horse's normal routine could wreak havoc with its digestive system. In the past two years, though, the practice hadn't caused any problems. Unexplained colics, like last night's, were the norm.

Two years. It was hard to believe I'd been at Foxdale that long. I rested my forearms on the fence. I ought to stop feeling sorry for myself. Waste of time.

The sun felt warm on my shoulders. The clatter of Mrs. Hill's voice over the P.A. system was an indistinct murmur. I looked over the horses. They were content, relaxed, happy to be outside. Farther down the hill, a bay pony pawed the ground in front of the automatic waterer. I hopped the fence and walked down the slope. She turned her big, old head and watched my approach with a calm eye.

"Hey there, girl. What's wrong?" I patted her neck, and she nuzzled my arm.

Her coat hadn't completely shed out, and I could smell the sharp odor of sweat and damp horse hair. I looked at the waterer and frowned. The lid was closed. I flipped it back onto the main housing. It wasn't easy to move, but if she'd been fooling with it, I supposed she could have accidentally closed it. She pursed her lips and drank greedily from the bowl.

I turned to leave. Movement in the implement building caught my eye. As far as I knew, Dave hadn't come in, and no one else should have been down there. I cut across the pasture.

Brian was sitting in the chair alongside Dave's workbench, his head bowed, elbows propped on his knees. A crumpled paper bag and an empty Miller's can lay on the ground by his feet. A second can dangled from his right hand. When I stepped into the shade of the roof overhang, he looked up and squinted at me through a haze of cigarette smoke.

"Well, if it ain't Sherlock Holmes." Brian gestured to a six-pack on the lower level of the mow. "Want some?"

When I didn't respond, he said, "Oh yeah. That's right. I forgot. You don't drink, don't smoke." He gulped some beer. "Let's see. You don't cuss. Not much anyway. You're polite as hell. Work like a dog."

He peered at me and rolled the cigarette filter between his lips. "Just what is it you do for fun?"

I gritted my teeth. "Get up."

"'Get up.'" He chuckled. "Get it up, you mean?" He took the cigarette from between his lips and spit, like he'd gotten a piece of tobacco on his tongue. "You *do* do that, don't you? Get it up with Mrs. Elsa 'if it moves, fuck it' Timbrook."

I lunged forward, twisted my fingers in his shirt, and hauled him to his feet. His chair toppled backward, and beer sloshed down the front of my jeans. His eyes were bloodshot, and he was having trouble focusing on my face.

Brian smirked. "So, I guess you're not so special after all."

I spun him around and leaned into him so that my mouth was close to his ear. "Fuck you." I shoved him outside.

He stumbled when his shoes hit the gravel in the lane.

"Pick up your check in the office," I said. "And don't come back."

"You gotta be kidding. Who'd want this job anyway, working for a self-righteous bastard like you? Slingin' shit all day long 'til you smell like it." His gaze drifted from my face to what was left of his six-pack. He looked back at me, his pale eyes wide and unblinking, and flicked his cigarette into the building. It landed on the ground behind me.

The skin on the back of my head contracted.

He gestured to the west wall where the graffiti had been. "Maybe they'll fix *you*."

I watched him start toward the office, then I spun around and searched for the cigarette. It was smoldering under the hay elevator. A couple more feet, and it would have landed in the chaff that littered the floor at the base of the mow.

I ground out the butt with the toe of my boot and exhaled breath I hadn't realized I'd been holding.

Brian hadn't wasted any time. By the time I got to the office, he'd already left.

The room was crowded. A thin woman with tanned, wiry arms and mousy brown hair held back with a bandanna was leaning on Mrs. Hill's desk with her fingers splayed across the bare metal. "...couldn't come, so one of my other girls wanted to take her place, and..."

A young girl had borrowed the office phone. She covered her ear with the palm of her hand and hunched forward while, behind her, three riders debated whether the times posted for their rides were running to schedule.

Mrs. Hill frowned at me, then waved me off. I knew she'd be irritated because we were short an employee on such a busy weekend, but she wouldn't want to talk about Brian then. I cut through the lounge and bought a Coke, then went outside and sat on one of the benches that were positioned down the length of the arena. Several clinic participants and a handful of boarders were working their horses in the sandy footing. On the far side of the judges' stand, a group of spectators were watching the clinic up close.

Someone sat down next to me. The wooden slats moved under my butt. I glanced to my right and was surprised to see that that someone was George Irons.

"Hey there, Mr. Irons. How ya doin'?"

"Not bad. Be a lot better if I was out on the bay, kickin' back a few, instead of watchin' a bunch of fancy horses trot round in circles." He gestured toward the dressage arena. "Got half my barn here today."

I turned the Coke can in my hands and pulled back on the tab.

Mr. Irons waved at a large gray that was being walked along the rail on a loose rein. The gelding's nose almost touched the ground, and his back looked supple and relaxed. "My daughter's up next. That's her new horse. Got an overstep you wouldn't believe."

"Nice looking animal," I said.

Irons nodded as a bay horse walked in front of us. "Paid too much for him of course, but..." His attention drifted from the bay to its rider, and he seemed to lose his train of thought. "Well, lookit that. Ol' Vic's gone from bad to worse. I know they don't care what jumpers look like, but really, that one's got a knot between its eyes, makes you think somebody'd hauled off and whacked it with a ball bat."

"You know Mr. Sanders, do you?"

"Yeah, I know 'im, all right. I'll tell you one thing, though. He sure as shit wishes he'd never heard of me. When those bastards stole my horses, they took his, too."

Mr. Irons continued speaking, oblivious to the fact that I'd become still or that my breathing had slowed even though my heart was pounding faster than a freight train, the blood swooshing past my eardrums.

"He'd hauled in his gelding," Irons continued, "looking for someplace temporary to keep it while he was waitin' to get in somewheres else. Then it goes and gets stolen. Only had a week to go before he was plannin' on movin' it, too."

I cleared my throat. "What was the gelding's name?"

"Portage something or other. Don't remember now. Some big ol' gray. Part draft, part thoroughbred. Ugly head, but not as bad as that." He gestured after Sanders' bay gelding.

"Light gray?" I said.

Irons shook his head. "Dark gray with dapples."

Sanders guided his horse between a pair of jump standards and circled toward us. Steel had been a dark gray, heavily dappled. A draft cross of some sort. His theft from Foxdale had netted Sanders twenty grand.

Sanders looked down his nose at us as he rode past. My face felt stiff.

"Was the horse insured?" I asked, though I expected I already knew the answer.

"You bet he was." Irons scowled. "Better'n I can say for myself."

"By chance," I said, "do you recall which insurance company?"

"Sure do. Same company that handles my liability coverage. Liberty South. He told me he was thinking 'bout gettin' his horse insured and asked me who I used and was I happy with 'em. I introduced him to my agent. Lucky timing for him, huh?"

I asked Irons if the gelding had any distinguishing marks or blemishes, but his description was vague and could have matched a thousand horses in any given county.

"Did the horse have any unusual behaviors," I said, "any quirks, weird habits?"

Irons squinted at me. "What you wantin' to know for?"

"Did he?" I said.

"Well, now. Let me think." He rubbed the bristles on his chin. "He was tense for his breedin'. Mouthy, too. Couldn't leave nothin' alone."

"What about when you handled him? Did he do anything out of the ordinary?"

"Now you mention it, he wasn't happy unless he had part of his lead in his mouth. Always had to have something to chew on."

A steel gray draft cross with a fetish for lead ropes, who just so happened to belong to Victor Sanders, gets stolen from George Irons' dressage barn only to show up at Foxdale two years later where he's stolen again. Even when Steel had been in the trailer that night, he had fooled with the chains the entire time. They had to be one and the same.

I wondered if he was still alive. If any of the others were. Were they being masqueraded somewhere else under different names, waiting for their turn to be "stolen"? I didn't know what Sanders did for a living, but it took a hunk of change to board a horse at a facility like Foxdale and keep it active on the show circuit. Sanders never wore anything that wasn't top-of-the-line, and the Mitsubishi 3000GT he owned had to have cost him a bundle, not to mention the money he shelled out entertaining the string of young women he brought to the farm. Then again, maybe they didn't cost him much.

"So, what you wantin' to know all this for?" Irons said.

I looked at the tightness around his eyes and the heavy lines crinkling his face. "I'll tell you when I know more."

"Tell me now."

I shook my head. "When I know more."

I checked that everything was running smoothly in the barns, then drove home. Greg's vetmobile was parked at the barn entrance with the compartment doors popped open. As I headed for the steps, he walked out of the barn and set a stainless steel bucket on the gravel.

He flipped a towel off his shoulder and wiped his hands. "Cuttin' out early?"

"Nah. I'm heading back in a couple minutes." I crossed the lot and stood alongside the back bumper. "Remember Victor Sanders' horse? That steel gray draft cross that got stolen?"

Greg frowned as he uncapped a green bottle and squirted some sharp-smelling disinfectant into the bucket. He stretched the hose out of the back of the truck and lifted a dental float out of the sudsy water. "Vaguely."

I told him my theory while he hosed off and dried the floats and stowed them in a bin.

He shook his head. "I don't know, Steve. Lots of horses have quirks like that, and now that the horse isn't around anymore, there's no way to prove it was the same one that was stolen from Ironsie's place."

Ironsie? "Well," I said, "I'll let the insurance company know, and they can take it from there."

I took the steps two at a time. When I reached the deck, I glanced over my shoulder. Greg had let the hose recoil back into the storage area under the compartment, and as he closed the lid, he looked up at me, his expression thoughtful.

I flipped through the clutter in the junk drawer until I found the packet Marilyn had sent me. I unfolded the copy of Sanders' insurance policy and smoothed out the pages on the countertop. On the first page of the mortality insurance application, question number fourteen asked: "Have you filed an insurance claim in the past three years for any of the proposed horses?" Sanders had answered no.

I got Marilyn's number from her brother and told her what I'd learned.

"And you said the company's name was…?"

"Liberty South." I gave her the agent's name. "What will happen now?"

"We'll contact them," she said. "Start an investigation. If we can't prove it was the same horse, or that he was involved in the thefts…I don't know. Maybe we can get him for intent to defraud." She sighed. "Depends on what we find."

Around five-thirty, I went into the lounge, snagged three sodas from the caterer, and walked over to the main dressage arena. Most of the auditors were clustered around the clinician who, according to Rachel, was short-listed for the Olympics.

Michael Burke was his name, and he was younger than I'd expected, somewhere in his late twenties, early thirties, and soft-spoken. He was slouched in his chair with his feet propped on an arena marker, his fingers laced together over his stomach. He'd tipped his cowboy hat low on his forehead and looked half asleep as he watched a rider guide her big chestnut across the diagonal in a leg yield.

When I scooted an empty chair up close behind Rachel's and sat down, she smiled slightly, and I knew she'd seen me. I passed the Coke over to Michael, then handed her a root beer.

"Keep the front of the horse straight," Michael called to the rider. "Point his nose at F and push his haunches to the outside."

I settled back into my seat. The girl on the chestnut straightened her horse at F, then guided him through the corner.

"Better," Michael said.

I popped the tab on my Coke and waited for the fizz to dissipate. Rachel had a yellow legal pad balanced on her thigh, and she'd been taking notes with a pink ink pen. Her handwriting was neat and precise and loopy and reminded me of love letters furtively passed in an afternoon geometry class.

As I looked up from the page, Elsa walked around the row of chairs and stopped in front of Michael. I glanced at Rachel's profile, then studied the Coke can in my hand. I took a gulp and glanced sideways at them.

Mrs. Timbrook was wearing a man's dress shirt. The sleeves were rolled up, and she'd twisted the shirttails together and knotted them above her navel. She hadn't bothered with the buttons.

Or a bra.

She leaned forward to offer Michael a food tray from the caterer, and I almost choked. I shifted in my seat and looked across the front field toward the old Ritter farm.

The scrapers had finished cutting and reshaping the land, and earlier that morning, the graders had begun smoothing gravel along the cul-de-sacs.

Elsa squeezed a chair into the space next to Michael and sat down.

I risked another glance. Michael was pretty much ignoring her, but Rachel's eyebrows were bunched together, and her lips were pursed as if she'd eaten something sour.

The close proximity was suddenly too much.

I got up and left.

In barn B, halfway down the aisle near the cut-through to the arena, I slouched onto a hay bale and leaned against a stall front. The barn was cool and dark, and as I sat there, listening to the slow, measured breaths of the horse dozing in the stall behind me, I was fairly certain I was the only one in the barn except, of course, for the horses. I finished the Coke, crumpled the can, and tossed it at the trash can positioned just inside the boarders' tack room. It bounced hollowly off the rim and rolled across the asphalt.

In the square of bright light at the end of the long aisle, Michael crossed the expanse of asphalt that shimmered under the late afternoon sun.

I pushed myself off the hay bale and picked up the can as Elsa passed the doorway. And she wasn't heading to her barn.

Chapter 17

The final ride of the evening was followed by a party of sorts. When the last of the participants headed for their lodgings, I walked through the barns. I had just finished checking on the clinic horses when Michael and Rachel entered the barn together.

She was gazing up at him with a faint smile on her lips. Her hair bounced on her shoulders when she nodded in response to something he'd said. I watched her with an odd mixture of love and sadness. I no longer cared that I'd gone from attraction to infatuation to love faster than was healthy. I loved her, and if she didn't feel the same, then I would just have to hope she'd catch up.

She said something I couldn't hear.

"That's right," Michael said, "and eventually the horse will respond to the release, which is absolutely phenomenal."

She smiled at him and brushed the bangs from her eyes. "I can imagine."

"Ask for a little shoulder-in and counter bending to get him soft, and like I said earlier, do lots of transitions within the gait to keep him focused."

I turned away from them and stared at one of the clinic horses without really seeing him.

They paused alongside me. "Rachel tells me you're going to lock the place up tonight."

"Yep."

"I'm going to sleep in the trailer. That okay?"

I jerked my head around. "You're kidding?"

"No. I always ask for the hotel's rate to be paid directly to me, so if I want to cut corners and keep the money myself, I can. Right now, every penny counts, and I'm used to sleeping just about anywhere....Don't look so surprised. Even with good sponsors, I'm still scrambling to pay the bills."

The thought of Michael staying on the grounds overnight normally wouldn't have bothered me one little bit. But nowadays...I could just see it: "Top Dressage Instructor Murdered at Local Horse Farm: Details Inside."

No one expects trouble until it's too late. I'm sure that woman in Pennsylvania never thought something so horrible would happen to her.

"You're welcome to stay in my apartment," I said. "I don't have a spare bed, but you could use my sleeping bag."

"I have one, but that's okay. I'll be comfortable enough in the trailer."

"It still gets cold at night, especially after midnight."

"I'm used to it."

"You'll be more comfortable in the apartment, even on the floor. In the morning, I'll drive you back whenever you want."

Michael frowned. "Do I have time to squeeze in a ride?" His face was flat, without emotion, but there was an edge to his voice that I hadn't heard before.

"Sure," I said.

"Your apartment it is, then." Michael spun around and walked down the aisle to get his bay horse ready.

He'd hauled two of his horses with him, and he'd only had time to work one of them during his lunch break.

Rachel stepped closer and peered at my face. "Is everything okay? You seem," she shrugged, "I don't know, tense."

"Not me." I jerked my head in Michael's direction. "You're impressed with him, aren't you?"

"He's great. Very insightful. He picks up on everything, the smallest detail. Everyone wa—" She frowned. "You're jealous."

"No, I'm not."

"Yes, you are."

When I didn't respond, Rachel slid her arms around my waist and pulled me against her. I grabbed a handful of her silky dark hair and kissed her hard on the mouth. There was a subtle shift in her demeanor, and it took me a minute to realize what it was. She may have been taken off guard, but she wasn't scared. Wasn't backed off by so much overt, irrepressible emotion.

She rested her head on my chest. Her mussed hair brushed against my chin. I kissed her sweet-smelling hair and whispered, half afraid to say it out loud, "I love you, Rachel."

She slowly lifted her head. Her eyes were dark and unreadable. "But you don't really know me."

"I know you well enough."

She slid her arms up my back and pulled me down to her level. She kissed me with passion, and I felt relief flood through my body. Maybe I wasn't totally off base after all.

I could have stayed there all night, but Michael, looking somewhat amused, wordlessly led his horse down the aisle and broke the spell.

Rachel stepped back and combed her fingers through her hair. "I'd better go, or I'll end up falling asleep on the drive home."

We walked out of the barn and headed down the lane. As we stepped beyond the protection of the buildings, a westerly breeze cut across the parking lot. Rachel wrapped her sweater tighter around her chest. Before she unlocked the door, she turned to face me, and I took her into my arms and kissed her again.

I wanted her so bad, I hurt, but I needed to stay in control. If all she felt from me was lust, she wouldn't believe in the love, and I wouldn't blame her.

Easier said than done.

She felt perfect in my arms, a perfect fit with all those wonderful curves that are so uniquely female. I stopped before I blew it, but she was smiling just the same. Amazing how the slightest tension, a subtle movement, little more than thought, could be sensed by an observant partner. I said good night before the love turned into good old-fashioned lust.

I watched her taillights disappear around a curve. She hadn't said "I love you." Not yet.

But I could wait.

Wait forever.

I didn't have to wait for Michael. By the time I'd finished checking the buildings, he was ready to go. I dumped his gear in the bed of my truck and cleared a space on the front seat. He climbed in without comment, and I drove past the gates.

After I'd locked them and pulled onto Rocky Ford, Michael said, "They must be a nuisance."

"Yes, but a necessary one."

He looked at me for a moment, then changed the subject. "That woman, the one who brought my dinner. She's a trip."

I grinned. "She is that. I saw her follow you to the barn. How'd you get rid of her?" I asked because Michael had returned to the arena almost immediately.

Michael chuckled. "I told her I preferred men…"

My fingers tightened on the steering wheel. "And do you?"

He chuckled. "Shit, no. Don't have a coronary on me, now." He leaned back in his seat and yawned. "I've dealt with women like her before. It's a weird sort of groupie thing. As soon as you're even moderately well-known, they put the make on you. Young girls, too."

My eyebrows rose. "I had no idea."

"Oh, I don't know about that. She got to you, didn't she?"

I glanced at him, and the Chevy's back tire dropped off the edge of the road. I gripped the steering wheel hard and dragged the truck back onto the pavement.

"Why do you think that?" If he could see it, so could everyone else. So could Rachel.

"I saw your face when you first caught sight of her. You looked, well…like you do now."

I sighed. "I didn't realize it was so obvious."

"Oh, don't get me wrong. It was just a timing thing. After that initial look of pure terror, I wouldn't have suspected a thing. Let's put it this way. I knew something was up, just didn't know what." He chuckled. "I was hard pressed to keep a straight face when I saw what had you shittin' your pants."

I groaned.

"She's somethin' else, I'll say that." He shook his head and shifted on the seat. "Enough to make you come just lookin' at her."

She was that.

"I take it Rachel doesn't know?" he said.

"No."

"Hmm. How many times?"

"Once."

He shrugged. "Maybe you'll be okay."

"I don't know." I slowed as we approached a sharp curve. "Girls are funny about stuff like that."

"True. It wouldn't do any good to tell her, but…Well, I wouldn't trust that woman. She might tell Rachel herself, or do something to make it obvious. Hell, she might even make it out to be more than it was."

Like those thoughts hadn't been squirreling round my head ever since that night in the feed room. I couldn't walk in there without thinking about it, though most of the time, I'd go over the entire encounter in my head and get horny as hell. Other times I'd walk in there and feel claustrophobic.

"Why didn't you, uh…take advantage of the opportunity?" I said.

"I'm serious about someone right now, plus, you do that too much, you end up with a reputation you—"

"You keep using your particular put-off, you'll have a different reputation to contend with."

"Come on, Steve. Don't you know that in this business, if you aren't a steer-ropin', tobacco-spittin', boot-stompin' cowboy, you've probably got that reputation already?"

I grinned.

I pulled into the parking space behind the foaling barn and turned off the engine. Since all the mares had foaled, Greg's foaling man no longer worked nights. The barn was dark.

"You don't," Michael said, "live in a barn?"

"Uh-huh."

"Jesus. I gave up sleeping in the trailer for this?"

"'Fraid so."

He jerked up on the door handle with more force than necessary and hopped out. His expectations rose slightly as we climbed the steps to the loft. The view across the horse pastures, even at night, was awe-inspiring. The moon had just crested the tree line and looked huge. A swath of white glimmered on the lake.

I opened the door and turned on the lights.

Michael stepped through the doorway and paused. "Well, who'd've thought?" He dumped his duffel bag on the floor and took off his jacket. "Nice place. No privacy though. You ever gonna hang curtains?"

"One day."

"I feel like I'm in a goddamned fish bowl." He walked into the living room/bedroom. "You have something against furniture, too?"

"Hardly."

Michael snorted.

"When it comes down to spending money on something to sit on or something to eat, I'll choose eat every time. Speaking of which…" I rummaged through the cabinets and settled on Spicy Doritos and microwaveable popcorn. I plunked two cans of Coke and the bag of chips on the island counter and filled two glasses with ice.

"What's this about?" Michael said.

A stack of fliers I hadn't gotten around to giving Greg was lying on top of a pile of magazines. Michael held one in his hand.

I told him about James Peters and the thefts and about Pennsylvania, then I asked him if he'd heard of anything that sounded even remotely related.

He shook his head as he gathered up the sheets and tapped them down on the countertop until they were organized into a neat pile. "No wonder you were so pigheaded about me sleeping in the trailer?"

"Yeah, well, now you know." I looked down at the popcorn in my hand and was no longer hungry. I dumped it in the trash.

"This guy, Peters. They didn't have to kill him, did they?" Michael said. "Not unless he could identify them." He ran his fingers up and down the smooth, cold surface of his glass. The ice shifted and settled. "They've got to have some horse connections, too. Some outlet for getting rid of the horses they take, and the tack. But you didn't recognize them?"

"No, but they were wearing masks." I stood abruptly. "I'm going to take a shower."

He glanced up at me and frowned. "Can I use your weights? Sitting all day drives me nuts."

"Sure," I said. "Want some music on?"

"What kind?"

"Pick something out."

He checked what was in the CD player and said it would do. When he turned it on, the volume was cranked way up.

He fumbled with the knobs and turned it down. "You deaf?"

"What?"

He grinned and shook his head. "At this rate, you'll be deaf by the time you're fifty."

"Yeah, well, what if I die when I'm forty-nine, and I've gone through life keeping the volume down to save my hearing?"

"You're crazy."

"So I've been told."

When I got out of the shower, Michael was finishing up a set. His hair was damp, and sweat glistened on his skin. He settled the bar in the rack and sat up. "Were you expecting company?"

"No." I glanced at the clock on the stove. It was well after midnight. "Why?"

He shrugged. "I heard a noise and thought there was someone on the deck, but—"

"How long ago?" My voice sounded tight.

"Five minutes, maybe less."

I yanked on my sneakers, grabbed a flashlight, and pushed through the kitchen door with Michael on my heels. I took the stairs two at a time and switched on the barn lights. The metal bracket by the light switch was empty.

"Shit." I spun around and almost knocked into Michael.

"What's wrong?" he said.

"Fire extinguisher's gone."

I scanned the parking lot, then ran around the corner of the barn and shone the light along the fence line. No fire extinguisher. I ran part-way down the narrow lawn between the fence and barn and panned the light across the grass. The extinguisher was lying in the darker shadows along the barn's foundation. I tossed the flashlight to Michael, scooped up the extinguisher, and ran into the barn aisle.

I stopped abruptly. "Do you smell that?"

Michael nodded. His face was pale.

The horses were out for the night. All the stall doors were open, and nothing looked out of place.

I turned slowly toward the feed room door, then flattened my palm on the smooth wood. It was cool to the touch. I put my hand on the doorknob. The metal felt warm against my skin, and I wondered if it was my imagination.

I stood to the side and opened the door.

A fire was smoldering in the far corner of the room. It flared with the inrush of air. Flames shot up the wall as I fumbled with the extinguisher's seal. I pulled out the pin and aimed the nozzle at the base of the fire. When the foam hit the flames, they hissed and billowed upward.

I yelled at Michael, "Run down the other end of the barn and see if that extinguisher's still there."

He took off, his face no longer white but orange in the fire's glow.

I gagged on the smoke.

I had never used an extinguisher before and had no idea how long it would last. I crouched down where the air was a bit clearer and squinted through the smoke. The heat was intense on my bare skin. I inched back toward the door. Greg didn't need this. And where the hell was Michael?

"Come on, Michael!" I yelled.

The extinguisher sputtered.

"Come on, damn it."

The light bulb in the ceiling fixture exploded, and I jumped.

Damn it, what was taking him so long?

Michael stepped through the doorway with the extinguisher in his hand. His face was covered with sweat, and he was out of breath. He fumbled with the pin.

A ceiling panel curled downward, then fell softly to the floor, bringing with it a shower of sparks. Michael got his extinguisher going just as mine emptied out.

"I'll be right back," I yelled.

I ran down the aisle and skidded to a stop alongside the spigot. I turned the pressure on full and ran backward, uncoiling the hose as I went. Michael was holding his own, but the fire was stubborn. I turned the nozzle full-on. The water sizzled when it hit the flames, and smoke mushroomed toward us. We backed up.

When the last of the fire was out, the barn was suddenly quiet except for our breathing and the sound of water dripping off the joists. We stared in at the gutted feed room as a stream of black water spread past our feet and meandered down the barn aisle.

I set the hose down.

Michael's sweat pants and shirt were streaked with soot. His face, too. I looked down at my bare chest and arms and legs, at my shorts that had once been white but would never be again and started to giggle. In a minute or two, we were both laughing so hard, my side hurt.

Michael set his extinguisher at the base of the wall and shivered. "God, that was awful."

I took a deep breath, which brought on a spasm of coughing. I nodded and braced my hands against the wall. When I caught my breath, I said, "Do you remember what the person looked like?"

"Hell, I wasn't even sure there was a person. It was more an impression that someone was there, it was that quick."

I went back into the feed room and examined the damage which, to my untrained eyes, appeared superficial. "They must not have planned this," I said.

"Why do you think that?"

"If they had, we wouldn't have had a prayer of stopping it ourselves." Or getting out alive, but I didn't say that. "They would have brought gasoline or something like it to speed up the process. Greg, the guy who owns this place, is fanatical about keeping the barn neat. He doesn't stockpile any chemicals or hay or let piles of junk accumulate around the barn. The fire hadn't spread much before I opened the door."

"What do you think they were planning?"

"I don't know."

He snorted. "When they saw you had company, they changed their plans."

I blinked.

"God, Steve. You'd better watch your back."

I rubbed my face. I didn't feel safe at work, not at night anyway, and now I wouldn't feel safe in my own home. Not until Ralston rounded them up. We went upstairs where I phoned Greg and told him to come down to the foaling barn. He didn't ask why.

We met in the parking lot. When he was close enough to see us, his face went white.

"What the hell?"

"Someone started a fire in the feed room."

He skirted past me and stopped in the doorway. He looked relieved, as well he might. "How do you know it wasn't electrical?"

"The fire extinguishers were outside," I said, "in the grass."

His face paled even more. He looked back into the feed room and muttered, "God."

That just about summed it up.

When Greg turned around, he seemed to notice Michael for the first time. I made introductions. Greg was still dressed in the navy blue coveralls he wore to work.

"How long have you been home?" I said.

"About an hour. Had an emergency colic."

"Did you notice any vehicles parked where they shouldn't have been? Anything that strikes you odd, now?"

He shook his head. "No. To tell the truth, I was half asleep. Three nights in a row I've been out on calls. If I'd seen anything unusual, I would've checked it out."

"No! Don't!"

They both looked at me in surprise, then Greg with understanding.

"You, more than anyone, ought to know." Greg stepped back into the feed room and tested the phone. The line ran up the wall along the doorjamb, and it still worked. He called the police.

Michael turned to me. "What did he mean by 'you ought to know'?"

I shrugged. "Beats me."

"You're a terrible liar, you know that?"

"No, I'm not."

"Yes, you are."

I crossed my arms over my chest. "Damn, it's cold."

Michael chuckled. "Stop changing the subject."

Greg stepped out of the feed room and gave him a look that shut him up pretty quick. Michael looked at the floor and cleared his throat. I suggested we go upstairs.

The authorities arrived in time, poked around the feed room, took statements, then left, leaving behind a clutter of empty coffee mugs and soft drink cans.

I picked the empties off the counter and tossed them in the trash. "I'm sorry about all this, Greg."

"It wasn't your fault. Hell, your quick reactions kept the whole barn from burning down." He stood up and stretched. "If you're worried about sleeping here, you could stay at the house for a while."

I thanked him for his offer but declined immediately. The skin around his eyes seemed to relax, and I realized he was relieved. His good nature had moved him to ask, but if danger was following me around, his house was the last place I should be. More than anything, he had his kids to think about.

Greg yawned. "What about your parents'?"

"I'll work something out." I had no clue what it would be.

Chapter 18

It was three-thirty by the time Greg headed home. I asked Michael if he still wanted to go in early.

"Might as well," he said. "Too late to get any sleep now."

He was right, of course. "Should have gone to a hotel, huh?"

"Damn right…but I'm glad I didn't."

"Why, for Christ's sake?"

"If we weren't talking, if I hadn't thought I'd seen someone on the deck, you might have been asleep when the fire broke out…or when they came through the door."

I didn't say anything.

I scrambled some eggs while Michael toasted half a loaf of bread.

When he'd downed his third slice, he said, "You trust your landlord?"

"What?"

"You said he knows some of the players. Maybe he's involved. Maybe he—"

"No way. You don't know what you're talking about. Plus, it's only natural that he'd know a lot of people in the industry."

Michael shrugged.

"He even offered me a place to stay."

"Sure. Forget it. Like you said, I don't know him. You going to tell Rachel what happened?"

"I don't think so."

"You should. She's a nice girl, and she cares for you, but she doesn't like it when you keep things from her. Especially your feelings. She senses that you're holding out on her, so—"

"How come *you* know so much?"

"We talked. Anyway," Michael continued, "I fixed it for you."

I lowered the glass of orange juice from my lips. "What, exactly, did you fix?"

"Let's see." He propped his elbows on the counter and yawned. "I told her that you're naturally reticent. That you avoid anything that even slightly resembles pity, that you have a major fear of failure despite the fact that you can't resist taking risks. You have an overwhelming desire to prove yourself. Oh, and you're embarrassed by strong emotions." He looked over the rim of his coffee mug. "And, your mouth's open."

I shut it. "Where the hell'd you come up with that load of crap?"

"Observing you. I took psych before I left school. Ultimately, I found that I prefer horses to most people. They're much nicer to work with."

"Good thing you gave it up. You're lousy at it."

"Not true." He wiped the corners of his mouth with his fingertips. "Keep that girl, Steve. And let her in more."

"Yes, sir."

I jammed my last bite of toast in my mouth and dumped the dishes in the sink. "Let's hit the road."

Michael frowned at his half-full cup of coffee. "Why the rush?"

"I want to check the farm, make sure your horses are okay."

He jumped up, and I saw that my alarm was infectious. "I now see why you've pursued an offensive."

At Foxdale, everything was secure. I fixed myself a cup of coffee and watched Michael run a quick brush over the horse's coat before sliding the saddle into place, seeing firsthand that the perfection evident in his horses' grooming had nothing to do with his efforts but with his groom's. When he led the chestnut down to the outdoor arena, I slumped onto a bench. My eyelids felt like sandpaper, and my head ached.

I closed my eyes and thought of all that had happened since that frigid morning in February. The three men and the fear they had wielded like a weapon. The horses on a fast trip to death. Sanders and his questionable remorse over a horse he'd thought of as an object and had been careful to insure. Harrison's driver and his drunken anger. Blood dripping from my nose. The bulldozers' throaty rumble as they cut into the brown earth and the realization that Foxdale would never be the same. Boris hanging from the rafters, his life blood draining from a slash in his throat.

I remembered the deafening sound of the cold rain hammering on the barn roof as I stared at the pile of charred wood that had once been an artful jump. The words "*Your dead motherfucker*" painted in red on ribbed metal siding and later, "Cats have nine lives. You don't" scrawled over my name. Tax write-offs and staring at newspaper clippings until my vision blurred.

I thought about James S. Peters in the cold hard ground and Mrs. Peters losing herself to senility, the mind's reflex to unbearable pain. Whitcombe's irritability building to the point of instability. Brian's probation hanging over his head like a scythe. Elsa and Rachel, lust and love. Flip sides of the need for intimacy.

I thought about the trailer search and how it had been thwarted by the Pennsylvania registration. And Randor L. Drake who appeared innocent but couldn't be. And where was he? Had he crouched over a pile of feed bags in Greg's barn and struck his match, or was he stalking rainbow trout in West Virginia?

Had he been in Pennsylvania last week? In a barn set back off the road?

I was thinking that I should call Ralston for an update when Rachel walked down the lane. She had arrived early, presumably to watch Michael ride his Olympic-caliber horse. I stood as she approached.

She flattened her hand on my chest. "Hey there, cutie."

I enveloped her in my arms and gave her a kiss that she encouraged and allowed to linger. All the possibilities were there.

Her hair was still damp from her shower and smelled of apples. I slid my hands over the swell of her buttocks. When I pulled her tight against me, I felt her grin and realized she had noticed the intense, physical reaction her closeness had generated.

Behind us, Michael and his wonder horse executed a ten meter circle at the trot, just the other side of the fence. After their third revolution, I looked up as they came close to the fence on yet another pass. Michael grinned and cued his horse into a canter.

On their next circuit, I mouthed, "Go get some of your own."

Apparently, he wasn't finished.

"He needed that," he yelled to Rachel, and then to me, "Tell her about last night."

Rachel tilted her head back and peered up at me. "What?"

"Umm." I kissed her face somewhere in the vicinity of her left eyebrow. "Someone started a fire in Greg's feed room."

"Oh, no." She leaned back so she could see my face better.

"Luckily there wasn't much damage," I said. "Michael and I were able to put it out quickly."

"Were any of the horses in the barn?"

"No, it was empty," I said.

"Not entirely."

"What do you mean?"

"You were in the barn. A little later, and you might have been asleep." She shivered. "And I see you've already thought of that."

"Uh-huh."

"Oh, Steve."

She tightened her arms around my waist. I felt comforted by her embrace and, best of all, wanted.

Maybe the fire had been a random act, some pyromaniac doing his thing. But they typically chose empty structures to torch.

They didn't check to make sure you were home first.

During my lunch break, I called Detective Ralston and was told he was still in Pennsylvania. I drove into town and purchased a heavy-duty dead bolt for the kitchen door. The second item took more effort to locate, but with the help of a knowledgeable salesclerk at an electronics store, I found a smoke/heat detector with a remote alarm. I installed the lock, but left the rest for later.

What I really needed was a gun. But I hated them. Always had. My father had one, and I still remembered the afternoon when I'd discovered it in his dresser, hidden beneath a stack of undershirts. I couldn't have been much older than seven. I had been surprised by its weight and the coldness of the black steel against my palm. It made me cold just thinking about it.

I made it back to work a little after two. Michael was slouched in a lawn chair with his cowboy hat pulled low on his forehead, and I wondered how he was holding up. I stopped in the office on my way to the barns. Mrs. Hill was on the phone, so I checked my bin. It was empty. The door behind me opened. Elsa Timbrook had her manicured hand on the doorknob. Her blond hair was gathered high on the back of her head and hung in curls down her neck. She glanced at me as she stepped into the room.

My initial impulse was to hightail it out of there, but I intercepted her instead. "Mrs. Timbrook?"

She ran the tip of her tongue across her lips. "Elsa," she said.

"You never answered me the other night," I said. "How do you know the guy I got into a fight with at the party—Mr. Harrison's driver?" When she didn't respond, I checked that Mrs. Hill was still on the phone, then said, "Please. It may be important."

She shifted a bulky canvas tote from one hand to the other and studied me with her smoky green eyes.

I waited.

She smoothed a finger down the side of her nose.

After a pause, in which I was certain she wasn't going to tell me, she said, "Robby's my brother."

"Your brother?"

Elsa nodded and clasped the tote's straps with both hands. The canvas rested against her bare thighs. Tightly rolled bandages for doing up her horse's legs stuck out from the depths of the bag. T&T Industries was embroidered diagonally across the tote. "Johnny, too."

I frowned. "You mean John Harrison?"

She nodded.

"You said Robby was dangerous. In what way?"

"They both are. But Robby…He's smart and he's sneaky, and he always gets what he wants." She brushed a strand of hair off her forehead. "And it doesn't matter who or what gets in his way."

I'd heard of one other Harrison. A name from the past. James Peters' past. "What's your father's name?"

She frowned. "John, Senior. Why?"

"Does he go by a nickname?" I said.

"Most people call him Buddy."

I gestured toward her tote. "What's T&T stand for?" I'd seen the logo somewhere before but couldn't place it.

Her hands clutched at the straps, and I had a sudden impression she was holding her breath. She glanced at the blue and gold letters. "I don't know. I got this from a friend."

Elsa excused herself, and as I watched her push through the door into the lounge, I remembered what Nick had said about Sanders. That he'd boarded his horse with Harrison before he'd moved it to Foxdale. Then, at the party, Sanders and Robby had argued, and I would have loved to have known what it had been about.

"I'm glad you're back," Mrs. Hill said before the receiver had come fully to rest in the cradle. She leaned back, and her chair's springs squeaked under the strain. "Mr. Ambrose has hired a security service."

"You're kidding?"

She shook her head and smiled broadly. "Someone will report in each night around ten and leave at six. Can you meet him tonight and show him around?"

"Sure. Will he be armed?"

"No." She picked up a piece of hard candy and rolled it between her fingers. "And think of any instructions you want to give him."

I stepped outside, paused, then leaned back into the office.

Mrs. Hill looked up from her paperwork.

"Thanks," I said.

She beamed at me, then waved me off.

I walked down to the barns and found that the crew was in the middle of turnouts. I led a bay gelding into the farthest paddock and turned him to face the gate. He stood perfectly still, his noble head held high as he waited for me to release him. When I slipped the chain from his halter, he wheeled around. His hindquarters bunched, and he propelled himself away from me, stretching full out, his hooves kicking up clods of earth. I draped the lead over my shoulder and walked back up the hill.

As I neared the barns, the scent of freshly mown grass and damp soil was replaced by the sharp odor of horses and the lighter fragrance of liniments that drifted from the wash racks. It occurred to me, then, that I hadn't felt this carefree in weeks. We now had a guard, and I assumed it was only a matter of time before Ralston had someone in custody.

After the last horse had been turned out, I drove to the construction site's wide dirt entrance. Dozers, backhoes, loaders, and a scraper or two were parked in a line beyond the trailer office. Sunday afternoon, the door was locked up tight, the equipment idle. I left the truck running and crossed the rough ground to the sign at the edge of the road. "Huntfield Estates," it read. "Luxury homes on one to three acre lots." It went on to list details, options, a 1-800 number, and in the lower right hand corner, "T&T Industries" was printed in blue and gold.

First Elsa's bag, now this. Yet, I was certain I'd seen it before. But where?

After work, I made it to the library five minutes before they locked the doors for the night. When I got home, I picked up the phone and flipped through the pages of my notebook until I found the number for James Peters' nephew. I punched in his number.

When he answered, I told him who I was and said, "Do you remember the name of the company that's developing the land that used to belong to your uncle?"

"No. Not offhand. Some kind of initials. Oh, wait a sec. There was something about the name, made me think of…Oh, yeah. Something to do with explosives. Something like that."

I exhaled through my mouth. "T&T Industries?"

"Yeah." I could almost see him nod. "That's it."

Despite having been up all of Saturday night, I spent most of Sunday night lying awake in the dark. Around three in the morning, I woke from a restless sleep and remembered where I'd first seen T&T Industries.

When I called Detective Ralston at seven o'clock Monday morning, I was told he was unavailable. I left a message for him to call me ASAP and got through the morning's work on auto pilot. During my lunch break, the phone rang in the office, and the answering machine picked up. I half-listened to a voice I didn't recognize. It took me a second to realize the message was for me and that the voice belonged to Ralston. I swallowed the last bite of my ham and cheese sandwich and snatched up the phone.

"Steve here."

"Officer Dorsett told me you mailed out a bunch of letters about the truck and trailer last week," Ralston said.

"Yeah, but—"

"You shouldn't have done that," he snapped.

"What does it matter? We found the trailer."

There was a long pause before he said, "I wish you'd talked to me first because I don't think Drake's trailer's the one."

"It is. I'm one hundred percent certain. Have you found him yet?"

"Maybe it is the trailer, but we haven't found the men who are behind it, and that letter was just plain stupid."

I clenched the phone cord in my hand. I wanted to scream that somebody had to do something, that he didn't know shit about what it felt like to be a target. I clamped down on my anger and said, "What about Drake? Have you talked to him?"

"I just finished interviewing him. He has an iron-clad alibi which I've already verified with his C.O. Every weekend a trailer was used in a theft, he was on duty."

"What about what happened in Pennsylvania?"

"He backed up his fishing trip with receipts for gas, food, and lodging. He was in West Virginia, all right."

"So," I heard the bite in my voice but didn't care, "he's lending the trailer to a buddy."

"That's a possibility I'm working on. But I tell you, Steve, it doesn't feel like it. In your own words, the guy's clueless."

"Who's the trailer registered to?"

Papers rustled in the background. "Laura Anne Covington, Drake's girlfriend. Mean anything to you?"

"No." I sat on the edge of Mrs. Hill's desk. "But I know who owns the truck—"

"What?"

"—and I think I know why they're going after Foxdale."
After a brief pause, I said, "Do you remember a guy named
Sanders, one of the owners who had his horse stolen back in
February?"

"Yes."

"I'm pretty sure he arranged for the theft or at least made
sure his horse was targeted by the thieves." I told Ralston
how he'd owned a horse that was stolen from a Carroll County
farm, and how I suspected that the same horse had ended up
at Foxdale two years later where it was stolen again. "He's
been making a habit of scamming insurance companies, and I
bet I know who helped him. In between the Carroll County
farm and Foxdale, he boarded his horse with our hay dealer,
John Harrison. Harrison's not above pulling scams of his own."

I told him how he and his brother had doctored the hay
invoices and that their own sister had warned me that they
were dangerous. "Her name's Elsa Timbrook. I checked the
files at the library. Her husband is part owner of a land
development company called T&T Industries. Remember
when you said that the obvious is often the most likely?"

"Yeah."

"Well, Foxdale sits on five hundred prime acres that back
up to the Patuxent River State Park, and—"

"The same park where Peters' body was found," Ralston
said.

"Yeah. Eighteen miles northwest from here. I checked,
but I think that was just a coincidence or an indicator that
they know the area. Anyway, over the past year or so, realtors
have been pressuring Foxdale to sell. The farm next door
already sold out and is being developed by—"

"T&T Industries," Ralston said.

"Yep."

"And the truck?"

"T&T industries owns a white, dual-axle pickup. It was
on your MVA list."

Ralston snorted.

"My guess is that Mr. Timbrook, knowing full well what kind of scum his wife's brothers are, went to them when he needed someone to damage Foxdale in an effort to force the owner to sell out. And if Harrison's been teaming up with Sanders in the insurance swindles like I think he has, it would only be natural for him to fall back on stealing horses as a way to shake up the boarders. Only problem is, Timbrook didn't bargain on running into an owner who couldn't care less if his profit margin went down the tubes. And guess what?"

When Ralston didn't respond, I said, "Harrison's father, Buddy Harrison, used to deliver hay to James Peters' farm which, by the way, just so happens to border Piney Run Park. John Harrison might have delivered to him as well, but I couldn't verify that because Mrs. Peters' mind is stuck in the past. Anyway, the farm was sold and is now being subdivided and developed by T&T Industries."

"Damn."

"Ask Drake," I said, "if he knows John Harrison."

◇◇◇

The six o'clock lesson had just begun, and I was on my way home when Mrs. Hill flagged me down.

"It looks like you were right about Harrison," Detective Ralston said when I took the phone from Mrs. Hill.

I turned my back to her and leaned against a filing cabinet. "He's involved, then?"

"John Harrison is Drake's cousin."

I exhaled slowly. "So Drake knew all along."

"I'm not so sure about that. I *do* think your visit got him thinking. He admitted that his cousins borrowed his trailer from time to time, but he never suspected it was being used for something illegal. What is clear is that he's afraid of them. If he knows something incriminating, I doubt he'll tell us. I'm on my way over to the Harrison farm now. It belongs to their father, but both brothers still live there." He paused. "Do you know where it is?"

"No idea."

"Montgomery County, about eight miles west of where you escaped from the trailer."

I didn't say anything.

"I'll let you know what I find out." He hung up.

I lowered the receiver onto the cradle.

When I didn't move, Mrs. Hill looked up from her paperwork. "How'd the guard work out last night?" she said.

I smoothed my palms down my jeans. "Good."

She leaned back in her chair and waited for me to continue. I walked into the lounge and stood in front of the soda machine. My throat was dry. I fumbled the coins into the slot and pressed the Coke button. The can rattled into the slot at the bottom.

I didn't go home. I watched a little TV, bits and pieces of the next three lessons, and otherwise hung around until the guard came in at ten. When the barns cleared out shortly afterward, I accompanied the guard on his first walk-through of the night. Like he'd done the night before, he had ignored the sign at the entrance to the lane and had parked his vehicle outside the office door. That was fine by me. It was more visible there and would hopefully serve as a deterrent.

I watched him settle into Mrs. Hill's chair, then headed home. I turned into Greg's driveway and was halfway down the lane when headlights flashed in my rearview mirror.

My grip tightened on the steering wheel. I turned off the main drive and drove down the short lane that circled around behind the foaling barn. When the car made the turn, too, I pressed my foot down on the accelerator.

I swung the truck in a tight circle, spewing gravel across the vacant lot, and pointed its nose toward the lane. The Chevy's engine idled as the car moved into sight. As it entered the last curve, I noticed the shape and position of the head-lights and realized it was Ralston's Crown Vic. I backed into my spot and rolled up the windows while Ralston climbed out and waited by the Ford's back fender.

"I was on my way to Foxdale when I saw you pull out in front of me," he said, and it bothered me that I hadn't noticed I was being followed. He jerked his head toward the steps. "Can I come up?"

"Sure. Did you talk to Harrison?"

"That's what I want to talk about."

He seemed prepared to wait until we were inside before he filled me in. We went up the stairs in silence. I braced open the screen door with my thigh and flipped through my keys.

Ralston stood behind me and fidgeted. "What'n the hell do you have so many keys for? You need to keep your house and truck keys separate so you can find them faster. And you should have your key in your hand before you get out of the truck." He glanced over his shoulder. "And you should lock your truck. I noticed you didn't."

I quit flipping through the keys.

"And," Ralston said, "when you pull into the parking lot, here or at work, look around before you get out. If you think you're being followed, head for the nearest police station, or a fire station if it's closer. Someone's always there, day or night."

I stood with my arms stiff at my sides.

"Come on, Steve. Open the door." He bent down and peered at the lock. "Is this new?"

I nodded.

"Good choice. But both the door and jamb are wood. They're your weak link. It wouldn't take much to kick the door in, even with the dead bolt." He shifted his weight. "Come on."

I found the right key, unlocked the door, and switched on the lights.

Ralston scanned the loft. When he walked around the far side of the island counter, he kept his hand near his gun. The skin on my arms tingled. I leaned against the island counter and crossed my arms over my chest while he checked to make sure no one was hiding on the other side of my bed.

After he'd given the bathroom and closet a once over, he walked to the far end of the loft and looked toward the road.

With his back to me, he said, "If you feel the least bit insecure when you walk in here, or have a feeling that something's not right, leave immediately."

"They're gone, aren't they?" I said and couldn't keep the tension out of my voice.

Ralston walked back into the kitchen. "Don't know for sure. Guy who works for them said they canceled a delivery scheduled for today. Something about the semi being out of commission, but as far as he knew, they hadn't called out the mechanic they use."

"Damn."

Ralston looked at my face, and his expression softened. "Let's sit down."

He slid a stool around the corner of the counter and settled onto the vinyl cushion. I sat with my back to the windows, and only then did it register that he'd moved his stool so he was facing the door. I turned and looked at the long stretch of glass, black with the night, and felt apprehension settle into my chest like a block of ice.

"I want to set up a protective detail here." Ralston tapped his fingers on the edge of the counter. It was quiet in the loft, and the sound got on my nerves.

"You think they're gonna come after me?"

"It's a possibility I'd like to use to advantage."

"They might have been here already." I told him about the fire.

Ralston glared at me, and I suddenly felt like a little kid who'd been caught out.

"Why in the hell didn't you tell me about this before now?"

"You were in Pennsylvania."

His eyes narrowed. "I wasn't there today."

I didn't say anything, and after a minute or two, he propped his elbows on the counter and rubbed his face. The overhead lights reflected off his blond hair.

"How'd it go up there, anyway?" I said.

"They found her late yesterday. Got some good trace, even DNA, but—"

"She's dead?"

Ralston nodded. "I don't think her case is related. It felt staged. Too many differences in the MO, and no signature. My money's on the boyfriend."

"What's a signature?"

"A compulsive behavior the killer doesn't vary from victim to victim."

I frowned. "How could there be a signature if Peters is your only victim?"

"He isn't. There are two other cases in the computer that closely match the MO in the Peters case—David Rowe and Larry Jacob. Only difference is, they weren't part of the horse community."

My skin felt clammy. "They sound familiar, but I can't think…"

"They were on my list the first time I interviewed you, mixed in with the grain dealers and fence companies."

"What's the…signature?" I said but wasn't sure I wanted to know.

"They were all bound with baling twine and beaten, and their throats were cut."

I swallowed and looked at my hands. "Like Boris."

"What?"

"The cat. They cut the cat's throat, too." I looked at his face. "Why are you telling me this?"

"I want you to take your situation seriously."

"Shit. I do."

"Have you still been going to the farm early, before anyone else?"

"Yeah," I said, "but now there's a guard."

"I mean before the guard."

I shrugged. "I can't let them run my life."

"Just end it?"

I looked down at the countertop.

"Which security firm?"

"Eastfield," I said.

Ralston grunted.

"Was James Peters' throat cut?"

Ralston nodded.

"I didn't know."

"Only partial information's released to the press," Ralston said. "Comes in handy when you're interviewing suspects or flakes who confess to crimes they didn't commit." Ralston pulled a notepad from his jacket pocket. "Go over your schedule with me so I can start working this out."

I told him what my normal routine was like, and he suggested some changes I could live with.

"And I'll talk to your boss and suggest they switch to Reinholdt Security. They're more professional, and they're armed."

Ralston picked up the phone and punched in a number. I propped my elbows on the counter, jammed my fingers in my hair, and rested my forehead against my palms. I listened as he tried to make arrangements and realized from the tone of his voice that his plans weren't working out. When he slammed down the receiver, I flinched.

"You're going to have to stay somewhere else until I can get a team together," Ralston said. "I don't have enough to justify having a detail stationed here without convincing my superiors first. I can't get it arranged tonight, but I will."

"Is it that bad?"

"I don't know. I don't want to find out the hard way." He looked me straight in the eye. "And neither do you."

The loft was so quiet, I could hear the second hand on the stove clock clicking like a metronome.

"Is there somewhere else you can stay?" Ralston said.

"It's almost midnight. I'll be back at work in five hours. In the morning, I'll ask a guy at the farm if I can stay with him. I'm sure he'll let me, at least for a while."

He frowned, then lifted the phone off the hook and held it out to me. "Wake him up."

I called Marty, and he said he would unlock his door and that I was damn lucky he didn't have company. I smiled as I hung up and said, "It's arranged."

"Do you have my card?"

I shook my head.

He fished a card out of his wallet, wrote down his pager number and Dorsett's, and handed it to me. "Call either one of us directly if you're worried about something, even if it seems insignificant, okay? And key in 911 after your number if you're in trouble."

I nodded.

Chapter 19

I closed the door quietly behind me and waited for my eyes to adjust to the dark. The whir of a fan drifted from the half-opened door to Marty's bedroom. After a minute or so, I dumped my duffel bag on the floor by the sofa and walked into the kitchen. The sink was cluttered with dirty dishes, and a collapsed Budweiser 24-pack and Domino's pizza box lay on the floor by the trash can. Chocolate ice cream from the bottom of an empty half-gallon carton had seeped across the counter and puddled on the floor. The room smelled of onions and beer.

My muscles were tense, and a dull ache had settled behind my eyes. I snagged two beers from the fridge, downed one, then set the empty on the counter. I flicked off the light switch and carried the unopened can into the darkened living room.

I slumped down on Marty's sagging sofa. After I polished off the second beer, I undressed, then wedged a pillow against the armrest and lay down. I hadn't eaten since lunch and already had a buzz going.

The phone's ringing brought me slowly back to consciousness, like mist rising off the surface of a lake. I had been dreaming. A nice dream, too. I opened my eyes and at first couldn't remember where I was, or why. Couldn't tell, from how I felt, whether I had been asleep for minutes or hours.

Marty's voice, thick with sleep, drifted through the open bedroom door. "Steve, it's for you."

I reached over the armrest and picked up the phone.

"This is Larry Oaks from Eastfield Security. There's something wrong with one of the horses."

His voice sounded hoarse, and I wondered if he'd been asleep. "What do you mean?" I mumbled.

"It keeps trying to get up but can't," he said, "like it's stuck."

"Shit. Which horse?"

"I don't know. A brown one."

Each stall was numbered, information cards hung on every stall door, and he didn't know which one. It figured. "Which barn, then?"

"The one with the arena in it."

"Okay, I'll be right there." I hung up. If the horse was simply cast, it would probably be up and fine by the time I got there. But if it had been rolling around in its stall because it was colicky with gas pain and had gotten itself jammed in the angle between the stall wall and the floor, it was an emergency. Even if the horse managed to get to its feet, colic didn't just go away by itself.

I pulled on my socks and yanked my jeans off the back of the sofa. Something thunked onto the floor between the sofa and wall. I checked that my wallet hadn't fallen out, then finished getting dressed. When I walked over to the bedroom door to tell Marty where I was going, he was snoring over the drone of the fan. I left him alone and headed for the front door.

It was pouring, and my truck was parked halfway down the block. I borrowed Marty's poncho off his coat tree and sped down rain-slicked streets with only a moderate try at caution. When I got to Foxdale, the gate was locked. It would be. I had locked it myself. I left it standing open and parked between the guard's car and the office door. The clock on the dash read one-thirty. I hadn't been asleep long. No wonder my brain felt fuzzy.

Barn B's lights blazed in the night, and a shaft of fluorescent light streamed through the office door, laying a wide rectangular patch across the wet ground. I walked into the office, but the guard wasn't there. The lights in the lounge were off, the room still. I crossed over to the desk. A half-empty coffee cup sat on the blotter alongside a yellow legal pad. The guard had listed his rounds. The first one was at ten o'clock, and he'd noted my name alongside the time. The next round was at eleven. At 11:55, he'd printed my name and phone number—Marty's phone number, actually—from when I'd called to tell him how he could get in touch with me. The last entry read 12:25 a.m.

There was no mention of his call about the colic. I touched the side of the Styrofoam cup. It was room temperature.

I went back outside and ran down the lane to barn B, avoiding the largest puddles on the way. He wasn't in the aisle. I switched on all the lights and walked quickly down aisle one. None of the horses looked upset. Some were even dozing. They wouldn't be. Not if one of their own was in trouble. They'd be wide awake and excited. I'd seen it often enough. I cut through the arena and checked aisle two just to make sure. No one there, either. I flicked on the lights on my way out and decided to call Ralston. I jogged toward the office.

I slowed to a walk at the sidewalk, and when I did, I noticed that the light was on in the men's room. That explained it.

I pushed open the door and stepped inside.

"Anybody here?" My voice echoed off the bare walls as a thought nagged at the edge of my consciousness. Something that wasn't right. Something the guard had said, but I couldn't think what.

As I turned to leave, the curtain to the shower stall moved and Robby Harrison stepped into the room.

He lunged toward me, and I briefly glimpsed another figure behind him. My muscles tensed as I grabbed the handle and pulled the door inward.

I stopped. There was nowhere to go.

At the threshold stood Mr. John Harrison, hay dealer, horse trader, and, according to our farrier, "a creepy bastard." He had severely beaten a horse with a whip, and he'd gotten away with it. His arm was outstretched, pointed at my face, and in his hand, he held a gun. Rain drops glistened on the black metal.

Harrison took a step forward. I had no choice but to back up. He directed me backward until my shoulder blades hit the first stall.

I had only glimpsed his face. What held my undivided attention was the small, round hole at the end of his gun. As black and final as death itself.

He latched his fingers around my throat and pressed the muzzle into my scalp above my left ear. Pressure began to build across the bridge of my nose, and the veins in my neck throbbed. It wasn't until then that I clearly saw Harrison's face. His lips were pulled back from his teeth like an animal's, and his eyes were stretched wide and unblinking. In the fluorescent light, they looked black.

I didn't have a chance.

I slid my fingers into my pocket and felt for my knife. It wasn't there. I remembered the thud as something had dropped behind Marty's couch.

Harrison licked his lips. "It's about time you and I got together, Mr. Stephen fucking Cline. You got away from me once, but you damn well won't this time."

He was leaning on my neck so hard, I thought I was going to pass out.

"How's that feel Steve? Huh?"

He tightened his grip, and I tried to move.

"Uh-uh." He pressed the gun's muzzle harder against my skin. "Don't try anything. You ain't goin' nowhere. What you are gonna do is learn. You're gonna fucking learn about it tonight. About fear and pain." He laughed. "And I'm gonna teach you."

Bastard.

Without taking his gaze off me, Harrison spoke over his shoulder to the man I thought I recognized from that night back in February. "Rich, hand over the rope."

The guy held the rope out to Harrison.

"Not me, you idiot. Give it to Robby." He gestured to his brother. "Now, go back outside and stand guard."

The guy was nervous, not as comfortable with the job as his buddies, and most ominous of all, he wouldn't look me in the eye.

The door thumped closed, leaving the room suddenly quiet. Harrison turned back to me. "All I hear is Foxdale this and Foxdale that, and I was getting damn sick of it. People leaving my place and comin' here. Saying 'Steve Cline's done this, and he's done that, and isn't the place nice.' Enough to make you puke." He clenched his teeth. "So when somebody wanted me to mess with your precious Foxdale, you think I needed askin' twice?"

No one answered.

He moved his face closer to mine. I could smell his sweat. His breath stank of cigarettes and beer as it slid across my skin. I looked past his face to the door.

"Shit, no," Harrison continued. "I didn't need askin'. Hell, he didn't even have to pay me, you being such a prick and all, checking the hay like it was your own damn money you was partin' with. And if that wasn't enough," his voice vibrated with anger, "I see your stupid little announcement stuck up on the bulletin board like you're some kinda Dick Tracy, and I can't use my truck and trailer no more, and all because of you, you fucking piece of shit. Imagine what I thought," he coughed and choked on his spit, "when I get your fucking stupid letter in the mail."

I didn't say anything.

"I decided, then and there, that I was gonna kill you. Kill you and make you pay. Make you suffer."

Behind him, Robby stood in a wide-legged stance, jiggling the coins in his pocket as he watched me with interest.

"Every day that went by," Harrison said, "it was all I could think of. Getting my hands on your scrawny neck and making you pay."

He let go of my throat and backed up. I could still feel his fingers on my neck.

"Lie on the floor, face down."

I took a shaky breath as Robby coiled the rope in his hands. He was wearing gloves. They both were. No fingerprints. No clues. I wondered if I'd end up in the woods, too.

"I said lie down, damn it!"

I wouldn't have a chance, not tied up.

"Lie down, or I'll shoot you right now." He raised the gun and pointed it at my face.

I got on the floor.

"Robby, make it tight," Harrison said. "I don't want him getting out of it this time."

Robby...Robert. Same as my father, same as my brother. Ironic. If they killed me—when they killed me—I wondered if the old man would somehow blame me. "He should have gotten an education and a good job, then none of this would have happened."

Robby was going to make sure this time. He yanked the poncho off and roughly tied my hands. When he was finished, he stood up and rubbed his hands together.

Harrison jammed his knee into the small of my back, grabbed a handful of my hair, and pulled my head off the floor.

Something touched my throat. It was cold and thin and sharp. I hadn't seen it coming. Maybe it was just as well. I closed my eyes. He pressed the knife harder against my skin. I tried to move away from the pressure but couldn't.

Blood trickled down my neck and soaked into my shirt.

Without warning, Harrison loosened his grip on my hair, and the blade cut deeper. I groaned with the effort of keeping my back arched. If I lowered my head, the knife would cut deeper. He shifted more weight onto my back. I gritted my teeth and grunted.

The bastard. I couldn't hold it much longer.

"Say something," he growled.

I wouldn't. Not if I could help it. He was going to kill me anyway. I would not give him the satisfaction of hearing me beg…or cry.

"You should of heard Peters," Harrison said as if he'd read my thoughts. "He cried like a baby, didn't he Robby? And boy could he scream. Screaming and crying for me not to hurt him, the old fart. Guess he shouldn't have reported me, the stupid son of a bitch."

Harrison took the knife away, and my face smashed against the cement.

He moved his face close to mine and whispered, "You're going to beg for mercy, scream for it, before the night's out."

My back and shoulder muscles trembled uncontrollably as the chill of the cement seeped into my sweat-soaked skin. I clenched my fists to stop the shaking.

Robby said, "Let's get going. It's not safe here. Anyway, you can take your time with him at the farm."

I closed my eyes and felt sick.

"Yeah, well…I want him to beg." Harrison kicked me in the ribs. The blow knocked the breath out of my lungs. He nailed me again, this time on my shoulder.

"Don't kick him in the head," Robby said. "I don't want to have to carry the bastard."

"Say something, damn it."

He kicked me again and again, and in a very short time, I lost count. I gritted my teeth to keep myself from groaning. Maybe I could talk my way out of it. It was worth a try.

I struggled to regulate my breathing and said, "The police know you murdered Peters."

"Yeah right." He punctuated his words with kicks. "They don't know shit."

Each blow seemed to merge with the next. My skin burned, and I could feel my heart pounding in my chest.

I gulped some air. "And they know that you helped Sanders with his insurance swindles. Do you think he's going to keep his mouth shut when they come down on him?"

Harrison became very still. Somewhere in the room, flies droned above the drip of a faucet. He began to pace, and it seemed that his agitation increased with each passing second. His boots scraped across the grit on the cement, and his breathing grew louder, faster, out of sync with the sound of my pulse pounding in my ears.

Maybe I should have kept my mouth shut. He came to an abrupt stop a foot away from my nose. I had a close-up view of his boots, scuffed up cowboy boots with sharply pointed toes.

"In that case, you're gonna pay. You're gonna wish you'd never been born."

He leaned over, and I felt his breath on my hair. "As a matter of fact, by mornin', you're gonna be in so much pain, you'll be beggin' me to put you down."

Robby laughed.

I closed my eyes and swallowed.

Harrison grabbed my arm, clenched his fingers in my hair, and yanked me to my feet. I could see the knife then. The blade was easily four inches long, a hunting knife.

"If you kill me, it'll be harder for you," I said and hated the tremor I heard in my voice.

"Awh...now he's worried about me. Better worry about yourself, you little shit. Where," he waved his arm, "where are they, huh? I don't see no cops round here."

He turned toward his brother. "They don't have squat."

"They know you're Drake's cousin," I said, "and Timbrook's brother-in-law and that T&T Industries has been wanting to buy Foxdale and—"

Harrison snatched the front of my shirt and shoved me against the wall. "It's all your fault."

I didn't say anything, and after a moment, he said, "Beg, damn it. Beg for your miserable life."

The faucet dripped into the lengthening silence.

Harrison looked over his shoulder. "You have something to soften him up, don't you, Robby?"

Robby had been watching us with about as much emotion as I would have expected if we'd been discussing a hay shipment.

Harrison yanked me off the wall and shoved me down the aisle toward the back of the room. He turned me to face the last stall.

"Kneel."

Oh, God. It can't be— I thought back to the guard's phone call. Why had I assumed it was him?

I stiffened.

"Kneel down," Harrison screamed. His words echoed in the tiny room.

He kicked the back of my knee and pushed down on my shoulders, forcing me onto my knees. In my peripheral vision, I saw the knife in his right hand, his fingers curled loosely around the handle.

"Robby, open the door."

A slow smile spread across Robby's face. His eyes were curiously blank as he watched my face. He pushed back the stall door.

The security guard was slumped in the narrow space between the wall and toilet.

I swallowed and clenched my teeth.

His throat had been cut, and his head hung at an angle that could only be achieved in death. His eyes were open, staring without sight at the top ledge of the door frame. The stall walls above him and to his left were streaked with a spray of blood.

Bastards.

Movement caught my eye. Every muscle in my body tensed. Something crawled across the glistening white cartilage where his trachea had been severed. A blowfly. Another crawled along his uniform's sharply creased collar. Others buzzed above our heads and bumped against the ceiling. Saliva flooded my mouth.

Fucking bastards! A scream in my mind.

Harrison grabbed my hair and pulled my head back so that I had to look. I closed my eyes, but it didn't make any difference. I could see him clearly in my mind, every detail.

That was it. What I'd missed. The guard wasn't a horseman. He wouldn't have known that the riding area in barn B was called an arena. It had been Harrison or Robby on the phone, not the guard.

I wondered how he'd felt when they'd marched him in here and thought I already knew. My stomach heaved. I swallowed hard and tasted bile at the back of my throat.

"Johnny," Robby said, "his eyes are closed. Think he's asleep?"

"Let's wake him up." Harrison leaned into me and placed the knife under my ear. "This is how Robby did it." He drew the blade across my throat. "Just like that. Shit, Cline, you're shaking so much, you made me cut you." He chuckled. "Next time it's gonna go all the way in, got it?"

"I think he's got it," Robby said.

Harrison pulled me to my feet and shoved me against the wall. He stuck the point of the knife under my chin and squinted at my face.

I forced myself to hold his gaze.

"Say something, damn it."

"Fuck you."

He pushed the knife in deeper, and I had nowhere to go. I think he would have killed me then and there. It was certainly in his eyes. But Robby yelled, "Don't kill him, Johnny. Not yet. We run into the cops, we can use him."

Harrison eased up on the knife.

More blood trickled down my neck.

After a moment, Robby said, "Come on, Johnny. We gotta get outta here."

Harrison wiped his knife off on my shirt and slid it into the sheath on his belt. He reached into his waistband, pulled out the gun, and casually aimed it at my chest. "Don't try anything, Cline."

Robby grabbed hold of my arm and steered me toward the door.

"Robby," Harrison said, "move over. You're blocking my aim. You—"

I swung round in front of Robby, kneed him in the balls, and wrenched free of his grasp. I bolted for the door.

Rich was outside, but I didn't give a shit. I was getting out of there.

As I twisted around to get hold of the door handle, Harrison slammed into me. I hit the wall so hard, my teeth rattled.

"Nice try, Cline." He gripped my chin and turned my face toward his. "But you're not gettin' outta this. Not until I put you in the ground." He shoved my face sideways. "And it ain't gonna be no easy trip, is it Robby?"

Robby grinned, though he was no longer standing upright. "Not for him, it ain't."

"You know," Harrison said, "he's gonna be fun the way he don't wanna give in."

My skin prickled.

He held the gun to my head and waved me outside. Rich spun around at the sound of the door opening.

It had stopped raining. As I stepped onto the sidewalk, it seemed as if time had become suspended, and I was overcome with a feeling of disbelief.

As we turned toward the barns, Robby screeched, "Rich, you stupid sonofabitch! All the time we were in there, and you couldn't think to turn off the lights?"

"But John told me to be a lookout," Rich whined.

"What?" Harrison said. "You couldn't watch the road *and* turn off the lights?" He shoved me toward the barn. "Jesus Christ. Put out a neon sign, why don't ya? Send out engraved invitations. Before you know it, everybody and his brother'll be down here."

Harrison yanked on my arm, and I stumbled. Rich followed alongside, glancing nervously from Harrison to Robby. He wasn't afraid for me, though. He couldn't care less. His only concern was for his own hide. We walked into the barn aisle and stopped in front of the feed room.

"Go turn off the lights," Robby said.

Rich ran down the lane. The lights went out in aisle two, and he was back in less than half a minute. "Come on, John," his voice was high-pitched, "we gotta get outta here. We've been here way too long and—"

"Shut up," Harrison said. "I'm sick of your sniveling and whining. You should take a lesson from Cline, here. He's gonna be dead soon, and he ain't whining like you." He turned to face me. "Ain't that right, boy?"

I stared at him with what I hoped was an expression devoid of emotion. The longer we were on the farm, the greater the chance someone would realize that something was wrong.

Harrison pulled me into him, then slammed me against the feed room wall. "I want to hear you beg, damn it."

"No."

He leaned into me. His facial muscles were stretched tight, and a fine sheen of sweat coated his skin.

"You will, you know." A thought moved in his eyes, and he smiled. "After you're dead and buried, I'll go visit that cute little honey of yours. Make her feel better."

Robby laughed.

I felt the blood drain from my face. I pushed against him. "You bastard!"

He swung the gun up hard and fast and broadsided me. I sagged against the wall and closed my eyes. Pain coursed through my head and settled in my eye. I heard a clicking sound—metal against metal—and instinctively knew what it was. I held my breath and opened my eyes. He was holding the gun in front of my nose, and the hammer was cocked.

He pressed the muzzle into my cheek. "Ask me not to."

Whatever I said, it wouldn't make any difference. The longer I held out, the longer I had to live. If I was wrong, if I had misread him, I would never know.

"Screw you."

Harrison looked over his shoulder at Robby.

"You've got his number," Robby said. "He doesn't like the thought of you doing his girl."

Harrison turned to face me. "You done it with her, boy? I can hardly wait to get my hands on her."

"Go to hell!" I choked on the words. Not her. Not Rachel.

Harrison studied my face, then nodded. "It's a start. Let's get the fuck outta here." He pulled me away from the wall, and Rich headed toward the doorway. "We'll drive by his apartment," Harrison said. "See if she's there."

Robby jiggled the coins in his pocket and cleared his throat. "Better not, Johnny. We gotta start tyin' up some loose ends, startin' with him."

Rich poked his head out the door, then jumped back as if he'd been shocked by a cattle prod. When he spun around, his eyes were wide with terror.

"There's a cop car parked outside the office." He almost screamed it.

"Shit." Harrison pushed me against the wall. "You're gonna get rid of him. If you don't, he's dead, and you're dead. Understand?"

I nodded.

Chapter 20

Harrison spun me around to face the wall, then cut through the rope that bound my wrists.

"Now," he said, "get rid of him. If I even think he's getting suspicious, I'll kill you both. Got it?"

I nodded.

"Good. Don't move out of my line of sight, or you're dead."

I concentrated on keeping my legs steady and stepped out of the barn.

Officer Walter Dorsett, tall, lean, and muscular, was headed straight for me. Fifteen yards separated us. He stopped when I did, and his hand moved instinctively to his gun.

I cleared my throat. "Hi, Harry. Nice night." My voice was hoarse.

Dorsett removed his gun from its holster and held it at his side. He looked toward the barn door and, without looking at me, said, "What are you doing here?"

"Just checking on a horse."

"Everything all right?"

"Couldn't be better, Harry."

He signaled for me to approach him. When I didn't move, he raised the gun with both hands and sighted on the barn door.

"I'll catch up with you tomorrow, Steve," he said loudly, then jerked his head toward the door. "What time?"

What time? What was he talking about? Oh…"Three… three o'clock."

Dorsett glanced at me, and in that instant, I saw movement in my peripheral vision. I turned toward the barn door in time to see Harrison squeeze off three shots. The muzzle flash was brilliant in the dark.

"No!" I screamed and spun around.

The force of the bullet slamming into Dorsett's chest knocked him off his feet. The gun slipped from his hand and clattered onto the asphalt.

"God, no," I sobbed. "No-o-o."

Harrison yanked me back into the barn. In my mind, I could still see Dorsett's lifeless form, dark and silent on the asphalt, his hand empty, palm face up, fingers curled toward the black sky.

"You killed a cop!" Rich screamed. "I can't believe it! You killed a fucking cop!"

"Shut up." Harrison shoved me against the wall.

"What are we gonna do now? We don't have a chance. They hunt—"

"Shut the fuck up." Harrison's voice cracked. "It's all your fault we're in this mess—"

"What?" Rich whined.

"If you hadn't done such a lousy job tying him up last time, he wouldn't of got away from us, and I wouldn't be here right now, finishing the job. A job *you* screwed up."

"It wasn't my fault. I did what you said. No one thought he'd get loose. At least I didn't do something stupid," Rich flailed his arms, "like kill a cop."

"Yeah, and I'd be stupider if I let you continue to fuck us up, wouldn't I?"

"Yeah," Rich suddenly became very still, "eh, I mean no."

Harrison casually pointed the gun at Rich and pulled the trigger.

The sound in the confines of the barn was deafening. The horse behind Rich crashed against the back wall of his stall.

All of the horses near us shied and whinnied. I hardly noticed. Rich slid down the wall and crumpled onto the floor.

The bullet had shattered the ridge of bone above his right eye. The other eye was wide open, seeing nothing. His head lolled to the side, and a stream of watery blood trickled from his nose and mouth. There was blood spatter on the grillwork of the stall front and on the horse that stood trembling at the back of his stall.

I swallowed. The bitter smell of burnt gunpowder hung so thickly in the air around us, I could taste it at the back of my throat.

"Damn it, Johnny. You shouldn't have popped him here. The police might be able to connect him with us. And you shouldn't have used your gun."

"So what? I'll dump it when we're done."

"Well, we can't leave him here," Robby said.

"You!" Harrison grabbed my arm. "Drag him down past the hay barn."

I thought about the old abandoned fire road and the gate Dave and I had never gotten around to installing.

"Good idea." Robby studied my face. "We'll put 'em both in the trunk. That oughta make for an interesting ride, huh lover-boy?"

Asshole. I looked down at Rich and couldn't imagine it.

"Go ahead." Harrison shoved me toward Rich's body. "Get movin'. We ain't got all night."

I gulped a lungful of air and gripped Rich's ankles. When I lifted his legs and stepped backward, his body slid the rest of the way down the stall front, and his head hit the asphalt with a sickening thud. My stomach churned. I leaned against the stall.

The gun's barrel butted against my shoulder. "Get movin', boy."

I kept my gaze on Rich's legs, tightened my grip on his ankles, and dragged him toward the end of the barn.

"Robby, go switch off the lights," Harrison said. "We can make the rest of the aisle in the dark."

I watched Robby saunter toward the doorway, then as unobtrusively as possible, I glanced behind me. I had forty-eight feet to go—the length of four stalls—before I was level with the cut-through to the arena. If I timed it right...

I slowed my pace. Robby was almost to the bank of light switches. He paused and peeked out the doorway. Hurry it up, I thought. I slowed even more.

Twenty-four feet to go.

Robby's hand moved down over the switches and plummeted the barn into darkness. I continued backward more slowly and forced myself to wait until the timing was in my favor.

Robby and Harrison were silhouetted by the sodium vapor light, and I hoped the lighting would work to my advantage. Hoped they couldn't see me as easily as I could them. I watched Robby move down the aisle toward us. I drew level with the cut-through as he reached the halfway mark between the lights and us. I quietly lowered Rich's legs to the asphalt, then bolted into the arena. I figured I had about eight seconds before Robby made it back to the light switch.

Harrison didn't wait for the lights. He bellowed and shot wildly. The bullet cracked harmlessly into the arena wall to my left as I neared the opposite cut-through that led into aisle two. As I turned the corner into the aisle, I grabbed a lead rope off its hook and thanked God that someone had hung it where it belonged for a change. Another gunshot. Wood splitting. Closer this time.

The lights in aisle one flashed on. I skidded to a halt in front of the third stall from the end and threw open the door. Chase stood in the center of the stall, legs splayed, eyes wide with fear. The only horse in the barn who wore a halter twenty-four hours a day. I clipped on the lead, grabbed a handful of mane, and vaulted onto his back.

I kicked him out of the stall and leaned to my right, knowing he would move to stay balanced under my weight. Out of the corner of my eye, I saw Harrison step into the aisle behind us. His arm came up. Almost fifty yards separated us, but it didn't much matter. Not with that gun of his. I ignored the fact that Chase's shoes were slipping on the asphalt and kicked him into a canter.

When Harrison fired again, Chase didn't need any encouragement. As we crossed the threshold, a bullet splintered the doorjamb at shoulder level. Only a foot away.

But it was enough.

In another second, we would be out of his line of sight. I leaned to my right, signaling to Chase that I wanted him to head down the corridor between the paddocks, when something hit my left side. I tipped forward over the horse's shoulder.

I had a clear view of his hooves skidding on the asphalt as he floundered under my shifting weight, uncertain what I wanted, and I nearly came off. I anchored my right hand in his mane, pressed my left hand against his shoulder, and pushed myself back into position. He had slowed to a trot. I kicked him into a gallop, and we sailed down the hill and slipped into darkness.

As we neared the woods, I straightened, weighted my seat, and brought him back to the trot. Where the lane emptied onto the trails, I spun him around and looked up the hill toward the barn.

Thinking that I wanted to go back, Chase bunched his hindquarters and lunged forward into a bouncy, agitated canter. The lead line was useless as far as brakes went. I yanked his head around, pointed him down the trail, and nailed him with my heels. He bolted into a frantic, disorganized gallop.

He was wound tight, snorting and blowing, every muscle in his body rigid with tension. I didn't fight him but let him go at his own pace. I gripped with my knees and prayed that his instincts would take us safely through the blackness. When he galloped down the section of trail that was little more than a ledge, I concentrated on keeping my balance and hoped he wouldn't step off into space.

Wet branches brushed against my arms and touched my hair as damp air, smelling richly of humus, buffeted my face. I crouched lower onto his neck. The woods passed by in a dizzying blur of dark shapes against black. I could not see the trail. Couldn't even see the ground beneath us. When we reached the stream crossing, he flew it, and I began to wonder if I would ever get him stopped.

Gradually, his stride evened out. When we hit the bottomland, I pulled him around to the left and headed west along the river bank. I sat up straighter, relaxed my lower back, and willed him to slow down. He dropped down to a trot, then to a walk, and I appreciated Anne's training skills more than ever.

My side ached. I lifted my arm and twisted around. My elbow and shirt were wet. I peeled the fabric off my waist. The air hit my skin, and the pain intensified. It felt like a burn, and I realized I'd been shot. I couldn't see the damage but decided it wasn't serious. I was breathing okay, and the pain wasn't too bad.

I thought about Dorsett, then, and urged Chase into a canter. If there was a chance he was still alive, I had to get him help. The gelding's gait was strung out and rough. I used my seat and legs to collect his stride and asked him to go faster across the uneven terrain. The tall grass dragged at his legs. He wasn't a cross-country horse, but he was willing nonetheless. A sharp contrast to his manners on the ground, where he was dangerous and unpredictable.

When we came to a wide drainage ditch that had deepened because of runoff from construction upslope, he slid awkwardly down the bank. I slipped forward, out of position, and when he heaved himself up the opposite bank and scrambled over the edge, I nearly came off.

Chase stopped.

The adrenaline rush had worn off, and my muscles trembled with fatigue and cold. I knotted the lead rope around my left wrist while, beneath me, the horse's body rocked with each ragged breath. Fear and exertion had taken a toll on both of us. I squeezed my calves and urged him forward.

It began to rain. A cold stinging rain.

I watched the terrain. An old trail, now unpopular because it dead-ended behind a newly constructed housing development, snaked uphill on the left.

I almost missed it. I pulled Chase sharply to the left, kicked him in the ribs, and he plowed through the thick undergrowth and bounded up the hill. His hooves slipped on the rain-soaked leaves. I grabbed mane and clucked to him. As we neared the ridge, I felt him abruptly focus his attention. I squinted through the rain.

Directly ahead stood a four-foot-high picket fence, its white planks gleaming in the darkness. Chase pricked his ears and extended his stride with enthusiasm. I gritted my teeth and held on tighter.

The horse cleared it with a foot to spare and landed neatly in someone's backyard. I pushed myself back into position as he zeroed in on the next fence. I had no control. With zero encouragement from me, he crossed the grass in six strides and sailed the front fence. I managed to stay with him, but he shied at a hose reel propped against the house. He veered to the left and crashed through the bowed branches of an ornamental tree. I ducked at the last second. Wet limbs gouged my shoulders and back, and my shirt tore. His next stride took us across the sidewalk, and when he slipped on the asphalt, he dropped down to a walk.

We had ended up in a cul-de-sac. Judging by the houses—all brick, expensive, convoluted affairs—we were in the relatively new subdivision just west of Foxdale. Deceptive considering the ride we'd just had. Except for one house at the mouth of the circle, all the homes were dark. When we reached the curb on the far side, I hopped off the gelding and led him onto the sidewalk. Chase snaked his neck around and tried to get a piece of my skin between his teeth, and I realized I should have stayed on his back.

I led him down the sidewalk and wondered how I would manage knocking on someone's door with Chase in tow.

As we turned toward the lighted house, where windows cast yellow squares onto an immaculate lawn, a car approached slowly from the main road. I looked over my shoulder and saw the lightbar on the roof and a shield on the door. I yanked Chase around and jogged toward the cruiser.

The gelding trotted sideways, back to his usual irritable self. It wasn't until we reached the length of sidewalk bordered by a decorative retaining wall that I was able to get him going in a straight line.

The cruiser angled across the road toward us and halted with its left front tire against the curb. The overhead lights flicked on. I glanced at Chase. He tensed his neck as the rotating blue and red lights flashed across his wide, liquid eyes. The driver turned on the spotlight and shone it in my face. I shaded my eyes and hoped Chase wouldn't bolt.

The wipers flicked across the windshield, flinging droplets through the glare of the spotlight. As the door creaked open, I noticed the cruiser's number painted on the front fender. Forty-six. Dorsett's number.

"Dorsett?" I squinted and stepped closer as he climbed from behind the wheel.

"Need some help, boy?"

Harrison leveled the barrel of his gun over the door frame and pulled the trigger as I spun away from him.

The impact slammed me into Chase's side.

A high-pitched whinny erupted from the horse's throat as I crashed onto the sidewalk. Chase wheeled around in the tight space. My arm jerked upward, and the lead rope tightened on my wrist. When the gelding felt the tension on his halter, he lowered his head, bunched his hindquarters, and kicked out with both hind legs. A hind hoof exploded through the driver's side window, and Harrison screamed.

I frantically worked at the rope.

Chase bolted, jerking me toward the cruiser. My chest bumped against the horse's hind legs as the rope unwound from my wrist. He kicked out again. His lethal hooves sliced high over my head and tangled with the open door before he galloped down the sidewalk.

Harrison was down on one knee between the cruiser's door and body, and he was groaning. I pushed myself to my knees, twisted around, and saw his gun on the sidewalk just beyond my feet. I lunged toward it and wrapped my fingers around the grip, then rolled away from the car. I pushed myself upright and propped my back against the retaining wall.

Harrison grunted to his feet and walked out from behind the car door, cradling his left arm against his ribs.

I raised the gun with both hands and pointed it at him.

I stared down the long black barrel and concentrated on the sight as it jumped wildly. Couldn't stop my hands from shaking. He turned sideways, and I forced myself to focus beyond the gun's sight. To focus on him.

His right arm moved.

When he turned back around, he held his hand behind his leg. I glanced at the leather sheath strapped to his belt. It was empty.

"You don't have the guts to use that," he said. "Do you, boy?"

"Don't." It came out a whisper.

He took a step forward. In my peripheral vision, I saw the flash of steel as he brought the knife around.

I squeezed the trigger.

Harrison staggered backward and collapsed against the cruiser. The door clicked shut as he slid to the ground, smearing a swath of red across the Howard County shield.

"Yes," I whispered. "I do."

I lowered my hand, and the gun clattered on the cement. Wetness soaked through my shirt. I looked at my side. Looked dispassionately at the blood seeping down a crack in the sidewalk.

Burning pain cut through me as if the thought created the reality. I leaned my head against the wall and listened to the monotonous whine as the wipers swept across the windshield. Listened to the low-pitched drone of the engine. It began to rain harder then, the drops pinging loudly on the hood. It soaked into my clothes and trickled through my hair.

I watched the rain move in sheets through the glare from the spotlight and became dizzy. Even though I was sweating, I shook from the cold.

Each breath was more difficult than the last. I closed my eyes and couldn't hear anything except my pulse banging in my ears. I wondered if I would hear the last beat and realize it.

Chapter 21

I had been drifting in and out of consciousness for what seemed a very long time. I had no idea what the time was, wasn't even certain of the day.

Someone cleared his throat. I opened my eyes. Detective Ralston was standing at the foot of the bed. His suit was wrinkled, and he'd loosened his tie.

"How's Dorsett?" I said.

"Better. He regained consciousness yesterday morning."

"What about brain…"

"He'll be fine. The bullet grazed his skull. He has one hell of a headache and bruised ribs where his vest stopped the other slug, but all in all, he was damn lucky."

"Hmm." My mouth felt like cotton.

Ralston gripped the footboard with both hands. His fingers were splayed and his skin looked pale against the industrial-steel gray. He gestured to the bed and medical gadgetry. "Sorry about this."

"It wasn't your fault."

"I should have handled it differently." He glanced at the ceiling, then rubbed his face. "I shouldn't have let another night go by without setting up a detail."

I shook my head. "If I hadn't left my new number with the…guard," I blinked, "I'd be downing some Millers and watching the Orioles."

Ralston grunted.

I fingered the cotton blanket that was draped across my lap. The damn thing must have been washed about a million times.

If I had only stayed in the loft that February night. An hour earlier, an hour later, would have made all the difference in the world. Harrison might still have targeted Foxdale, but he wouldn't have cared about me. Wouldn't have become fixated.

My lungs felt as if they had collapsed into a tight ball in the center of my chest.

Ralston straightened and walked around the room. He looked at the IV bag, the monitors mounted on a trolley, the curtains that provided privacy. He briefly looked at my chart, then he dragged a chair closer to the bed and sat down. Light brown bristles darkened his chin, and his eyes were bloodshot behind his wire-rimmed glasses.

"Are you up to giving me a statement," he said, "start to finish?"

I nodded.

He had a tape recorder with him that I hadn't noticed. He checked the cassette and switched it on. "Did you see who shot Richard Harper?"

"Yes." My voice was hoarse. "Harrison did."

"Which one?"

"Oh, John."

He hesitated. "Do you know which one of them killed the guard?"

"No. Harrison," I shook my head, "I mean, John Harrison said that Robby cut the guard's throat." I swallowed. "Any word on Robby, yet?"

"No. His car's been recovered. The Virginia State Police found it disabled on 211, just west of Warrenton. What happened after you went to your friend's house?"

I told Ralston about the phone call and the rest of it, and when I was finished, I was exhausted. "I was thinking," I said. "Something Mrs. Peters mentioned. I think her husband reported Harrison. Maybe to the AHSA or—"

"The what?" Ralston said.

"American Horse Show Association. Maybe Harrison was scamming insurance companies, too, and Peters caught on. Or maybe Peters reported him to the Humane Society." I told him what Nick had said about Harrison whipping a horse.

Ralston scribbled the information down and closed his notebook. "I'll let you get some rest."

"Wait," I said as he turned to leave. "Did the horse make it back okay?"

He shook his head. "He slipped as he turned onto Rocky Ford and broke his hip. Had to be destroyed."

"Damn," I mumbled.

"I'm sorry, Steve." Ralston turned toward the door and said, more to himself than to me, "About everything."

The door swung shut and, in a moment, the resultant current of air swirled across my skin. I stared at the faded pattern in the curtain and remembered the thrill I'd felt when Chase had caught sight of that white picket fence. I thought about the joy I'd felt flowing from his mind when faced with a fence and the torment he'd lived with otherwise. A sad, screwed up horse.

I leaned back on the pillow. More than anything, I wanted to go back to sleep. But Harrison kept getting in the way, and a hundred other things I would have just as soon forgotten.

On the sidewalk that night, as I had lain against the cold block wall, I had looked at Harrison's face after he'd died. His mouth had hung slackly open, his eyes staring blankly toward the sky. Raindrops fell on his face and trickled into his mouth, but what I remembered most was that his expression had been one of pure astonishment. His sick, perverted mind had driven him to take one more risk.

The next day, they removed another tube and moved me into a regular room. I pressed them about a release date, but they said it was still too soon to tell, so instead, I wondered when they would allow visitors. Rachel in particular.

My next visitor was not Rachel, however, but Detective Ralston.

He snagged a chair and dragged it over to the bed. "You're looking a damn sight better than the last time I saw you."

"Yeah. I can hardly wait to get out of here."

"Your doctor says you're doing well, all things considered."

"Did he say when I'd be getting out?"

He chuckled. "No. Dorsett's out of ICU."

"I know. When they wheeled him down the hall, they let him stop in for a minute."

Ralston swung the chair around backward and straddled it. "The investigation's moving along nicely. Besides what happened at Foxdale, we've linked John Harrison to the murder of James Peters and to your abduction in February. It's also looking good for connecting him with the murders of David Rowe and Larry Jacob, the two I mentioned the other night."

I shut my mouth with a snap. "How'd you do that?"

"When we searched their farm, we found some interesting things. Your wallet, for one. The older brother, John, kept something from each victim in a bedroom dresser."

"Jesus." I swallowed and closed my eyes. "What about Pennsylvania?"

"The boyfriend confessed. They'd been arguing all weekend, and apparently it escalated into a physical confrontation. He struck her hard enough that it killed her. Afterward, he remembered reading about the Peters case in the newspaper and pretended his girlfriend was victim number two."

"What about the stolen horses?" I said.

"There wasn't a theft. They'd sold the horses a month earlier, and apparently that's what they were arguing about." Ralston pulled a plastic evidence bag out of his jacket pocket and tossed it on the bed. "You might be interested in this."

Inside was an envelope addressed to my Post Office box and a wrinkled sheet of white, lined paper. I smoothed the plastic on my thigh, flattened the paper with my fingers, and squinted at the small script. Although the note was unsigned, whoever had written it had identified John Harrison as someone who used a rig that matched the description of the one I'd been looking for. I looked up at Ralston.

"It came in yesterday's mail," he said. "We impounded the truck owned by T&T Industries and compared the tire tread with the casts taken in the Rowe case." Ralston smiled briefly. "They matched."

"Good."

"As soon as we confronted Timbrook with that bit of information, we couldn't shut him up. It seems that John Harrison had tipped him off about the Peters farm being for sale, but he had no idea Harrison had been involved in Peters' disappearance and death. Because the land butted up against Piney Run Park, T&T Industries made more on the deal than they'd expected, so Timbrook actively began pursuing land bordering the state park system."

"Which led him to the Ritter farm," I said.

Ralston nodded. "That deal went through smoothly, but Timbrook was greedy. Like you suspected, when he couldn't persuade Foxdale's owner to sell, he asked John and Robert to make trouble for the farm, but he swears up, down, and sideways that he never meant for anyone to get hurt."

I handed the letter back to Ralston and thought about Elsa. Had she known what was going on? Was that why she had warned me about Robby even though she lied about her tote.

"And you were right about something else. "June of last year, Peters reported Harrison to the Montgomery County Humane Society for cruelty."

"God." After a while, I said, "How could it happen? How could two people become so...twisted?"

Detective Ralston rubbed his chin. There was more color to his face, and he was freshly shaven. He wasn't wearing the wire-rims of the day before, and I wondered if he wore contacts. "Maybe they learned by example. The father's done time for sexual battery, assault with a deadly weapon, aggravated assault. Right now, he's in for statutory rape. John had a few minor brushes with the law when he was younger, all misdemeanors—"

"He got smarter."

"What? Oh, yeah. Robert managed to stay clean until now."

The fluorescent tube above my head hummed softly. "What about Elsa?"

Ralston shrugged. "There's nothing to indicate she knew what her husband and brothers were up to, but the fact that she warned you implies otherwise. As far as the cousin's concerned, the one who owns the trailer, I don't think he knew they were using it for anything illegal. Oh, and the District Attorney's office is investigating Sanders. So far, they've found claims on four different horses."

"Wow." I shifted my pillow. "Heard anything about Robby?"

Ralston shook his head. "Nothing."

After lunch, I fell asleep. Sometime during my nap, the pain medication wore off. I floated upward on a rising wave of pain and jerked awake with a start. Rachel was sitting beside my bed, her fingers entwined in mine, and she looked scared. Her face looked stiff, and a tremor worked at the corner of her mouth. I could only guess how my face must have looked before I'd come fully awake.

"Hey," I mumbled.

She stood up. Her skin was pale in the fluorescent light. "Oh God, Steve. Should I get a nurse?"

"No." I squeezed her hand. "I'm okay, really. When I first wake up, sometimes it's rough, but I'm better now."

"Oh, Steve." She hugged me.

I put my arm around her shoulders and pulled her close. She rested her head on my chest. Her arms trembled in little spasms, and I could tell she was crying. I ran my fingers through her hair and closed my eyes. Her warm tears seeped through the hospital gown.

"Hey, it's okay," I said.

She lifted her head, and her black hair swung forward and brushed against my chin. When I smoothed it back behind her ear and kissed her cheek, she moved her lips over mine and kissed me, then she looked into my eyes.

"I love you," she whispered.

To receive a free catalog of other Poisoned Pen Press titles, please contact us in one of the following ways:

Phone: 1-800-421-3976
Facsimile: 1-480-949-1707
Email: info@poisonedpenpress.com
Website: www.poisonedpenpress.com

Poisoned Pen Press
6962 E. First Ave. Ste 103
Scottsdale, AZ 85251